TWIN LIGHTS

TWIN LIGHTS

A NOVEL BY

CHUCK DOWDLE

LUMINARE PRESS

WWW.LUMINAREPRESS.COM

Twin Lights
Copyright © 2021 by Chuck Dowdle

Printed in the United States of America

Luminare Press
442 Charnelton St.
Eugene, OR 97401
www.luminarepress.com

LCCN: 2021923340
ISBN: 978-1-64388-912-2

"Twin Lights" would not have been
completed in its present form without the creative
and determined editorial assistance of my kind, patient
and understanding daughter, Allie LeCaux.

PROLOGUE

"Twin Lights" was written by Chuck Dowdle to help him imagine what life might have been like had his twin sons lived and been his only children. Michael Charles and Mark Edward Dowdle were born prematurely at five-and-a-half months' gestation on August 9th, 1953. They died an hour apart the following day.

At the time the twins were born, the Dowdles had one daughter, Kathleen, who was two. After the twins died, the Dowdles had four more daughters over the next thirteen years: Laure, Allie, Genevieve and Mary.

"DOCTOR," WHISPERED SISTER GIOVANNI WITH A SENSE OF URGENCY as he slid the tiny newborn infant into her outstretched hands, "I think there's another one!"

It wasn't until after Chuck's wife, Marty, was finally able to come home from the hospital that she gave him the details of the twins' delivery: *After Michael was born and Sister Giovanni told Dr. Schoeneberger she thought there was a second baby, he turned his attention away from Michael and began helping me give birth to Mark. At that point a warm feeling filled my body and I began observing everything that was happening from about five feet above the delivery table. After Mark was born, my body continued feeling comfortably warm and I was drawn toward a distant white light. I had a sense of peace and no pain as Dr. Schoeneberger and Sister Giovanni began working frantically on my body, pounding on it, it seemed, to help keep me alive. I heard Sister Giovanni say, "I think she's coming around, Doctor," and then heard Dr. Schoeneberger breathe a sigh of relief as he said, "Thank God!"*

As Dr. Schoeneberger left the delivery room and met Chuck, he extended his hand and said, "Congratulations, Mr. Dowdle, you're the father of twin boys! You'll be able to see them soon. They're extremely small since your wife was only seven months along, but they're mighty little fighters, and with time in the hospital and the loving care of the nuns, I think they'll make it. We'll keep a very close watch."

Just as Dr. Schoeneberger turned to leave, Sister Giovanni came out of the delivery room.

"Would you like to see your boys, Mr. Dowdle?" she asked with a smile.

"I sure would!" said Chuck, as she ushered him into the newborn area. There they were, lying side by side, looking perfectly normal, all pink and no parts missing. They were indeed very small, a little under two and a half pounds each. They were quiet and still in their bassinets, the warm air of the nursery wafting over their naked little bodies. Sister Giovanni had cupped their tiny heads in separate oxygen masks to help them breathe since the hospital didn't have incubators. Chuck stared down at his sons in love-filled awe and said a silent prayer.

"If you don't mind, Mr. Dowdle," Sister Giovanni interrupted, "I think we should baptize your sons. I don't know if you and your wife finalized a name beforehand, but now, of course, we need a second one as well!"

"The last time we talked about names, Marty and I had a hard time choosing between Michael Charles or Mark Edward for a boy's name," Chuck said, "but since there are two babies, those names will be perfect. Let's use them!" he said eagerly.

Sister M. Giovanni Becker, OSF, was a woman of action, and before Chuck knew it, his boys were baptized and he was off to see Marty.

"Hi, sweetheart," he whispered softly as he entered her room and walked slowly to her bedside. "How are you feeling?"

"I'm hurting a little," she said weakly, "but that's to be expected. I'm sure I'll feel better in a day or two." She smiled as Chuck clasped her warm hands in his and kissed her tenderly on the forehead. "Have you had a chance to see your new sons?" she asked.

"I just did!" he said proudly. "They're beautiful! Two little identical boys! I can hardly believe it! And before I forget to tell you, honey, they've already been named and baptized!"

Marty's mouth fell open. "You're not kidding, are you?" she asked.

"No, I'm not! I guess things got a little dicey in the delivery room, so Sister Giovanni decided it would be a good idea to baptize them as soon as they were settled in the nursery. She asked me what we wanted to name them, and I just blurted out, 'Michael and Mark.' I didn't know what to say, so I picked the names we'd narrowed down to and then chose my own first and middle names for their middle names. They're Michael Charles Dowdle and Mark Edward Dowdle, born August 9, 1953 at St. James Hospital in Perham, Minnesota," said Chuck proudly. "Our little twin lights!"

"Those names are perfect," said Marty as she smiled at him.

"They're also the boys' confirmation names," he said. "Sister Giovanni called Father Donnay from St. Henry's when she sensed things were critical, and he rushed over and confirmed them, too."

"I think that's wonderful," Marty said. "By the way, Sister Giovanni told me I could go home in a couple of days, but the boys are going to have to stay in the hospital for several weeks until they gain some weight. We're lucky to live right across the street; it's so convenient for us to see them and especially for me to feed them."

When Marty was discharged a few days later, she was able to catch up on some much-needed rest, and finally, a long two months later, the Dowdles were more than ready to bring their sons home from the hospital. The nuns had taken excellent care of them, and each of the boys had doubled in weight since their birth.

It was a typical cold November afternoon when the twins got to come home, and it was a Friday, so Chuck was able to spend the weekend helping Marty. The basement apartment they rented from Otto and Evelyn Krueger was comfortable and warm. It was like any other apartment with a kitchen, bathroom, living room, laundry and bedroom, but one had to walk up a flight of stairs to get outside. The boys would love the apartment once they started crawling, the kitchen with its slick vinyl floors and the rest of the flooring smooth and shiny hardwood.

Michael and Mark were bundled in warm blankets for the short walk across the street. Chuck carried a newborn in each arm, and neither let out a peep until they got home and began examining their new surroundings. Before too long they started making "mm, mm, mm," sounds. Chuck thought those were happy responses to all the new objects, but Marty knew better. She had heard those sounds in the hospital many times before and they only meant one thing, dirty diapers! "Well, Chuck," she said mischievously, "I think it's time for you to get acquainted with your sons in a very intimate way, so you take Michael, I'll take Mark and we'll do this together."

The counter space on either side of the kitchen sink was perfect for changing diapers, so that's where the new parents lay the twins, ever so gently, and began the unpinning. Marty went about her work like a journeyman, as she had been changing the boys for the past couple of months on her many daily visits to the hospital. Chuck, on the other hand, acted like a new hire at work, hesitant and a little heavy-handed, as he had never changed a baby's diaper in his life. This time he was in luck, as the boys had only urinated.

"OK, Chuck," Marty said, "all you have to do is wipe Michael's little butt and testicles with this warm, damp washcloth, rub on some lotion, pin on a fresh diaper and you're all done. Just follow my lead."

Both parents went to work, Chuck watching and copying Marty's every move. They had just finished the pinning when the boys once again began making their "mm, mm, mm," sounds, a duet with which the new parents were both now familiar. "Oh, no, it can't be!" said Chuck. Marty just smiled as they began unpinning their sons' diapers for the second time.

That's when the unexpected happened—both boys spouting urine geysers into the air as soon as their diapers were removed. Twin fountains! "You've got to be kidding!" Chuck yelled as he jumped back.

"I'm afraid not, honey," Marty laughed. "I had that happen to me many a time at the hospital. You'll get used to it. It's part of the deal with little boys. All you can do is grin and bear it—and try not to take a direct hit!"

"OK, Michael," Chuck whispered as he nuzzled his son's downy, warm head against his cheek, "let's you and me try this again and see if we can do it without any more accidents."

That was just the beginning of the first day at home. Next was feeding time, which usually took place shortly after they were all clean. Marty knew the routine well. She had been doing it at the hospital, and though it was quite a challenge, the nurses helped out and she had managed. The twins sang a different song when they wanted to eat, "ah, ah, ah, ah, ah, ah," and they didn't let up until they were fed!

Sure enough, Mark and Michael started singing as soon as their diapers were changed. "OK, Chuck," said Marty, "it sounds like they're hungry, their first feeding away from the hospital, so it's going to take two of us. I'll get settled in the rocking chair and you can hand me Michael. He's usually more ravenous than Mark."

Marty unbuttoned her blouse, exposing her bulging milk-filled breasts. "I'm ready," she said. "You can hand him to me now." As soon as Michael got settled into her arms and she placed his tiny, warm head against her breast, he began anxiously waving his head back and forth with his mouth wide open, like a baby bird searching for a worm from its mother. He knew food was coming! Marty helped Michael latch on and he immediately began sucking and smacking for milk. "OK," Marty said patiently, "now you can hand me Mark." It was a welcome sight for Chuck, seeing his little babies taking nourishment from their mother's breasts in order to survive, and seeing his wife very much alive, smiling and savoring the moment. When the boys were finished, Marty let out a big sigh. "This is exhausting!" she said with a good-natured laugh. "I sure wish you had breasts that could help!"

"I'm sure glad I don't!" laughed Chuck.

"Marty noticed Michael's eyes beginning to close. "OK," she said in a whisper, "you can take him from me now." She eased Michael gently into Chuck's arms. "I'll follow you into the bedroom with Mark," she said.

They gently placed the boys into their crib, and it wasn't long before they were both fast asleep. "I can't believe it!" Chuck whispered. "We have peace and quiet on our first day home! We're pros already, Mart!"

"You might not want to start bragging quite yet," Marty cautioned as they walked into the kitchen to get dinner ready. "You may be brought back to earth sooner than you think!"

Chuck could hardly contain himself. Everything was peaceful and warm in their basement apartment, a casserole prepared for them by Otto and Evelyn had just come out of the oven, and the twins were snug in their crib and sleeping like lambs! What could be more perfect for their first day at home?

Chuck and Marty held hands as he said a prayer…"*and thank you for this delicious food. Amen!*" They were about to take their first bites when Chuck thought he heard a murmur coming from the boys' bedroom. "Did you hear that?" he asked, his fork stopping abruptly midway to his mouth.

"I sure did," she said, frowning.

Chuck rose from the table and tiptoed towards the twins' room. Not a sound! But then, as he walked away, he heard "mm, mm, mm," and then a second little voice joined the first with its "mm, mm, mm." Chuck couldn't believe his ears. Could it be? Dirty diapers? They'd just gotten the twins cleaned and changed before they fed them! "Again?" he said aloud.

"I think," Marty said with a knowing smile as she walked toward their bedroom, "that our little troopers have pooped in their diapers.

At least that's the way it happened at the hospital. Time for us to do some investigating."

Chuck wasn't eager to do any sleuthing, especially with his dinner getting cold, but he knew it had to be done. "Here we go," he said with a resigned smile.

"Mm, mm, mm!" came the call again, this time more persistent. "I can smell it!" Chuck groaned as he moved his head inside the door and looked back at Marty. "No doubt about it, they've done something special!"

"You take Michael and I'll take Mark," said Marty as she reached down into the crib.

Chuck soon found out that changing a poop-filled diaper was very different from changing one that was merely wet. This was a much messier job! "Now what do I do with it?" Chuck asked, the full diaper in his hands. "Here, take this one, too," said Marty as she handed him Mark's. "You can rinse them out in the toilet and then put them in the diaper pail next to the washing machine." By the time Chuck returned, Marty had both boys cleaned up and changed and tucked in once again. They clearly loved their mother's tender touch. "Hopefully that's it for a while," she said in a whisper, "at least for another four hours."

By the time they finished eating and had done the dishes, it was already seven o'clock. "I can't believe how fast the hours have rolled by," Chuck said. "We'll be feeding those two again before long! When do we get to rest?" he asked.

"I'm afraid rest isn't part of the deal," said Marty. "I'm going to keep pumping breast milk like I was doing at the hospital. When I wake up at ten and two and six you can help me with their bottle feedings."

"I'll be happy to do that and anything else you need, honey," said Chuck. "If you're going to have to get up at night and early in the morning, I will, too."

"It'll be worth it for me and for them," she said. "It's exhausting trying to breastfeed two babies, and Sister Giovanni told me it's important to keep pace with their appetites."

"Well, let's try to get some sleep!" she said as they got ready for bed. They crawled in, exhausted, and were out like a light as soon as their heads hit the pillows.

In the morning, after three diaper changes and the ten, two and six o'clock feedings, Chuck said, "I never realized being a parent was so much work! And this is times two!"

Life in Perham, Minnesota sure was different from life in Karlsruhe, North Dakota where Chuck taught his first year. Perham was a beautiful lake community with friendly, welcoming residents. Karlsruhe was a dot on the map, way out in the country, and everyone was clannish and spoke German. In Karlsruhe, Chuck had taught General Science, General Math, World History, Business Law and Psychology to different grades. In Perham, it was English and World Geography to seventh graders. Suffice it to say, near the end of that first school year in Karlsruhe, the Dowdles were antsy to leave, and Chuck was applying for teaching jobs elsewhere. They were elated when he was offered the position in Perham.

A gentle "mm, mm, mm," began sounding around nine a.m., shortly after Chuck and Marty had finished breakfast and were reading the paper. By nine-thirty the single "mm, mm, mm," was joined by another, and by ten a.m. it was an insistent duet. The boys were ready to eat—again!

"Where did that three hours go?" Chuck muttered before getting up and joining Marty in the nursery.

"I think my biological clock has been set to go off every four hours ever since they were born," said Marty. "I sure can anticipate when they're getting hungry. After this feeding I think we'll be able to get in our own nap, hopefully until two o'clock or so. I'll switch them to the bottle at that feeding and see how it goes."

"Sounds like a good plan," said Chuck enthusiastically, "especially the part about our nap!"

With the twins fed and nestled back in their crib, quiet filled the warm and cozy apartment, and a light snow began to fall. Chuck and Marty crawled back into bed and nestled under the comforter, kissed one another tenderly and immediately fell asleep. The cold November wind began picking up speed and piled the swirling snow against the small rectangular windows, the only means of letting outside light into their basement apartment.

"Chuck!" Marty whispered excitedly as she nudged him awake. "Look at what time it is!"

"Holy cow! Five thirty!" Chuck said, at once wide awake. "I'm sorry I wasn't up to help with the two o'clock feeding!"

"I wasn't either!" she said. "They must have slept through it or else we were so sound asleep we just didn't hear them!"

"I can't believe it!" said Chuck as they both crawled out of bed. They moved quietly across the floor and down the hall in their slippers to check on the twins. "They're still sleeping, Mart!" he said in disbelief.

"Those little angels!" she said. "They must have known we were exhausted. Let's go eat while they're still sleeping. I can heat up the casserole leftovers."

No sooner had they taken their first bites when, you guessed it, the familiar "ah, ah, ahs" filled the air, slow and solo at first, soon joined by a more demanding second voice. "We'd better get cracking!" Chuck said as left the table. "Those little guys must be hungry!"

"You change their diapers," Marty called after him, "and I'll get the bottles ready."

"OK, boys," said Chuck as he entered their bedroom and went to work on diaper change number one. "I'm getting pretty good at this, don't you think?" he said to a wide-eyed Michael. He was just about to pin on his clean diaper when a stream hit him right in the eye. "Damn! Bullseye!" Chuck yelled, urine dripping down his cheek.

Marty came rushing from the kitchen. "What's the matter, honey?" she said.

"The little squirt got me!" Chuck laughed as he started over with a clean diaper. Like Michael, Mark gurgled as his dad turned his attention to him and pinned the soft cloth around his tiny bottom. "Good boy, buddy," Chuck said, "no squirting!"

The twins were fed and back in bed without further incident. "We've got it made," Chuck whispered as he watched their little blue eyes droop and close. "Now maybe we can sit and enjoy our dinner!"

It was quite a first 24 hours at home with their newborn family. After all the weekend excitement with the boys, Monday morning was a welcome relief for Chuck. He helped Marty with the six o'clock feeding, downed a quick breakfast and headed out the door and off to school. Marty was going to spend her first full day alone with the twins, but she was clearly very capable and didn't foresee any problems.

"How'd it go?" Chuck asked when he got home.

"Just fine!" she said. "They were little angels. I fed them one at a time at ten and again at two and they haven't let out a peep since. Tiptoe in and take a look, just don't wake them!"

THE DAYS PASSED RAPIDLY AND THANKSGIVING DAY SOON ARRIVED. Their parents, Bill and Beth Kirkwood and Frank and Grace Dowdle, drove down from Crookston for the weekend, excited about seeing their grandsons for the first time. Chuck's parents didn't own a car, so they traveled with the Kirkwoods. Their lodging needs were handily taken care of, as two single teachers who rented upstairs rooms from landlords Otto and Evelyn Kreuger told Chuck and Marty their parents were welcome to stay in their rooms, as both planned to be out of town for Thanksgiving.

The grandparents were eager to meet their new grandchildren, also curious about what basement apartment living was like for Chuck and Marty. "I hear footsteps on the stairs," said Chuck. "I think they've arrived!"

Marty was busy in the kitchen, but eager to see her parents, so she wiped her hands on her apron and rushed to the bottom of the stairs to greet them. Her mother, Beth, gave her a warm hug. "Oh, Marilyn, it's so good to see you! How are you feeling?" she asked.

"I'm feeling good, Mom," she said. "How was the drive down?"

"It was good, Marilyn. Bill did the driving and it didn't take long at all."

Marty's "daddy" (as she was fond of calling her father) stepped down from the stairs and gave his daughter a loving embrace. "It sure is good to see you again, Marilyn!" he said. "We left at ten o'clock, stopped at Detroit Lakes for coffee, and it only took us about two hours to get here. It was a nice relaxing drive, and I know the Dowdles enjoyed it as well."

Chuck's mother approached Marty, and reaching out to her said, "My, but you look lovely, Marilyn. The glow of motherhood!" She turned towards her son and said, "Hi, Charlie!" as they exchanged warm hugs.

Chuck and his dad embraced and picked up the rear as the exuberant caravan headed to the twins' bedroom. "This is a nice place you've got here, Charlie," Frank said. "I didn't know what to expect, but this is comfortable, lots of nice light from those windows. I guess you'll have to get out there and shovel the snow once it starts blowing and shifting against the house."

"I know," said Chuck laughing. "Here's hoping for a mild winter! We sure do like it here. I think the boys will, too, especially once they start crawling around." They caught up with the others, all of them peeking into the twins' crib.

"They're beautiful!" exclaimed Mrs. Dowdle in a joyful whisper. "With their blond, downy hair they look just like you did as a newborn, Chuck!"

"Poor little guys," he joked.

"And they have his blue eyes, too," Marilyn said. The twins were oblivious to all the admiration and observation and just kept sleeping, one at each end of the crib.

"My, Marilyn," said her mother as they all walked into the living room. "It sure is warm and cozy in here."

"We like this apartment a lot," said Marty. "The Kruegers are wonderful landlords. Evelyn is a nurse for the doctor who delivered the boys, and her husband, Otto, is a long-distance hauler."

"Very nice place indeed," said Frank, "and it sure smells good around here!"

"That would be turkey!" said Marilyn. "Would it be okay if we ate around four o'clock? I put the bird in early, so it should be done by then. I figured if the boys stayed on schedule and ate at two and six, we might just be able to have a leisurely, peaceful dinner. What do you think?"

"That sounds wonderful, Marilyn," her mother said. "Maybe while you're busy in the kitchen, you'll let us feed the twins."

"Oh, Mom," she gushed. "Of course!"

"I'd love to and I'll bet Grace would, too! A baby for each of us! It may have been a while, but I think it will come back to us."

"Count me in!" Chuck's mom said enthusiastically.

The women busied themselves with helping Marty in the kitchen while the men visited in the living room. "Well, Frank, how do you like our new president now that he's been in office for a year?" asked Mr. Kirkwood. Chuck listened closely, as his dad had been a Democrat all his life and Mr. Kirkwood was an independent.

"Well," Frank said, "I liked Roosevelt and I think Truman did a great job taking over and helping us win World War II when Roosevelt died in '45, but I like Dwight Eisenhower, too. He did a good job leading us to victory in Europe."

"Tough for Truman to become President after being Vice President for just a few months, and then to have to decide to use the atomic bomb against Japan to end the war," Mr. Kirkwood said. The men mulled over the many decisions "Ike" was going to have to make regarding the Communist influence in government and civil rights issues, then began talking about Crookston politics. Marilyn's dad was an attorney and had been mayor of Crookston for twelve years. Chuck's dad was a barber, and it seemed politics was all men talked about when they came in for a shave or a haircut.

Time flew by, and then everyone heard the twin chorus begin, the gentle "um, um, um" growing to insistent "Um! Um! Um!"

"Sounds like it's time for those boys to eat!" Marilyn said. "Are you ladies ready?"

"Oh, yes!" both grandmothers said in unison.

"Okay," Marty said with a smile. "They'll need changing first, so why don't you go in and do that while I'm heating the bottles."

The women slowly entered the twins' bedroom and began cooing baby talk to their new grandsons. The boys' deep-blue eyes darted from one woman to the other, their heads moving back and forth as they searched for "Mom" in the two beaming faces. "Which one do you want, Grace?" asked Beth.

"I'll take this little guy…Michael…at least I think it's Michael!" she laughed as she gently picked him up. "He looks just like Charlie did as a newborn."

Beth lovingly lifted Mark from the crib and the grandmothers placed the boys side by side on the changing table. "Oh my!" said Beth. "Mark's diaper is soaked!"

"So is Michael's!" said Grace.

"Of course," laughed Beth. "Twin bladders!"

The women expertly went about their work. It had been a long time since either had changed a diaper, but both were experienced and not about to let one outdo the other. Chuck's mom had given birth to five children, three of them boys, and Mrs. Kirkwood had a boy and two girls.

The women stood and admired the twins, their beloved new grandsons. The boys stared up at them and waited for their mom's familiar hands to gently caress their soft, pink bodies. Michael began singing his mm, mm, mm's as Chuck's mother began rubbing his clean little behind with lotion. "Aren't you adorable," she cooed…just as she was squirted in the face! "Oh, my!" she cried as she jumped back. "I had forgotten about that possibility! The little dickens really got me!" she said as a laughing Beth handed her a damp cloth.

Both ladies had a good chuckle as Beth began rubbing Mark with lotion. Sure enough, he just then let loose with a stream of his own, but Beth was watching for it and backed up with a loud, "Oh no!" in time to avoid the attack. Both women erupted in laughter.

"Everything okay in there?" Marty called from the kitchen. "You two are having an awful lot of fun changing diapers! The bottles are just about ready out here." The grandmothers entered the living room and settled onto the couch, each with a twin bundled comfortably in their arms.

"What was all the commotion in there, Grace?" asked Frank.

"I got a hearty squirt in the face while I was changing this little one," she said, "and then Mark tried the same thing on Beth, but she was quick enough to move out of the line of fire! It was so long ago with Bill and Charlie and Jerry that I forgot what happens with little boys." The men chuckled and walked into the kitchen where Marty and Chuck were setting the table for Thanksgiving dinner.

"Anything we can do to help out, Charlie?" Chuck's dad asked.

"Sure," said Chuck. "How about you and Mr. Kirkwood carve the turkey?" The men were happy to oblige, thankful to not have been delegated the diaper-changing duty, and went about their task like professionals. They had carved many a Thanksgiving turkey in their lifetimes, and while they were doing their handiwork, Chuck and Marty went to work on the mashed potatoes and gravy.

"I think we'll be ready to eat as soon as the boys are fed," said Marty.

Their three o'clock bottles were soon drained and the doting grandmothers were busily settling the grandsons down for an afternoon nap when they detected a certain odor filling the air… definitely not turkey!…followed by Michael's "mm, mm, mm." Mark soon joined in. "I hear that chorus," yelled Marty from the kitchen. "They often need a diaper change soon after eating, you might want to check."

Beth bent down to smell Mark's diaper. "Whew!" she exclaimed as she backed away. "I'm afraid it's more than just urine this time!"

"Michael, too!" said Grace as she quickly raised her head away from his diaper. In no time at all, the experienced grandmothers had the twins cleaned and diapered and nestled back into the crib. The content babies were soon sound asleep.

"My, what a lovely Thanksgiving celebration!" said Marty's mother as she admired the beautifully-set table with the exquisite cream-colored linen tablecloth, a family heirloom.

Everyone expressed their praises as they settled into their places. "Lord, we have so much for which to be thankful," said Chuck as he began to pray. "Thank you for making it possible for our parents to be here with us to share in Thanksgiving and thank you for our two beautiful and healthy boys! And Lord, thank you for my loving wife, who has prepared this magnificent meal. Amen!"

After enjoying the scrumptious meal, everyone pitched in with the cleanup and then retired to the living room to relax and enjoy a piece of Marty's homemade pumpkin pie with fresh whipped cream. It was about six o'clock when they finished, time once again for the twins to be fed. "We shouldn't have to worry about the boys after this feeding," said Marty cheerily. "They've been sleeping through the night and that's been a real blessing."

Just as anticipated, the twins woke up right on schedule, were fed by their mom and went to sleep immediately afterwards, calmed as they were by hearing the familiar voice, seeing the familiar face and feeling the familiar touch. The grandparents tiptoed into the boys' bedroom to sneak a quick good-night peek and then headed upstairs to their rooms. "Thank you so much for preparing that fantastic meal, Marilyn," said Chuck's mother.

"Yes," Chuck's dad added, "it was delicious, Marilyn. Thank you."

"Marilyn," Marty's mother said, "we loved every bite! And so thoughtful of you and Chuck and the Kruegers to make arrangements for us to sleep here. Please thank them for us."

"I sure will, Mom," said Marty. "I hope you all sleep well up there. Good night to everyone!"

The next morning the twins were up bright and early at six o'clock. Chuck changed and fed them while Marty fixed a hearty breakfast of fresh orange juice, bacon and eggs, hash browns, toast and coffee. She knew this was her dad's favorite breakfast and she wanted to please him. And pleased he was. Mr. Kirkwood must have smelled the bacon frying, as he was the first one to come downstairs. "Well, Marilyn," he said brightly, "you must be making something good in here. I could smell it all the way up in our room!"

"It's your favorite breakfast, Daddy," she said. "I wanted you to have it before you started the drive home; that way you won't have to stop along the way." It wasn't long before her mother and Chuck's parents came down as well, and everyone sat and enjoyed breakfast. Before finishing, a familiar sound echoed from the twins' bedroom. Chuck and Marty had the routine down and both hopped into action. Chuck headed to the bedroom to change the boys' diapers, Marty to the kitchen to heat the bottles. "Daddy," Marty asked, "would you and Mr. Dowdle like to feed the twins this morning?"

"Oh, I don't know, Marilyn," he said, hesitating. "The last baby I fed was you, twenty-five years ago. I'm not sure I'll remember how!"

"Sure you will, Bill," encouraged Mrs. Kirkwood. "I remember how you loved feeding Marilyn and she loved being fed by you. Go ahead!"

"OK, Marilyn. I'll give it a try," said her father.

"I will, too," Chuck's dad said. "It will be fun to see if I remember how."

"Thank you!" said Marty as she removed the twins' bottles from the pan of warm water. She loved her dad, and it made her happy that he agreed to take on the feeding, as she wanted him to feel as close to his grandsons as she felt to him.

The grandfathers could hear one noisy baby as Chuck headed into the living room with a twin in each arm. "OK," Chuck said cheerily, "who wants the hungry one? That would be Michael!"

"I'll take him, Charlie," Chuck's dad said as he reached out for the handoff. Michael kicked his little legs in all directions in anticipation of being fed as Marty handed Chuck's dad the bottle. "All right, little guy, it's just you and me now," said Chuck's dad as the nipple found its way to Michael's open mouth. Michael began sucking wildly and stared into his grandpa's face with his inquisitive, baby-blue eyes. "Who are you and why are you feeding me?" they seemed to ask.

Next up was Mark, and Chuck placed him gently into Mr. Kirkwood's outstretched arms. "Okay, Daddy, your turn," Marilyn said with a smile as she handed him the warm bottle. Mark didn't seem as ravenous as his brother nor did he reach out for the bottle when it was held in front of him. However, when Marty's dad held the nipple near his lips, he latched onto it and began sucking with the same vigor as Michael. Marilyn beamed at her dad and Mr. Dowdle and said, "You two certainly haven't lost your touch. You can come back here and handle feedings any time you want!" Grace and Beth marveled at how well-behaved Michael and Mark were while being fed by strangers, but then, these strangers were two men who loved their grandsons very much, and that was surely sensed by the boys as they gazed up into their grandfathers' faces.

The twins were back in their crib and sleeping by the time the grandparents climbed the stairs to their bedrooms to pack up before the drive back to Crookston. Chuck helped them carry their suitcases to the car, and everyone exchanged a round of hugs and expressed appreciation for the lovely visit.

"This has been a wonderful Thanksgiving for us, Marilyn," her mom said. "It sure would be fun to come back for Christmas next month and see how the twins are doing. They change so rapidly at this age."

"Oh, Mom, would you and dad like to do that?" Marty asked enthusiastically. "We'd love to have you all back! The teachers upstairs will probably go home for the holidays and I'm sure you could stay there again. Maybe Chuck's parents could drive with you again as well!"

Everything was soon arranged. Chuck talked to Otto and Evelyn, they talked to their tenants and all was in place for Chuck and Marty's parents to use the rooms again during Christmas vacation. Chuck's parents thought it would be fun to spend Christmas in Perham and were looking forward to sharing the trip again with Marty's parents. Frank and Grace didn't own a car, never had, and it was always a pleasure for them to sit and enjoy the passing countryside.

All seemed calm and bright for Chuck and Marty. However, two weeks before Christmas a minor tragedy befell the small family. Marilyn was the first to write her parents and give them the difficult news.

December 10, 1953

Dear Mom and Daddy,

Thank you for taking the time to drive to Perham to celebrate Thanksgiving with us and to meet your grandsons. We loved it and they loved you! And thanks so much for sharing the journey with Mr. and Mrs. Dowdle. Chuck really appreciated that. We're very much looking forward to seeing you all again at Christmas!

There is something I must tell you before you come, something very sad. We took the twins to Dr. Schoeneberger yesterday for their four-month checkup, and he asked us if we'd noticed any unusual behavior from either of the boys. I told him the only thing I'd noticed was that Mark was rubbing his eyes a lot and didn't reach out for the bottle during feedings the way Michael did. The doctor told us there may be an explanation and wanted us to have the boys seen by Dr. O.E. Bertelson, an eye, ear, nose and throat specialist. He called ahead and we got right in.

When Dr. Bertelson checked Michael's eyes, he said everything looked fine, but after checking Mark's eyes, he told us Mark had developed a mild form of a disease called *Retinopathy of Prematurity*. It happens when there's abnormal blood vessel development in the retina of the eye in a premature infant. He gave us some literature on the disease and wants us to check back in a week to see if it's worsened and whether we're going to have to do anything about it. Right now it's a game of wait and see.

That's all I can tell you at this point. We don't want to let ourselves get too worried until we know what we're dealing with. I'll let you know as soon as we find out anything more. Chuck's been busy at school, trying to get everything wrapped up before Christmas vacation so he can relax and enjoy the time off. We're looking forward to seeing you again!

—Love, Marilyn

After Chuck and Marty came home from seeing Dr. Bertelson, they sat together after supper and the boys' last feeding and began reading all the materials he'd given them. When they learned that 12,000 babies worldwide had not only been born with Retinopathy of Prematurity since 1941, but blinded by it as well, they became concerned. They became even more concerned when they read that two British scientists suggested it was oxygen toxicity that caused the disease, remembering how Michael and Mark's tiny heads were placed in oxygen masks immediately after they were born just to help them survive.

Marty began to cry softly as she was reading. Chuck looked at her lovingly as he pulled her close. "What's the matter, honey?" he asked. He knew Marty had been deeply affected by Dr. Bertelson's diagnosis for Mark, more so than he had at this point, perhaps because she had been a medical secretary and was more aware of the consequences of the disease. That and the fact that she was a mother.

"Oh, Chuck!" she sighed. "What are we going to do if Mark loses his sight?"

"Honey," said Chuck gently, "he won't, don't worry."

"But it says right here," said Marty tearfully, "I'll read it. '*When the excess oxygen environment is removed, the blood vessels begin forming rapidly and begin growing into the vitreous humor of the eye from the retina, which can cause blindness!*' What if that happens to Mark?"

"Honey, that's something we'll have to learn more about when we see Dr. Bertelson again," said Chuck. "It's getting late; it's been a long day and we're both tired. Let's go to bed." Chuck's anxiety was growing. He didn't know what to say to comfort his wife, and he was worried as well.

It seemed like the following week would never end, both parents constantly observing Mark for any signs that his sight might be deteriorating. It was cold outside and snow covered the ground when they brought the twins back in to see Dr. Bertelson for the follow-up appointment.

"Good afternoon, Mr. and Mrs. Dowdle," he said. "How have the boys been?"

"I've been watching Mark closely all week, Doctor," Marty said, "but I haven't noticed anything different about his eyes. He still rubs them quite a bit and he still searches for his bottle in the air with his hands when I'm ready to feed him. I don't think he's seeing the bottle clearly, because his reach has been way off."

"Well, with his condition that's to be expected, Mrs. Dowdle," he said. "I'll take a good look at him today and see if I can give you an update on his condition. Did you and your husband have a chance to read the Retinopathy of Prematurity literature?"

"Yes, we did, doctor," Chuck said soberly, "and it's pretty scary to think our son may end up going blind."

"I don't want us to jump to any conclusions until we've had more time to assess any changes," said Dr. Bertelson as he bent over Mark on the examining table and peered into his eyes with a special ophthalmic lens. Mark just lay there and didn't let out a peep. "This is a good little guy," said the doctor, stepping back. "He's going to be okay for now because the disease is only mild, at what we call Stage I. I want to go into observation mode and I'll see you back in a month. We'll hope the disease hasn't progressed. It may have even disappeared," he said as Chuck and Marty looked notably relieved. "Do either of you have any questions?"

"I don't think I do, Doctor," Marty said as she wrapped a heavy blanket around Mark and cuddled him close to her body. "You've explained Mark's condition to us thoroughly and it's a big relief to learn this stage of the disease doesn't lead directly to blindness. We appreciate your time and concern and will be back in a month. Maybe Chuck has some questions?"

"No, not right now at least," said Chuck. "Thank you very much for taking care of Mark for us."

"It's my pleasure, Mr. Dowdle," said the doctor as he shook Chuck's hand. "If you and your wife will stop at the front desk and make the return appointment, we'll be all set. Enjoy those boys and stay warm!"

Once they got into the car and began driving home, Chuck let out a heavy sigh of relief and exclaimed, "Wow! I'm so happy that Mark's condition isn't serious!"

"Me, too," said Marty, closing her eyes and exhaling deeply, "but we'll have to watch him closely for any new signs of the disease."

Both parents were silent the rest of the way home and so were the twins. Michael had slept through his brother's entire appointment, and began to wake up just as Chuck was tucking him into his crib. "Dada, Dada, Dada," he said. Chuck and Marty had been working with the boys to teach them how to say Dada and Mama, and their efforts had paid off! Now when they had dirty diapers or were hungry, it was no longer mm, mm, mm or ah, ah, ah, instead they called out "Dada! Mama!" Sometimes it got a little confusing, but they were very young for even being able to say those words, so it didn't matter. Chuck and Marty were as proud as two young parents could be! That night Chuck sat down to write his folks a letter to let them know what had transpired:

December 16, 1953

Dear Mom and Dad,

Marilyn and I are sure looking forward to having you here for Christmas! You'll be able to travel with Mr. and Mrs. Kirkwood and stay in the same room as before. You and the Kirkwoods are going to have something new to talk about on the drive, because we just got back from the doctor and learned Mark has a mild form of a disease called Retinopathy of Prematurity.

We knew he had a problem of some sort with his eyes when we took the twins in for their four-month checkup a week ago. Dr. Schoeneberger noticed something different at that time and had us take the boys to an eye specialist that afternoon, Dr. O.E. Bertelson. He examined both boys' eyes and told us Mark had the disease. Retinopathy of Prematurity is an eye disorder that primarily affects premature infants, and it can cause blindness. Michael seems to be OK, but Mark is going to have to be watched closely to see if the disease progresses. By the time you and Dad and the Kirkwoods get here for Christmas, our hope is that Mark will be on his way to a total recovery!

The only other news I have to share is that we made a down payment on a home lot about two blocks from the school. If everything goes according to plan, we'll be building in the spring and moving into our new house before classes start in the fall! That's about it in the way of news from here. I hope all's well with both of you. We'll see you soon!

—Love, Charlie

The first morning of Christmas vacation, a Saturday, began as usual, lots of tender-loving care for the twins. Chuck was looking forward to having two weeks to spend with his boys and Marty was happily anticipating some alone time away from the house, a chance to finally accomplish her Christmas shopping! There were piles of snow on the ground and it was cold outside, but that didn't matter to her. She was ready!

Around noon, shortly after they had changed and fed the boys, the doorbell rang. When Chuck went up the stairs and opened the door, all the members of his Current Events Club were there to greet him: Judy Mondt, Patty Moltzan, Margaret Radke, Eileen Wallace, Jocelyn Frank, Janice Lillis, Sharon Samp, Charles Meyer, Eugene Klinnert, Kenneth Anderson, Gary West, Linda & Laurie Hertel, Rose Hammers, Jean Wendt, Jo Ann Langston, Ruth Ann Silbernagel, Colleen Belka, Barbara Bahls, Janice Stollenwerk, Sharon Rosen, Cleo Schmidt, Evalin Cavalier, Ann Schatschneider and Lorraine Lueders! "Hi, Mr. Dowdle!" they yelled in unison. "We came to wish you a Merry Christmas and to see your twins!" gushed Lorraine.

"Well, don't just stand out there in the cold!" Chuck said cheerily, his breath turning a crisp, cold white. "Come on down! We just put the boys in bed, but I don't think they're sleeping yet. Be careful and hold onto the railing! These stairs get pretty slippery when they're wet."

Chuck taught World Geography to seventh graders, and shortly after the beginning of the school year he started a new club for interested students, the Current Events Club. Once a week in the evening the kids, some of whom had to be driven in quite a distance from the country, gathered at the school to discuss topics of current interest. It was amazing how, in spite of the miles some parents had to drive, they were willing to get their kids to the meetings, even in the dead of winter. And now the kids were at his home, thoughtful enough to come by on a cold December night.

"Mr. Dowdle," Judy said, beaming as she handed him a large package wrapped in festive holiday paper, "we wanted to get you something to show our appreciation for all the extra time you've spent with us in the Current Events Club."

Chuck sat down on the couch and opened the present, and when he saw it was a beautifully-embossed World Atlas, he was thrilled. "Thank you very much!" he said appreciatively. When he opened the cover and saw each of them had written and signed a short message, he began to tear up. "You kids are too much," he said, his face flushed. "Thank you, truly. Now let's go in and see the twins." None of them had seen the little guys before, and the boys' heads moved from side to side as they tried to take in the large group stepping into their bedroom. That's when the fun began!

Michael was first. "Dada, Dada, Dada," he cooed and the kids began to giggle. Then Mark began singing, "Mama, Mama, Mama," and the group erupted in laughter. Everyone was still amused when they filed out of the bedroom and headed up the stairs to leave. "Thanks for letting us see your boys, Mr. and Mrs. Dowdle! They're adorable!" they called back cheerfully as they left the house. "Have a Merry Christmas!"

"Those sure are some great kids, Chuck," Marty said. "I can see why you love being around them."

"They are special," said Chuck beaming. "So thoughtful and energetic, and they love getting together to discuss what's happening in the world. It makes me happy to see how interested they are in what's going on around them."

After lunch, an ebullient Marty left to do some holiday shopping. She got back late, her cheeks flushed from the cold, her arms laden with packages. Chuck had supper ready and the twins fed and tucked in for the night. "This is heaven!" gushed Marty as she sat down at the table and filled her plate, "I feel like a queen!" After a peaceful meal, she and Chuck retired to the living room and prayed the Rosary before bed, asking that Mark's eyes would be healed. It had been a busy day, and they were more than ready to settle in under the cozy comforter for a good night's sleep.

"Mama, Mama, Mama!" came the familiar chorus at six the next morning. Marty had decided to start feeding the boys solid food while Chuck was home on vacation so as to take advantage of his help, and there was no time like the present! After the diaper change, Marty took Mark and Chuck took Michael. Instead of bottles, they each had a small bowl of oatmeal Marty had prepared ahead of time. Chuck was first to give it a try. When he held the small spoonful up to Michael's lips, Michael just stared at him, and then suddenly slapped at the spoon, sending oatmeal in every direction! It was quite different with Mark. When Marty held the spoon to his lips, he took a small taste, and then opened his mouth and waited until Marty gently placed a spoonful of oatmeal into his mouth. He moved it around and then swallowed. He liked it!

"I'll be damned!" Chuck said laughing. "If you can do it, I can, too!" It was quite a challenge for the next few bites, but before long, both boys were eagerly opening their mouths for more breakfast!

After the twins were fed, Marty decided it would be fun to lay them on a thick comforter on the living room floor where they could take in the Christmas tree fanfare. It turned out to be a good idea. Chuck brought the tree in, and the boys gazed up at it, turning their heads from side to side. Next, came stringing of the lights, colorful red, green, yellow, blue and white bulbs, and then strands of silver tinsel. The boys were spellbound, kept staring upward, perhaps wondering what was going to happen next. Chuck plugged in the lights, and the tree came to life! The boys twisted and squirmed to get a better look. Then they did a first! Simultaneously, they turned from their backs to their tummies and began cooing and kicking, their heads bobbing up and down as they took in the festive scene before them.

"Will you look at that!" said Chuck. "Only four months old and they're already rolling over! They'll be crawling all over the place soon!"

"I don't think it will happen quite that fast," said Marty. "You're just a proud papa!"

"I am! I am!" yelled Chuck, his face glowing. His startled sons turned their gazes away from the tree long enough to say, "Dada, Dada, Dada," then back to the sparkling tree.

Time passed rapidly as the days rolled by, and December 24th soon arrived. It was noon when Marty heard the doorbell ring. That must be them, Chuck!" she said.

Chuck leapt up the stairs, flung open the door and called out, "Merry Christmas!"

"Merry Christmas to you!" their parents said in joyful unison.

"Come in! Come in!" Chuck said. "Be careful when you head down the stairs; hang onto the railing. The stairs can be slippery when they're wet."

Marty was at the bottom of the stairs to greet her parents. "It's so good to see you again, Marilyn," said her father. "How are the twins?"

"Oh, wait until you see them, Daddy! They've grown and changed quite a bit in just a month!" she said cheerfully. Then she looked mischievously at her mother and Mrs. Dowdle. "I know you just got here. Are you ladies up for some more diaper changing this visit?"

"Sure we are! Right, Grace?" said Marty's mother confidently.

"Of course!" said Chuck's mom. "And this time we'll be on guard for those two little squirters!"

"We recently began feeding them oatmeal before their bottles, and it's presented quite a messy challenge," Marty said. "You'll see! For now, why don't you all give me your coats and come into the living room and make yourselves comfortable. I'll serve you lunch out there. We can just eat and talk. We'll bring your things in from the car and up to your rooms after we're done. Let's just relax, especially now while the boys are still sleeping!"

"This sure is a nice tree," Mrs. Kirkwood said as she walked around the grand perimeter.

"You should have seen the boys' eyes when it was being decorated," said Chuck. We had them lying on their backs on a comforter, and when we plugged the lights in, they rolled onto their stomachs for the first time and began kicking their legs. Michael even began moving his arms like he wanted to swim towards it and touch it!"

"How precious!" Chuck's mom said. "I bet they've grown a lot since we last saw them a month ago!"

"They sure have, Mom," he said. "Wait until you see them!"

"Here we are, folks," Marty said as she entered the living room with a tray of tuna sandwiches and fresh fruit. "Help yourselves and I'll make some coffee."

"This looks wonderful, Marilyn," said her dad. "Thank you!"

"Just you wait, Daddy," she said. "I made some of your favorite Christmas sugar cookies. You can have them with your coffee."

Everyone enjoyed lunch, and then sat and chatted. "We left Crookston at about nine this morning," Mr. Kirkwood said. "There was quite a bit of snow on the ground, and it took us longer to get here this time even though we didn't stop to eat."

"Good thing you didn't stop!" Marty laughed as her dad reached for a second sandwich.

"I'll say!" said her dad. "I wouldn't be able to enjoy this delicious lunch like I am!"

"Oh, Daddy," I'm glad you like it," beamed Marty.

"How about I go out and get your luggage so you folks can get settled in upstairs before the boys wake up?" suggested Chuck.

"That'd be great, Charlie," said Chuck's dad. "I'll come with you and help."

It was beginning to snow, and the wind was picking up as Chuck and his dad lugged the suitcases into the house and up the stairs. Chuck noticed his dad breathing quite heavily as they neared the landing. "Why don't you stay up here and unpack, Dad," he said, "and I'll get the rest of the luggage."

"OK, Charlie, thank you," he said breathlessly.

Chuck left the room and headed downstairs. It didn't take long for him to get the rest of the suitcases upstairs. "You're all set up there," he announced as he entered the dining room. "Why don't you all take your time unpacking and rest up a bit. I'm sure you'll hear the boys once they wake up!"

"That sounds like a good idea, Chuck," Mrs. Kirkwood said as they headed to the stairs.

"Well, honey, I think this is our chance for a rest as well," Chuck said as he caught Marty in the middle of a yawn. "Why don't we sit and figure out our plan?"

"Sure," said Marty, "though I don't think there's much to figure out. "I've got a beef roast in the oven. We can have that tonight and tomorrow. My mom loves to play cards; maybe we can do that after dinner tonight."

"Sounds good to me," he said affectionately as he nuzzled up behind her and kissed her tenderly on the nape of the neck.

Both new parents were exhausted. It wasn't long before they dozed off in each other's arms, and it seemed like only a short time after that when they heard the all-too-familiar, "Dada! Dada! Mama! Mama!"

"Did you hear what I just heard?" Chuck whispered softly into Marty's ear. She didn't move, was fast asleep. Chuck slipped off his shoes, eased gently away from her warm body and shuffled quietly across the hardwood floor and into the nursery. He closed the door so the twin noisemakers wouldn't wake their mom, and began changing their wet diapers. "Boys," he whispered, "it's almost time to go see your grandparents. Michael, do you want to see your grandmas and grandpas?"

"Da, da, da, da, dada!" Michael blurted.

After the twins were clean and dry, Chuck laid them back in the crib and went to see if Marty was still sleeping. Quite the contrary! She was wide awake, sitting and talking with her parents and Chuck's mom and dad. "It's feeding time!" he announced. "I'll get the boys and see if they'll do the tummy flip act for you before they're fed."

With Mark cooing in his arms, Chuck returned to a chorus of oohs and aahs from the admiring grandparents. He placed Mark on his back on the soft comforter in front of the Christmas tree and then brought Michael out and placed him on his back a short distance from Mark. "OK, everybody ready? Here we go!" With that he plugged in the Christmas tree lights and it sparkled to life.

"Oh, my! How beautiful, Charlie!" Chuck's mother exclaimed.

"It sure is, Charlie," Chuck's dad said appreciatively.

"It's so lovely with all those colors and the silver tinsel," said Mrs. Kirkwood. "I remember that angel dressed in white on top of the tree. Is that the one that used to be ours, Marilyn?"

"Yes, Mother," she said. "You gave that to me when I left home so I'd always have a piece of Christmas memory with our family."

"Oh, yes, now I remember," she said nostalgically.

Michael had been rolling from side to side on his back, and when he finally made it over and onto his tummy, Mr. Kirkwood said, "Good boy, Michael! Good boy!" Mark was still lying on his back, but when he heard Michael call out, "Dada, Dada, Dada," he began rolling with vigor, and when he made it onto his tummy, everyone clapped and cheered. Both boys began kicking their legs and moving their arms in a swimming motion in a determined attempt to reach the tree. "Crawl, boys, crawl!" Mr. Kirkwood called out as he bent down towards his grandsons and urged them on.

"Oh, Bill," Mrs. Kirkwood said laughing, "I hardly think those little guys are going to get up just for you! What they probably want more than anything is dinner! Grace, how about you and I feed them?"

"Good idea," Mrs. Dowdle said eagerly.

"I say great idea!" said Marilyn.

The women bent over the boys, picked them up and cradled them gently in their arms, cooing at them like the fond grandmothers they were. They sat on the sofa with their little charges while Marty heated their bottles. Mrs. Dowdle had Michael and Mrs. Kirkwood had Mark. "Okay, ladies, ready or not!" Marty said jovially as she entered the room with a bottle in each hand.

"This little guy saw you coming and started kicking!" Chuck's mother said as Marty handed her the bottle. As soon as the nipple touched Michael's lips, he latched on and began gulping down the milk as if he hadn't eaten in days. Mark wasn't quite as enthusiastic for Mrs. Kirkwood. He fumbled with the nipple and finally began sucking, but it took him longer than usual, notably longer than it had his brother.

While the grandmothers were busily feeding the boys, the men went into the kitchen and helped Marty with dinner. "We're having roast beef tonight, Daddy," she said, "and then I thought tomorrow afternoon you could make roast beef sandwiches for us just the way you used to when I was home."

"That sounds wonderful, Marilyn," he said smiling. "I'd be happy to."

After the boys were fed and tucked in for the night, everyone sat down to enjoy the delicious roast. Chuck and Marty and the four grandparents were tired after their long day, and instead of playing cards after dinner as planned, they decided to call it an early night and headed off to bed.

Like clockwork, the twins were wide awake and ready for breakfast at six o'clock the next morning. It was going to be a very busy Christmas Day! Marty and Chuck were going to the eight o'clock Mass at St. Henry's Church, returning in time for their parents to attend the ten o'clock service. After church, everyone would sit down for a hearty brunch, hopefully with the twins fed by that time and back down for their mid-morning nap.

Chuck could hear the grandparent parade headed down the stairs at seven o'clock. "Good morning and Merry Christmas!" he said enthusiastically. How'd everybody sleep?"

"We slept good and hard!" Chuck's mom said. "It's so comfortable and quiet up there."

"Yes, Chuck, I agree," Beth added. "Bill and I slept really well. There's nothing like a good night's rest."

"Happy to hear it," Chuck said. "Now I have a question for all of you. Would you mind staying with the twins while Marty and I go to the eight o'clock Mass at St. Henry's? We'd be back around 9:15, and then you folks could easily make it to the ten o'clock Mass if that sounds all right with you."

"That sounds fine, Chuck," Beth said. "How far is the church from here?"

"It's only three blocks," Chuck said, "within walking distance, but you'll want to drive in this weather. While you're at church, Marty and I will fix Christmas brunch, the twins will have had their breakfast, and we can all sit down for a peaceful meal together when you get back."

While Chuck and Marty were at church, the grandmothers enjoyed their time of doting on their grandsons. They placed them on their backs in front of the glowing Christmas tree to see if they'd flip onto their tummies. Sure enough, they did, and in record time! "These two are fast learners!" Grace said.

"Bill," Beth said, "why don't you and Frank bring the twins' gifts in from the car and put them under the tree. We'll surprise Chuck and Marilyn when they get home from church."

"Good idea, Beth," said Bill as he and Frank headed for the chilly outdoors. It wasn't an easy task to maneuver the two heavy cardboard boxes from the trunk to the house and down the steep steps, but they did it! Michael and Mark greeted their return with a chorus of coos as the grandfathers placed the merrily-decorated packages under the tree. On each was a large printed label: MERRY CHRISTMAS!

All was calm when Chuck and Marty returned from church. "What's this?" Chuck asked when he saw the oversized boxes under the tree.

"Santa stopped by while you were out, Chuck," laughed Mrs. Kirkwood. "They're presents for the boys. We can open them when we get back from church, maybe after brunch. Until then, no peeking!"

"Thank you very much, Mother!" said Marilyn. "I'm so curious! You all should probably head off now. You'll like our pastor, Father Nicholas Donnay."

"We'll see you later, Charlie," Mrs. Dowdle said as the grandparents made their way up the stairs and headed outdoors to their car.

Time was of the essence. Chuck and Marty began scurrying around like ants on a mission. Chuck began setting the dinette table in the kitchen, the only dining area in the apartment. Next, he joined Marty in scrubbing and dicing potatoes to accompany the scrambled eggs and ham. "Mama, Mama, Mama," came the twin chorus from the bedroom. "I'll tend to those two. You carry on here," said Marty as she washed her hands at the sink and headed down the hall.

A few minutes before eleven, the grandparents could be heard returning from church, chattering happily as they made their way down the stairs. Chuck and Marty were ready! The twins were fed and back down for a nap, and brunch was prepared. "Sure smells good in here, Charlie!" Chuck's dad said as he entered the kitchen and eyed the sliced ham.

Marty pulled a batch of her dad's favorite baking powder biscuits from the oven, golden brown, just the way he liked them. "Oh, Marilyn," Mr. Kirkwood gushed, "you're going to spoil us rotten with your cooking!"

"I hope so, Daddy!" she said as she hugged him. "Let's sit down and eat while everything is hot." In addition to the ham and eggs and potatoes and biscuits, Marty had fixed a fruit salad, vibrant in color with its array of melons and berries. Chuck set a percolator of freshly-brewed coffee on the table and the feast was about to begin!

"Lord, thank you for letting us all be together this Christmas Day to celebrate the birth of Jesus Christ and to share our family love," said Chuck as all heads bowed, "and thank you for this bountiful food, deliciously prepared by my beautiful wife. Amen!"

"Nice short prayer, Chuck," his dad said jokingly.

"Just the kind I like when I'm hungry!" laughed Mrs. Kirkwood. "Marilyn, this ham looks delicious!" she added as she forked a generous slice onto her plate.

"I hope it is!" said Marty.

"No need to wonder about that," her dad said as he took his first bite. "It's perfect! And please pass that basket of beautiful biscuits. They're calling my name!"

"I thought you'd like them, Daddy," said a beaming Marty. "What did you think of Father Donnay?"

"We all liked him," said her mother, "and his sermon was very good. He seemed like a very gentle and spiritual man. We chatted with him a bit after Mass and talked about our common French backgrounds. You're fortunate to have him as your parish priest."

"I agree. Chuck and I love him," said Marty.

After their hearty and satisfying breakfast, they left the piles of dishes behind and headed into the living room to open presents. It turned out to be an unusually synchronistic gift giving Christmas for the adults, as everyone received sweaters, nothing else, just sweaters! "Well," said Chuck as he held up two of his for everyone to see, "we're all going to be warm this winter!"

"Time to open the big boxes," said Chuck's mother.

"I can't imagine what they are," said Chuck.

"Why don't you try guessing, Charlie," she teased.

"Okay," he said as he lifted the box slightly to assess its weight, "I think it's an indoor swing set!"

"No, that's not it," she laughed.

"Go ahead, open it, Charlie," Chuck's dad said.

"Here goes!" said Chuck as he ripped off the fancy paper. On the side of the box was a colorful picture of a red wagon with built-up wooden sides. "Wow! The boys sure are going to love this! Thank you very much!"

"Your mom and I thought you and Marilyn could use a wagon this summer when you go out for walks with the boys," said Chuck's dad. "They can even stand up in it and hold onto the sides with no danger of falling out."

"It's wonderful!" said Marty. "I love it! Thank you both!"

"It'll be perfect," Chuck said as he began unwrapping the other large box containing the gift from Mr. and Mrs. Kirkwood.

Marty was thrilled when she saw the picture on the box. A highchair for twins! "Oh, my! How wonderful!" she gushed as she got up and embraced her mother and father and kissed them both. "I've never seen anything like this built especially for twins! I can't wait until they're able to feed themselves, maybe even feed each other!"

"Tell you what," Mrs. Kirkwood said, "why don't you men assemble the wagon and highchair while Grace and I help Marilyn with the dishes and kitchen cleanup. By the time we're finished, the twins will probably be waking for their afternoon feeding."

The plan worked like a finely-tuned machine. Just as anticipated, at 2:00 p.m. the kitchen was spic and span, the boys began singing their familiar refrain and the highchair and wagon were ready to go. "They really look nice," Chuck said as he stood back and admired the gifts. "We're going to make very good use of these, such generous and thoughtful presents. Thank you!"

"Yes, thank you! They're beautiful!" said Marty as she hugged her dad and then Chuck's dad.

Marty's dad beamed happily, but Chuck's dad blushed shyly. He wasn't used to receiving that kind of affection. "As soon as the snow melts," he said, "you and Charlie should be able to start using the wagon, and I wouldn't think it would be too long before you can have the twins sitting up in the highchair."

"I can hardly wait!" said Marty.

Mrs. Kirkwood looked admiringly at her daughter and said, "You've been working so hard all morning, Marilyn, why don't you let Grace and me take care of the twins for this feeding."

"That's sure OK with me, Mother," said Marty with a contented sigh. "And maybe if Daddy's not too tired, he can make us roast beef sandwiches like we always had on Sunday afternoons when I was home!"

"I'd be delighted, Marilyn," said her dad. "We can do it together, just like we used to."

After the grandmothers had finished feeding the twins, they laid them on their backs on the comforter in front of the Christmas tree. Michael began carrying on a conversation with the colored bulbs, his head darting up and down and left to right, while Mark turned towards his brother, seemingly more drawn to Michael's voice than to the glittering show.

Out in the kitchen, Marty was admiring the way her dad patiently carved the thin slices of roast beef for their sandwiches. He had her spread mayonnaise on the whole wheat bread, right up to the corners. Marty knew the drill. She had the lettuce, dill pickles and olives ready to go. Her dad sliced the pickles, nice and thin, just like the roast beef. "OK, Marilyn," he said as he masterfully layered the beef onto the first slice of bread, "let the building begin!" The pickles, lettuce and cover of bread came next. The last step was Marilyn's favorite, watching her dad slice each sandwich into four sections and then pierce each quarter with a crowning toothpicked olive.

"Perfect, Daddy! Just the way I remember! Thank you so much for making them," she said affectionately. "Guess what I made for dessert?" Her dad stood back as Marilyn opened the oven door and removed a beautiful lemon meringue pie, its stiff egg whites browned to perfection.

"Oh, Marilyn," her dad sighed, patting his stomach, "I love you!"

"I love you, too, Daddy," she said as she embraced her father.

After eating, the house was wonderfully quiet. The twins were fed and down for their naps, and everyone gathered in the living room to relax and take advantage of the peaceful time together. Chuck brought out the plans for the house they'd begin building in the spring. It would be a one-story open plan with three large bedrooms, each with its own bathroom, all bedrooms located in the back of the house. The front of the house would have a spacious rectangular kitchen with an abundance of windows, perfect for viewing the outside action. The kitchen would open to a large informal dining room/den where family activities would take place. A double garage would be attached to the front of the house.

"That's going to be one big house, Charlie," said Chuck's dad, looking slightly worried. "Are you sure you're going to be able to afford it?"

"It's not like the olden days, Dad," said Chuck. "We've already got a G.I. loan and I have a secure teaching job in Perham. We'll be ready to go as soon as the ground thaws!"

"It's great that you and Marilyn are getting off to such a wonderful start with your family, and in such a friendly town, Chuck," said Mrs. Kirkwood.

Everyone examined the housing plans in detail and then played some Whist, the grandparents' favorite card game. Time whizzed by, and it was soon six o'clock and time to feed the twins again, especially judging by the persistent sounds coming from down the hall. "Marilyn, what would you think about trying out the new high chair?" Mrs. Kirkwood asked.

"Oh, Mother, I don't know," said Marilyn. "Do you think the boys are ready? They're still so small."

"Small and mighty!" said Marty's mom. "I think it might work if we prop them up with some pillows."

"OK, let's try it," said Marty. After the boys were freshly diapered and the grandmothers had the pillows positioned, Chuck took Michael and Marty took Mark and gently placed them side-by-side into the highchair. The boys had never experienced sitting up in this way and had no clue as to what was happening, but seemed to like it. The grandmothers tied a long dish towel around each of their tummies and around the back of the high chair to help them stay upright, and it worked! When Chuck and Marty began feeding them pureed beef and vegetables, it was like watching baby birds opening their mouths for food.

"You can see why these little guys have been gaining some serious weight," Chuck said as he refilled spoonful after spoonful for Michael.

"How much do they weigh now?" his mother asked.

"The last time I weighed them they were both about thirteen pounds, which is quite good when you consider how tiny they were at birth," said Marty.

"I'll say so," said Mrs. Dowdle.

The boys were soon down for the night, and later in the evening everyone gathered around the kitchen table to enjoy a slice of lemon meringue pie. "Extraordinary!" said Mr. Kirkwood, smacking his lips. "Thank you, Marilyn! The next time we see you will probably be in April," he added. "Your mother and I will be traveling to Minneapolis for a meeting I have with other mayors April 26th through 28th, and we were thinking we could stop here on our way back."

"Oh, Daddy, that would be great if you could," said Marty. "School will still be in session, so you won't be able to stay upstairs, but we'd love to have you stop and visit."

"All right," he said smiling, "it's a deal."

The grandparents were up early the next morning, eating breakfast at the same time as the twins, and they were soon packed and ready to leave. They kissed their grandsons goodbye with hugs and tickles as Michael and Mark laughed with glee.

"Marilyn, we had a beautiful visit," said Mr. Kirkwood. "Looks like the wind's come up and it's beginning to snow a bit. We'd best get going if we expect to make it home by noon."

"Yes, I guess you'd better, Daddy," said Marty, her eyes glistening with tears. "We enjoyed having all of you so much. Thank you for coming. I love you all!"

After all the goodbyes were said and the grandparents were headed on their way, Chuck and Marty stretched out on their bed for a much-needed rest. "It's not so easy entertaining company when we've got two little ones," said Marty. "I love seeing them, and of course appreciate all the wonderful gifts and all they did to help, but it is a bit exhausting, especially during the holidays."

"Let's try to take it easy during the rest of our vacation," Chuck said as he hugged his wife. "Just think, 1954, the beginning of a new year!"

It seemed like they'd barely had time to relax when they heard a familiar cry from down the hall, "Mama! Mama! Mama!" Time for the ten o'clock bottle feeding! Marty settled onto the couch with Mark and Chuck began feeding Michael. Mark had always been different than Michael during feedings, but he seemed to have become more finicky over the past couple of weeks. On this particular morning he actually pushed the bottle away, so Marty set it aside and tried breastfeeding. Mark latched on immediately and sucked contentedly.

"Something seems not quite right with Mark and the bottle," said Marty. "He's never pushed it away before, seems to almost unsettle him." What she didn't realize is that all of their lives were soon going to be dramatically changed.

"Good afternoon, Mr. and Mrs. Dowdle," Dr. Bertelson said cheerfully when Marty and Chuck brought the twins in for their next eye exam. "How have the boys been?"

"Fine, doctor," she said, "but Mark seems to have become more irritable recently. I've gone back to breastfeeding him because he often pushes the bottle away."

"It's been a month since I last saw the boys," he said, flipping through the medical file.

"That's right, doctor," said Marty, cuddling Mark in her arms.

"I'll take a look at Michael first," he said, "and then we'll see if there have been any changes in Mark's eyes." Michael lay quietly on the examining table as Dr. Bertelson directed the bright light into his eyes.

"His eyes seem to be just fine," he said after a few minutes, pushing back his chair. He handed Michael to Chuck and then took Mark from Marty's arms, placing him gently on the examining table. He peered deeply into Mark's eyes and quickly stopped. "Mrs. Dowdle," he said frowning, "would you mind steadying Mark on the table so I can get a better look?" Marty gently held Mark's shoulders down so he wouldn't squirm, and Dr. Bertelson continued with his examination. When he rose to face Chuck and Marty, Mark began crying. Dr. Bertelson picked him up and placed him in Marty's arms, where he was soon consoled. "Some things have changed since I last examined Mark" he said in a serious tone. "It seems his mildly-abnormal blood vessel growth has worsened notably, causing the retinas to become completely detached. What apparently happened during the past month is that the abnormal blood vessels began growing toward the center of his eyes instead of following their normal growth pattern along the surface of the retinas. Sometimes when this happens, the blood vessels of the retinas become enlarged and twisted and bleed. Scarring usually takes place, and traction from the scarring causes the abnormal vessels to pull the retinas away from the walls of the eyes. This happens in a small number of babies and Mark is one of them. There's nothing I could have done to prevent it, and at this point there's not much I'm able to do for him. I'm very sorry to tell you that he has lost vision in both eyes."

When Marty heard those words, nothing else Dr. Bertelson had to say mattered. Tears filled her eyes and she drew Mark closer to her breast. Chuck put his arm around her shoulder. "It's going to be OK, honey," he said, his eyes welling up with tears as well.

"I know this is a lot to take in," said Dr. Bertelson quietly. "I'd like to see the boys again in a month. Meanwhile, please call or come in sooner if you have any questions or problems."

When they pulled up in front of the house, neighbors John and Ruthie Klug stopped to ask how Mark was doing. They knew he had a minor issue with his eyes, but their faces dropped when Chuck told them Mark was now blind. They couldn't believe what they were hearing, but they could sympathize, as they'd had their hearts broken as well. Ruthie had suffered two miscarriages and they were without children. As the Klugs walked slowly away, Marty and Chuck hugged the twins close to their bodies and walked quickly toward the house.

Neither of the new parents had an inkling they would be receiving this devastating news. Yes, they knew Mark had a problem with his eyes when Dr. Bertelson first saw him, but the way he had described it to them, as a *mildly-abnormal* blood vessel growth that usually resolves on its own without further progression, well, that had set their minds at ease. As soon as they got downstairs to the warm basement, Michael began singing, "Mama, Mama, Mama," and Mark began crying. He hardly ever cried. Perhaps this was a sign of the challenges ahead.

"It's been a long day, honey," Chuck said. "Why don't we get the boys ready for bed and feed them early tonight so we can have some time to ourselves."

"Sounds like a good idea," said Marty. "I'm emotionally drained. If you wouldn't mind, I think I'd like to have some time alone to write to my parents and tell them what we just learned."

"Sure, Marty," he said. "How about I give the boys their baths and get them ready to eat? You take your time. If you feel the way I do, you'll want to have a good cry." Marty did want to shed buckets of tears, to let them flow freely and to have some quiet time to think. It was hard to imagine what was in store for their little family.

January 7, 1954

Dear Mother and Daddy,

I have some very sad news. When we went to Mark's eye doctor today for his monthly check-up, we learned that his Retinopathy of Prematurity had taken a rapid turn for the worse. We were stunned when Dr. Bertelson described how the disease had advanced and caused the retinas of both of his eyes to become completely detached, leaving him completely blind. Needless to say, Chuck and I are shocked and saddened. We left the office about an hour ago.

I know tragedies happen in families all the time, and as difficult as it is to even begin to digest this news, I feel so fortunate to have my two beautiful boys. I'm grateful Mark has his twin brother, as I expect that will make the road ahead easier for him.

Thanks again for the lovely Christmas gifts. You'll be happy to know we've been using the highchair every day. We prop the boys up with pillows, secure them with the ties and they're very happy being fed side-by-side. It's going to be interesting when they start feeding themselves!

We're looking forward to seeing you on your return trip to Minneapolis. By then the boys should be crawling all around the house and we'll have a better idea of what we're up against! I'm sorry to be the bearer of sad news. I hope things are good with both of you. It will be wonderful to see you in April.

—Love, Marilyn

"Oh, honey, thank you!" Marty said as she entered the bedroom and saw Chuck had the boys freshly diapered and bundled in his arms. "I'll take Mark so you can give Michael his bottle," she said as she reached out for him and they all walked into the kitchen. She rubbed Mark's face against her warm breast and he searched persistently for her nipple, locating it and settling in. "Will you look at that," said Marty, observing how strongly he was sucking. "This little guy may not be able to see, but he certainly isn't going to starve! He's not usually such an enthusiastic eater."

"I think it's a good sign," Chuck said as he set down Michael's empty bottle and propped him up in the highchair. "I know we haven't done this before, honey, but what would you think about letting the boys try feeding themselves tonight? It would be interesting to see how Mark reacts."

"Oh, I don't know, Chuck," said Marty hesitantly as she nestled Mark alongside Michael in the highchair. "That may be rushing it, not to mention the frustration for Mark in not being able to see his food!"

Her husband could be very persuasive at times, and this would one of those times. "I think the sooner he figures it out, the better," said Chuck, "and this will be great entertainment!" Sure enough, the fun commenced as soon as he handed the boys their little spoons. Michael clutched his with both hands and immediately began pounding the rubber-coated drumstick on the highchair tray. Mark held his spoon tightly with one hand and waved it around in the air. Next came the real test as Chuck placed Michael's bowl of oatmeal in front of him on the tray. Michael immediately pounded on it with his hand, splattering oatmeal onto the tray and floor. He then managed to spoon up a bit of oatmeal and tried directing the utensil to his mouth, but didn't quite hit the target, instead depositing oatmeal on his cheeks, nose and eyelids. As for Mark, he just held the spoon in the air until his arm grew tired, then rested his hand on the tray before pounding on it just as his brother had. After several minutes, Marty could see the feeding was going nowhere fast and decided she'd had enough of this foolishness. She gently pried the spoons from the boys' hands. "I guess it is a little too soon," Chuck said sheepishly as he wiped the oatmeal from the floor.

That evening after supper there was a knock at their door. Evelyn Kreuger, their landlord, was standing there, tears streaming down her face. "Oh, Chuck, Marilyn, I'm so sorry!" she said. After you left Dr. Bertelson's office, he called Dr. Schoeneberger's office and told me about Mark. Everybody is feeling so sad. Please let Otto and me know if there's anything we can do."

"We will, Evelyn," Marty said as they embraced. "Thank you so much for coming by."

When Chuck went back to school Monday morning, he learned that not only did Evelyn know about Mark, so did the teachers and many of his students, and they all expressed their heartfelt sympathy. That's the way it was in a small town like Perham. News traveled fast, and when a local family was going through a difficult time, the townspeople were most often aware of it and always ready to help. When Chuck got home from school that afternoon, he sat down and wrote a letter to his parents.

January 12, 1954

Dear Mom and Dad,

Maybe the Kirkwoods have already called and given you the sad news on Mark's eyes, but in case not, I'm writing to tell you about it now. When we took him to the eye doctor Friday afternoon, we learned that his retinopathy of prematurity had taken a rapid turn for the worse. It has caused the retinas of both eyes to become completely detached, leaving him blind. Marty and I were devastated when he told us there was nothing that could be done. We're still trying to digest the news, doing our best to adjust to our son's new reality. We're determined to help him become just as happy and successful in life without sight as he might have been with it.

Thanks again for the beautiful wagon you gave the boys. We can't wait to try it out. We'll let you know how it goes after the snow melts and we're able to get them outside and wheeling around the neighborhood. That's the news for now. I know you won't be able to come along with the Kirkwoods when they stop here in April, so maybe we'll make the drive to Crookston this summer!

—Love, Charlie

THE NEXT COUPLE OF MONTHS WERE BOTH EXCITING AND challenging. The boys gained more weight and had become extremely energetic since learning to crawl. One evening, shortly after their six o'clock feeding, something very interesting happened. They were lying on the comforter on the floor in the living room when they turned over from their backs to their stomachs and were facing one another. Michael said, "Bra, Bra!" and Mark lifted his head and said, "Bra, Bra!" back to him. Although "bra" sounds like a woman's accoutrement, to them it meant brother. Michael said, "Bra, Bra!" again, this time with a greater sense of urgency, and Mark's legs started working. He began crawling towards his brother and yelling, "Bra, Bra, Bra, Bra!" It was a precious sight to behold. When Mark reached Michael, he leaned his head in next to his brother's and both remained silent for a few seconds, and then they were off, Michael in the lead singing, "Bra, Bra, Bra!" and Mark making impressive speed close behind.

The Dowdles celebrated the twins' first Easter and their eighth month of life on April 18th, 1954. Both parents wondered how their sons' relationship would develop, especially over the next several years. With Mark's blindness, would they grow closer or would they tend to grow apart? Only time would tell.

Chuck headed back to school after enjoying a relaxed Easter vacation, and many things began happening. Both Marty and he were thrilled when the snow finally melted and the contractor began excavating for the basement of their new house. Whenever she had time, Marty bundled up the boys, tucked them into their wagon and pulled it over to the building site, which was only four blocks from their rented basement apartment and just a couple of blocks from the school and downtown. The twins loved being out in the fresh air. Michael's head darted from left to right as he observed the colors and action of everything around him, while Mark seemed very content to feel the breeze on his face and take in the cacophony of sounds along their route. Some days when Marty needed groceries, she'd pull the wagon to the store and load it up. The food-laden wagon with an identical toddler seated at each end was a sight to see—and hear! "Bra, Bra, Bra!" the boys sang out as Marty pulled them along.

It had been a while since they had heard from either of their parents, and Marty was happy to find a letter waiting for her from her dad when she returned one afternoon after an outing with the boys.

April 21, 1954

Dear Marilyn,

Your mom and I were very sorry to hear the update regarding Mark's vision. We'll be able to talk at length about it when we see you at the end of the month. We'll drive down there on the 25th and stop on the way back after my meeting with the Minnesota League of Municipalities.

Marilyn, it's going to be a tough road ahead for you and Chuck, but with all the love you have to share with your boys, and with Mark having a twin brother who loves him and vice versa, I know he'll not only survive, he'll thrive! It's going to be an interesting journey for your family, no doubt about that.

Beth and I are very much looking forward to seeing you and Chuck and our grandsons again. Until then, be assured that all of you have all of our love.

—Love, Dad

Marty was thrilled to hear from her dad and was looking forward to the upcoming visit. Facing the reality of Mark's blindness was difficult, and she and Chuck found deep comfort in the love of their parents. Everyone was being so kind, especially Chuck's fellow teachers at Perham High School. Just last Saturday, Richard McKay and his wife invited them for dinner while Otto and Evelyn Krueger babysat the boys. It was a relaxing visit, a delightful meal shared with teacher friends and a much-appreciated break from their usual evening bustle of feedings and activity with the twins. Sadly, their happiness was to be short lived, clouded over with the news of a tragic family event.

On the morning Marty's parents were driving to Minneapolis, the telephone rang while she was feeding the twins. Her mother was on the other end of the line. "Marilyn," she said in a strained whisper, "I'm afraid I have some very difficult news. Perhaps you should sit down."

"Mother! What is it?" Marty asked, her heart pounding. She could tell by her mother's tone that it was something very bad.

"It's Daddy," she said in a weakened voice. "On the way to Minneapolis this morning he suffered a massive heart attack and died." The tragic news packed a sickening punch to Marty's stomach and literally took her breath away, rendering her unable to speak as she gripped the phone and began to sob. "I'm so sorry to have to make this call, Marilyn," her mother said soberly. "The husband of another couple with whom we were traveling was behind the wheel, so luckily there was no accident. Daddy received emergency care on the scene and was rushed to the hospital, but it was too late. It happened right outside Saint Cloud, so I'll be here today, and then will be driving back to Crookston tomorrow with our friends. I'm in a bit of a daze, as you might imagine."

"Oh, Mother!" Marty sobbed. "I can't believe this has happened. What are you going to do? I need to be there!"

"It all feels very unreal, Marilyn," said her mother. "When I get home, I'll start making funeral arrangements. I will have to take it one day at a time. That's all I can do right now."

They hung up a few minutes later, and Marty felt like she'd been slammed in the gut. She managed to get the twins down for a morning nap and then sat on the couch and cried her heart out. The tears were still flowing by the time Chuck arrived home from school.

"Oh, honey, I'm so sorry," he said, holding her close after she gave him the news.

Marty's mother called again the next evening and said arrangements had been made. The funeral would be at the Cathedral of the Immaculate Conception in Crookston at eleven o'clock on Friday, May 7th, and she wanted Chuck to be a pallbearer and to give a eulogy, if he would. When Marty told him, Chuck said he would, of course, do that for her father. Before they drove to Crookston, they bought a buggy for the twins so they would have something to put them in on the drive up and easily move them from place to place if they were walking. The upper part of the carriage was detachable and fit into the back seat of the car. The diaper pail fit conveniently on the back floor and the rest of the carriage in the trunk with their luggage. When Friday rolled around they were ready to go.

When they pulled up in front of the Kirkwoods' house, Marty's mom came out to greet them and the trio shared an emotional embrace. "Chuck," she said gratefully, "thank you so much for agreeing to give a eulogy for Bill. I feel very out of sorts. Everything just happened so suddenly."

"I appreciate that you asked me," said Chuck. "I consider it an honor."

While Chuck was putting the carriage together for the twins, Marty and her mother walked into the house, heads together, expressing their sorrow to one another over what had happened. When they were ready to leave, Chuck drove to the church, as he needed to arrive early, and Marty and her mother decided to walk the three short blocks with the twins in their buggy. When they turned the corner, they were deeply touched to see the church parking lot overflowing with vehicles, and upon entering the Cathedral, the pews filled to capacity.

Reverend William Keefe, a longtime friend of the Kirkwood family, said the funeral Mass, and then expressed a few personal thoughts of condolence before introducing Chuck. "Now, Charlie Dowdle, Bill Kirkwood's son-in-law, would like to say a few words." Chuck left his pew and approached the ambo near the altar. Reaching it, he turned slowly and looked out at Mrs. Kirkwood, Marty and the filled church.

"I'd like to tell you about the man Mrs. Kirkwood, Marty and I admired and loved very much," said Chuck, his voice wavering with emotion. "When I first met Marty's father and asked his permission to marry her, he gave it to me along with a little friendly advice. *'It doesn't matter what you do in life, Chuck,'* I remember him saying, *'as long as you're happy doing it.'* I think Mr. Kirkwood lived that advice because he was a very happy man. Unfortunately, that happiness was cut short way too soon."

"Bill Kirkwood was a special person," he continued. "He accomplished a lot in his fifty-nine years, was a rural schoolteacher in North Dakota, attended Business College in Fargo, worked as a law clerk and studied law independently, and in 1921 was admitted to the Minnesota Bar, practicing law in Crookston until his untimely death on April 25th. He was mayor of Crookston for twelve years, during which time he was President of the Minnesota League of Municipalities. Much of what I learned about Mr. Kirkwood I learned before I met Marty, gleaned from reading frequent articles that appeared in the Crookston Daily Times featuring his accomplishments and dedicated community involvement. Some of you may not know Mr. Kirkwood was instrumental in bringing an airport to Crookston, the aptly-named Kirkwood Municipal Airport, a landmark dedicated to a man who truly dedicated his life to this town."

All eyes and ears were on Chuck as he spoke. "What I learned about Mr. Kirkwood from my wife after we were married was that he was a real survivor! All the time he was mayor and working earnestly for the growth and development of the Crookston community, he was suffering from tuberculosis. At one point he was quarantined in the Crookston Sanitarium for an entire year. During that time, his wife, Beth, made frequent treks out to the 'san,' as we used to call it, to confer with her husband about business matters, which enabled the family to stay afloat financially. She often walked there from her Woods Addition home in all kinds of inclement weather when she needed to confer with Mr. Kirkwood. One determined woman, Beth Kirkwood, and Mr. Kirkwood was always proud to have her by his side. Theirs was a mighty love. And I'd be remiss," added Chuck, "if I didn't mention the deep love my wife, Marty, had for her father, 'Daddy,' as she fondly called him, and he for her, his beloved 'Marilyn.' They shared many a fine evening singing Irish lullabies with Marty at the piano, just as Mr. Kirkwood had done with his mother, Mary Ellen O'Sullivan, when he was a youngster. In closing, we all know legs and arms and eyes and lungs are vitally important and help us live and succeed, certainly more easily when we have them and they're working properly! For those who don't have them or find theirs to be out of kilter for one reason or another, a special strong and resilient few are able to rise above the challenges, to dig deep into their souls and generate a spirit of gratefulness and determination that enables them not only to survive, but to thrive. That's Bill Kirkwood, a loved and respected husband, father and human being. He will be greatly missed."

One could have heard a pin drop after Chuck's eulogy came to an end. "Thank you for those thoughtful words," said Father Keefe as he stepped up to the ambo. "Houske Funeral Home will now be moving the casket out to Calvary Cemetery for the burial and you're all welcome to attend."

Chuck wheeled the buggy out of the vestibule, and with his dad's help, broke it down and got the twins settled into the back seat of the car. They were quiet angels during the funeral Mass, not a peep out of either, and were sleeping up to the moment Chuck started the car. Michael looked up at Grandpa Dowdle and said, "Dada! Dada! Dada!"

"No, Michael," Chuck's mother said, "that's Grandpa."

Michael stared up at his grandpa. "Grandpa, Grandpa," he said after a few moments, and you should have seen the surprised looks on everyone's faces!

"Mark listens especially well since losing his eyesight," Chuck explained, "and he's picking up new words all the time." Chuck's dad just smiled and remained silent.

Mrs. Kirkwood and Marilyn drove to the cemetery with Father Keefe, and after the burial accepted his kind offer of a ride home. Marilyn stayed overnight with her mother, and Chuck and the twins stayed with his parents. They figured this was a more convenient plan since they had Chuck's old crib set up in an upstairs bedroom and knew Marilyn would appreciate some time alone with her mother. It would also give Chuck a chance to rest while Grandma and Grandpa Dowdle spent time with their grandsons.

Grandma Dowdle was especially solicitous of the boys when they got home. She wanted to wash them, feed them, cuddle them, play with them, get them into their pajamas and put them to bed when the time came, and that was all okay with Chuck. He was looking forward to a break in the action, a chance to sit quietly and talk with his dad. "Well, Charlie, what's on your schedule when you get back to Perham?" asked his dad once they finally had a chance to relax in the living room.

"Another month of school, Dad," he said, "and then I'll be looking for a summer job. The new house is coming right along, and we'll hopefully be moved in by the time classes start again in September. It's going to be interesting to see how the twins adjust to their new surroundings. It's huge compared to the basement apartment. Mark will be back to square zero in familiarizing himself with the layout, but I think he'll do fine. He's always right on his brother's tail. Wherever Michael goes, he goes. We'll just have to wait and see. Of course, Marty and I would love to have you and Mom come for a visit once we're in the new house. You could take a bus or the train since they both stop in Perham."

"We'll see, Charlie," his dad said. "We'll see."

On their way back to Perham the next afternoon, Chuck and Marty smelled something hot coming from the car when they got near Detroit Lakes, so they pulled off the highway and onto a frontage road, slowly making their way to a nearby farmhouse. It was none too soon, as steam was coming from under the hood by the time they pulled up near the front porch. "Looks like you two may have a bit of a radiator problem," said a jovial farmer as he pushed open the screened door.

"It sure does," Chuck said as he got out of the car. He lifted the hood and both he and the farmer jumped back as the hissing steam billowed and spewed into the air.

"Watch that radiator cap," warned the farmer. "Don't touch it or you'll have one burned hand. Wait here and I'll go fetch some water."

The farmer's wife soon came out onto the porch to investigate all the commotion. "Is that a baby you have there in the back?" she asked as she came closer to the car.

"Two of them!" said Chuck smiling.

"Mama! Mama! Mama!" the boys began chanting, and the farmer's wife laughed heartily.

"Twins! My, aren't they just the sweetest things," she said. "John and I were never able to have children, broke my heart. I sure do love babies. Your boys look so much alike, they must be identical."

"That they are," Marty said, "and they're a real handful! They were born prematurely, and this little one developed a disease called Retinopathy of Prematurity," she added as she looked over the back seat at Mark. "He recently became totally blind."

"Oh, I'm so sorry to hear that," the farmer's wife said sympathetically, "though I don't expect it's going to hold him back one bit!" She took another admiring look at the twins. "Let me go see what's taking John so long," she said as she headed back into the house.

When he came out of the house with his wife, John had a pail of water in one hand and a bundle of old rags in the other. With the cloth covering his hand he slowly unscrewed the radiator cap as steam hissed into the air. "You can see how hot that is," he said as he began to slowly funnel fresh cold water into the radiator. It eventually stopped bubbling up, and the farmer put the cap back on. "I don't think I'd drive a whole lot further with this car before a mechanic takes a look at it," he said. "It obviously has some sort of engine problem."

"We only have a short way to go," Chuck said. "Hopefully we'll be all right between here and Perham. Thanks a lot for your help!" As they drove away, Chuck and Marty waved farewell to the friendly farmer and his wife, and they were soon back on the highway and headed home. After driving for about fifteen miles, steam began hissing once again from the radiator. "Damn!" said Chuck. "It looks like we've got the same problem, but I'm not going to stop now. Just two more miles and we'll be home!" he said.

As they reached the outskirts of Perham and began driving through town, the engine began making an obnoxiously-loud clanking sound. Everyone who saw them stared, then smiled and looked knowingly at their car. These were all people they knew, and it was embarrassing! "Chuck," said Marty, "it sounds the same way the old black Nash did before we traded it in. Do you think this one has the same problem?"

"Maybe so," said Chuck. "We're so close to home, I think we can make it. I don't want to stop!"

The car Marty remembered was a four-door, stick-shift, 30's Nash sedan that looked like a hearse. It was Chuck's first car, one he'd bought the summer of '52 after graduating from St. John's University. The car had been sitting all winter in the snow on a vacant lot in St. Cloud, Minnesota, had an old trailer attached, just what they needed! When the bargaining began, the owner said he wanted $50.00 for both the Nash and the trailer, which Chuck couldn't afford, so he asked the seller if he'd take $25.00. The answer was a resounding no. Chuck then mentioned he had a real nice alligator-covered portable radio, perhaps the owner would accept that and $25.00 for the car and trailer. Chuck made a point of telling him he'd just graduated from St. John's, was married and on his way to his first teaching assignment at Karlsruhe, North Dakota, needed a car and could definitely make good use of the trailer to haul their belongings. Long story short, they reached a deal and Chuck found himself smiling behind the wheel of the vintage Nash. The joy was short-lived, however. Driving from St. Cloud to Crookston, they were forced to stop a half dozen times at small towns and farmhouses to fill up the radiator because the engine kept overheating and spewing steam *from under the hood. "Guess that's what I get for $25 and a portable radio," Chuck remembered saying to Marty, who'd been taking it all in stride and wondering what was going to happen next. They finally made it home to Crookston, and luckily the journey to Karlsruhe went okay; the Nash just required the frequent addition of water to the radiator. A week later, though, after driving to Minot, North Dakota, on a Saturday morning, the engine started making a loud clanking sound as they headed down Main Street. Sounds like you broke a rod," Chuck remembered the service station attendant saying. He was right, so Chuck had simply limped the big old black sedan to the Nash dealership, broken rod and all, and traded it in for another used Nash, the one they were currently driving that was now making the same ominous sound. Talk about déjà vu!*

It felt like a lot of things were happening in too short a time. They'd had this Nash for a little over a year and a half, so when they got home, got unpacked and got the boys fed and in bed, they talked cars. They both decided they'd had it! For now they would simply walk wherever they needed to be until they could afford a new vehicle. Moving into their new home would eat up any money they'd save by not having a car, and since everything was close by in small-town Perham, it wouldn't be a hardship to walk. It just made good sense. They junked the car and took to their feet. It wasn't bad at all, especially now that they had the buggy and the wagon for the twins, who were happy travelers when they were outside and privy to human-powered modes of transport.

THE DAY AFTER SCHOOL LET OUT IN JUNE, CHUCK SATISFIED IN A big way the twins' desire to be outdoors. Otto Krueger mentioned to Chuck that he and Evelyn weren't going to be planting a garden that summer, and that he and Marty were welcome to use their garden space. It was a large area, about fifty feet wide and a hundred feet long! Chuck and Marty talked it over and decided to go for it. They could just picture all the fresh vegetables they'd be eating every week. However, there was a lot more to gardening than just harvesting. For the twins, this was a whole new adventure, and they were ready for some fun!

"Okay, boys," Chuck said as he hoisted the happy duo into his arms and headed up the basement stairs, "today you're going to learn about gardening!" Ten-month-old babies certainly recognized nothing about the word 'gardening,' but they sensed they were headed for some outdoor action, and that was all they needed to know.

The first step in the process was to turn over the soil, and with a garden this size, that wasn't going to be easy. Chuck plunked the twins down in the middle of the plot and began working the black, loamy dirt. This was a first for the twins, never having touched or smelled dirt before, and they were easily entertained. The rich soil was loaded with earthworms, so when Chuck found a fat long one, he brought it over to the boys to see what they'd do. He handed it to Michael first, who examined it closely as it squirmed around in his hands. Something very different happened when Chuck took the earthworm from Michael and placed it in Mark's hands. At first, Mark seemed to want to pet it, then laughed when it first moved. When it moved again, Mark grasped it with his little fingers and brought it straight to his mouth!

"No, Mark!" Chuck said as he snatched the worm and tossed it away. "You can't eat that!" Mark was not happy. He had discovered a new toy and liked the motion of the squiggly worm, but it was soon forgotten when Chuck took him and Michael over to where he'd been digging and let them play in the freshly tilled soil. It was warm and soft, and the boys liked sifting it through their fingers. While they were happily entertaining themselves with the dirt, Chuck went back to his digging… until he heard the boys coughing and choking! You guessed it. They had both decided to eat dirt! Chuck grabbed a twin under each arm and rushed to the faucet at the side of the house. It didn't take long to clear the small amount of dirt from their mouths. "Okay, boys," he said as he plopped the boys into their wagon, "you're going to have to watch me from there so I can get some work done!"

The twins were able to stand up in the wagon while clutching its high sides, but that wasn't good enough. They wanted out! They wanted earthworms and dirt! Michael started screaming and was soon joined by a crying Mark. Chuck decided he'd better take them both inside before the neighbors came over to check on their well-being. He plucked them out of the wagon and carried them down the basement stairs to

Marty. "What in heaven's name!" said Marty when she saw their dirty, tear-stained faces. "What happened out there?"

"Well," Chuck said with a smile, "turns out these two explorers like to eat earthworms and dirt! And they definitely don't like standing in their wagon when they could be playing in the garden. Between their crying and screaming and my not getting anything done, I decided it would be best to bring them back inside."

"So I see," said Marty laughing. "I'll clean them up and you can go back to work."

"What a relief!" Chuck thought as he headed up the stairs. He attacked the garden with gusto, and by the time it started getting dark and he came back inside, he had the entire plot dug up, smoothed out with the rake and ready for planting.

"Perfect timing," said Marty. "The twins are fed and down for the night and supper's almost ready."

"Great, honey, thank you!" said an exhausted Chuck. "Happy to say I'm done out there, at least the first step. Tomorrow we can buy some different kinds of seeds, maybe some tomato plants. Have you thought about what veggies you might want to plant?"

"Not really," she said, "but I think it would be nice to have a little bit of everything. Tomatoes, radishes, lettuce, cucumbers, maybe some peas and beans if it's not too late in the season. Maybe even some flowers."

"I don't see why not," he said smiling.

Both parents had been so busy they'd almost forgotten that Wednesday, June 9th, would be their third wedding anniversary. They were pondering how they might celebrate the occasion when Chuck received a phone call from the school that definitely gave them a second good reason to plan something special. Superintendent Harold Kraft, who knew that Har Sandholm, a science teacher, and Chuck, were looking for work, called them and asked if they'd be interested in painting the school classrooms over the summer, all twenty of them! They said they would, so Mr. Kraft told them, "You boys go over to Welter's Hardware, pick out whatever paint colors you want, charge it to the school and go to work!" Har and Chuck took Superintendent Kraft at his word, and while they listened to the baseball games all summer, they painted every classroom: peach, chartreuse, lilac, pink, beige, pastel yellows, greens, browns and purples! It was going to be interesting to watch the kids' reaction when they came back to school in the fall, but that was a long way off, and a lot would be happening between June and September of 1954.

One incident Chuck and Marty could have easily done without that summer occurred two months after their anniversary on August 9th, the twins' first birthday. By this time the boys were walking, though rather unsteadily, and Mark kept bumping into things while following Michael around the apartment, so Marty tied each end of a dishtowel to them to see if that would help. It was about four feet long and did the job admirably. It did inhibit Michael's freedom, but he didn't seem to mind having his brother following so closely on his heels. As a matter of fact, he seemed to enjoy being the leader as the two of them moved in tandem from room to room. Late in the afternoon, Marty finished frosting the twins' angel food birthday cake. She placed two white candles in the middle and wrote the words, 'Michael & Mark, Twin Lights.' Chuck was busy wrapping the boys' presents in the living room when he heard them call out, "Mama! Mama! Mama!"

"Chuck," she called, "would you mind seeing what they're up to?"

He peeked into their bedroom, but they weren't there, and then he saw the apartment door leading to the stairs had been left open. A chill filled his body. He rushed through the laundry room and out towards the stairs. There at the top of the landing were his boys, standing with the dish towel tied between them and looking down at him. "Daddy! Daddy!" they called gleefully, both seeming to sense they had performed a mighty feat.

Chuck very calmly climbed the twenty or so stairs, two at a time, all the time looking into Michael's eyes and praying he wouldn't decide to leap down. If he did, Mark would be pulled right with him, and it would be a long, hard tumble. When Chuck reached the top of the stairs, he stretched his arms out and grasped the boys as they greeted him again with their joyous chorus, "Daddy! Daddy! Daddy!" Relief was written all over Chuck's face. He breathed deeply, hugged the boys gratefully and called out, "Marty, come to the stairs! You'll have to see this to believe it. It's a first!"

Marty came rushing from the kitchen, and when she saw Chuck kneeling at the top of the landing with his arms wrapped around his young sons, she immediately realized what had transpired. "For heavens sakes!" she exclaimed.

"Can you believe they crawled up these stairs while they were tied together?" said Chuck. "Get the camera, honey, we've got to have a picture of this!"

Marty ran for the camera and snapped a photo of the three of them at the top of the stairs. "Mama! Mama!" Michael called down excitedly as Mark joined in.

"It's time for birthday cake if you want to get those little mischief makers down the stairs," said Marty.

Chuck picked up the boys, one in each arm, and slowly made his way down the steep steps with the two brazen adventure seekers. Marty tied them securely into their highchair and then carried over the angel food cake she'd made for the occasion as Chuck sang a rousing rendition of Happy Birthday. "Should have been devil's food for these two!" he laughed as Marty lit the two candles, one for each twin. Chuck bent down in front of the boys, and while blowing into their faces, said, "Blow, boys, blow your candles!" The twins didn't so much like the feel of their dad blowing at them, and they both rubbed their eyes and turned away.

"Let me have a go at it," said Marty. She blew softly in their direction, accompanied by an exaggerated blowing sound effect. "You can do it!" she said to the twins. "Try it!" This time the boys imitated her breaths with several short, choppy puffs of air, Chuck in position behind them so as to lend a little help. The candles flickered and went out, trailing two thin streams of white smoke.

"I'll bet neither of them will have any trouble eating the cake," Marty said as she cut each a small piece and placed it in their hands.

"That's good cake, boys!" said Chuck. "Go ahead, try it!"

Mark was first to give it a go. He lifted his piece to his mouth and nibbled off a small frosted corner, eating it delicately as was his usual manner. Michael looked over at his brother, and then thought the better of that technique as he attempted to jam his entire piece into his mouth, ending up with pink frosted cheeks and chin! Chuck and Marty couldn't help but laugh, Michael joined in, and Mark contributed an enthusiastic nonsensical chatter. The party was in full swing! Several minutes later the twins were still going strong, practically eating their fingers to get to every last bit of frosting. "OK, boys, that's the end of the celebrating for today," said Marty as she cleaned their hands and faces with a damp washcloth. "It's time for your bottles."

Moments later there was a knock at the door. Chuck opened it to find Tom Schmitz, a fellow St. John's University graduate, standing there. Tom's dad owned the local Perham Ford agency, and Chuck surmised Tom was paying them a visit for one reason, to sell them a car! "Hi, Charlie!" said Tom with a smile. "Could I come in and talk with you and Marty for a minute or two?"

"Of course, Tom," Chuck said. "We just finished a party for the twins' first birthday. Come on in and have a piece of cake."

"Happy to oblige," said Tom cheerfully as he greeted Marty and the twins in the kitchen. "Those sure are two good-looking little guys you have."

"Thanks, Tom," she said. "Chuck will get you a piece of cake. The boys are just finishing up their bottles and then will go down for a nap, so I'll be with you two in just a couple of minutes."

"Take your time, no hurry," said Tom as Chuck served him a generous slab of cake.

Chuck began telling him about his summer job, painting every classroom at the school. "With all that experience, you must be getting pretty good at it," said Tom. "How'd you like to paint our cabin out at Big Pine Lake?"

"Let me think about it, Tom," Chuck said as Marty entered the kitchen.

"Think about what?" she asked.

"I just asked Charlie if he'd be interested in painting our cabin out at Big Pine Lake," said Tom, "but that's not why I'm here. I see you walking all over town and I think you need a car!" Chuck told him he didn't think they could afford one right now, and that the buggy and wagon were making things easier with the twins. Tom, the ultimate salesman, looked directly into Chuck's eyes, and in his most persuasive voice said, "How does $25.00 down and $25.00 a month sound?"

Actually, that sounded pretty darn good and it was a payment they could swing. Before they knew what had hit them, they'd ordered a brand new, four-door, fire-engine red, Ford country sedan! "It'll take a couple of months to get here, but you should have it by the end of September," said Tom as Chuck and Marty followed him to the stairs to say goodbye. "Oh, and by the way," he added as he headed up, "Joanie and I are planning on starting a family and we'd like to get in a little practice. If you two would like to go away for an overnighter to the St. John's Homecoming football game in September, you can use our car and we'll babysit for you that weekend."

All of this excitement was a bit overwhelming in the most wonderful of ways, especially with the twins' birthday celebration on top of it! After Tom left, Chuck and Marty sat on the couch and replayed the afternoon. They couldn't believe they'd just bought a new car! "That friend of yours is quite a salesman, Chuck," she said.

"I know," said Chuck, his voice showing a bit of buyer's remorse. "I sure didn't wake up this morning thinking I'd be buying a new car today, but we're going to need one sooner or later, and he's a 'Johnnie,' so I'm glad we bought it from him."

The twins were sleeping soundly, and Chuck and Marty took advantage of the peaceful block of time to talk about everything that was going to be happening over the summer and into September. Chuck would be finishing the classroom painting project near the end of August and might be painting the cabin of Tom Schmitz before school started back up. In addition, Evelyn and Otto Kreuger asked him if he'd be interested in painting one of the rooms of their house. Everything seemed to be piling up, but it all amounted to his making some much-needed money, so Chuck decided to take on the additional two projects. He and Marty even decided to take Tom and Joanie up on their babysitting offer for Homecoming weekend. Indeed, it was going to be an action-packed several weeks.

With all the action that had taken place on the twins' birthday, it wasn't until the next morning that they all sat together in the living room and opened presents. Chuck rolled a round package towards Mark, a package which obviously contained a big ball, bigger than Mark! Mark felt the paper and moved the package around on the floor. He pushed it away and Michael scrambled after it as it rolled past him. Michael rolled it back to Mark, who pushed it away again. Then Chuck unwrapped it, but when it didn't come back right way to Mark, he grew annoyed and began screaming until Chuck placed the large rubber ball right in front of him. Mark felt the smooth surface and laughed as he attempted to pull the unwieldly ball close to his body. Then he pushed it away and sat without moving, listening for any sound it might make. No sound from the ball, but he did hear Michael chasing after it, and he called out loudly to him until Michael rolled it up against him. Mark pushed it away again, laughing, and the twins had a new game!

Chuck sat down on the floor next to Mark and slowly began unwrapping another present, one he had special ordered. It was a set of 26 oversized blocks, each with a raised capital letter of the alphabet and a raised braille equivalent. The A had a single dot, the B two vertical dots, the C two horizontal dots, etc. Chuck put several blocks down in front of Mark, who carefully felt each of them, didn't push them away like he did the ball. As Mark held a block in his hand, Chuck guided it into position atop another block, demonstrating for him the 'building' aspect of the blocks. Michael was keeping a close eye on the action and of course wanted to join the fun. He very gingerly placed a block on top of the other two. Pretty soon the twins were building up the blocks together. They had discovered yet another game!

That afternoon, Marty picked fresh vegetables from the garden for their supper, but it was no easy task. First she had to haul the twins upstairs. They were heavy, twenty pounds apiece! After bringing Michael upstairs and plunking him down in the center of the garden, she ran back down to get Mark and hurried back upstairs. She often mused how sweet it would be when their new house was finished and they were living on one floor!

The twins sat contentedly as Marty began harvesting peas. Occasionally she would hand a shelled pea to each of the boys, which they immediately placed in their mouth. They had teeth now, six each, and took advantage of every opportunity to put their chewers to work. The boys ate almost everything they were fed these days, with most things cut into small pieces or mashed. They had good appetites and their rapid growth showed it. They were getting strong as well, so strong that Marty and Chuck traded in the dishtowel for a leather tether for those times when they needed to be kept together. The tether was three feet long and hooked onto the loops of the boys' pants. It would come in very handy once they moved into their spacious new house!

The next three weeks flew by. Chuck and Har finished painting the classrooms the last Friday in August, and the money they earned helped tide them over until school began. A few days later Tom Schmitz dropped Chuck off at Big Pine Lake, where he spent all day painting Tom's cabin. When Tom picked Chuck up late that afternoon, he was quite impressed with Chuck's work and gave him one hundred dollars! "Thanks a lot, Tom," said Chuck, exhausted, but gleeful. "This will be enough for the $25.00 down payment on the car and the first three payments!"

"Think nothing of it, Charlie," Tom said. "Besides, you earned it! You worked all day and the cabin looks great!"

"By the way," Chuck said. "Marty and I decided to take you up on that babysitting offer and the use of your car for the St. John's Homecoming weekend."

"Great, Charlie! Joanie and I were hoping you would. You two deserve a break, and like I said, it'll be good experience for us before we have our own little one. Joanie will be thrilled!"

When Chuck got home, the tantalizing aroma of chicken broccoli casserole filled the air. "Honey," he gushed as he walked into the kitchen and gave Marty a big hug and a kiss, "I am one lucky man and a very hungry one!"

"Everything is ready," she said cheerily. "Wash up and we can eat."

"Daddy! Daddy!" Michael and Mark yelled from their highchair. Chuck walked over and gave each a smacking kiss on the cheek. Michael laughed at his dad, who had paint on his face, in his hair, on his clothes, pretty much everywhere! Mark sensed the strange smell. He just wrinkled his nose and turned away.

"I'll be just a couple of minutes, honey," said Chuck as he headed down the hall.

That evening, Chuck and Marty talked about how next week, their last precious few days of vacation, would be spent before school started up again. It was going to be a busy time! The contractor told them they could move into their new home during the first week in September, and there was plenty that needed to be accomplished in preparation for that. First and foremost, Chuck hired a company to install a cyclone fence around the entire perimeter of the backyard so the twins would be safe. It was expensive, but worth the investment for the peace of mind alone.

"Honey, I opt for calling tomorrow a total day of rest after church," Chuck said, "and then on Monday we can start making the most of the week. I think I'll paint that room upstairs for Otto and Evelyn first thing; that will be a day-long project. What's on your schedule?"

"Well, I'd like to move into the new house as soon as possible," said Marty, "so I'll get to packing the rest of the stuff. Maybe we can start bringing things over on Tuesday?"

"I don't see why not," said Chuck enthusiastically. "We don't have much, not a lot of heavy furniture. I think we can be out of here in a day."

"I'd love that!" said Marty. "I'm so ready. It's been a long year living in this basement."

"All right, Tuesday it is!" he said. "I'll rent a truck and see if I can get a couple of teachers to help out. We'll be out of here in no time!"

Sunday morning came around, a beautiful Indian-summer day and perfect weather for the three-block walk to St. Henry's Church. The family carefully made their way up the basement stairs, and with the move into their new home just two days away, it was thankfully the last time they would ever have to do that for Sunday church. The boys rode happily in their wagon, standing up and hanging onto the sides most of the way. The warm breeze felt good against their faces and the fall leaves crunched and crackled as the wagon rolled along. Michael's head darted from side to side, taking it all in, while Mark listened intently to every sound, his head held high. When Chuck and Marty entered the church, each one carrying one of the boys, Father Donnay greeted them enthusiastically. "Good morning, Mr. and Mrs. Dowdle! Good morning, boys! How are my favorite little angels today?" he asked.

Michael and Mark liked Father Donnay. Much to the amusement of Chuck and Marty, and Father Donnay, they reached out to him and said, "Daddy! Daddy!"

"They sure are growing up," he said as he laughed and gave each a gentle pat on the head.

"They're like their dad," Marty said. "They love to eat!"

The men chuckled and Father Donnay said, "Don't we all! Don't we all!"

As touted, Father Donnay's 'angel' boys were perfectly behaved during Mass. Michael liked to look around at the beautiful stained-glass windows and was mesmerized by the candles on the alter. Mark was entertained by the sounds of the organ and singing, not such a fan of incense, crinkling his nose whenever Father Donnay used the censer. After Mass, the parishioners stopped to talk and always made a special effort to communicate with Mark through touch. Perham was a special little community, and Chuck and Marty felt blessed to be able to work and raise their children in such a friendly and supportive town.

Chuck was up early on Monday morning and started painting the Kruegers' bedroom right after breakfast. The small space was a piece of cake compared to the high-ceilinged classrooms, and he finished the job shortly before supper. Otto and Evelyn were pleased as could be and insisted that Chuck not pay any rent for August in exchange for the job.

"Well, honey, I'm happy to say that's done," Chuck said as he came into the kitchen, "and the best part is Otto & Evelyn are trading the work for this month's rent!"

"That's great news!" said Marty. "And I imagine you're one hungry painter. The twins are already down for the night. Go ahead and wash up and I'll pull the meatloaf from the oven."

She'd said the magic word. Meatloaf! Chuck was seated at the table in a matter of minutes. "Looks delicious, honey, thank you!" he said as he helped himself to a hearty slab.

"I can hardly wait for tomorrow!" Marty gushed. "Can you believe we'll be in our new house?"

"The boys are going to like it!" said Chuck.

"I'm going to love it!" said Marty.

Tuesday morning after breakfast Marty loaded the twins into the wagon and walked them to their new home. She was curious to see how they would react in the unfamiliar surroundings. The double garage door was open when they arrived, so she wheeled the wagon in and tethered the boys so Michael could lead Mark around the space. When they went into the house and into the large family room, Michael grew excited and took off running across the floor, immediately yanking Mark to the ground. This stopped both of them in their tracks, of course. Michael paused while his surprised brother got to his feet, and then took off again, slower this time, pulling good-natured Mark along with him from room to room.

"Isn't this nice, boys!" Marty said as she entered their bedroom. Mark knew by the tone of her voice that she was very pleased. Of course, it didn't mean much to him since he didn't know what it was all about, and, for that matter, it didn't mean much to Michael, either. What Michael did appreciate was the sight of a whole lot of open space and the shiny salt and pepper vinyl floor, perfect for sliding as the boys quickly found out! "OK, enough of that," said Marty after their tenth run across it. "Let's go take a look at the back yard." She led them out of the house and through the garage. "Now," she said gleefully as they stepped outside into the huge, sunny space, "you two can run your little feet off!"

It wasn't long before Chuck pulled up in the moving truck with his two teacher friends and the furniture. It only took a quick morning to unload since there was so little: the pearl-gray dinette set, the hide-a-bed they'd been using for their combined bed/sofa, the large mohair easy chair Marty's mom had given them, the Maytag wringer washing machine, the boys' crib, highchair and buggy, and the family's clothes, dishes, books and other boxed-up belongings. It was a little after noon by the time the job was done, and definitely time to feed three hungry movers! "Chuck, why don't Wally, Bill and you wash up while I set up lunch," said Marty. "We'll celebrate our first meal in our new house!"

"Excellent!" Chuck said. While they were cleaning up, Marty set the just-moved-in dining room table with paper plates and cups and loaded a just-unpacked serving platter with ham & cheese sandwich squares. She added a jar of crisp dill pickles and a couple of bags of potato chips and they had the makings of a grand indoor picnic!

It didn't take the men long to emerge from the bathroom. They had worked up mighty appetites. "This looks great, Marty!" said Bill. "Thanks for fixing us lunch."

"Ditto that, Marty," Wally said. "We really appreciate it." As he looked around the family room, he said, "I was so busy moving furniture, I didn't notice how big the rooms are!"

"Well," said Chuck, "we wanted an open floor plan, friendly and informal, a big kitchen for Marty, space for guests and a lot of room for the boys to run around. It is a big place, but I know we'll use every inch of it! By the way, where are the boys?" asked Chuck.

"Oh, my goodness!" exclaimed Marty as she ran from the table to look out the back window. "I left them playing in the yard! I was thinking they were napping, I'm so conditioned to this being their time for that! Everyone jumped up and ran to the window to see if the twins were okay. There they were, sitting happily together on the fresh grass, completely enthralled by their new environment. "Well," Marty said with a relieved sigh, "I guess they didn't worry about me any more than I did about them. That big fenced back yard may prove to be the best part of this house!"

As the men polished off the last of the sandwiches, Marty produced a metal container filled with Chuck's favorite triple chocolate chip cookies. "Anyone for dessert?" she said with a smile. Needless to say, she didn't have to ask twice. After they'd all eaten their share, Chuck thanked Wally and Bill for the moving help and asked if they'd like a lift home in the truck.

"No need for that, Chuck," said Wally. It's nice outside and just a few short blocks."

"And we need to walk off those cookies!" said Bill, patting his stomach.

"Thank you both for all your help. We so appreciate it," said Marty.

"I'm glad we could do it. You and Chuck and the boys have a lot of new house to get used to, so have fun with that!" said Wally.

"We'll see you next Monday at school, Chuck," said Bill as they parted ways in the front yard and headed on down the sunny, tree-lined street.

"Thanks again!" Chuck called after them. Marty, meanwhile, brought the boys in from the back yard and began feeding them lunch.

"Daddy! Daddy! Daddy!" Mark yelled when Chuck came back in.

"How do my boys like their new house?" he asked playfully.

"If the back yard is any indication, they love it!" Marty said. The twins spent the next few hours exploring every room in the house. They were tethered, but unusually quiet at one point, and then wild laughter erupted. Marty walked down the hall and into the master bedroom. There they were in the bathroom, having a grand time splashing water out of the toilet bowl and onto themselves and the floor. "Boys! What are you doing?" said Marty in a serious tone, working hard to contain her laughter at the sight of the twins, doused from head to toe. "There's water everywhere!"

That evening, after everything had quieted down and the twins were sleeping soundly in their new bedroom, the two exhausted, but very happy parents sat down and talked about things they would need to buy for their home. "I say the first thing we get is a king-sized bed!" Chuck said. "I've had enough of opening and closing the hide-a-bed. How about tomorrow we go shopping at Schoeneberger's Furniture Store?" he said as he leaned over and kissed a smiling Marty.

"Sounds good to me!" she said.

The next morning Chuck and Marty loaded the boys in the wagon and wheeled down to Schoeneberger's. With a big new house and a lot of empty rooms to fill, they looked longingly at all the furniture, but both knew some things would just have to wait, as they simply didn't have the money. They did find the perfect bed and had it delivered to the house that very afternoon!

As fate would have it, a letter arrived in the mail that day that would soon solve their lack-of-furnishings dilemma.

September 3, 1954

Dear Marilyn and Chuck,

I have some big news. I'm moving! Since Bill died, I've been thinking a lot about relocating from Crookston to California so I can be closer to Bette and Billy. Don McKenzie, who owns the Crookston Daily Times, said he'd be interested in buying the house if I decided to move, so I'm going to sell it to him and also sell Daddy's Credit Union business. I plan to lease the farm to the Caouette brothers, so I'll keep getting an annual income from that.

Marilyn, you're the one who learned to play the piano, so I want you to have it. Also, you and Chuck can have any of the furniture from the house you'd like since I don't want to haul it out to California. The sooner you can come and get it, the better, since I'm wanting to head west before the end of June. I know this will be a big change for all of us and I hope you feel OK about my decision. I know it's what is best for me.

Hugs to you and my two beautiful grandsons!

—*Love, Mom*

It surprised Marilyn to learn her mother had decided to move to California, but in a way it didn't. She knew her mother had always been closer to Billy and Bette than to her. She was more like her dad and had always felt closer to him than anyone else in the family. When she told Chuck the news, he was surprised, but understood.

"Mother doesn't want to haul a bunch of furniture to California," Marty told him. "She said we can have whatever we'd like. What do you think?"

"I think the timing couldn't be better," he said, "and it would save us a lot of money. This house is so big and empty it echoes. I say let's go for it! I'll call Wally and Bill and see if they'd be willing to help again while I still have the truck." He called the next day and both men happily offered their services, so early Friday morning the trio of movers headed off to Crookston. By 9:00 a.m. they were parked in front of the Kirkwood house and ready to load.

"My, Chuck!" Mrs. Kirkwood said when she greeted him. "You and your friends must have left at the crack of dawn! Can I get you a cup of coffee or something to eat before you start in?"

"Thanks, Beth," said Chuck. "Maybe after we get it all loaded, and by the way, thank you very much for the furniture! We'll both treasure these things you're giving us, as will the boys as they grow up. It all holds precious memories for Marty, especially the piano."

Although they'd brought along a dolly to move the piano, it was still quite a struggle, but the rest of the pieces felt easy in comparison. Chuck had learned a few tricks about moving and packing furniture on those occasions when he had helped Otto Krueger, who was a long-distance hauler. By noon, they had everything in the truck and ready to go. "You gentlemen made short work of that!" said Mrs. Kirkwood. "Can I interest you in some food and drinks?"

"You've just spoken magic words to three hungry men, Beth," Chuck said. "Give us a few minutes to clean up and we'll be right there!"

After enjoying a delicious meal, Wally and Bill thanked Mrs. Kirkwood and headed for the truck while Chuck stayed a minute to say goodbye. "Thanks again for all the furniture, Beth," he said. "We can sure use it! Marty and I appreciate it so much. Thank you, too, for the sandwiches and apple pie!"

"You're welcome, Chuck," she said as he gave her a big hug. "You'd better get going before you get me crying. Give Marilyn a big hug for me and all my love to her and the boys!"

"I will! I will!" Chuck said as he jogged out to the truck. "And they send their love to you!"

Bill was already in the driver's seat with the engine running when Chuck hopped in next to Wally. It made him feel a bit sad to see Beth standing alone on the porch without her husband by her side. He hoped she would be happy in California. He and the boys waved goodbye as the truck headed down the street and out of sight. "Thanks for driving, Bill," Chuck said.

"You drove here; thought I'd give you a break and drive back," said Bill.

It didn't take long for them to get home. It was three o'clock when they pulled up in front of the new house. "That was a quick trip! How did everything go?" Marty asked when she came out to greet them, pulling the twins in their wagon.

"Just fine, honey," Chuck said. "Your mother sends her love to you and the boys. When I said goodbye and gave her a big hug, she said to give you one, too, so here's that," he said as he held her in a warm embrace.

"OK, you two lovebirds," said Wally. "Enough of that. Time to get this rig unloaded!"

"All right, kids," Marty said to Michael and Mark, "it's time for us to get out of the way and let these movers do their work." The boys loved being with their mother. She played with them, read to them and taught them new things every day. When she saw how much they enjoyed learning, she decided to try a new game, one that would teach them new words. The first step was to search for good books at the Perham library. The librarian asked her if she would be interested in renting a 'braillewriter' for Mark from the Otter Tail County Office of Education. Marty had never seen or even heard of such a thing and was very enthusiastic when the librarian explained that if would enable her to write in braille on a six-key machine. "That sounds wonderful!" she exclaimed. "I'd certainly like to try it!"

Unloading the furniture went a lot faster than loading it, piano and all. By five o'clock the truck was empty and the house was full! "Thank you very much, guys," Chuck said to Wally and Bill. "I owe you one!"

"We are so grateful for your help," said Marty as they headed off. "Thank you!"

The family spent Saturday and Sunday just getting used to their new house. It was luxurious compared to the basement apartment, so spacious. Michael and Mark got plenty of exercise running from room and room and especially playing outside in the back yard. Marty loved having them out there knowing they were fenced in and couldn't get into any trouble. Or so she had hoped. That's where they were on Monday afternoon when Marty heard them screaming, "Mama! Mama! Mama!" She raced out of the kitchen to the back, where the twins were sitting side by side on the ground in the middle of a small army of ants, the stinging variety! She quickly undressed the boys, flung their clothes aside and brushed the ants from their little bodies. All was peaceful by the time Chuck came home from school.

"How'd your day go, honey?" he asked cheerfully. "Things seem pretty quiet around here."

"If only you knew!" Marty said, and then proceeded to tell him about the stinging ant episode.

"I feel bad for the boys," said Chuck, "but it's all part of getting used to the new house. We can't protect them from everything, that's for sure."

On Wednesday, the librarian called and told Marty she could come in and pick up the braillewriter when she had a chance. Marty was so excited she pulled the boys over in the wagon that afternoon. This was going to be fun! She decided the first word she'd teach the boys was BALL. They loved their ball and were always having fun rolling it around the house. The second word was ANT. And it wasn't long before a third word was to become an important part of the twins' growing vocabulary. PUPPY!

Tom Dubay, a fellow teacher, had a beloved Welsh Corgi that got impregnated by a terrier. "Charlie," said Tom one day as they were walking home from school, "how would you and Marty like to have a dog? Suzie had seven pups this summer. They're ten weeks old, adorable little things, just about ready to be let go. I'll give you the pick of the litter!"

"Wow! I don't know, Tom," Chuck said. "That's something I'd have to talk over with Marty."

"Well," he said, "mention it to her this weekend and see what she says. Just let me know. They're great little dogs. Good family dogs. I expect all seven will go fast."

"I'll do that, Tom. Thanks a lot for the offer!" Chuck said as he reached the house and Tom walked on.

"Hi, honey," Chuck called out as he came in the front door.

"I'm in here!" Marty answered from the kitchen.

"Where are the twins?" he asked as he gave her a hug and a kiss.

"They're playing out in back," she said. "Here's hoping they've learned to stay away from the ants! I haven't heard any screaming."

"Yet…," they replied in unison, laughing.

"Guess what?" Chuck said. "I walked home today with Tom Dubay and he offered us a puppy. His dog, Suzie, had seven pups. They're ten weeks old, a Welsh Corgi/terrier mix, and just about ready to go. He wants to give us pick of the litter."

"Wow," said Marty, the only comment she could come up with at that moment.

"I told him we'd talk it over and I'd let him know," said Chuck, sensing her apprehension. What do you think?"

"Oh, Chuck, I don't know," she sighed. "I have my hands pretty full with the twins, and as much as I think they'd enjoy having a puppy, as would we all, I'm afraid it would be like having another toddler in the house!"

"Well, think it over. We can talk more about it later," he said. "Tom told me he didn't have to know until Monday, so whatever we decide, I'll tell him then. I'm going to change my clothes and hang out with the boys for a bit," he said as he headed down the hall.

While he sat by the twins and watched them happily entertaining themselves in the warm afternoon sun, he reminisced about the fun times he and his friend, Howie Pederson, used to have with their neighborhood dog…*Bess was a brown and white English Springer Spaniel, strong and energetic, loved to follow them around the neighborhood and on the wooded trails along the Red Lake River. One fall day when she saw them headed for the river, she ran after them and quickly led the way. Bess* was a hunter, and as soon as she reached the river trail she began running ahead. They could hear her barking playfully in the distance as she gave chase to one small critter or another. At one point her barking sounded more serious and commanding than usual, so Howie and Chuck jogged to catch up with her. The crisp autumn air filled their lungs and was exhilarating. As her barking grew louder, they knew they had just about reached her, but still couldn't see her.

"Here, Bess! Come here, girl!" Chuck shouted, expecting her to come running back to them as she always did. The trail turned towards an open area with a tangle of scattered branches, sticks and twigs. Among the pile were some freshly-cut trees, mounds of wood chips and Bess, barking fiercely at a king-sized beaver she'd cornered!

"Sic him, Bess!" Howie yelled, and Bess unleashed a ferocious attack, which was met head on by the beaver's sharp four frontal teeth. Bess yelped in pain and leapt away from the beaver, which swished its large, leathery tail on the ground and bolted for the river. Bess's ear had a ragged tear and was dripping blood!

"Get him, girl!" Chuck shouted as Bess took off after the beaver. Just as the two animals reached the riverbank, Beth lunged forward and clamped her strong jaws onto the thick, furry neck of the beaver. It snapped backwards at her in an attempt to make her release her grip, but Bess had no intention of letting go. Dirt and woodchips flew wildly as the beaver clawed at the ground with all its might in an attempt to access the water, Bess pulling with all her might in the opposite direction. The beaver's tug-of-war power soon proved to be too much, and the two animals toppled from the edge of the riverbank into the swirling water, Bess still clinging to the beaver's neck.

"No, Bess, no!" Howie shouted. "Here, girl!" he yelled as he made a daring attempt to grab for her collar. It was too late! The river water churned into a muddy gray as Bess and the beaver struggled with one another and were soon carried away by the current. Within seconds the action ceased and the tumbling bodies disappeared. Howie and Chuck ran along the riverside trail in a panic, scanning the water for any sign of the two animals, hoping that Bess hadn't drowned!

After what felt like an eternity, Chuck saw a thin line of bubbles on the surface angling downstream. "Howie, look!" he yelled. Just then, both the dog and beaver burst through the surface, locked in a thrashing life and death struggle. Chuck and Howie called out frantically for Bess to come to them, but to no avail. In the boys' eagerness to have their dog playfully attack the beaver, they had provoked something very stupid! True, they were only ten years old, but they knew better. They had matched their neighbor's fun-loving dog with a wild animal, a very strong wild animal at that! The beaver had reached its natural habitat, and with its webbed feet and powerful flattened tail, the swimming advantage was on its side, especially under the water.

Bess and the beaver disappeared beneath the surface once again. Chuck and Howie ran along the riverbank in a panic, scanning the water in search of the two animals. They had been under for what seemed like an eternity, no bubbles, no splashing, no sign of struggle. Chuck felt numb as he stumbled after Howie. Was Bess still alive? His heart was pounding and began to ache, his eyes tearing up. He'd never forgive himself if Bess died! He asked God to please not let that happen.

God must have been listening. Just then the two animals broke the surface, Bess with the beaver's neck still clenched in her jaws! The boys couldn't believe it. Not only was Bess alive, she was trying to bring the beaver ashore! Howie and Chuck jumped up and down and yelled for her to swim towards them as she fought against the current, both running along the riverbank and shouting encouragement as she drew near. Bess finally engineered the few remaining feet and managed to pull herself onto a protruding sandbar, dropping the motionless beaver at Chuck and Howie's feet. Both boys began petting her and praising her lavishly, but she was too exhausted to respond. "Good girl, Bess," Chuck whispered, his voice choking. She had done battle at the boys' bidding and she had won, but she was one tired dog! Seemingly lifeless, the beaver just lay where Bess dropped it, but after several minutes it began inching its way from the sandbar back to the water. The boys watched as the beaver turned upstream and swam away. Bess could only muster a weak whine as she rose slowly on wobbly legs.

"Time for supper!" Marty called out the living room window, and Chuck was abruptly jerked back to reality.

"OK, honey!" he answered as he regained his sense of time and place. "I hope you boys are hungry," he said as he hoisted the twins into his arms and headed into the house. "I smell pork chops!" The boys ate just about everything Chuck and Marty did at this point, and they had mighty appetites!

"While you were outside I was thinking about all the good times I used to have with my dog, Muggsie," Marty said, "and of course that got me thinking about Tom Dubay's offer."

When Marty was a child her family owned a Boston Terrier. She loved that little dog, with its cute pug nose and cuddly little black and white body. Maybe she was weakening! "It's funny you should mention that," Chuck said. "While I was out in the back I was reliving my time with Bess, the neighborhood dog we used to play with when I was a kid."

After they finished eating and had the twins down for the night, Chuck and Marty curled up on the couch and talked about Tom's puppy offer. "The more I think about it, the more I think it could be a good thing for the twins," said Marty. "We could try tethering it to Mark on occasion; it would give Michael more freedom and give Mark the opportunity to develop a close relationship with a pet. Puppies aren't easy, and I sure don't need more to worry about, but I think in the long run it would be worth it, especially for Mark. What do you think?"

Chuck couldn't believe what he had just heard. "Honey, that makes perfect sense to me," he said, barely able to contain his excitement. "I agree with everything you just said. Let's do it!"

"Well, Chuck," Tom said when they saw each other between classes on Monday, "any decision about the puppy?"

"I can't believe I'm saying this," Chuck laughed, "but we're going to take you up on your offer! Marty wasn't so sure at first, thought it might be too much to handle on top of the twins, but then she got around to thinking how a puppy might actually be more helpful with the boys than anything, and it would give Michael some freedom and Mark the chance to bond with a pet. So, yes, we want one!"

"That's great news!" said Tom. "The only hard part will be choosing just one. You'll be able to take the puppy home on October 1st at twelve weeks, and like I said, you can have pick of the litter."

That night when Chuck got home from school, he told Marty what Tom had said. I'm so excited," said Marty. She was a dog lover through and through. "It'll be interesting to see how the boys respond. Oh, by the way," she added, "Tom Schmitz called and said our new car will be here the first week in October."

"Wow, a new puppy and a new car in the same week! That will make for an exciting few days," Chuck said.

"And did you remember we get to use Tom's car for the Saint John's Homecoming game this Saturday?" Marty said.

"I almost forgot!" said Chuck. "So much has been going on, I haven't had time to even think about it. What would you think of having Tom and his wife over for dinner on Friday? It would give them some time with the twins while we're here."

"Good idea," said Marty. "Sounds like they've never taken care of one young one, much less two, so they may be in for a big surprise with our active little duo!"

When Tom and Joannie arrived for dinner that Friday, Michael pulled Mark towards the door and they chorused, "Open, Daddy!" Michael quickly backed away when he saw two unfamiliar adults standing there.

"Hello there, boys!" Tom said enthusiastically as Chuck greeted Joannie and him.

The twins stood and said nothing; then Michael turned and ran towards the kitchen, Mark in tow. "Mama! Mama!" he yelled.

Marty came out of the kitchen and welcomed the guests. "Come in! Come in!" she said. "We're really glad you could make it."

"It was very kind of you to have us over," said Joannie.

"Very wise to give us a head start!" laughed Tom. "Who gets to teach me how to change a diaper?"

"Well, Tom, you can get your babysitting feet wet right now! Time for the boys' dinner," said Chuck as he untied Mark's tether and lifted him up. "There you go, Son," he said as he placed him in the highchair and then lifted Michael to his spot beside him.

"Lord," Chuck prayed after everyone was gathered around the table, "we're so grateful for this food and for all of our blessings, especially grateful that Tom and Joannie are sharing this meal and will be watching the boys tomorrow and giving Marty and me the opportunity to go to the homecoming game. Heaven help them!" he said as everyone laughed.

Marty showed Tom how to feed Michael in between taking bites of his own dinner, which was not an easy task with Michael's hearty appetite. Joanne tried her hand at feeding Mark, but he sensed something was different in the way the spoon was being held and kept his mouth firmly closed. "Open, Brother, open!" urged Michael, having often heard his dad and mom speak those words.

"I can see I have a lot to learn!" laughed Joannie. "This isn't going to be as easy as I thought!"

After dinner, everyone sat in the family room and talked while the boys played with their building blocks. "Do you have any questions?" asked Marty.

"When's bedtime?" asked Joannie.

"Theirs or mine?" laughed Tom.

"We start getting them ready shortly after they've eaten," said Marty. "It's always easier once they're fed and in a happy mood. Right about now, as a matter of fact. Would you like to join in the fun?"

"Sure!" said Tom and Joannie in unison.

"First thing is the double diaper change," said Chuck. "Each of you can bring one of the boys and follow me." Chuck got everything ready as Tom and Joannie went to work on the boys' diapers. Their careful and dainty undressing process and cautious unpinning reminded Chuck of his first several weeks of diaper changes with the twins, every move carried out in meticulously- slow fashion.

"There you go, little fella," Tom said proudly as he rubbed lotion on Michael's soft bottom and started to pin on a clean diaper, "just about ready for bed." That's when it happened! Michael stared up into Tom's face and let loose with a robust stream of urine. "Whoa!" yelled Tom as he backed away. "That was a surprise!"

"And now you get to start all over with a clean diaper," said Chuck laughing.

Luckily for Joannie, she didn't have the same experience with Mark. She had him freshly diapered and settled in bed in no time. Marty came in for the round of good-night kisses and it was lights out, the twins soon fast asleep.

"That wasn't so hard!" said Joannie as they sat in the family room.

"Speak for yourself!" laughed Tom as he collapsed onto the couch in exaggerated fashion.

"They're good little boys," said Marty. "I don't think you'll have any problems."

"I'm sure we'll do okay," said Joannie smiling. "We'll get here right after breakfast tomorrow so you can get an early start. You'll have about a two-hour drive."

Everything went as planned. The Schmitz's took over early in the morning as promised and Chuck and Marty headed for St. John's. It was a typical fall day, pleasantly warm, leaves turning a lovely array of orange, brown, red and yellow autumn colors. "This is heavenly!" gushed Marty as she settled back in the passenger seat and marveled at the passing scenery.

The game was a thriller. St. John's beat Gustavus Adolphus 21-7 and remained unbeaten for the year. Chuck and Marty stopped for dinner before heading back to Perham, and it was just getting dark when they rolled up to the house. Everything was quiet when they opened the door, so they tiptoed in and didn't say a word. Joannie and Tom were sitting on the sofa, Tom fast asleep and Joannie wide awake, both looking like they'd been put through a wringer.

"How'd things go?" Marty whispered.

"Just fine," Joannie said smiling, the fatigue in her voice giving her away. "Two babies are a handful, that's for sure!" she admitted. She roused Tom, and the four of them sat and shared the tales of their day.

"That was great training for us," Tom said. "And we waited until you got home to tell you our big news. Joannie's three-months pregnant!"

"Congratulations!" Chuck and Marty exclaimed, forgetting to lower their voices with the excitement of Tom's announcement.

Just then they heard sounds coming from down the hall. "SHHHHH!" reprimanded the harried babysitters as everyone laughed.

After the Schmitzes left, Chuck and Marty headed to bed. It had been a fantastic, action-packed day, and they were more than ready for a good night's sleep.

The familiar routine began the next morning after Sunday Mass. "Why don't you boys go out and play," Marty said as the two were running in circles around the house. Mark and Michael were familiar with those words, as Marty often included that phrase with their braille typewriter lessons. She had begun to teach them many words, such as OPEN and

BROTHER. Above each word she typed in braille, she also printed the letters in large manuscript for Michael.

Many new experiences took place during the last week in September. Chuck and Marty bought a large playpen and two potty chairs from Schoeneberger's Furniture Store. The twins were not happy when they were put in the playpen, especially when Chuck tried putting the chairs into the playpen and strapped the boys in with encouragement to go. The twins made it clear they just wanted out! It seemed they weren't ready, and Chuck and Marty decided their first attempt had been made a bit too soon. It was going to be interesting to see what would happen when the new puppy's housebreaking effort was added to the potty-training equation.

Tom Schmitz pulled up in front of their house early the next Saturday morning with a sparkling new, fire-hydrant red, four-door Ford country sedan. "There's your beautiful set of wheels, Charlie!" said Tom enthusiastically as he greeted Chuck. "Let's take her for a ride with the family and see how you like it!"

"Marty!" Chuck called out. "Come here, honey! Something out front I want you to see!"

When she came to the door and saw Tom standing there, she knew. He just pointed and smiled at the shiny red car parked at the curb. "Wow! It's wonderful!" Marty exclaimed.

"Tom wants to take the family out for a little spin to see how we like it," said Chuck.

"Okay," Marty said enthusiastically. "You get the twins and I'll be right there."

Their purchase included a thick, forest green cotton pad that filled the whole back of the car when the back seat was down, including the wheel wells, and the twins just lay on it while Marty held their leather tether. Tom drove them out to Big Pine Lake and had Chuck drive back. "This baby really moves!" Chuck gushed as he stepped on the accelerator and the car surged forward. When they got home, Tom said they could pick up the car any time they wanted after they came in and signed the necessary forms. Needless to say, the paperwork was completed and the new sedan parked in their garage by the end of the day! The next week passed quickly. Chuck and Marty were enjoying trying out their new car, driving to church, driving to the grocery store and taking a spin with the twins after Chuck got home from school. With their gleaming new vehicle, just being in it was entertainment enough!

When school let out on Friday, Tom Dubay told Chuck the puppies were ready, so the family drove over Saturday morning to take a look. When Michael saw them squirming around on a blanket by their mother, he flew towards them, jerking Mark to the floor and then falling backwards on top of him. "Now that's what I call eager!" said Tom as the boys made their way to their feet. Michael started petting all of the puppies, but one in particular crawled right onto Mark's lap as he sat on the floor. Mark could feel something soft and warm and cuddled it against his chest. The little pup licked his face again and again as Mark giggled. "I think that might be the one, Charlie," Tom said.

"I think you're right," Chuck said. "I like that one, too! He's energetic and friendly, just like the boys." The adorable pup had soft, rust-colored fur, bright brown eyes, floppy little ears and handsome snow-white markings on his chest and paws. "What do you think, Marty?" Chuck asked.

"I think that puppy chose us," said Marty smiling. "What do you think, boys?" she asked.

"Yes! Yes!" the twins yelled exuberantly.

"Well, then, it's settled." said Tom. "He's all yours!"

When they got home, they put the puppy in the boys' playpen and watched as he moved about the small space, busily taking in the new smells and no doubt curious about the absence of his mother and siblings. "Let's have Mark sit in the playpen with him for a bit and see what happens," said Chuck as he lifted Mark over the side rail.

Well, something happened all right! The little pup immediately jumped into Mark's lap. "Puppy!" Mark laughed, and began moving his hands all around the puppy's face. As his fingers explored the puppy's open mouth, the puppy bit into Mark's thumb with its little needle-like teeth. Mark screamed bloody murder, then cupped the puppy's head in his hands and bit into one of its ears, at which point the puppy responded with an ear-piercing yelp of its own. It was pure bedlam until Marty was able to unclench Mark's teeth from the puppy's ear.

"Doggie ouch!" said Mark.

"I'll make it better," said Marty as she lifted Mark from the playpen and gently kissed his thumb.

"So much for my great idea," said Chuck. "Now I'm in the doghouse!"

The kids' vocabulary was increasing at a rapid pace. Marty added DOG to the braille list of words to be learned, and she was soon to add CAT. That evening they took the puppy out of the playpen after he'd eaten and let him run around on the vinyl floor with the twins chasing after him. They were all getting some exercise and the twins were happy as can be, Mark having quickly forgotten about the finger-biting episode.

That night everyone slept well, even the new furry family member, but on Sunday morning Chuck and Marty were shocked to find the puppy wasn't in the playpen! It seems he had squeezed through the narrow wooden bars, and there he was, fast asleep under the dining room table. And that's not all they found! Around the house were a number of little puddles, including a fresh stain on the new family room drapes. "Enough of that!" said Marty emphatically. "We need to get this little guy used to the great outdoors." And that's exactly what happened. They put the puppy and his blanket out in the back yard while they were at church, and when they returned they found him curled up in the sunshine, snoozing the morning away as if nothing had happened.

"Good dog," said Chuck as he bent down to pet him. "We need to get you housebroken!"

"Him and the boys," said Marty laughing. "Hopefully we can train them all at once!"

The puppy loved its time in the back yard, its time anywhere for that matter. He was one happy little dog and the family grew quickly attached. The puppy play was cut short one afternoon when the puppy noticed a stately black cat rubbing its back against the cyclone fence. The twins and the puppy ran innocently towards it, but when the puppy pressed its face up against the fence, the cat hissed and ran a sharp claw down the puppy's nose. The puppy let out a sharp, shrill cry and Chuck and Marty came running. When they saw the cat and drops of blood on the puppy's nose, they knew immediately what had happened and shooed the big cat away. Now the twins had a new word added to their vocabulary, but all Mark knew about the confrontation was that CAT was somehow associated with a whole lot of hissing and crying.

For now, the number one priority was housebreaking the puppy. As it turned out, their Corgi was a quick study. Chuck studied the *World Book Encyclopedia* for its recommended technique and it worked! It was called the *den-bed* method. He made a den-bed for the puppy by getting a lidded cardboard box from the grocery store and punching air holes in the side. The puppy, of course, preferred not to be in the small box, but he wanted it to stay clean, so when he was confined and needed to do his duty, he would whine and Chuck would carry him to the chosen spot in the back yard. After that, whenever the puppy whined, whether in the box or not, everyone knew what he wanted and opened the back door for him. Mission accomplished! By the way, the puppy now had a name, Lord Tregnor, 'Treg' or 'Treggie' for short. Since he was a Welsh Corgi, Chuck and Marty decided a title from Welsh nobility was perfect for their honorable canine.

Given their success in housebreaking the rambunctious little puppy, Chuck and Marty figured it was time to retry their potty-training effort with the boys. One day in December when the twins were sixteen months old, they struck gold! Thanks to patient encouragement from his dad, Mark not only peed in the potty, he did the double duty! "Good for you!" Chuck said exuberantly. Not to be outdone, Michael's face turned an intense red as he sat on his chair, and sure enough, he had success as well! It was amazing how competitive the boys were. Whatever one did, the other wanted to imitate, especially if praise from their dad followed the action. Their twin achievements on the potty definitely garnered congratulatory words from both parents!

"Now I have four new words to add to their vocabulary," Marty said after Chuck shared the big news. "POTTY, PEE PEE, POOP and GOOD!" That made more than twenty words the boys were learning, and they especially enjoyed working on the braille versions. Marty and Chuck were learning the braille versions right along with the twins, making them all the more appreciative of the effort involved for their young sons.

ALTHOUGH THE HOLIDAYS WERE ALWAYS A WONDERFUL TIME FOR the family, they would never be quite as bright for Marty with her dad gone and her mother living in California. Thanksgiving had been lovely, and Chuck and Marty deeply appreciated all they had for which to be thankful, but Christmas just wouldn't be the same this year. Chuck wasn't sure what to do about it, whether or not to invite his mom and dad, but his dilemma was solved a couple of days before Christmas vacation. "Chuck, why don't you call your parents and ask if they'd like to come for Christmas," said Marty.

"I've been thinking about that," said Chuck. "I was afraid it might make you sad."

"I think it would be wonderful to have them here," said Marty. "I'd enjoy seeing them and it's been a whole year since they've seen the twins. I know the boys would love for them to be here as well."

When Chuck made the call, Frank and Grace were delighted to be asked, and would make plans to take the train to Perham on Christmas Eve. "My parents would love to accept the invitation," Chuck told Marty after he hung up. "They're coming on the train, so I won't need to drive up to Crookston. I can go to work on a surprise backyard project I planned for Christmas vacation."

"Uh oh," Marty laughed. "And just what might that be?" she asked suspiciously. "This is the first I've heard of any such project."

"Well," he said, "I was thinking it would be neat to flood the back yard and make an ice rink. What do you think?"

"Wow!" said Marty laughing. "I wasn't expecting that! I actually think it would be a lot of fun," she said enthusiastically, "and I'm sure the boys would agree! They may not be able to skate quite yet, but they'll have a good time sliding around. Do you remember how each neighborhood in Crookston used to flood a vacant lot every winter? We got such a kick out of sliding around!"

"That's exactly what I was thinking about when I came up with the idea for our yard," he said, "just like one of the neighborhood rinks." It didn't take long for Chuck's plan to come to fruition, a mere two days as a matter of fact. On December 17th, 1954, the temperature plunged to zero, perfect for his backyard flooding project and the creation of a smooth sheet of ice. That night Mother Nature obliged with several inches of fresh snow, which Chuck shoveled to the edges of the rink the next morning, creating a nice bank around the perimeter.

"Beautiful!" Marty exclaimed when she saw what he had done.

That afternoon Chuck went down to Welter's Hardware Store and bought a sled for the twins. They were going to get ice skates, too, but that would have to wait for a Christmas Eve delivery from Santa Claus. When Chuck got home, he put on his skates and pulled the empty sled around the rink. Michael could hardly contain his excitement as he watched through the window, so Marty gathered up the twins' snow pants, scarves, caps, mittens and boots. "Okay, boys," she said after they were all bundled up, "it's time for some fun on the ice rink!"

Michael and Mark were tethered to one another, and although Mark had no idea what was happening, he let himself be pulled onto the ice behind his brother with his typical good-natured enthusiasm. "Ouch!" he yelled in surprise as he immediately slipped and fell onto his rear end, pulling Michael down on top of him. "Brother! Okay?" asked Michael as the boys laughed.

"Okay!" said Mark. He was accustomed to falling and wasn't about to let a little ice defeat him. He slid his gloved hand around on the surface and then put it to his face and licked it.

"That's ice, Mark!" said Chuck, laughing as he bent down to help the boys to their feet. "Do you like it? It's cold!"

"Ice, Brother!" repeated Michael. "Cold!"

"Cold!" said Mark, licking his glove.

"Let's go for a ride!" said Chuck as he lifted the boys onto the sled. "Hold on!" The boys squealed with delight as the sled began moving and slowly picked up speed. Around and around they went as their dad circled the rink, the wind brushing against their faces and their cheeks alive with the rosy glow of winter fun. The boys still had a week before Grandpa and Grandma Dowdle's arrival, and all they wanted to do every morning after breakfast (and all day, for that matter) was spend time playing on the backyard ice. That was fine with Marty as long is it wasn't too windy or cold outside. She could keep an eye on their antics through the window and get things done in the house without interruption, sometimes even take a few precious minutes of quiet time to unwind and relax.

Tregnor was growing bigger every day. He was a friendly, energetic and playful puppy, equally enthusiastic about spending time outdoors, especially when the twins were involved. He didn't quite know what to make of the rink, as every time he ran across the ice he'd slide right past the boys when he attempted to stop, his little paws churning fruitlessly in an effort to apply the brakes. It became a game of sorts, definitely amusing to watch, and everyone was having a good time!

On Christmas Eve, Chuck drove to the train station with the twins to pick up Grandma and Grandpa Dowdle. Mark loved hearing the steam engine chugging and hissing as the train approached and Michael loved waving to the engineer as it pulled into the station. Chuck brought the boys up close when the train arrived so they could feel the steam against their faces. TRAIN! Another new word for Marty to add to their rapidly-increasing braille vocabulary. The brakes screeched metal on metal and Mark covered his ears with mittened hands to buffer the sound.

Grandma Dowdle was the first to step from the train, Grandpa Dowdle close behind. "Oh, there are my precious little grandsons!" she exclaimed when she saw the twins. Mark was only four months old the last time he heard his grandma's voice, but he seemed to remember it and grinned broadly as she bent down and picked him up, hugging him warmly.

"And now this one wants some of that," laughed Chuck as she set Mark down and he lifted a smiling Michael to her open arms.

"It's good to see you, Charlie. Those boys of yours are something special," said Frank as he shook hands with his son.

"Thanks, Dad. It's great to see you, too. How was the train ride?" asked Chuck.

"It was really enjoyable," he said, "a little slow, but fun to see all the small towns and the accumulation of snow along the way. First time we've taken the train to Perham."

"Well, let's pile into the car and get home for lunch," Chuck said enthusiastically. "Thanks to my lovely wife, we have homemade turkey vegetable soup and buttermilk biscuits on the menu!"

"That sounds real good on a day like today," said his dad with a big grin.

When they pulled up in front of the house, Chuck's mother was overwhelmed. "I never dreamed you had such a big place, Charlie!" she said. "It's beautiful!"

"Wait until you see the inside, Mom," he said as they walked up the freshly-shoveled path to the front door. Marty greeted Frank and Grace enthusiastically, as did Tregnor from his playpen in the kitchen.

"Oh, I hear your doggie!" Grandma said to the twins.

"Twegnor!" Mark said.

"Chuck, why don't you show your mom and dad the house while I finish getting lunch ready," Marty said.

"Follow me," said a beaming Chuck as he led his parents on a grand tour. Needless to say, they were impressed as he escorted them from room to room.

"You've got a great place here, Charlie," said his dad as they rounded the final turn and headed into the dining room. "It's spacious and must be very well insulated. So nice and warm."

"It is simply lovely," said his mom. "I'm so happy for you and Marilyn and the boys."

"We sure are happy here," said Chuck. "It was worth the wait!"

"If everyone's ready, let's sit down and eat while everything's hot," said Marty.

"It looks wonderful, Marilyn," said Chuck's dad as they all found their places.

"My, how those boys have grown!" Chuck's mother said. "When we were here last Christmas, they had to be propped up in their highchair. Before long they'll be sitting at the table!"

"You're right! said Chuck. "They feed themselves now and eat what we eat, and they're not afraid of packing the food in as you'll soon see."

"Let's say a prayer so we can get to packing in some of this food ourselves!" laughed Chuck's dad.

"*Father*," Chuck began, "*thank you for bringing my parents here safely, for us being together to celebrate the birth of your Son, and thank you for my wonderful wife who prepared this delicious lunch. Amen.*"

Marty placed two small bowls of warm soup on the tray in front of the twins and handed them their spoons. They immediately began to slurp it up, dribbling some of it on their bibs in the process. "My goodness, look at that!" said Grandma Dowdle. "Neither of them has any problem with that spoon!"

"Not at all," Chuck said, "and you can see Mark keeps right up with his brother."

After lunch, Chuck's parents got settled into their guest bedroom and then the grownups sat in the family room and talked while the twins were napping. "There certainly have been a lot of changes for you since last Christmas," Chuck's mother said. "How does your mother like living in California, Marilyn?" she asked.

"She's really enjoying it," Marty said. "We got a Christmas card from her this week, and she said the weather in San Gabriel has been sunny and warm just about every day since she got there. There are orange groves everywhere and she can see the snow-covered San Gabriel mountains from her back yard. I know she misses spending Christmas with all of us, but she's not missing the Minnesota winter weather at all!"

"It's nice to be with family during the holidays if you can, but I certainly understand why she's so happy there!" Chuck's mother said.

The time passed quickly as they sat and chatted. "I think I hear some double action from down the hall," said Marty as she got up and went to check on the boys.

"How'd you like to see your grandsons skate around the rink in their overshoes?" Chuck asked.

"Oh, it may be too cold for them out there!" Chuck's mother said.

"Heck no!" Chuck said. "They like this weather!"

Michael and Mark were soon bundled up and enthusiastically headed out the back door with their dad, Tregnor bounding close behind. "We'll be watching from in here where it's nice and warm!" said Grace.

Chuck helped the boys onto the sled and began pulling them around the rink while Tregnor did his best to keep up. After a dozen laps he set the sled aside and helped the twins to their feet on the ice. Off they went! The grandparents waved through the window as the twin and dog trio slid and slipped their way around the rink.

Skating without skates was hard work, and before long the boys were ready to go inside, no doubt tempted by the opportunity to spend time with Grandma and Grandpa. They ran into the kitchen, where Grace was helping their mom prepare the turkey fixings for Christmas Eve dinner. "Gramma! Gramma!" Mark yelled. "Me and Michael skated!"

"I was watching you!" said their grandma. "You both did great! Now let me help you get out of those bulky clothes." With the winter layers removed, Grandma took a hand of each of the twins and whispered, "Let's go take a peek at Grandpa! I think he's sleeping!" That he was, sprawled contentedly in Chuck's oversized easy chair in front of the blazing fire. He had his feet propped up on the ottoman and was snoring, which fascinated the twins. When Grandma led them closer to him, Mark stopped and listened. He slowly approached the side of the chair and reached up to Grandpa's face, but couldn't quite stretch his arm high enough. Grandma lifted him, and he reached to where the sound was coming from, Grandpa's nose and mouth! When Grandpa felt the touch of the soft little hand fingering his face, he roused himself with a mighty snort. The boys began laughing, and Grandma laughed, too. "I'll let you entertain these two while I help Marilyn in the kitchen," Grace said to Frank as she lifted the twins up onto her husband's lap.

"Fine with me!" he said, and with his grandsons cuddled comfortably in his arms, he began telling them the story of the birth of Jesus. "Well, boys," he began, "a long, long time ago a little boy just like you was born. His name was Jesus and he was called the Son of God. He was a very important little boy, and after he was born, three wise men came to visit him." That's as far as Grandpa got, as the twins' eyes slowly drooped and they were soon fast asleep.

"Good work, Dad," Chuck whispered when he came into the room and saw the twins cuddled fast asleep in the chair with their grandfather. "You have the touch! If it's okay with you, let's just let them stay there. When they wake up, Marty and Mom will join us and we'll open presents."

"That's just fine," Chuck's dad said quietly. "This chair is real comfortable and it's nice to be so close to my grandsons." The aroma from the roasting turkey was beginning to fill the house, and Marty and Grace were just putting the pumpkin pies into the oven. "Sure smells good around here," Frank said quietly as he inhaled deeply.

"It sure does," Chuck said. "Reminds me of those Christmas dinners we used to have at home. Turkey, dressing, mashed potatoes and gravy, cranberries, and sweet potatoes covered with brown sugar, which tasted just like candy."

"And to top it off, pumpkin pie with real whipped cream!" said his dad. "We were pretty lucky, Charlie."

"And continue to be, Dad," Chuck said. "Marty is one great cook! By the way, does Santa Claus still come to the Grand Theater in Crookston on Christmas Eve and give bags of candy to the kids? I used to love that!"

"He sure does. That's one tradition that's still with us. I remember how all the kids in town were invited to that matinee," he said as he began reliving the experience. "The *Crookston Daily Times* would announce the event by saying something like, "Santa Claus will be arriving this Saturday afternoon at the Grand Theater to wish all Crookston children a Merry Christmas! Free movies will be shown and bags of candy will be given to all who attend!"

"Were they kidding? Who wouldn't attend?" laughed Chuck. He was right. It was the 1930's, the time of the Great Depression, a time when anything free was unheard of. "The only Crookston kid I knew who missed that matinee had pneumonia and a 105-degree temperature!" Chuck said.

"It was a big deal," reminisced his dad. "Free cartoons, big bags of candy, nuts and fruit. Everyone wanted to be there; it's still very popular to this day."

"I remember right after they finished showing animations like Bugs Bunny, Porky Pig, Donald Duck and Micky Mouse and all that," said Chuck, "the theater owner, Mr. Hiller, would walk onto the stage and thank everyone for coming. He'd wish everyone a Merry Christmas and then we'd hear bells jingling from the lobby. It got louder and louder, and then HO! HO! HO! MERRY CHRISTMAS!"

So much for whispering! The twins awoke with a start with his enthusiastic Santa imitation. "Uh oh, Charlie," said his dad, "I think you've done it now."

"That's okay," he said. "It's about time to open presents, and the twins will want to be center stage for that!"

"Looks like everybody's awake!" said Chuck's mom as she came into the room. "Marilyn is fixing us a delicious-looking meal! We've got the pumpkin pies in the oven and dinner will be ready in about an hour."

"Sure smells good!" said Chuck. "Do you remember how Mr. Hiller used to invite all of us kids for free movies and bags of goodies from Santa Claus?" he asked his mom.

"Oh, yes, of course," she said, "and they still do it every year!"

"Dad and I were just talking about it, reminiscing about those good old times," Chuck told her. "But enough of that. I think it's time to open some presents!"

The twins weren't quite ready to move out of the easy chair, warm and comfortable as they were on Grandpa's lap. "C'mon, boys," Chuck said enticingly as he lifted them into his arms, "it's time to see what Santa Claus brought you!"

Everyone settled in the family room as the gift unveiling began. The first present was from Grandma to the twins, matching pajama sets she'd sewn. "Jamas!" shouted Michael, holding his up. Mark was drawn to the softness of the fabric and sat quietly, rubbing the flannel against his face.

"Well, boys," Marty said, "what do you say to Grandma?"

"Thank you, Grandma!" they said in unison.

When the adults exchanged their gifts, none of them received sweaters this year! Instead, there was a lovely glass bowl Marty had picked out for Chuck's mother and a plush navy-blue robe she'd chosen for Chuck's dad.

"It's just beautiful, Marilyn!" Chuck's mother gushed as she gave her daughter-in-law a hug. "Thank you very much! It will be so lovely for special occasions."

"This robe isn't going to wait for special occasions!" Chuck's dad said as he stood and held his gift up for everyone to admire. "I'll be putting it on every morning and every evening and maybe in between. Thank you very much, Marilyn!" he said as he walked to the couch and gave her a hug.

Chuck picked up the gift from his parents to Marty and him. "I wonder what this might be," he said. "It's heavy! Do you want me to open it or would you like to?" he asked Marty.

"Go ahead," she said cheerily.

"We hope you like it," his mom said. "It's something we noticed you didn't have last time we were here."

Chuck tore away the colorful Christmas paper from the box, exposing an image of a fancy standing mixer. "Wow!" he said. "We don't have one of these! This is great!" He opened the box and pulled out the shiny white appliance and its three accompanying glass bowls.

"Thank you so much!" said Marty as she gazed at the Sunbeam beauty. "It's nice and big. I love it!"

"Lucky me!" said Chuck. "Now Marty will be making desserts nonstop! Thank you! Thank you!" he said as he and Marty embraced his parents.

"Let's have the boys open their presents and then it will be just about time to eat," said Marty.

Chuck placed a small, unwrapped gift in Mark's lap and said, "Go ahead and open it, Son." Mark fumbled with the lid a bit and then lifted it off. Chuck placed Mark's hands on a pair of shiny new skates. Mark smiled broadly as he glided his little fingers gently over the soft leather boot and hard metal blades.

"Daddy!" Michael yelled, "I want skates, too!" When Chuck handed Michael his box, he ripped off the cover and discovered he had a pair of shiny new skates. "Skates, Brother!" he said gleefully.

"Yes, skates!" said Mark.

"Thank you, Daddy!" they both said.

"Remember to thank your mother, too," said their dad.

"Thank you, Mommy!" the boys said in unison as she hugged them both.

"Marty and I got skates for each other this year, too," Chuck said. "Our skates were old and worn, the same ones we've had since ninth grade, so we decided to get new ones."

"Especially now that we have an ice rink in our back yard!" Marty laughed. "I think it's time to head to the dining room," she said as she stood up. "That turkey smells like it's ready!"

Everyone was soon seated around the table, the twins settled into their highchair with bibs on and spoons at the ready. Chuck prayed, "*Lord, thank you for letting us be together with Grandma and Grandpa this Christmas Eve, about to enjoy this delicious meal Marty has prepared.*"

"With a lot of help!" Marty interjected.

"*...and thank you for our health and the mighty appetites with which you've blessed us. AMEN!*" finished Chuck with a flourish. As soon as Marty placed plates of turkey, mashed potatoes and gravy, cranberries and sweet potatoes on the tray in front of the twins, they wasted no time digging in! Mark had no problem locating his food or his mouth. He bent over the plate more closely than Michael, but kept right up as far as speed of the shovel.

"Those little guys sure are hungry!" Grandma said.

"They're hearty eaters," Chuck said. "Mark sometimes needs a little assistance, but he figures out where the food is by touching it with his spoon. They're not even eighteen months old and already weigh about 30 pounds each. We thought being born prematurely might affect their growth, but no sign of that. It certainly hasn't held either of them back. They have great appetites and are a couple of healthy, happy kids. We're very lucky," he said proudly.

"Did Chuck mention he and the boys and I are all learning braille?" Marty asked Chuck's parents.

"That's wonderful!" Chuck's mom said.

"It's a family affair," said Chuck. "We decided since Mark was learning braille, then of course we all should. I can hardly keep up with the boys! It's been a humbling experience for me, and it takes a lot of work!"

After everyone finished eating, including polishing off generous portions of fresh-baked pumpkin pie, Marty said, "It's been a long day for all of us. I don't know about the rest of you, but by the time the twins are cleaned up and ready for bed, I think I'll be ready, too."

"I'm sure you will, Marilyn," Chuck's mom said. "Frank and I relaxed on the train all morning, so how about you and Chuck let us put the boys to bed?"

"That would be wonderful!" said Marty with an appreciative sigh.

Grandma and Grandpa got the twins washed up and into their new Christmas pajamas, tucked them in and had just finished telling them a bedtime story when Marty and Chuck tiptoed into their bedroom. The eyes of both boys were already closed and they were fast asleep. "That's a beautiful site to see! Thank you!" Marty whispered as they left the room. "Now it's time for all of us to get some sleep. We have a big day tomorrow."

"Marty and I are going to nine o'clock Mass, and we take the twins to church, so you don't have to worry about them," said Chuck. "You two can sleep in!"

"Sounds like a great idea," said his dad, smiling.

"Have a good sleep!" said Chuck as they all headed off to bed.

As planned, Chuck and Marty and the boys were up early, out the door and at St. Henry's for Christmas morning Mass. After the service, Father Donnay stood at the back of the church and greeted all of his parishioners as they filed out. When he saw the twins, he leaned down and gave each of them a big hug. "Merry Christmas, my little angels, Merry Christmas!" he said cheerily. The twins beamed up at him, Mark by now well familiar with his friendly voice.

When they got home, Chuck's parents were relaxing in the family room with a cup of coffee. With all hands pitching in, they were soon gathered around the table enjoying delicious fresh fruit salad, ham & eggs, potatoes, and toast with strawberry jam. The boys had already eaten an early-morning breakfast before church, but they were more than ready for a second round.

After they'd eaten, Chuck asked Marty if she was game to try out her new skates with the twins. "It would be fun!" she said. "The sun's shining and it's not too cold outside. Let's do it!" Chuck loved his wife's enthusiasm. She was one good sport and a great mother, too!

While Marty was putting on her skates, Chuck's mom helped bundle up the twins, and before long all of them were ready to go. "This is going to be interesting!" said Chuck as he took Mark by the hand and led him outside. Mark walked slowly on wobbly ankles to the ice rink. He was no doubt wondering what his dad was doing to him, strapping foreign things to his feet that made it difficult for him to walk and keep his balance. When they reached the ice, Chuck faced him and held him by both hands as he gently pulled him forward. Mark was smiling, then laughing! He loved it, especially the ease with which he was gliding along. "That's the way to do it, Mark!" Chuck said as he increased the speed of their lap. "You're doing great!"

When Michael saw how much fun Mark was having with his dad, he yelled, "Mom, skate with me!" Marty took him by the hand and led him to the rink. Off they went! For his first time on skates, he was a natural! "Hi Brother!" he yelled as they skated alongside his dad and brother.

"Hi Brother!" Mark yelled back.

"Michael, you're doing so well for your first time!" Marty said as they circled the rink. "It won't be long before you and your brother will be skating by yourselves!"

"Can Treggie skate?" Michael asked.

"I'm afraid not," she said, "but I'll go get him and he can run around with us. Wait here and I'll be right back."

While she was in the house, Michael watched his dad moving around the rink with Mark, and he wasn't about to just stand there and wait for his mom, not Michael! Instead, he started running on his skates to see if he could catch them. He fell one, two, three times, and when he was just getting to his feet to try again, Chuck and Mark skated up to him. "Okay, Michael, it's your turn," announced Chuck. "Wait here, Mark, he said as he let go of his hand. "Here comes Mom to skate with you.

"Fast, Dad, fast!" yelled Michael as he circled the rink with his father. Marty held onto Mark as they made their way around, Treg clawing at the ice for traction as he slipped and slid his way along behind them.

After several minutes of skating with Michael, Chuck said, "How'd you like to try skating with your brother?"

"Yes!" Michael yelled.

Marty and Mark glided up to them. "First things first," said Chuck as he attached the tether to the twins, Michael on the inside and Mark on the outside. "Okay, boys," he said, "keep the tether taut between you the same way you do when you're in the house. You'll do fine!"

Michael was eager to get started, and when he pulled forward a bit too vigorously, both boys went down. "Wait for me, Brother!" Mark said as they got to their feet. On the second attempt, they moved slowly forward until the tether was straight and taut, then made the turn at the end of the rink and headed down the straightaway. Tregnor made a gallant effort to run alongside, barking playfully and doing his best to be part of the team.

Grandma and Grandpa had come outdoors and were standing near the house, observing the action. The boys improved with every lap, and each time they skated by, Grandma clapped and cheered and Grandpa yelled out, "That's the way to do it, boys! Keep it up!"

"It's just amazing how rapidly those two have caught on," Chuck's mother said. "They're not even two!"

"It's interesting how determined they are," said Chuck's dad. "They fall down and bounce right back up like rubber balls. Gutsy little guys, and natural athletes just like Charlie."

"I think that's enough skating for today, Chuck," said Marty after about thirty minutes of around and around action. "We can do it again tomorrow."

Everyone came indoors for some warmth and relaxation. Time rolled by and it was soon time to think about lunch. "I feel like all I've done is eat since we arrived yesterday!" laughed Chuck's mom as she headed into the kitchen with Marty.

"Me, too," hollered his dad from the living room, "and I like it!"

"And I bet I know what we're having," said Chuck as he came into the kitchen with the twins. "Turkey sandwiches and cranberries! My favorite combination!"

"I know, I know," Marty said, laughing, "as I'm sure your mom does as well."

"Yes, that goes all the way back to when he was a little boy," said Grace, "more so than any of the other kids in the family."

"I don't think he'll ever tire of eating turkey and cranberries," said Marty. "Whenever we're travelling and stop at a deli for lunch, you can guess what he orders every time."

"And don't forget how much I love pumpkin pie and whipped cream!" said Chuck. "My other favorite meal!"

"All I can say," Marty said to Chuck's mom, "is that your son sure loves to eat!"

"And after watching my grandsons, I think they're on track to be just like their father," laughed Grace.

Everyone sat down for a hearty lunch, after which the twins napped and the adults sat and chatted. "What are you planning on doing next summer, Charlie?" Chuck's dad asked.

"I really don't know yet, Dad," he said. "I'm going to have to get work somewhere to help with the car and house payments, but I don't have a job lined up yet. Last summer was great. Our superintendent hired Har Sandholm and me to paint all the school classrooms. It was a big job, a lot of fun and we made good money. I don't yet know what this summer will bring."

"I'm sure you'll find something good, Charlie," Chuck's mom said. She always thought positively about her sons, as did his dad.

"Yes, Charlie," he said, "I'm sure you'll be able to find some kind of work around here."

"I think so, too," Chuck said, "and I've got the rest of the school year to think about it and make it happen, so I'm not worried."

Enough talk about work, this was Christmas! The rest of the afternoon was spent playing with the twins and enjoying a festive afternoon. In the evening, after a second feast of turkey with all the trimmings and Chuck's favorite pumpkin pie dessert, it was soon time for everyone to head off to bed in anticipation of a restful night's sleep.

The grandparents were up early the next morning, as the train to Crookston was scheduled to depart at nine o'clock. The twins were emphatic in their pleas to see the train again, so everyone loaded into the car and drove to the station together. After the typical farewell commotion of hugs and kisses, the grandparents waved from the window, and the train chugged away. Chuck and Marty drove home, put the twins down for a nap and breathed sighs of relief. It had all been wonderful, but it would be good to settle back into their normal routine.

AFTER CHRISTMAS VACATION, THE NEXT FIVE MONTHS OF SCHOOL flew by. Summer break arrived and Chuck hadn't yet found a job. The local mill hired a couple of guys the first week, but those jobs went fast. During the middle of the second week of summer vacation, he heard an extra gang on the railroad was hiring 'gandy dancers.' He applied, got the job, and that's how he spent the summer of 1955. Gandy dancing wasn't something new to Chuck. He had worked with a railroad gang of older men and 15 to 16 year-old Crookston kids during the summers of 1943 and 1944 when World War II was still being fought and there was a shortage of men on the home front. He had enjoyed the hard work and loved to tell the tale:

The Great Northern Railroad needed workers badly, so after our freshman year of high school, a gang of us went over to the railroad office and applied for work. We were supposed to be at least sixteen years old, thus some of us lied about our age. The railroad didn't care. They needed men to work an extra gang on the track and never did check our ages. Had they done so, they would have discovered that many of us were only fifteen and had just finished ninth grade.

Our boss's nickname was 'Scrap Iron.' He was a hunched-over old guy, his face tanned and cracked like aged brown shoe leather. He was a very gentle man for a railroad foreman. Before we were hired, he lined us up and looked us over. When he came to me, he asked, "Son, are you ready to go to work?" I remember standing as straight and tall as I could and answering, "Yes, sir!" I was hired on the spot and told to report to the depot at seven o'clock the next morning. I was thrilled! 'Scrappy' thought I looked good enough to work for man's pay, which I learned would be fifty dollars every two weeks! That was a lot of money in 1943, considering a private in the Army was paid only twenty-one dollars a month at that time for fighting in a war.

The pay may have been real good, but we earned it! First, we pulled out the spikes, which were driven into the holes on each side of a heavy iron plate which sat on the railroad tie under the rail. Heavy six-foot iron crowbars with hammer-like claws on one end were used to pull the spikes. Next, heavy iron jacks, weighing about seventy pounds each, were forced under the rail, hoisting it two to three inches above the railroad ties. This made it possible for the next procedure, pulling the old, rotten, heavily-creosoted ties out from under the rail. One worker would get inside the rails, one outside, and using tongs, the two men would tug at the tie until it loosened and came out, just like a dentist pulling a tooth. For some reason I developed a real liking for the strong-smelling creosote, which was used as a wood preservative.

We typically worked in pairs when we pulled out ties. 'Gandy dancing' was the next step in the procedure. Bill Monroe was my dance partner. He and I would pull new creosoted ties under the rails with our ice tongs and then commence 'tamping' dirt and crushed rock beneath them with our shovels until they were tight against the underside of the rails. Before 'dressing down' the track, the last step in the gandy dancing process, heavy mauls were used to pound spikes into the ties. That's when the fun began!

The old hands watched as we kids tapped the spikes into the ties and then raised the mauls over our heads and took full-fledged swings. Of course, just like when you're pounding nails into boards, if you didn't hit the spike heads flush, they'd go zinging through the air like shrapnel. Watching our feeble attempts to drive the spikes into the ties, taking five, six or sometimes seven swings before success, provided the old hands with lots of laughs. Before the end of the summer, most of us could drive a spike into a tie in four or five swings. You can understand why we all stood and watched in awe while a very strong adult named Frank Sherak drove a spike into a tie with two and sometimes one swing!

There is some uncertainty as to the origin of the term 'gandy dancer.' Some believe it may have derived from 'gander' due to the flat-footed 'goose' steps of the workmen, some suggest it may have come from a 'Gandy' tool company providing railroad equipment, but there's a lack of consensus or evidence to prove either. I always thought it must have come from the way we had to tamp the ties up under the rails. Bill Monroe and I would stand facing each other, one on each side of a tie. We'd stand on our left legs and together force the dirt and crushed rock under the tie, using our right legs on the shovels in sort of a rocking, 'gandy dancing' motion.

We labored all morning and most of the afternoon under the scorching Minnesota sun. It was miserable in that sense, and many of us had to take salt tablets so we wouldn't faint. We were sort of an odd crew, half men too old for World War II and half kids too young for it, but we all got along. The older men joked and kidded with us to help lighten our days, and that helped.

Near the end of the afternoon, the entire crew of fifty men and boys would line the track. Each took a heavy six-foot iron crowbar and forced it under the rail. At that point, Scrappy called out, "Yo!" and the whole line pulled their guts out until the rail moved to where he wanted it. We'd put the finishing touches on the job by smoothing rock down from the track in a gentle slope towards the ground, after which it was time to call it a day.

We were transported to and from a worksite from the Great Northern Railroad in a big grain truck. It was covered and seated forty men, twenty on two rows in the middle and ten on each side. The smell was overpowering at day's end, with cigarette smoke, chewing tobacco and sweat filling the packed space. Sometimes the ride back home took a pleasant turn when Scrappy decided to make a beer stop. The first time this happened, I couldn't believe it. We'd all pile out of the truck and file into a bar. "Boys, you put in a fine day's work today!" he'd announce as he approached the bartender. "Set 'em up!" he'd say, and we were all served glasses of cold Grain Belt Beer. Sure tasted good after working all day in the blazing sun.

Some of the boys quit during the first week of work; they couldn't take the heat and blistered hands. My 'gandy dancing' partner, Bill Monroe, hung in there, and I got to know him real well. I liked him a lot. Strong bonds are formed when you sweat in somebody's face for three months! Bill went to Central High School and I went to Cathedral, and we became the best of buddies. Many new friendships were forged among young and old alike that summer.

I learned a lot about myself. In spite of being only 120 pounds and pretty much a weakling when I started, I learned I had a lot of perseverance and could stick with a job under some pretty severe conditions. I also learned I was extremely shy, but that I was just as shrewd as the next guy at weaseling *out of some of the more difficult jobs. Perhaps the biggest plus resulting from a summer of hard labor was a new self-image, a new sense of confidence, one I certainly lacked at the beginning of my freshman year. I liked the feeling of being strong and in control of my body. I also liked the independent feeling of having my own money. I'd had money before from selling the Crookston Daily Times on the streets and home routes delivering the Minneapolis Star Journal, the Saint Paul Pioneer Press and the Grand Forks Herald, but I'd never had this much money coming in on a regular basis. It made quite an impact on my style of living! I was able to purchase all my own school clothes at J.C. Penny, play pool at the Playhouse and have ice cream sundaes at Schreiter's Drug Store on my way home from school. Life was good!*

CHUCK WAS BEGINNING TO TASTE A NEW KIND OF FREEDOM DURING that summer of 1943, the kind that went with holding down a man's job, earning a man's pay and buying things he wanted. He loved the discipline of work as well. It all made him very happy. He was becoming a man! Twelve years later, 1955, he *was* a man, a family man with a wife and twin sons to support. He needed the summer job he got working on the railroad, but what he hadn't thought about beforehand was how much the work may have changed over the years. Two guys no longer faced each other on opposite sides of a tie, tamping it with their shovels. It was all done mechanically now by heavy steel shovels attached to a machine. There was no longer any dirt tamped under the ties; it was now all large pieces of crushed rock. The heavy part of the work now consisted of constantly picking up jacks and moving them ahead of one another and raising the track so the old ties could be pulled out and the new ones pulled in. That was still done by hand, as was lining the track and dressing it down, not easy tasks in the blistering sun. When Chuck got home after the first day on the job, his back hurt, he was sunburned and he was beat! Working on the railroad was worlds away from teaching.

"Daddy, can we go swimming?" the twins pleaded when he entered the house after his first long day back on the railroad. Usually he would have happily obliged, would have been ready and eager to play with his sons, but this day was different. He was dirty and sweaty and exhausted! Nevertheless, he was willing.

"Okay, boys," he said, mustering up some enthusiasm, "just give me a few minutes to clean up."

The Dowdles had purchased a large plastic swimming pool and placed it in the center of their backyard. The boys took to the water like fish! Mark was a little leery at first, but before long he was swishing around and keeping up with his brother. The pool was good sized, thirty feet in diameter and two feet deep, and Marty and Chuck took advantage of it as well. As for Tregnor, he found entertainment in running around the perimeter, but wasn't fond of water and wasn't about to be enticed to give swimming a try.

June passed quickly, Chuck away all day at his railroad job, Marty tending to the house and errands and trying to keep the twins out of mischief. On the Fourth of July holiday, the whole family was home and enjoying the pool. Tregnor was running around it and barking as usual when the first big bang went off. He suddenly disappeared. No one paid any attention at first, but then Mark said, "Where's Treggie?"

Chuck went to look for him, and when he came back he laughed and said, "You're not going to believe it. Guess where I found that dog?"

"Where?" Marty asked.

"He was in the garage in the washing machine, shivering like crazy! He somehow jumped up into it! I think the fireworks and smell of smoke scared him half to death!" said Chuck.

"The poor thing!" said Marty.

"I left him in the garage and closed the door so it wouldn't be so loud and wrapped him in a blanket to keep him warm," said Chuck. "Next year we'll have to get some sort of tranquilizers so he doesn't get so terrified."

"Is he all right, Dad?" asked Mark.

"Yes, he's okay. He just doesn't like the big noises and the smell of the smoke. He'll be happy when it's all over!"

A LITTLE OVER A MONTH LATER, ON AUGUST 9TH, 1955, THE TWINS turned two and life was about as good as it gets. Chuck had adjusted to his summer railroad job but was looking forward to going back to teaching. Marty loved the new house, and the twins loved swimming and playing outdoors with Treg.

Late that afternoon, after everyone had eaten, Marty said, "Boys, we decided to get one big present for all of our birthdays this year."

"What is it, Mommy?" Michael yelled.

"You'll see," she said.

"C'mon with me," said their dad as he took the twins' hands. "It's in the garage. We'll let Mark feel it first and see if he can guess what it is." Inside the garage they approached a shiny red custom tandem bicycle, two seats in front for Chuck and Marty, two child seats at the rear for the twins.

"I know," Michael yelled excitedly.

"Don't say it, Michael," said Chuck. "Let Mark make a guess."

Mark placed his hands on the bike's metal crossbar and slowly rubbed the smooth finish. He fingered the spokes of the front wheel and yelled, "I know! A bicycle!"

"That's right!" said Chuck. "And all of us can ride together! Would you two like to try it out with Mom and me?" he asked.

"Yes!" the boys yelled in unison.

With helmets secured, safety harnesses attached and the garage door open, they were ready to roll! "Whooeeeee!" the boys hollered as they headed down the driveway.

Chuck was a strong captain at the helm thanks to his summer of manual labor, and the shiny new bicycle glided along with seemingly little effort. "We're going by the hospital where you and Michael were born," Marty called back as they passed the familiar building. Next, they pedaled across the street and stopped to talk to Evelyn Krueger, their former landlady, who happened to be working outside in her yard.

"My, my," she exclaimed, "isn't that something! A bicycle built for four! You boys are sprouting up so fast I can hardly believe it! Are you enjoying your ride?"

"Yes!" they yelled.

"It's our birthday!" said Mark.

"Well, well, happy birthday!" said Evelyn enthusiastically.

"Let's go, Dad!" said Michael impatiently.

"See you later, Evelyn!" Chuck said as he pushed off and they pedaled on down the street. Three more blocks took them past St. Henry's

Church and then home. While Marty held the bike steady, Chuck lifted Mark out of his seat. "How'd you like that ride, Son?" he asked.

"I loved it, Dad!" said Mark. Chuck smiled to himself, noting that Mark had taken to calling him Dad instead of Daddy. His boys were growing up!

That evening, Marty and Chuck decided to say their Rosary in the kids' bedroom. "Can I touch your rosary?" Mark asked.

"Me, too," said Michael. Marty handed her rosary to Mark and Chuck handed his to Michael. The parents smiled as they watched their curious sons move their fingers from bead to bead.

"When Jesus was two years old like you, His mother loved Him just like I love you," said Marty.

"Did he have cake and ice cream?" Michael asked.

"No," Marty laughed, "but his mommy cared for Him just like I care for you."

Did she go swimming with Him?" Mark asked.

"I don't think so," Marty said, "but she taught Him all about God."

"Who's God?" Mark asked.

"God is the one who made everything," she said.

"Did he make me?" Michael asked.

"Yes," she said.

"Your mom and I helped him," said Chuck as he winked at his wife.

"Okay, boys, that's all the talking about Jesus for tonight," said Marty. "You can hold our rosaries while we say our prayers."

While Mark fingered his crucifix and Michael was examining his, Chuck and Marty began: *I believe in God the Father Almighty, Creator of heaven and earth, and in Jesus Christ, his only son, our Lord, who was conceived by the Holy Spirit, born of the Virgin Mary, suffered under Pontius Pilate, was crucified, died, and was buried.* Michael's eyes began to close as did Mark's, his fingers falling from the crucifix as his parents continued: *He descended into hell; the third day He arose again from the dead; He ascended into heaven, is seated at the right hand of God, the Father Almighty; from thence He shall come to judge the living and the dead.*

The boys were sleeping soundly when the last line of the Apostles' Creed was said…*I believe in the Holy Spirit, the Holy Catholic Church, the Communion of Saints, the forgiveness of sins, the resurrection of the body, and life everlasting. Amen.*

"Gee," Chuck whispered as he retrieved the rosaries and Marty and he tiptoed out of the bedroom, "isn't it amazing the questions those two come up with?"

"It sure is," Marty said. "I think they're a little too young for us to explain God."

"I think you're right," he agreed.

<hr />

AFTER WORKING ON THE RAILROAD ALL SUMMER, CHUCK DECIDED he wasn't going to take on that kind of work again. It may have been fun when he was sixteen, but not when he was twenty-seven, too backbreaking. He would need to find a better way to make extra money next summer.

As luck would have it, he didn't have to wait until next summer. Just after school started, he read about a part-time job selling *World Book Encyclopedia*. That appealed to him, so one Saturday he interviewed with the representative for the Perham area, Harry Burnham, a manager from Minneapolis who drove up to talk with him. The company wanted a teacher, and Chuck was the only teacher who applied for the job, so Harry gave him a starter kit, showed him how to fill out an order blank, signed a contract and said, "You're now a *World Book* representative, Mr. Dowdle. Congratulations!" What the manager didn't tell him was that he'd have to go after his own leads, which meant cold calling prospective customers. That was something Chuck had never done, and he wondered what he had gotten himself into after walking the streets for hours one Saturday and selling nothing. To say it was disappointing was an understatement. He had never received so many rejections in his life. All he heard all day was, "No, I'm sorry, we're not interested."

The second Saturday had a different ending. It had been a long one and he was tired and frustrated. He hadn't sold a thing. It was near suppertime when he knocked on the last door. "Please, come in!" said the woman cordially when he told her he was a representative for *World Book Encyclopedia*. "We've been wanting to buy a set, have used them many times at the library, just haven't had time to pursue it for our home. I'm glad you found us!" Chuck couldn't believe his ears as she continued. "We're just finishing up dinner," she said as she led him into the living room. "You can have a seat here and write up the order and I'll be with you in just a few minutes. We'd like the dictionaries as well."

Chuck was stunned and elated. He could hardly think straight; he was so nervous he made a mistake on the order blank and had to tear it up. On the second try he made another mistake and had to start over yet again. He was working up a sweat, wondering if he'd have the simple order completed by the time the woman returned. Finally, on his third try, success! "How are you doing with that?" the woman said as she walked into the room.

"I'm all ready," he said. "All I need is your signature and a check." Just like that, his first sale! As Chuck left the house, he realized he'd made as much money in an hour as he would have made from teaching all day. He was giddy!

Later in the year, after Chuck had made a number of sales to both parents and schools, he learned the company was producing braille sets of *World Book Encyclopedia* and schools could apply to receive a free set. When he mentioned this to his school librarian, she said, "That would be very interesting, Mr. Dowdle, but we don't have any blind students here."

THAT FACT WAS TO CHANGE DRAMATICALLY WHEN CHUCK WENT back to school in the fall of 1956. Mrs. Naomi Pederson, an exceptional English and Speech teacher, had talked to him the previous year about teaching English. "I think you'd like teaching high school English, Mr. Dowdle," she said enthusiastically. She handed him a book which contained the complete works of William Shakespeare. "Take this book home with you and see what you think." He did, was hooked by the time he finished it, and everything else fell into place.

Teaching English wasn't all that was going to be new on his first day of school in September. While he was alone in his classroom in the morning, preparing to greet his first period ninth grade English class, a tall boy carrying a heavy case burst into the room and said rather loudly, "Good morning, Mr. Dowdle!" My name's David Overton. Where do I sit?" When Chuck looked up from what he was doing, the first thing he noticed was that the young student had no eyeballs. He was blind!

After the initial surprise, Chuck walked over to him, put his hand on his shoulder and said, "Right over here, David," as he led him to an empty desk at the front of the room. David didn't waste any time getting settled in. He placed his braille typewriter case on top of his desk, opened it and took out the machine. Chuck certainly hadn't anticipated he would be teaching a student who was blind. He watched David curiously and thought, "This is going to be a new challenge!"

The months rolled by, and having David in the classroom became one of the best teaching experiences of Chuck's career. David was a real gem. He listened attentively and actively participated in discussion. When it came time for writing, David would insert a card in his braille machine and go for it! He'd bring the completed assignment to his braille teacher, who would translate it and place a copy in Chuck's mailbox by the following morning. The process worked like a charm. Both Chuck and David's fellow students were amazed at how confident and successful he was, outside of the classroom as well. He would weave in and out among the students in the crowded halls, clicking his tongue against his palate and using the echo to determine if he risked bumping into anyone. It was amazing to watch him maneuver from one class to another.

Chuck loved working with David Overton, he loved teaching ninth grade English, and he became very successful selling *World Book Encyclopedia*. All that had to happen now to make him any happier was for the school to apply for a free braille set. When that happened and the application was accepted, he was ecstatic. He knew how beneficial the books would be for David during the rest of his high school years, and for his son, Mark, when he got older.

The set of braille encyclopedia arrived shortly after the end of the school year. Agnes Welter contacted him and had him come and help her open the boxes and shelve the books in the library. It turned out to be an all-day job, as there were many volumes to unpack. When they finished the task, Mrs. Welter asked Chuck if he wanted to take a volume home to examine, and he jumped at the opportunity. Up until now, Marty had been having Mark tell her stories, which she then typed up on the braille machine. Reading an article from the braille encyclopedia would be a giant leap forward. "Which volume would you like to take home, Mr. Dowdle?" asked Mrs. Welter.

Chuck pondered the decision for a moment. For his sales pitch with prospective buyers, he always carried the 'A' volume for demonstration. Many times he would open the volume to the **Animal** or **Ant** article and have the children in the family read aloud in front of their parents. "I think I'll take the 'A' volume," he said. The twins had a memorable experience with ants in our back yard, and I know they'd be interested to read about them in the encyclopedia."

"Sounds like a good idea," she said, pulling out the 'A' volume and handing it to Chuck.

Chuck flipped quickly through the pages. "Here it is," he said, "**Ant**." "How did you know?" she asked.

"Braille isn't easy," he said, "but when we began having Mark study his letters and first words in braille, we decided we'd take on the challenge as a family, Michael, too. We're all learning together. Look at that first paragraph of dots, Agnes," Chuck said enthusiastically as he placed the open book next to her. "I'll illustrate by reading it to you," he said, and slowly began to move his fingers across the page. '*An ant is an insect that lives in organized communities. Ants are therefore known as social insects. Other social insects include some kinds of bees, all termites and certain wasps. However, ants are perhaps the most highly developed social insects.*'

"My!" she said after Chuck made his way through the first few lines. "I'm impressed!"

When he brought the 'A' volume home that afternoon and showed it to Marty, she was elated. "This is going to be so wonderful for Mark!" she said. "I can hardly wait to get started."

That evening everyone sat down together at the kitchen table to check it out. "Let's read about ants!" suggested Chuck.

Marty opened the volume to the **Ant** article and gently moved Mark's fingers over the raised dots of the first few words so he could get the feel of it. "Let me see if I can read it," she said. A broad smile broke over his face as his mother slowly worked her way through the first couple of sentences.

"What's a termite, Mom?" asked Michael, who had been patiently watching and listening. And thus the inquisitive fun began! Chuck and Marty spent the next hour reading and answering question after question from their sons. By bedtime they were all tired, but hooked on braille!

You can see how Marty spent many summer hours with the boys while Chuck was busy selling encyclopedias. It took almost all of June for the trio to read through the entire article on ants, but by the end of the month they had all advanced their braille-reading skills and were a trio of ant experts! Michael would find ants in the back yard and describe to Mark how they were scurrying about and dragging materials along for building their nests, just as they'd learned in the encyclopedia! Michael was intrigued by the ants' bodies, their tiny heads and trunks and sense organs, Mark more interested in how they interacted and communicated with their antennae. They were bright and curious little boys!

THE REST OF THE SUMMER WAS SPENT PLAYING IN THE POOL AND pedaling into town and around the neighborhood on the tandem. The boys waited eagerly each day for their dad to come home from book selling so the family could ride together.

One day, shortly after the Fourth of July, Marty was outside enjoying a rare moment of relaxation in the sun while the twins played with Tregnor.

"Can we read about animals in *World Book* tonight?" asked Mark.

"Of course," said Marty, since Chuck hadn't yet returned the 'A' braille volume to the school. The **Animal** article took up a good number of pages, and the boys couldn't get enough. They were always excited to tell their dad everything they'd learned each day.

For Chuck, selling *World Book Encyclopedia* during the summer sure beat laboring on the railroad. It was often disappointing work, hiking up and down block after block in the heat of the day, knocking on doors and encountering frequent rejection, but every so often he met a family that welcomed him into their home and ended up buying a set. That made it all worthwhile for Chuck, as he knew interests would be sparked when children read, and he loved promoting learning.

As a teacher, he was, of course, earning money doing just that, but not the kind of money he earned one hot summer afternoon near the end of July when an elementary school principal from a town near Perham called him. "Mr. Dowdle," she said, "my name is Mrs. Bernice Johnson. I'm the new principal at Vista Elementary School in Detroit Lakes, and I was given your name by another principal. We'd like to order the *World Book Encyclopedia* for our school."

"That's wonderful," Chuck said. "When would be a convenient time for me to come by?"

"Well," she said, "we'd like to have them in time for the opening of school. Could you possibly make it today?"

"Let's see," he answered. "It's eleven o'clock now. I could be there at noon if that works for you."

"That would be fine," she said. "We can talk over lunch."

"Sounds great," he said. "I'll see you at twelve and we can write up the order."

"Who was that?" Marty asked. "Sounded like a good call!"

"A principal from Detroit Lakes who wants to purchase a set of *World Book Encyclopedia* for her new school in Detroit Lakes," he said.

"That's great news!" said Marty.

"I need to be there at noon," said Chuck. "How would you and the kids like to join me for the drive?"

"That would be fun!" said Marty enthusiastically. "We can play by the lake while you're at the school, and you can join us when you're done," she said as she hurried off to round up the boys.

Detroit Lakes was only twenty miles from Perham, so it took them no time at all to make the short trip. Chuck dropped Marty and the twins off at a sandy beach area and then headed on to his appointment. "See you soon!" he yelled as he waved out the window.

"It's nice to meet you, Mr. Dowdle," Mrs. Johnson said when he arrived. "I'm so glad you were able to make it here today. Let's go down to the lunch room. We can grab a sandwich and I'll explain what I need."

"Sounds good," Chuck said as she rose from her desk. He couldn't help but wonder what she meant by, 'I'll explain what I need.' Wasn't this just a straightforward sale of a set of encyclopedias? He would soon find out it was far from that.

They sat together at one of the long student lunch tables near the back of the cafeteria. "You certainly have a nice school here, Mrs. Johnson," he said.

"Thank you. We're very proud of it," she said, "and we want to get off to a good start. That's why I called you. We have eighteen classrooms, and I'd like a set of *World Book* for each of them, also two sets for our library." Chuck forced himself to stay focused to keep his jaw from dropping to the floor. "Do you think we could have them by the start of the school year?" she continued.

"Definitely!" Chuck said, aware of the obvious glee in his own voice. "I'll fill out the order and bring it up to your office. If you fill out a requisition, I can send the order in tonight; that will ensure the books are here in time."

"That would be just wonderful!" she said.

As he was driving away from Vista Elementary School and toward the lake to join Marty and the boys, Chuck could hardly contain himself. He had just sold more sets of *World Book* in five minutes than he had all summer!

"Hi, honey!" Marty called as he got out of the car and jogged towards her and the boys. She could see the lightness in his step. "How'd it go?" she asked.

"Wait until I tell you!" he said as he plopped down beside her on the warm sand. Michael and Mark looked up briefly, managed quick smiles and a 'Hi, Dad,' but were busily building a sand tower, oblivious to the big announcement about to be delivered.

"I sure hope it's good news," said Marty.

"It's good all right!" said Chuck. "The principal just ordered twenty sets of books! Can you believe it? Twenty sets! That means we just made five hundred dollars, honey, as much as I usually make in a whole month of teaching!"

"Twenty?" Marty said in complete shock. "Twenty sets?" she said again, shaking her head in disbelief.

"That's right, honey," said her beaming husband.

"That's wonderful!" she exclaimed as she hugged him.

"It sure is! And I'm ready to celebrate!" said Chuck. "Let's pack up and head home!"

Mark was quick to sense the utter elation in the air. "You're happy, Daddy," he said as they were driving along.

"I sure am, Mark," Chuck said. "I'm happy because I have two special little guys and your beautiful mother to love!"

That evening after the boys were in bed and Marty and he were getting ready to say the Rosary, Mark whispered sleepily, "Dad, I'd like a rosary."

"Okay, Mark," he said softly so as not to waken Michael, who had already fallen asleep. "Your mom and I will see what we can do."

Chuck made the Sign of the Cross and began to pray...*In the name of the Father, and of the Son, and of the Holy Spirit...*He smiled as he saw Mark's lips moving. Marty noticed this, too. As Chuck began saying the Apostles' Creed, Mark's lips stopped moving and he fell asleep just like his brother. He and Marty tiptoed from the boys' bedroom and headed to the family room to finish their Rosary.

"Interesting how Mark seemed to be following along with the words," said Marty as they sat down. "We can get them little rosaries for their birthday."

"I think that would be great," said Chuck. "I remember how Mark fingered the cross and felt the beads of your rosary a year ago. It's probably a good time to try again. There's something else I'd like to get them," he said.

"What's that?" she asked.

"I was thinking I'd like to buy fishing poles for all of us and take them to Little Pine Lake," said Chuck.

"I think they'd love that!" said Marty. "Let's finish our Rosary and talk about it tomorrow. We've still got a couple of days."

When the boys' birthday arrived, they were excited to open their presents. Chuck had wrapped the two fishing poles in separate packages and Marty had wrapped two rosaries in separate packages, so they each had two gifts to open. Chuck handed them their poles first. Mark slid his hands up and down the long, narrow object before tearing off the paper, and when he began feeling the skinny bamboo pole he didn't know what to make of it. "What is this?" he asked.

"It's a fishing pole, Brother!" Michael yelled as he unwrapped his. "Thank you, Dad! Now we can catch fish!" Michael had seen his dad's rod and reel quite often when he headed out to Big Pine Lake after supper, alone, to go fishing. He knew what a fishing pole looked like, but he'd never been able to go along with his dad. Chuck was afraid the energetic twins might annoy the men who lined the shore after work, men who liked it quiet and peaceful while they were casting out after walleyes and northern pike. The boys were older now, and Chuck thought if he could get them out a little earlier in the afternoon, he could not only teach them how to fish, but also instill a bit of fishing etiquette.

"Thank you, Dad," said Mark as he examined every inch of his new pole. "Are you going to take us fishing with you?"

"I think you're old enough to give it a try," he said. "Would you like that?"

"I think so," said Mark.

"It will be fun, Brother!" said Michael.

"Here's one more present for each of you," Marty said as she handed them their wrapped rosaries.

"Is it something for fishing, Mom?" Michael asked.

"Open it and you'll find out," said Marty.

Mark had his package open just before his brother, and when he fingered the crucifix, he smiled and said, "It's a rosary!"

"Thank you!" said the boys in unison.

"Would you like to learn the *Sign of the Cross*?" Marty asked.

"Yes, I would," Mark answered.

"Me, too," Michael said.

"All right," she said, "let's do it right now." She sat next to Mark and took his hands in hers, and Chuck did the same with Michael. When each of the boys had the cross in their right hand, Marty raised Mark's hand with hers to his forehead and said, '*In the name of the Father*,' as Chuck and Michael imitated her. Marty moved Mark's hand and hers over his heart and continued, '*and of the Son*,' and again Chuck and Michael followed, '*and of the Holy Spirit. Amen.*' She and Chuck were beaming as they touched the crucifix to each of the boys' left and right shoulders.

"That's the *Sign of the Cross*," said Chuck.

"When can we say the rest of it with you?" Mark asked solemnly.

"We'll start with the *Sign of the Cross* for now," said Marty. "You can practice that and we'll add a little more every day."

That evening at bedtime the twins had the crosses of their rosaries poised in their hands. "Okay, boys, here we go," Chuck said. As he and Marty raised the crosses of their rosaries to their foreheads, so did Mark and Michael, and in family chorus they said, '*In the name of the Father*.' The rest of the *Sign of the Cross* was completed in unison, and it brought smiles to their parents' faces. "You two sure learned that quickly," said Chuck. "I'm so proud of you. Now Mom and I will finish and you can hold your rosaries." As soon as they began the *Apostle's Creed*, Michael nodded off, but Mark's lips kept moving along with them. He didn't fall asleep until they were almost finished and ready to move on to the *Our Father*.

"I sure would like to know what's going on in Mark's head," Marty said after they'd tiptoed out. "His lips kept moving until you were almost finished!"

"I noticed that," said Chuck. "Hard to know what he's thinking. Every day sure is a new adventure with those little guys. I'll take them to Big Pine Lake tomorrow and see how they like fishing."

"Good idea," said Marty. "I imagine it's all they'll be thinking about when they wake up."

It wasn't! They wanted breakfast—bananas and peaches and a big bowl of oatmeal with cinnamon and raisins and walnuts! Next up was running out to the back yard to play with Treg as they did most every morning. He loved having the boys race after him after he retrieved a thrown ball, prancing proudly around with it in his mouth with an expression on his face that said, "Get it if you can!" Mark was tethered to Michael, but the boys were used to that and had learned to move as one body. It was like watching a couple of Border Collies as they tried to herd Treg, except of course they were never successful. He was too aware and too quick for them, until he eventually tired and came to them with a panting smile, dropping the saliva-laden ball at their feet.

After getting hot and sweaty from the morning dog action, the twins always wanted to get in the pool to cool off. "Only three years old, and look at them!" Chuck said to Marty as they sat and watched their sons. "They thrash around in that water like fish on a hook!"

"On that subject, I wonder if they've forgotten all about their new poles," said Marty.

No sooner had she spoken when Michael yelled out, "Hey, Dad, can we go fishing today?"

Chuck and Marty laughed at the coincidental timing. "Good idea!" said Chuck.

"Great idea!" said Marty, anticipating a peaceful afternoon to herself.

"We'll go to the lake after you and Mark have had lunch and time to rest. I'll dig up some earthworms for bait."

"What's bait?" yelled Michael.

"You'll see," Chuck called back. "You'll see soon enough."

After they'd eaten lunch and taken a nap, the boys woke up ready and raring to go. "Is it time to leave?" asked Mark as he and Michael ran into the kitchen.

"It sure is," said Chuck. "Your poles are out in the car already."

"Hold on," said Marty. "Let's get some mosquito lotion on you two. Those bugs at the lake like to bite!"

After they arrived at Big Pine, Chuck took out three lawn chairs and set them in a shady spot under a group of trees. He got the twins settled in and began explaining the finer points of fishing. "I'll start with setting up your pole, Mark," he said. "Michael can watch and then we'll get his ready."

"Okay, Dad," said the boys.

Chuck took out some black nylon fishing line and ran it through Mark's fingers. "The first thing I'm going to do is tie the fishing line to your pole, Mark," he said.

"Okay," Mark said, patiently waiting to see what would happen next.

"Now I'm going to tie a hook on the end of your fishing line," he said. "It's sharp and pointy, and it'll stick you if you're not careful. I'm going to let you touch it very gently." He took one of Mark's fingers in his hand and rubbed it very lightly across the point of the hook. "Can you feel how sharp that is?" he asked.

"Yes!" exclaimed Mark. "It's very sharp!"

"It has to be like that in order to catch a fish," he said. "Now I'm going to put a worm on the end of your hook. Fish like to eat worms, so they bite into them, and when they do, that's how you catch them!"

"Okay, Dad," Mark said.

"When's it my turn, Dad?" asked Michael.

"Coming right up, Michael," Chuck said as he took out a sinker and bobber and attached them near the end of Mark's fishing line. "This heavy little thing is called a sinker," he said as he placed it in Mark's hands. "It's tied to your fishing line near your hook, and it will make sure your hook goes down in the water near the fish." Next, Chuck placed the cork bobber in

Mark's hands. "This is called a bobber, Mark," he said. "It's tied to your line above the sinker and floats on top of the water. When you catch a fish, you won't see it because it will go under the water. You'll feel a tug on your pole, and that's how you'll know you have a fish on the hook! When that happens, just hang onto your pole so the fish doesn't yank it out of your hands, okay?"

"Okay, Dad," said Mark with a serious face. "I'm ready."

Chuck tossed Mark's line into the water and then began helping Michael. "You've been real good to wait so patiently, Michael," Chuck said. "Let's get you rolling."

"Can I put the worm on the hook, Dad?" he asked.

"Sure," said Chuck, a bit surprised that his young son would want to do that, "just be careful not to stick yourself on the point of the hook." Michael reached into the can of worms and pulled out a long, wiggly, fat one, and then began threading it onto his hook like a pro. Chuck was amazed when he saw how easily Michael baited the hook. "Wow! You did that really well, Michael," he said.

"Can I fish now?" he asked.

"You bet, Son," Chuck said. He threw Michael's line into the water and turned to fixing up his own.

"Dad! I think Mark has a fish!" Michael yelled as he saw his brother's bobber plunge under the water.

Mark had a fish all right, a big one! His bamboo pole doubled over, and he might have lost it if his dad hadn't run over to help. Mark grew very excited when he felt the fish trying to tug the pole out of his hands, but he held onto it, and after a brief struggle, he and his dad landed a large walleyed pike. It looked like it weighed about six pounds.

"I caught a fish, Brother!" yelled Mark.

"I see it! I see it!" said Michael. "It's a huge one!"

Chuck got the fish off the hook and held it near Mark's hands. "Touch it so you'll know what a fish feels like, Mark," he said.

Mark rubbed his hands along the side of the walleyed. "It's big!" he said proudly. "And it's slippery!" Then he rubbed the top of the fish, which raised its spiny dorsal fin. "Ouch! That hurt!" he yelled as he jerked his hand away.

"I'm sorry, Mark," Chuck said. "That was my fault. I should have made sure your hand didn't get near that dorsal fin."

Just then Michael yelled, "Dad! I think I've got one!"

Chuck couldn't believe it. There were many days when he sat all afternoon and caught nothing, and his boys had hooked two fish in two minutes! He didn't know quite what to do first. He was still holding Mark's walleyed, and Michael's bobber had plunged under the water. "Just hang onto your pole until I get Mark's fish on the stringer," Chuck yelled. "I'll be right there!"

"Dad!" Michael yelled. "I can't hold it! It's pulling hard!"

Chuck threw Mark's walleyed and the stringer behind the lawn chairs and ran over and grabbed onto Michael's pole with him. "I think you caught a whopper!" he said excitedly as they saw the water ripple near the surface. Then the line went slack and Chuck said, "I hope we didn't lose him!"

They hadn't! The fish was trying to outsmart them, easing up and waiting for an opportunity to shake the dangling hook from its mouth. "Do you think…," Michael started to say, when a northern pike burst out of the water and leaped about three feet into the air, twisting its body back and forth in a valiant attempt to free itself from the hook.

"Hang on, Michael!" Chuck yelled.

"Hang on, Brother!" yelled Mark excitedly.

"He's still on the hook and he's a big one all right!" said Chuck. It seemed like a very long time before the large northern finally tired and he and Michael were able to drag it out of the water and onto the shore, where it flopped around and gasped for air. "Don't touch it!" Chuck cautioned as Michael reached out to rub its side as he'd seen his brother do with the walleyed. "It's still very much alive, and if those sharp teeth bite your fingers, it will feel like needles!"

After a few minutes of struggle, they succeeded in getting both fish on the stringer. "That sure was fun!" said Michael.

"You two are born fishermen!" said Chuck proudly.

"Do you think we'll catch more today, Dad?" Mark asked. He had been listening to all the action and was eager to reel in another one.

"Maybe," said Chuck. "You never know. Sometimes they keep biting and sometimes not. We'll just have to wait and see."

The three of them settled into round two and waited for an hour, but nothing happened, nary a nibble. "Well, boys, it looks like that's about it for today. Let's pack up and head home," said Chuck.

The boys were eager to tell their mom about their fishing adventure, but Mark wanted nothing to do with cleaning the fish. Instead, he stayed in the house and described in detail every little touch and sound he had experienced while pulling in his walleyed.

Michael, on the other hand, was fascinated as he watched his dad scale the fish, cut their heads off and gut them. "Wow!" he said as his eyes grew big. "When are we going to eat them, Dad?"

"Tonight for dinner!" said a beaming Chuck.

That evening Marty fried up potatoes with onions, and when the family took their first bites of the golden-brown fish, it was a gastronomic delight that topped even the adventure of catching them. The boys loved the taste of the fish, especially the walleyed, Marty making sure they were free of any bones. Dad helped out, of course, but he seemed more interested in eating than looking for bones!

That night as Marty was readying the boys for bed, Mark asked, "Mom, can we read about fish tomorrow?"

"That's a great idea," she said. "It will be fun for you now that you've been out fishing for the first time. I'll go to the school library tomorrow and pick up the braille 'F' volume." Accomplished salesman that he was, Chuck had earned a free set of *World Book Encyclopedia* for their home, thus the twins could learn together.

When Marty came home with the braille volume the next day, she sat down with the twins and began reading the article about fish: *'Fish are vertebrates (backboned animals) that live in water. There are more kinds of fish than all other kinds of water and land vertebrates put together. The various kinds of fish differ so greatly in shape, color and size that it is hard to believe they all belong to the same animal group. For example, some fish look like lumpy rocks and others like wriggly worms. Some fish are nearly as flat as pancakes and others can blow themselves up like balloons. Fish have all the colors of the rainbow, many as bright as the most vibrant-colored birds. Their rich reds, yellows, blues and purples form hundreds of beautiful patterns, from stripes and lace-like designs to polka dots.'*

"What I don't understand is how fish breathe so long under the water," Mark said. "We can't do that!"

"That's true," she said, "but fish can't breathe out of the water and we can. Would you like me to read about how fish breathe?"

"Yes, Mom," Mark said. "I want to know."

"And I want to read about how people breathe," said Michael.

Marty had her hands full that afternoon, reading first about how fish use their gills to breathe the oxygen dissolved in water, and then about how humans use their lungs to breathe air. As soon as Michael saw pictures showing the insides of the human body, he was hooked. He was especially interested in the heart, as his dad had shown him the fish hearts while they were being cleaned. "Read more!" he said to his mom as she turned the page.

Although Mark had initially shown interest in learning how fish and humans breathe, he soon grew tired of listening and trying to follow along in the braille volume as Marty was reading aloud. He called Tregnor, who came running to his side. Treg was good company for Mark, always a comfort when he felt frustrated or in need of companionship. Just being able to hold Treg's warm, furry body close to his own was all Mark needed. It settled Tregnor as well, and he seemed to treasure the soft, gentle touch of Mark's hands. "Mom," Mark said as he pulled Treg close to his chest, "I can feel Treg's heart beating. It's fast!"

"Dogs are a lot like us, but their hearts beat faster than ours," said Marty.

"They breathe faster, too," said Michael, "with their tongues hanging out."

"That's how they stay cool," she said, "especially when it's hot like this in the summer."

"How does that keep them cool?" Mark asked.

"Well," Marty said, wondering what she'd gotten herself into with her inquisitive sons, "dogs can't sweat like us when they get hot, so they stick out their tongues and pant, and when the water in their mouths evaporates, it cools their bodies, just like you get cool after you've been running and get sweaty and the water dries on your body when you stop to rest."

"Can we read about dogs next?" asked Mark.

"Of course," she said, and that's exactly what they did as they began learning all about dogs. The twins were surprised to learn a six-month-old puppy generally compares in development to a ten-year-old child, and that a two-year-old dog is like a 24-year-old person. "After a dog's second year," said Marty, "each year equals about four or five years of a person's life, so right now Treg is about 24, and next year he'll be almost 30! That's older than me and Dad!" she laughed.

"Wow! No wonder he's so smart!" said Michael.

Michael was right. Treg was bright and quick. When Chuck threw his ball up onto the roof, regardless of where it came down, Treg was right there, waiting to catch it in his mouth, and then, of course, he would run away and play the predictable game of catch-me-if-you can until he tired and relinquished the ball, dropping it at Chuck's feet. One day Chuck saw him with a bird in his mouth, and yelled at him to let it go. Treg simply opened his mouth and the bird flew away. He had evidently snatched it out of a nearby bush, a common resting place for the birds.

Now that the twins were three years old, they were allowed to take Treg around the block on a leash. It was an interesting sight, Treg in the lead, Michael behind Treg, leash in hand, and Mark behind Michael, the tether between them. Treg led the caravan around the block and right back to their front door, just like a seeing eye dog. As time passed, the twins were allowed to go further from home with Treg, until they were finally able to make it all the way downtown and back. Of course, all the way was only three blocks from home, and Perham was a very small and safe town where everyone knew and watched over them. And besides, their fearless, four-legged leader was older than them and very dependable!

BY THE TIME THE TWINS WERE FIVE YEARS OLD, BOTH WERE accomplished readers and more than kindergarten-ready, so they were placed in Pauline Bernauer's first grade class, where they excelled. Mark's young classmates were curious about his blindness and intrigued by his braille machine, and before the school year ended they would have the chance to learn and understand more about his condition and try out the braille machine for themselves.

School wasn't the only new learning experience for the twins when they turned five. This was also when they made their First Holy Communion, and they were prepared! Mark had listened to the words of the Rosary since he was three years old, mouthing the words with his mom and dad at bedtime. Michael was usually fast asleep after the first few lines, not so with Mark. He worked hard to stay awake until it was finished, and then would finally let himself doze off.

"Can I say the Rosary with you?" Mark asked quietly one evening, Michael already sleeping soundly.

This took his parents by surprise. "Yes, of course you can, Mark," Marty whispered. What they soon learned was that their son had memorized every prayer. When Michael found out the next day, he was not happy! He wanted to do everything Mark did, only better. That night and for many to come, he tried very hard to stay awake to learn to pray the Rosary just like his brother. Sometimes he'd fall asleep during the Apostles' Creed, but as time passed, he, too, memorized all of the prayers.

During this same time period, Marty and Chuck began teaching the boys about Jesus and the Blessed Virgin Mary. Father Donnay was impressed by how well they could say the Rosary, so impressed that he had them help teach the other children. The twins would stand in front of the First Holy Communion class and begin each prayer together, the other children listening and joining in as they learned the words. Before long, the entire class was saying the Rosary aloud together, Father Donnay beaming as he listened to their words.

With the twins now in school, Marty happily found a few spare hours to play the piano. She loved her time at the keyboard, and sometimes when the twins came home from school they would find her playing, transfixed by the music, as if she was in a different world. Michael usually headed out the back door to play with Treg, but Mark was drawn to the sound of the piano, and usually cuddled up alongside his mom while she was playing. One day when this happened, she said, "Mark, would you like to learn to play?"

"Do you think I could do it?" Mark asked.

"Absolutely!" she said as she lifted him up onto her lap. "Let's try it." She placed her left hand on the keyboard and placed his little left hand on top of hers. "Keep your fingers on top of mine," she instructed, "and when I move a finger, you move that same finger; try to keep it right on top of mine." She played a note, and Mark's finger went down on the key with hers. "That's the way to do it, Mark!" she said encouragingly. "Before long you'll be playing a whole song all on your own!" That was the understatement of the day. Within a month, Mark was picking out melodies and composing simple tunes. He loved the piano!

Michael, on the other hand, wasn't such a fan. He wanted to play something, of course, when he saw his brother getting so much attention, but he didn't want anything to do with playing the keyboard. It seemed far too complicated to him and took a lot of patience, and he and Marty quickly realized it wasn't to be. She thought about what instrument might interest her energetic son. Drums came to mind, but the more she thought about the constant banging, the more she decided it was a bad idea. "What would you think about learning to play the trumpet, Michael?" she asked one afternoon. "Once you get good enough you can play in the school band."

Now that idea appealed to Michael! He had seen the Perham High School band march up and down the street in front of their house during practice, and he often ran outside to fall in step alongside the action for a block or two. "Yes!" he yelled. "I want to play the trumpet!"

"I'll talk it over with your dad tonight," said Marty. "We'll see what we can do."

Michael couldn't endure the wait. As soon as Chuck walked in the door from school, Michael ran up to him and yelled "Dad! Dad! Guess what?"

"Whoa! Must be something exciting!" he said as he took off his jacket.

"I'm going to play the trumpet!" Michael said, his face beaming.

"Is that so?" he said. "Have you talked this over with your mom?"

"Mom said she'd tell you about it tonight!" he said excitedly.

That evening while everyone was enjoying a delicious chicken-broccoli casserole, Marty said, "Well, Chuck, as you heard, Michael would like to play the trumpet. What do you think?"

"Hmmm," he said, looking at Michael, "you'd have to put in a lot of hours of practice. Are you willing to do that?"

"Yes, Dad!" he said. "I'll play it every day! I promise!"

The next day at school, Chuck talked to Ralph Meyerdirk, the music teacher, and Ralph described the type of trumpet that would be appropriate for a five year old. Chuck and Marty made the decision to buy one and Michael was thrilled, but try as he might, he wasn't able to get a single sound out of it. At Ralph's suggestion, Chuck brought Michael to the school one Friday afternoon for some tutoring. Ralph showed him what he was doing wrong, and Michael immediately pursed his lips against the mouthpiece and went toot, toot, tooting around the band room, marching just like the high school kids he had observed in front of the house.

"There you go! You've got it!" said Chuck proudly. His son was taking to the trumpet like a duck to water. "I may never get him to stop blowing on that thing now!" laughed Chuck.

"At the rate he's going it won't be long before he's ready for the school band," said Ralph.

That got Michael's attention, and when Ralph asked him if he'd like to come to the school every Friday afternoon after classes for a half hour or so to learn more, he became very excited. "Can I, Dad?" he asked, looking imploringly at his father.

"You're willing to do that, Ralph?" Chuck asked his teacher friend.

"Sure!" said Ralph. "There's nothing like catching them young, and who knows, we may have a virtuoso trumpet player in our midst."

"Well, OK. We'll take you up on your offer! Thanks a lot, Ralph," Chuck said appreciatively. "The two of us will see you after school next Friday."

"Thank you, Mr. Meyerdirk," Michael said as they were leaving.

"You're welcome, Michael," he said. "I'll be looking forward to seeing you Friday."

Michael couldn't wait to tell his mom the good news. He ran ahead of his dad and burst through the front door. "Mom! Mom!" he yelled excitedly.

Marty was fixing supper and came quickly from the kitchen when she heard him calling. "My goodness, Michael!" she said. "What is it?"

"Mom, you won't believe it! Mr. Meyerdirk showed me how to play! Listen!" he said as he put the trumpet mouthpiece to his lips and produced a couple of shrill squeaks.

"Good for you!" said Marty, as she applauded and did her best to sound genuinely impressed. Mark came into the room with Treg, and Michael demonstrated a few more blasts.

"Good, Brother!" said Mark. Treg was a bit less enthusiastic, using his paws in an attempt to rub the sound from his ears.

By Christmas, the boys had advanced their piano and trumpet-playing skills and played a '*Silent Night*' duet for visiting Grandma and Grandpa Dowdle. There were a few pauses here and there and the boys weren't always in sync, but at least one could tell which song it was, and the audience of four could not have been more appreciative. "It's just wonderful you boys have learned to play music!" gushed Grandma Dowdle.

"Mark turned his head from the piano, faced her and said, "Mom taught me, Grandma."

"Mr. Meyerdirk taught me," said Michael proudly. "He's the music teacher at school and he said when I get good enough I can march with the band!"

"Well, that will be a big day!" said his grandmother.

Chuck's dad got a kick out of the twins' enthusiasm. "You boys keep at it," he said encouragingly, "and you can perform more songs for us when we visit again this summer."

"OK!" they said in unison.

IN THE SPRING, AFTER ALL THE SNOW HAD MELTED AND EVERYTHING had dried out, Chuck took his sons to the high school track. They, of course, had the urge to run! At first Michael sped off by himself while Chuck held onto Mark's hand and ran slowly with him.

"C'mon, Mark!" said Michael as he ran back to his brother. "You and I can run together!"

Chuck took the leather strap out of his pocket and snapped the ends to the loops of the boys' pants. Off they went, slowly at first, and then picked up speed as they adjusted to each other's stride. They'd had lots of practice over their few short years, and with little effort were able to keep the strap taut between them, even as they were making the turns around the oval. They passed members of the high school relay team who were doing post-practice stretching on the outer edge of the track, and that speedy foursome marveled at how fast the twins were able to run without tripping over each other's feet. When the twins came around the final turn, the trackmen clapped and cheered, just the motivation the boys needed to go faster and faster. By the end of the season, after many trips to the track with their dad, Michael and Mark had become quite an impressive tandem team. Their specialty was the 440, one time around, as they couldn't resist putting every bit of energy they had into that first lap and were always too pooped to do more.

Chuck and Marty were pleased to note that as exhausted as Michael and Mark may have been from their outdoor activities, they remained enthusiastic about practicing their musical instruments. Since Grandma and Grandpa's time with them over Christmas, Marty had begun teaching Mark a more complicated piece on the piano, 'Summertime,' and Mr. Meyerdirk had been helping Michael learn the same piece on the trumpet. The boys could hardly wait for their grandparents to visit again. Not only were they excited to play their duet and show them how much their playing had improved, they could also have them come to the track to see them run.

April 9, 1959

Dear Mom and Dad,

The twins keep talking about your visit with us last Christmas and are looking forward to seeing you again this summer. They'll have a lot to talk about when you come. They'll soon be making their First Holy Communion. Father Donnay explained to them that he acts in Jesus' name when the bread and wine on the altar are changed into Christ's body and blood, and the twins, as young as they are, have already developed a deep faith and love of Jesus Christ. The boys are not only baptized, but they've also gone to confession, and, like I said, will soon be making their First Holy Communion. They've also learned to say the Rosary and have done so well that Father Donnay asked them to help teach it to the other kids in the class.

And you should see them run around the track tethered together. The high school track team cheers them on, adds fuel to their fire. They run the 440, one lap around at full speed, and seem to be getting faster and faster every week.

Something else they'll be eager to show you is how well they can read. Mrs. Bernauer, their first-grade teacher, has been doing a fantastic job with them in both braille and regular reading.

Last but not least is their latest musical accomplishment, 'Summertime,' a tune I know you love. Marty's been teaching Mark the piece on the piano, and Mr. Meyerdirk, the high school music teacher, has been tutoring Mark on the trumpet. Those boys will be putting on quite a concert for you when you come to visit, hopefully in August. You might want to pack some earplugs!

That's the update on things around here. If by chance you can make it here for the twins' birthday on the ninth, I know they'd be happy about that. You can surprise them! No problem if that date doesn't work out. We'd love to have you come whenever you can.

—Love, Charlie

The rest of the school year whizzed by. The twins made their First Holy Communion, dressed in identical charcoal suits, black patent leather oxfords, white shirts and red ties. They held hands when they received the host. It was a spiritual milestone.

The boys continued running around the high school track during the summer, and Marty loved it as much as they did. The vigorous exercise drained off some of their excess energy, and she very much appreciated the quiet time in the house when they came home ready to rest. After they wakened from a nap, she would give them a snack, and then it was time to practice their instruments, which they did with no prodding. They wanted '*Summertime*' to sound perfect for Grandma and Grandpa!

July 28, 1959

Dear Marilyn and Charlie,

Frank and I talked it over and have decided to make it for the twins' sixth birthday. If it's okay with you, we'd like to stay for a couple of days instead of coming right back. We'll take the train on August 8th and stay with you until the 10th if that works out with your schedule. We're looking forward to seeing you!

—Love, Mom

August 1, 1959

Dear Mom and Dad,

It's great you'll be here for the boys' birthday. You're welcome to stay with us as long as you wish. I'll meet you at the train station in the afternoon. Be sure to pack some old clothes so you can go fishing with me and the boys. We've been doing a lot of it this summer. We'll see you soon!

—Love, Charlie

When the train came chugging into the Perham station, the twins were eagerly waiting to greet their grandparents. "There they are, Mark!" Michael shouted to his brother. "They're waving out the window!" Mark wasn't too eager to rush up close to the train. He could hear the steam hissing from the engine, and it sounded pretty scary, even though he'd heard it a few times before.

"There are my two favorite grandsons!" Grandma Dowdle said cheerfully when she and Grandpa Dowdle stepped down from the passenger car and greeted Chuck and the twins. "Look how much you've grown!" she said as she hugged the boys.

"We're big now!" said Mark.

"You certainly are!" said Grandpa.

"C'mon, Grandma," Michael said as he clasped his grandma's hand and tugged her towards the car. "We've got to get home! Mom's waiting for us!"

"Well, Charlie," Chuck's dad said as the two of them walked side by side. "How's everything been going?"

"Just great, Dad," he said. "We've been spending more time outdoors than inside, that's for sure! You'll get a kick seeing how well the twins are doing with their running, not to mention playing their musical instruments."

It didn't take them long to get home, and Marty had the table set and supper in the oven when they arrived. "Hello, Marilyn," said Grace as they exchanged hugs.

"Something smells real good in here," said Frank as he and Marty embraced.

"It's so good to see both of you," said Marty. "I hope you're hungry! The beef roast is almost ready and we have lots of fresh garden vegetables to eat up."

"Sounds great!" said Frank.

"It sure does," said Grace.

"I didn't know you had a garden, Charlie," said Chuck's dad.

"We sure do," said Chuck. "Our back yard is big and the whole family loves veggies, so we decided to use part of the space to grow some food! Marty and I have fond memories of the garden we planted in the back yard of our basement apartment.

"Let's go take a look, Charlie," said his dad as they headed to the back.

"C'mon, Grandma! Me and Mark will show you!" said Michael. Each grandson took a hand and led Grandma out the back door.

"Oh, my, it's lovely! Look at all those peas! And green beans! And so many beautiful marigolds! I wish you could see it, Mark," she said.

"That's all right, Grandma," Mark said softly. "You can see it for me." Grace looked down at her grandson and squeezed his hand, feeling the love pass between them.

"You've all done a real fine job out here," Chuck's dad said. "I'll bet it took some time and a whole lot of backbreaking labor to get that soil ready."

"It wasn't bad, Dad," Chuck said. "Just wait until you taste those garden tomatoes with some of that green leaf lettuce. The work was all worth it. I learned how to garden from you, you know. It was all from you."

"Yes, I guess that's right," he said. "I always liked to garden."

"Look," Grandma said. "There's some rhubarb, my favorite!"

"I heard that, Grace," said Marty with a smile as she came to the back door. "You'll be happy to know we're having vanilla ice cream topped with fresh rhubarb sauce for dessert tonight! The roast just came out of the oven," she called out to everyone, "time to head inside and get washed up for dinner."

After everyone was seated around the table, Marty said, "Mark, would you like to say grace?"

"Sure," said Mark. "Thank you, Jesus, for letting Grandma and Grandpa come to visit us," he said solemnly, "and thank you for my mom for fixing us such a good supper. Amen."

The meal was thoroughly enjoyed by all. After the table was cleared and the dishes done, everyone gathered in the living room to hear the boys' long-practiced tune, '*Summertime*.' Mark seated himself at the piano and placed his hands in the starting position after feeling the keys. Michael raised the trumpet to his pursed lips and they began to play, with their dad joining in song: '*Summertime, and the living is easy, fish are jumping and the cotton is high.'* Tregnor quickly decided to seek out a quiet space and trotted out of the room.

"That was absolutely marvelous!" Grandma said as the boys finished.

"Bravo!" cheered Grandpa. "Excellent indeed!"

"Thank you, Grandma and Grandpa," the twins chorused. "We practiced for a long time!"

"You did a great job," said Chuck.

"You sure did," Marty agreed. They all sat around and chatted for a while until first the boys yawned, then Grandpa, then Grandma. "I think it's time for everyone to think about getting ready for bed!" said Marty.

"Do you want to say the Rosary with us first, Grandma?" Mark asked, both he and Michael wanting to spend all the time they could with her.

"Yes, of course, that would be very nice," she said.

Marty was proud of how confident and outgoing her sons were, especially with their grandparents. The boys ran and got their rosaries from their room and settled onto the couch next to their grandma, one on each side. Mark began: *'In the name of the Father, and of the Son, and of the Holy Spirit.'* He led the whole first decade of the *Sorrowful Mysteries* and Michael followed with the second decade.

"You boys certainly know how to say your Rosary," said Grandpa when they were finished.

"We learned it by listening to Mom and Dad," Mark said, "and then we taught the kids in our First Communion class."

"That's just wonderful," said their Grandpa. "I'm very proud of you."

"Well, boys," Marty said to the beaming twins, "I know Grandma and Grandpa are tired after traveling here on the train, so let's all get ready for bed. We want to be rested up for your big day tomorrow."

"Okay, Mom," Michael said as he took Mark's hand and led him over to their grandparents. "We need to give everybody a kiss goodnight."

"And big hugs for you!" said Grandma as they embraced.

The boys were the first ones up in the morning. Chuck told them the night before that they'd be able to go fishing at Big Pine Lake if they were out of bed early. He didn't have to say it twice! The birthday boys were in the kitchen at eight o'clock, dressed and ready to go.

"Happy Birthday, you two!" said Grandma as she and Grandpa walked in.

"Yes, Happy Birthday, boys!" said Grandpa. "You sure are up bright and early!"

"Dad said we could go fishing this morning after breakfast, Grandpa!" Michael said enthusiastically.

"Well, let's get started eating then," Grandpa said. Everyone sat down to a hearty breakfast of bananas, fresh strawberries, oranges, and a big bowl of oatmeal with cinnamon, raisins and walnuts, and last but not least, steaming mugs of black coffee for the adults. "Before we head off to the lake, I'd like to give you boys something Grandma and I brought from Crookston for your birthdays," he said.

Michael watched eagerly as his grandpa walked down the hall to the guest bedroom. "What do you think it is?" asked Mark, sitting patiently next to his brother.

"I don't know," Michael said excitedly, "but he sure had a big smile on his face."

When Grandpa came back, he was holding two steel rods with South Bend reels attached, each with a black nylon line with sinkers, leaders and shiny silver spoons dangling from their ends. He handed one to Michael and then sat down next to Mark and placed the second rod and reel in his hands.

"Wow!" said the boys in unison. "Fishing rods!"

"I'll have your dad show you the fancy parts and I'll explain it to Mark," said Grandpa to Michael.

"What do you boys say?" said Chuck.

"Thank you, Grandma and Grandpa!" they yelled out enthusiastically.

"I think you're going to like this lure, Mark," said Grandpa as he took Mark's hand and rubbed it on top of the smooth silver spoon. "It's called a Weed Eater." Then Grandpa took Mark's hand and let him feel underneath the spoon where the hook was shielded by a thin metal spring. "You'll be able to reel this in among the weeds where all the fish are hiding," he said, "and you won't get a snag. When a fish strikes, the thin metal strip springs and you've got your fish!"

"Let's go, Grandpa!" Mark said excitedly. "Let's go fishing!"

Before long, everyone had all piled into the station wagon and they were off for the quick ten-minute drive to Big Pine Lake. It was a perfect morning for fishing. The sun was shining and all was quiet, as they were the first to arrive. Chuck set up the lawn chairs under a big tree near the water so Grandma and Marty could take in the action in the comfort of the shade.

Michael ran down to the edge of the lake and right away began casting out and reeling in his line. Grandpa held Mark's hand as they walked slowly to the water's edge. "Do you think we'll catch anything, Grandpa?" Mark asked as he methodically tipped his rod behind his back and whipped it forward. Without his knowing it, his lure landed in the water just on the outside of a cluster of tall grasses. He began reeling in his line very slowly, right through the weedy plants, and his Weed Eater lure didn't snag on any of them. When he was about halfway through, the tip of his rod doubled forward and a huge northern pike burst through the water! Everyone but Mark could see it was trying to wriggle loose from the shiny silver lure in its mouth. Mark didn't let out a peep. He was calm and a perfect study of intense concentration as he clung to his rod and reel and began playing the fish, letting the line out a little when it tugged hard and reeling it in slowly when it went slack. This kid may have just turned six, but he was a fisherman!

"Good work, Mark!" said Grandpa. "Keep playing him and you'll bring him in!"

"It looks like Mark is going to be the first one to catch a fish," Grandma said.

"I'm not surprised," Marty said with a smile. "He goes about it so slowly and gently. I think his blindness gives him a special feel."

While the women were talking, Michael saw what was transpiring with Mark. "Dad!" he yelled as he ran up to where he was sitting on his lawn chair. "I need the net so I can help Mark!"

"Okay, okay, Son," he said. "Take it easy. Mark hasn't caught that fish yet."

"Thanks, Dad," yelled Michael as he took the net from his dad's hands and raced back to help his brother. The big fish was already tiring and Mark was methodically reeling it in to shore. "Just a little bit closer, Mark," Michael said excitedly, "and I'll be able to net him."

About six feet from the shoreline, the northern turned on its side as if to attempt an escape, but it was obvious that all fight had left its body. As Mark reeled it ever-closer, Michael dipped the net around its body and dragged it, still wiggling and swishing, up onto the shore. "Wow! It's huge, Mark!" he exclaimed.

Now it was time for Dad to get into the action. "Good job, boys!" he yelled as he headed down to check out the catch. "You've got a nice northern, Mark," he said, bending down to give the fish a closer look. "I think this has to be the biggest one for any of us this year, I'm guessing about thirteen pounds!" Mark beamed as his dad untangled the fish from the net and placed it in his hands so he could feel the weight of it.

Meanwhile, Michael was hoping for a repeat of Mark's good fortune and cast his lure at the same weedy spot his brother had chosen. He imitated Mark's style of fishing and began reeling slowly through the weeds. It worked! He got a strike immediately, and judging by the deep bend of his rod, it was another whopper. "Dad! Brother! I've got one!" he yelled.

"Wow! Way to go!" Chuck yelled as Michael began playing the fish. Michael was less patient and more aggressive than his brother and came close to losing it, but didn't. "Another beauty!" Chuck said as he assisted by netting the big walleyed pike. "You boys must be carrying horseshoes in your pockets today!"

Grandpa tried his luck in the weeds, too, but all he got was a pile of snags. After putting the two fish on a stringer and staking it to the shoreline so the catch could be in the water until they were ready to leave, Chuck decided to go back up and sit with his mother and Marty. After all, he'd have plenty of opportunities to go fishing when his parents weren't in town for a visit. "Today is the twins' lucky day," he said. "Neither of them has ever caught fish that big. And did you see how excited Michael was to help Mark? That was real kind of him."

"It sure was," said Grandma.

"It does my heart good to see them care so much for one another the way they do," said Marty.

After another hour of casting and no further strikes, it was time to head home. "I bet I know what you two would like for your birthday supper," Marty said as they were driving.

"Fish!" said Mark. "That's what I want!"

"Me, too!" said Michael.

"Nothing better than a fresh catch!" said Grandpa.

"Sounds good to me," said Grandma, "as long as I don't have to clean them!"

As soon as they got home, the men went to work cleaning the fish while the women planned the meal. The twins were fans of fried potatoes, so Marty decided they would fry the fish as well. "How about some fresh-picked green beans and a garden salad to go with it?" Marty asked.

"Sounds heavenly," said Grandma, "a meal fit for a king!"

While they busied themselves prepping the supper and baking the twins' birthday cake, Chuck, Grandpa and the boys walked to the high school. Michael and Mark wanted to show Grandpa how fast they could run. "Okay, Grandpa," Michael yelled. "We're ready for you to time us!"

"OK!" Grandpa yelled back from alongside the track. "Let's see what you can do! On your marks, get set, go!" The tethered duo blasted off as Grandpa's jaw dropped in amazement. "Wow! Those two can really move!" he said to Chuck. They hit the halfway mark at two minutes, and when they headed down the straightaway, Grandpa yelled, "C'mon, boys! Go! Go!"

The twins were panting heavily, pushing themselves harder than ever before. They could hear their Grandpa's encouragement and were giving it their all to impress him. "Four and half minutes!" yelled Chuck as they ran across the finish line. "I can't believe it," he said to his dad. "That's the fastest they've ever run!"

After the boys caught their breath and basked in the praises of their achievement, they were ready to show Grandpa yet another of their accomplishments. "Grandpa," Mark said as they headed home, "when we get back can I show you and Grandma how I read braille?"

"I'd love to see that, Mark," he said.

"Can I show you how I read, too, Grandpa?" Michael asked.

"Of course," he answered. "I'd love to hear both of you and I know Grandma would as well."

"They're not very competitive, are they?" quipped Chuck.

"Competitive is an understatement," Grandpa chuckled, "but I've also noticed how much they look out for each other."

As soon as they got home and opened the door, the aroma of fresh fish frying filled their nostrils as they all breathed deeply. "Supper will be ready soon," Marty said. "Why don't you all get cleaned up and we'll get to celebrating this birthday dinner!"

"First can we show Grandpa and Grandma how we can read?" Michael asked.

"OK, birthday boys," she said, "but just for a few minutes. Dinner is close to ready. Get washed up first," she hollered after them as Michael took Mark's hand and they rushed down the hall to the bathroom.

"This is going to be fun!" Michael said as he began washing his hands and face. "Grandpa used to ride horses when he lived on the farm, so I'm sure he'd like to hear us read about horses!" The boys had fond memories of their own recent visit to a farm where the farmer had hoisted them up onto a big, gentle workhorse and led them around the pasture. Of course, when they got home, they wanted to read all about horses, and Marty had picked up the braille volume from school and brought it home for the summer.

After they had washed up, the boys ran hand in hand to the living room where Grandma and Grandpa were waiting for them. "Okay," Marty said, "go get your books!"

They rushed out and quickly returned with the regular and braille 'H' volumes of the encyclopedia. Mark opened his volume to the horse article, gently placed his fingers on the page and asked, "Are you ready?"

"Yes!" said Grandma and Grandpa in unison. "Go ahead!"

With that, Mark began. *The horse has been one of the most useful animals for thousands of years. Horses once provided the fastest and surest way to travel on land. Hunters on horseback chased animals and killed them for food and sport.* The grandparents beamed as Mark continued. *Soldiers charged into battle on sturdy war horses. The pioneers used horses when they settled the American West in the days of stagecoaches, covered wagons and the Pony Express.*

"Mark, that's wonderful!" said Grandma as Mark paused and looked up. "You read beautifully!"

"You certainly do!" said Grandpa.

"He's one avid reader, no doubt about that!" said Chuck proudly.

"Let's have Michael read a bit now," said Marty, and then it will be time to eat."

Both the braille and regular volume had the same wording, thus Michael was able to pick up where his brother left off: '*The horse is not as important as it once was as a means of transportation,*' he read. '*In most countries, the iron horse (train) and horseless carriage (automobile) have replaced the horse almost entirely. People still use horses for recreation, sport and work. Children and adults ride horses for fun and exercise. Large crowds thrill to the excitement of horse races. Horses perform in circuses, rodeos, carnivals, parades and horse shows. They help ranchers round up herds of cattle and are sometimes used to pull plows and perform other farm work.*'

"Well done!" said Marty as Michael paused. "I think we'd best stop there since dinner is ready."

"I'm very impressed!" said Grandpa. "I could listen to you two read all day!"

"My goodness!" said a beaming Grandma. "That was wonderful! I'm very proud of both of you!"

"Enough reading for now! Time to eat some fried fish!" said Chuck.

"Sure smells good!' said Grandpa. "You don't have to tell me twice!"

Everyone soon found their places around the table. "Heavenly Father," Chuck prayed as they sat with heads bowed, "thank you for this beautiful day and for this special meal prepared with love, and thank you, Lord, for bringing Grandpa and Grandma here to spend this time with us. Thank you for my beautiful wife and two sons, the mighty fishermen who are celebrating six years of life today. Amen."

"Amen!" came the exuberant chorus.

The fish was prepared to perfection, golden brown and crispy on top, soft and flaky on the inside. "This is quite a feast!" said Grandpa as he helped himself to a hearty portion of fried potatoes and onions.

"The garden vegetables are beautiful, Marty!" said Grandma.

It didn't take long for the food to disappear, and after everyone finished eating, Marty said, "Why don't you boys go visit in the living room with Dad and Grandpa for a while and Grandma and I will clean up and get the birthday cake ready."

While they were doing that, Tregnor came to the back screen door and began scratching it and sniffing the air. "I think someone's ready for dinner," said Grandma.

"He's always ready!" laughed Marty. "I'll give him a few leftover fried potatoes with his canned food."

The women outdid themselves with the birthday cake. Or cakes! They decided to make two, a devil's food with chocolate fudge frosting and an angel food cake with blue butter frosting, both to be served, of course, with vanilla ice cream. "OK, we're ready for you!" Marty called out.

"All those boys do love their sweets!" said Grandma smiling. Needless to say, one announcement was all it took as the men hustled into the dining room and joined in a rousing rendition of "Happy Birthday!"

"Wow!" Michael yelled as he took in the cakes. "Mark! Mom and Grandma made two cakes, one with chocolate frosting and one with blue frosting! They each have six candles!"

"I'm going to have a big piece of each one!" said Mark.

"First, you two get to make a wish and blow out your candles," said Marty as she moved Mark in front of the angel food cake. Mark stood quietly for a moment, then took a deep breath and kept blowing until all six were extinguished.

"Great job, Mark! You got all of them!" said Chuck. "Your turn, Michael."

"Don't forget to make a wish!" said Grandma just as he cut loose with one big blast of air and all the candles went out.

"Wow! Just like that!" said Grandpa.

Marty and Grandma began cutting the two cakes and served up generous double portions. "Anyone for a scoop of vanilla ice cream?" asked Chuck as everyone held out their plates.

"These cakes sure are good!" said Mark.

"Yummy!" said Michael as he dug in.

It had been quite a day, and a successful one, too. With bellies full, everyone headed into the living room. Chuck told his dad the twins wanted to show him how well they could say the Rosary. Grandpa loved saying the Rosary, and he beamed when his grandsons took out their rosaries, made the Sign of the Cross with their crucifixes and said, '*In the name of the Father, and of the Son, and of the Holy Spirit. Amen.*' After saying the prayers for all five decades of the *Joyful Mysteries*, Grandpa moved towards his grandsons, reached to them with outstretched arms and embraced them both. A tear ran down his cheek. "You boys have made me very proud," he said. "You recited that beautifully."

Early the next morning, Chuck drove his parents to the railroad station, and before boarding the train and heading back to Crookston, his mom said, "Thank you so much for everything, Charlie. We enjoyed our visit with you and Marty and the boys very much."

"We sure did, Charlie," his dad said. "Give our love to Marilyn and our grandsons, and thanks again for inviting us."

"It was great having you here," Chuck said as his mom and dad climbed aboard.

------◆◆◆------

THE NEXT THREE YEARS WERE A BIT OF A BLUR, SO MUCH HAPPENING. The main concern was that Chuck's dad had been having a lot of medical challenges. Chuck, Marty and the boys drove up to Crookston during the summer of 1962, and that was the last time Chuck would see his dad.

"Is Grandpa going to be okay, Dad?" asked Mark on the drive home from Perham.

"Grandpa's not doing very well, Mark," said Chuck. "I think that may be the last time you'll see him." When Chuck said that, tears formed in Mark's eyes, and when he began to quietly cry, Michael did, too.

"We love him so much," said Mark.

"I know. And he sure loves both of you," said Chuck, his voice edged with emotion. "Maybe now would be a good time to say the Rosary for Grandpa," Chuck said. "You boys know how he loved hearing you say it."

Without hesitation, Mark dug into his pocket for his rosary and began. *'In the name of the Father, and of the Son, and of the Holy Spirit. Amen.'* It wasn't long after they had finished saying the Rosary that they reached the outskirts of Perham and were home. The first thing the boys did was run to the back yard and hug Tregnor, who clearly sensed their sadness and welcomed their affection as always.

When school started in September, the twins had the same teacher they'd had in 4th grade, Mrs. LaVerne Lefman, thus they picked up right where they'd left off the previous year. By this time, Mark was devouring the braille *World Book Encyclopedia* articles in addition to his regular classroom work, and Michael of course was determined to keep up with him.

Early in November, when all the leaves started to fall and winter began to set in, Chuck received a letter from his mom:

November 7, 1962

Dear Charlie,

Your dad had to be taken by ambulance to the Veterans Administration Hospital in Fargo this morning. He's been getting weaker and weaker, and the doctors here thought he needed to be hospitalized. If you and Marilyn can make it up here for Thanksgiving with the boys, I know he would like to see everyone again.

—Love, Mom

Chuck's dad died in the hospital a week after his mom had written. He was 73. When Chuck went to Michael and Mark's room and told them the sad news, the boys clung to one another and cried quietly. When they came out of their room, Marty was there to comfort them. "Do you think Grandpa's in heaven?" Michael asked.

"Yes, I'm sure he is," she said. "He was a good man, your grandpa, and I know God loved him and will want to be with him. You can remember him in your prayers tonight."

"God," Michael said before he went to sleep that night, "please take care of Grandpa."

"And please help Grandma to not be too sad," Mark added.

When Chuck heard his sons express their loving thoughts, it tugged at his heart. "I'm sure God is listening to you tonight," he whispered, his voice hoarse with emotion.

Mrs. Lefman was immediately aware that something was amiss when the boys walked into class the next morning. Michael wasn't his usual robust self and Mark didn't greet her in his typical friendly fashion. "What's going on with you two boys today?" she asked. "Did something happen?"

"Our grandpa died yesterday," said Mark sadly.

"Oh, I'm so sorry," she said. "I know how much he meant to you." The rest of the day passed in sort of a daze, and when the twins got home they headed straight to the back yard to be with Tregnor. He laid quietly as they petted him and talked about Grandpa, and this comforted them.

The next day was Saturday, and the family drove up to Crookston to be with Chuck's mother for the weekend and funeral on Monday. The boys had never seen a dead person, thus Grandpa would be their first. When they drove up to Norman's Funeral Home that afternoon, a lot of Grandpa's friends were in the room. Chuck slowly led Michael and Mark to the open casket. "Grandpa's face looks all white, Dad," whispered Michael as he peered in. This remark aroused Mark's curiosity, and he did what one might expect from one who's unable to see. He reached down with his hand until he was able to touch his grandpa's face, and then he leaned over the edge and kissed him on the cheek.

About an hour later, after everyone had the opportunity to view the body, socialize and offer their condolences, they gathered around the casket and the twins led them in saying the *Glorious Mysteries of the Rosary*.

The funeral Mass on Monday was held at the Cathedral of the Immaculate Conception. After the funeral, everyone drove out to the cemetery for the burial. Chuck and Marty were in for quite a shock, as they quickly realized Chuck's dad and mom had burial sites right next to Marty's dad and mom. On their drive back to Perham, they talked about it, wondering how that had come about.

On Tuesday morning, Mrs. Lefman met the twins at her classroom door. They were still downcast, so she talked with them and listened as they told her about the funeral and burial. Later in the day, while the class was practicing letter writing, she noticed Michael and Mark were having trouble getting started, so she went over to them and suggested they might like to compose a letter to their grandpa. Both were soon writing up a storm.

Dear Grandpa,

Pretty soon it will be Thanksgiving. Michael and I are going to miss you. I'll always remember the huge northern pike I caught with the new rod and reel you gave me. I'll think of you whenever I'm fishing. I'll also think of you whenever I say my Rosary, Grandpa, because I know how much you liked it. I hope God is gentle and kind to you in heaven just like you were always gentle and kind with me and Michael. I love you!

—Your grandson, Mark

Dear Grandpa,

We're writing letters in school today, and our teacher said Mark and I could write to you, so that's what I'm doing. It's hard for me because I know you're not here anymore. I'm going to try anyway. On the way home from Crookston, I heard Mom and Dad talking about how you are buried right next to Mom's dad, and I thought that was pretty neat. I don't know where I'll be buried when I die, but I hope it's close to you. I guess I have plenty of time to think about it. I hope God is taking good care of you in heaven.

—Your grandson, Michael

CHRISTMAS WAS GOING TO BE VERY DIFFERENT THIS YEAR WITH NO grandpas to join in the celebration, but the boys were happy they would be seeing their grandmas. Grandma Kirkwood was flying in from California for a few days and Grandma Dowdle planned to travel to Perham by train. Chuck picked up Marty's mother at the Minneapolis-St. Paul International Airport on December 23rd, and on the way home they made a stop in St. Cloud where Mrs. Kirkwood bought bicycles for the entire family for Christmas.

"I really appreciate your taking the time to do this, Chuck," said Mrs. Kirkwood as they pulled up to the Schwinn bicycle shop. "I'll be quick!"

"No problem!" said Chuck enthusiastically. "Take as long as you need."

"I've been wanting to buy bicycles for you and Marilyn and the boys for a long time," she said.

"It's very generous of you," said Chuck. "Thank you so much!"

"I was sorry to learn about your dad, Chuck," she added as they sat quietly in the car for a moment.

"It seemed pretty sudden," he said, "but I guess he hadn't been feeling well for a while. By the way, did you know my folks have burial plots right next to yours and Bill's?"

"I didn't know that!" said Mrs. Kirkwood, looking stunned. "I wonder how that happened!"

"I don't know," he said, 'but it sure was a surprise when we went out to the cemetery for my dad's burial."

"My goodness, I should say so," said Mrs. Kirkwood softly.

They made their way into the bike shop and walked up and down the rows of shiny new bicycles. "I'm thinking one for you, one for Marilyn, a junior bicycle for Michael and a junior tandem bicycle Michael and Mark can ride together," said Mrs. Kirkwood.

"You really want to buy four bicycles?" Chuck asked incredulously.

"Yes," she said. "I really do. I've been thinking about how much enjoyment Marilyn and you and the boys would get out of riding them next summer. And half the fun of a gift is being able to anticipate the fun of using it," she said. They hadn't been in the store for more than thirty minutes before they had a beautiful canary yellow bicycle picked out for Marty, a regal blue for Chuck and two fire-hydrant-red junior bicycles for the boys.

A worker headed to the warehouse to pick up the four boxed, unassembled bicycles, the only way Chuck would be able to get them home to Perham in the station wagon. "When you get ready to use the bikes this spring," the store manager said, "just bring them back and we'll be happy to put them together free of charge."

"Sounds good," Chuck said, but he knew he wouldn't be driving back to St. Cloud several times to have each of the bicycles assembled. He'd get someone in Perham to help if he couldn't do it himself.

After driving for a couple of hours on the icy highway, they made it home without incident by late afternoon. "Oh, Mom, it's so good to see you!" gushed Marty as she greeted her mother. "It's been a long time, too long! How do you like California by now?"

"Oh, Marilyn, I do love it," she said. "San Gabriel is a very nice city surrounded by orange groves and the San Gabriel mountains. I feel like I made a wise choice."

"I'm so glad to hear that," said Marty as they embraced.

After supper, the twins showed Grandma Kirkwood how well they could play the piano and trumpet. They proudly performed '*Jingle Bells*,' which they'd practiced many a time at school before Christmas vacation.

"My, but you boys have certainly learned how to get some fine music from those instruments!" she said enthusiastically.

"Do you want to hear me read, Grandma?" Mark asked.

"Why, yes, Mark," she said, "that would be very nice."

Mark had brought home the braille 'C' volume from school because it had an article about Christmas, and that's what he began reading to her: *'Christmas is a Christian holiday that celebrates the birth of Jesus Christ. No one knows the exact date of Christ's birth, but most Christians observe Christmas on December 25th. On this day many go to church where they take part in special religious services. During the Christmas season, they also exchange gifts and decorate their homes with Christmas trees, holly and mistletoe. The word Christmas comes from Cristes Maesse, an early English phrase that means Mass of Christ.'*

"My goodness, Mark," said Grandma, "you read that beautifully!"

"What's mistletoe, Grandma?" Michael asked.

"It's a green plant that grows on trunks and branches of different trees," she said. "People hang it in their homes, and if you accidentally stand beneath it, you're going to get kissed! I don't know how that tradition started."

"I'll find out from the encyclopedia!" yelled Michael as he ran to get the 'M' volume. "I can read it to you!" He quickly returned and Grandma helped him locate the page as he settled in next to her on the couch and began to read: *'Mistletoe is associated with many traditions and holidays, especially Christmas. Historians say the Druids, or ancient priests of the Celts, cut the mistletoe that grew on the sacred oak and gave it to the people for charms. In Teutonic mythology, an arrow made of mistletoe killed Balder, son of the goddess Frigg. Early European peoples used mistletoe as a ceremonial plant. The custom of using mistletoe at Christmas probably comes from this practice. In many countries, tradition says that a person caught standing beneath mistletoe must forfeit a kiss.'*

"Just like you said, Grandma!" said Mark.

Mrs. Kirkwood fought back a yawn as Michael was about to continue reading. "I think that's enough reading for tonight, Michael," said Marty. "Grandma's had a long day. You and Mark can read more for her tomorrow after we've all had a good night's sleep."

"Okay," said Michael, and after the boys gave their grandma a big hug and a kiss, she yawned again and they all headed off to bed.

"I love Grandma," Mark whispered in his mother's ear before he went to sleep that night. Marty smiled broadly, touched to hear her son express such fondness for her mother.

"That's so nice, Mark," she whispered back to him. "I know she loves you and Michael, too."

The next day, Christmas Eve, was very busy. After breakfast, while Marty, her mother and the twins went downtown for a morning of last-minute holiday shopping, Chuck called his friend, Bruno Zanoni, a shop teacher at Perham High School, and asked him if he'd have time to help him assemble some bicycles. Bruno came right over, and in less than two hours the two of them had all four bikes put together and standing in the garage, ready to ride! "You have one generous mother-in-law," said Bruno. "Those are some real beauties!"

Chuck thanked Bruno profusely for helping him as they shook hands and parted ways. "Any time, my friend," said Bruno, "any time." That was the neat thing about living in a small town like Perham. It seemed everyone was friendly and helpful.

It wasn't more than fifteen minutes after Bruno left when the station wagon pulled into the driveway. Good timing! After helping to unload packages and groceries, Chuck asked the boys if they wanted to drive to the train depot with him to pick up Grandma Dowdle.

"I want to!" Michael yelled.

"Me, too!" Mark yelled. Tregnor began barking and wanted to be involved when he heard the twins excited voices, so they took him along as well. He was well trained and used to riding in the car just about everywhere with the family, so it was no big deal for him to join in the action. And getting them all out of the house to pick up Grandma Dowdle would be a good diversion so the twins wouldn't be wondering what it was that was now hidden under the draped bedsheets in the garage.

In spite of the heavy snow that had fallen during the night, the train came chugging into the station right on time at half past twelve. Steam hissed from the snow-covered engine, icicles hanging from its edges. When it finally came to a screeching halt and the conductor put the foot stand down for arriving passengers, Michael was the first to see Grandma Dowdle. "There she is!" he yelled.

Everyone rushed to meet her, Michael in the lead, Chuck close behind with Mark holding one hand and Tregnor's leash in the other. "This is quite a greeting!" said Chuck's mother as they surrounded her. "Even Treg is here!"

"Did you have a nice train ride, Grandma?" asked Mark as the threesome exchanged hugs.

"I sure did," she said. She took Mark's hand and they began walking towards the station with Chuck and Michael.

"I'm surprised the train was here right on time given the heavy snow we had last night, Mom," said Chuck.

"It snowed last night in Crookston as well," she said. After picking up her luggage, everyone piled into the station wagon, Grandma in the front seat with Chuck, the boys and Treg in the back, and they were off for the short drive home.

When they arrived, Marty and her mother had lunch ready, so after more greetings and hugs, they sat down and ate and chatted. It was great to have family, what remained of it, together again for Christmas.

That evening, after everyone enjoyed a delicious ham supper, Michael said, "When are we going to open presents?"

"Not until all these dishes are cleaned up and you two are ready for bed," Marty said. "Why don't you go down to the bathroom with your dad, and while he's helping you, we'll finish up here."

It didn't take the boys long. They were eager to open their gifts! Of course, Mark couldn't see his presents, but he sure could feel them. "I'd like to give Mark and Michael their presents first," Grandma Dowdle said as she picked up two packages and placed them on the twins' laps. Mark moved his fingers slowly along the smooth paper and ribbon. However, when he heard Michael rip his package open, it didn't take him long to do the same. He could feel something soft, and by this time Michael had already tried on his navy blue watch cap and mittens knitted by Grandma Dowdle.

"Thank you, Grandma!" said the boys in unison.

"They fit real good and sure feel nice and warm!" said Mark.

Chuck's mom had also knitted each of the boys a navy blue V-neck sweater, and after they slipped into them, the twins put on an impromptu fashion show. "Wow! Those are pretty neat, Mom," Chuck said as the boys paraded around the living room.

"They're wonderful, Grace," said Marty. "I can't imagine how much time it took to make two beautiful sets."

"Well, if you like them, I think you'll like your presents, too," said Grace as she handed Chuck and Marty their gifts.

"Why don't you open yours first, honey," Chuck said.

Marty slowly unraveled the red ribbon from around her colorful green package. "Hurry up, Mom, so we can see what you got!" Michael yelled.

When Marty opened her present, she saw another beautifully-knit navy blue sweater. "Oh, Grace," she said, "it's absolutely lovely! Thank you so much!"

Chuck was right behind in opening his gift, and you guessed it, yet another! "Wow! Thanks a lot, Mom! I love it!" said Chuck. "I can't believe you made four sweaters! It must have taken forever."

"Well, yes, it took a little time," she said. "If you like them, it was all worth it."

"We love them!" everybody chimed.

"I guess I should have made one for Tregnor, too!" laughed Grandma Dowdle.

"OK, time to open your presents," said Marty as she handed her mom and Chuck's mother their gifts. The grandmas smiled at each other as they began to unwrap their presents.

"What did you get?" Mark asked excitedly.

"Just a minute, Mark; your grandma's a little slow," Grandma Kirkwood said laughing. "What a beautiful gift!" she exclaimed when she saw the black, calf-skin purse.

"Oh my, it certainly is!" said Grandma Dowdle as she removed the layer of tissue.

"It's a purse, Mark. Feel how soft it is," said Grandma Kirkwood as she held it out.

Mark ran his hands over the fur. "It's so smooth, Grandma," he said. "Do you like it?"

"I adore it!" she said. "Thank you, Marilyn!"

"I love mine, too, Marilyn," said Mrs. Dowdle. "It's just what I needed. Thank you!"

"Well, boys, are you ready to see what else you got for Christmas?" Chuck asked.

"Yes!" they yelled in unison.

"We'll have to go out to the garage," he said.

"How come the garage, Dad?" Mark asked as Chuck took his hand and led the way.

"You'll see!" he said, and this really aroused Mark's curiosity.

"C'mon, Brother!" said Michael excitedly as he ran ahead.

"Don't say anything when you see your present, Michael," Chuck cautioned. "I want Mark to discover for himself what it is."

"Okay, Dad," said Michael.

They walked into the garage and Chuck lifted a white bed sheet off shiny new skis stacked in the corner. Michael's face broke into a big grin. His dad stood one of the skis up in front of Mark so he could feel it. As Mark ran his hands up and down the varnished surface, a puzzled look crossed his face until he felt the leather strap in the middle of the ski. He reached up to the tip and said, "I know!"

"What do you think it is?" asked Marty.

"It's a ski!" he yelled.

"You're right!' yelled Michael. "You guessed it!"

"Your dad and I decided to get cross country skis for the whole family. We can all go out and have a good time in the snow and get some exercise this winter," said Marty.

"Wow! That will be fun, Brother!" said Michael as Chuck handed him his pair. "Thanks, Dad, thanks, Mom!" he said.

"Yes, thank you!" said Mark. "I can hardly wait to try them!"

"Oh, boys, I think there might be something else," said Chuck.

"What? Where?" said Michael excitedly.

"Why don't you take your brother over to the other corner where the sheets are covering something," said Chuck teasingly.

When Michael lifted the first sheet, he couldn't believe his eyes. There sat a men's Schwinn bicycle, shiny and new. "Mark, reach out and touch this!" he yelled. "It's a big bicycle!" Michael immediately tugged off a second sheet and there sat a women's Schwinn bicycle. "Mark, you won't believe it!" he yelled. "It's another bicycle, a big yellow one!" Michael rushed over to the last sheet, and when he yanked it off, he saw two fire-hydrant red bicycles, just the right size for him and his brother! "Mark! Mark!" he yelled. "There are two new red bicycles! One of them has two seats so we can ride it together!"

This brought a huge smile to Mark's face as Michael led him up to the tandem. He began feeling the leather seats and cool steel of the handlebars. "Wow!" he said. "I get to ride a bike. I can't believe it!"

"Skiing in the winter and biking in the summer," laughed Marty. "This family is going to be in great shape!"

"Boys, would you like to know who bought us these bicycles?" asked Chuck.

"Who?" Mark asked.

"Your Grandma Kirkwood," Chuck said. "Every one of them."

"Indeed, I did," said Grandma Kirkwood, "and I was delighted to do so!"

Mark reached out to give her a big hug and Michael hugged her at the same time, their enthusiastic embraces just about knocking her off her feet. "Thank you, Grandma!" the boys chorused gleefully.

"You are very welcome," she said, smiling as she regained her balance.

"Such a thoughtful and generous gift for all of us," said Marty. "Thank you!"

"Yes, thanks, Mom!" said Chuck. "We'll get so much use out of these!"

Thus marked the exciting finale to the family's Christmas celebration. The next morning after breakfast, the grandmas left together on the train for Crookston. Mrs. Kirkwood had some Crookston business to attend to regarding the sale of her farm and home, and when finished she'd be flying back to California from the nearby airport in Grand Forks, North Dakota.

After seeing their grandmas off at the depot, the first thing the twins wanted to do was rush back and try out their new skis. There was plenty of snow on the ground, and they could hardly wait. "Can we all go skiing when we get home, Dad?" Michael asked excitedly.

"I don't see why not," Chuck said. "School's out; let's have some fun!"

When they walked in the house, the twins found their mom sewing metal loops onto their jackets. She didn't want to do it before they got their skis because they'd be asking all kinds of questions, but now it was all right for them to know the plan. "Your dad and I thought if we sewed loops onto your jackets and then hooked a bungee cord between the loops, you boys could ski together much like you do when you run together. The only difference is that Mark will be following in your tracks through the snow, Michael."

"That's a good idea, Mom," he said. "We like running that way and skiing shouldn't be much different."

Mark heard what his brother said and a big smile broke across his face. "Let's go now, Michael! It'll be fun!"

The sun was shining and the snow was crisp under their skis as they slid away from the house, tethered by the bungee cord. It became taut as Michael quickly picked up speed. They soon passed the school and were skiing on a country road. "This is great!" Mark yelled as the cold air filled his lungs and he labored to stay in his brother's tracks. "Slow down a little, Brother!" he yelled again. "I'm having a hard time keeping up!"

Michael slowed a little, but then kept plowing ahead, pulling his brother along whenever he felt the bungee cord tighten. "We're coming to a downhill, Mark!" he yelled. "Try to keep your balance and we'll make it to the bottom without falling!" As soon as they began descending, Mark could feel the cold air rush against his cheeks. Both boys were quiet as they picked up speed, the tips of their skis plowing through the fresh snow as they concentrated on staying upright. Halfway down the hill, something suddenly caught on the underside of Michael's skis. He lost his balance and yelled, "Watch out, Mark!" But it was too late. Michael flew forward and did a big belly flop into the snow, and when the underside of Mark's skis hit the same patch of snow, he went down, too.

As they struggled to their feet, Michael brushed the snow from his brother's jacket and said, "Sorry, Brother. I'll have to be more on the lookout for bad spots like that. Are you okay?"

"Yeah, I'm fine," Mark said. "A little snow never hurt anybody."

"Wait a minute, Brother," said Michael as he noticed a red splotch in the snow and a tear in Mark's jeans. "There's some blood soaking through your pants by your right knee!" He looked down at the place where Mark had fallen and saw shards of brown glass. "I think you were cut by a broken bottle that was buried in the snow!" he said. "Let me see how bad it is, Brother," he said as he bent down and pulled up Mark's pant leg. What he saw was an ugly gash. It was jagged and deep, about two inches long and oozing blood. As calmly as he could, so as not to arouse his brother's fears, he said, "Let's get back so Mom can clean it and bandage it up. It's cut pretty bad."

"Do we have to?" said Mark. "It doesn't hurt that much and we just got started."

"Let's get it fixed up and then we can ski some more," said Michael in his most convincing voice. He didn't waste any time heading for home. He was worried! He had read in *World Book* that a person could bleed to death if they lost too much blood. What would happen if Mark fainted and fell? How would he get him home? What if he died? All of these thoughts were racing through his head as he picked up speed. "How are you doing?" he yelled to Mark. There was no reply, so Michael slowed down and yelled again, "Are you okay back there?"

"Yes!" Mark yelled back. "I think I was dreaming or something. I felt a little dizzy."

Mark's face was notably pale against the flush of his cold cheeks, and Michael began to get scared. "You're doing real good, Brother," he said as they moved along. "We'll be home in no time."

They reached the high school and Michael breathed a sigh of relief. Cars began passing them, and he knew that help would be near if they needed it. They were only a couple of blocks from their house, and when they finally reached the front door, Michael opened it and yelled, "Mom! Mom! Mark fell on some broken glass in the snow and cut his knee!"

Marty ran to the door and immediately saw Mark's blood-soaked pant leg. "Oh my!" she said, trying to remain calm. "There's a good deal of blood there, Son. You must have taken quite a tumble. Did you both go down?"

"First Michael, then me," said Mark, "but I fell on the glass."

This wasn't the first time either of the boys had fallen and bruised or cut themselves. Frankly, Marty was surprised they'd avoided any broken bones up to this point, active as was her dynamic duo. "I think we should have Dr. Schoeneberger take a look at it, Mark," she said softly as she observed the still-oozing wound. "There's a pretty good cut on your knee. Does it hurt?"

"It stings a little, Mom," he said, "but it doesn't hurt too much."

Chuck was busy over at the school, so Marty placed a call to Dr. Schoeneberger's office. Evelyn, his nurse, suggested Marty take Mark to the Emergency Room at the hospital, as that's where they'd find the doctor, and she'd let him know they were headed his way.

"Well, well, what do we have here, Mark?" Dr. Schoeneberger asked when he saw his young patient sitting on the examining table.

"Michael and I were trying out our new skis and we fell when we were going down a hill," he said. "I cut my knee on some glass that was under the snow."

"Well, Mark," Dr. Schoeneberger said as he examined the wound. "It doesn't look too bad, but it looks like I'll have to put a few sutures in it to close it up."

Mark didn't let out a whimper as Dr. Schoeneberger went to work. Michael's eyes never left Dr. Schoeneberger's hands as the highly-skilled physician put on a show of stitching expertise. "Just keep that clean and dry for a couple of days, Mark," Dr. Schoeneberger said as he finished up, "and you'll be back on the skis again before you know it."

"Maybe later today?" asked Mark enthusiastically.

"Hold off for a few days," laughed Dr. Schoeneberger. "Give things time to heal before you hit the slopes again."

Treg came bouncing up to the boys when they came in the door. Mark cuddled up with him on the couch and began telling him everything that had happened.

Michael was more interested in the blood his brother had lost. The first thing he did was get the 'B' volume of *World Book* and began reading about blood!

'Blood is the river of life that flows through the human body. We cannot live without it. The heart pumps blood to all our body cells, supplying them with oxygen and food. At the same time, blood carries carbon dioxide and other waste products from the cells. Blood also fights infection, keeps our temperature steady and carries chemicals that regulate many bodily functions. Finally, blood has substances that plug broken blood vessels and thus prevent us from bleeding to death.'

That night at supper, Michael told his father every detail of his day with Mark. "His leg was bleeding really bad, Dad!" he said. "He got pale and dizzy and I was scared!"

"Well, you did a great job of getting him home safely so Mom could take care of him, Michael," he said, "and you were very brave, Mark. I'm proud of both of you."

"Thanks, Dad," said the boys.

"I want you to limit your skiing to the neighborhood for now," he said. "Better to be where more people are around until you have a little more experience."

After the dishes were done and the twins had taken their baths and were ready for bed, the family sat in the living room with their rosaries. "Well, boys, this has been quite a day. What would you think about thanking God tonight for getting you home safely?"

"Good idea, Dad," Michael said.

"And I can thank God for Dr. Schoeneberger fixing my knee," Mark said.

After saying the Rosary and getting tucked into bed, Michael wanted to know how Dr. Schoeneberger learned how to be such a good doctor.

"He went to school for many years and had a lot of training, Michael," said his father. "The next time you see him you can ask him about that."

"I want to be a doctor, Dad," said Michael. "I want to be like Dr. Schoeneberger and sew people up when they get hurt."

"I think you'd be an excellent doctor," he said. "You have a lot of time to think it over. The best thing you can do now is study hard in school and learn as much as you can. When I was your age," he added, "I remember reading a book about a man named Albert Schweitzer. It made a big impression on me. He became a doctor and spent his entire life serving others. I knew I wanted to be like him in that way, helping people. Like I said, you have some years to think about what you want to do with your life."

"Guess I wouldn't be able to be a doctor since I can't see, right Dad?" asked Mark.

"It would be challenging, but there are many kinds of doctors, Mark," said Chuck. "I have no doubt you'll achieve whatever you set your mind on accomplishing," he added. "Maybe you'd like to be a lawyer like your Grandpa Kirkwood or a teacher like me," he added.

"Maybe," said Mark. "What do lawyers do?"

"Let's save that discussion for tomorrow," he said as he noticed Michael's eyes fighting to stay open. "It's time for you two to get some sleep." Once their heads hit the pillows, the boys were out like a light. They had had quite an emotional and energy-draining day. As Chuck walked out to the living room, he was thinking it would be fun to take the boys to the Otter Tail County Courthouse at Fergus Falls and sit in on a lawyer doing his work. It was a short 30-40 mile drive and would be an interesting family outing. He'd talk to them in the morning and see how they felt about the idea.

"How would you all like to take a drive to Fergus Falls this morning and drop in at the courthouse so you boys can learn firsthand what lawyers do?" Chuck asked at breakfast.

"Oh, honey," Marty said, "it would be fun; I just don't have the time today. I bet the boys would enjoy it, though."

"Sorry, Dad, not me," said Michael. "I'm playing hockey this morning over at the school. Plus, I've already decided I'm going to be a doctor like Dr. Schoeneberger."

"Well, Mark," Chuck said, "I guess that leaves us. How about it?"

Mark smiled and said, "Sure, Dad. I think it would be fun. Just you and me."

After breakfast, while Michael was getting ready for hockey and Mark was getting dressed for Fergus Falls, Marty asked Chuck, "What brought on the idea of going to the courthouse?"

"Well," he said, "last night before the boys went to sleep, Michael said he wanted to be a surgeon so he could sew people up. Mark said he didn't think being a doctor of any type was for him, and I suggested he might like to be a lawyer like his Grandpa Kirkwood; I thought it would be interesting for him to observe lawyers doing their work at the Fergus Falls courthouse."

"I think it's a great idea!" said Marty. "Mark will enjoy having you all to himself, and I can just see my dad smiling down on the two of you at the courthouse. He sure would have loved being there with you."

Before they left for Fergus Falls, Michael was already out the door with his skates slung over his shoulder and Marty was in the kitchen rolling out a crust for an apple pie. "I don't think I want to leave!" said Chuck.

"Let's go, Dad!" Mark said as he walked into the kitchen, dressed and ready to go.

"Don't worry, the pie will be waiting," said Marty as Chuck took his son's hand and led him toward the door.

"Wait a minute," Marty said. "Aren't you two forgetting a little something for the baker?" They both rushed back to the kitchen and gave her a big hug and a kiss.

"Bye, Mom!" Mark called back over his shoulder as he and his dad left the house.

It didn't take long for the duo to arrive in Fergus Falls. "Here we are, Mark," said Chuck as they pulled into the courthouse parking lot. "Now you'll get to learn all about lawyers!" They left the car and began crunching their way over the packed snow towards a three-story, cream-colored brick and limestone building. Chuck described it to Mark and told him going inside would be a first for him, too.

As they entered, Chuck read aloud the signage directing visitors to the law enforcement center, sheriff's office, county jail, probation, administration, judicial offices and three courtrooms. "Which way do we go, Dad?" asked Mark.

"Courtrooms are on the third floor. Let's use the stairs," he said, taking Mark's hand.

"Okay, Dad," he said. "By the way, why does it smell like trees in here?"

Chuck laughed and said, "I think they use a lot of pine-scented disinfectant in these places to keep them clean. You're right; it does smell like pine trees!"

When they reached the third-story landing, the door to Superior Courtroom 1 was open, so they walked in and sat in the back of the room. "This is an old courtroom, Mark," Chuck said, "but it's really nice. We're sitting in the visitors' section. There are four raised tables in front for the lawyers and their clients, and in front of that there's a large bench where the judge sits. Over on the side of the room is where the bad guys sit." No sooner had Chuck said the words "bad guys," when the side door opened and a heavy-set bailiff led a shackled prisoner into the hushed room. Chuck could see his ankles were chained together as well as his hands.

Mark leaned toward his dad and whispered, "What's that clanging sound?"

"The bailiff just brought in a prisoner. He has chains on his ankles and hands," Chuck said quietly. "He must be one of the real bad ones! We'll have to be quiet now," he added. "Here comes the judge, and the court will soon be in session."

"Please rise," the bailiff announced. "Otter Tail Superior Court, the Honorable Joseph P. Murphy presiding." Chuck and Mark stood, and before they sat down, Chuck looked around and sensed they were the only observers in the room. You could have heard a pin drop when the judge began reading the prisoner his rights. Mark's face grew tense, and he gripped his dad's hand as he listened intently. After about a half hour, the proceedings were finished. The judge stepped down from his bench and left for his chambers. The bailiff led the prisoner back out the side door to the jail, and Chuck and Mark got up and walked out of the courtroom.

Mark didn't utter a word until they began walking slowly down the three flights of stairs. "Dad, do you think we could go to the jail where they're keeping that bad guy?"

"I'll ask when we get downstairs," he said. "Why do you want to go there?"

"I want to feel what it's like," said Mark.

When they got downstairs, they walked to the reception area of the jail. Chuck explained to the jailer on duty that his son was considering becoming a lawyer, that he was blind and wanted to feel what a jail cell was like. The jailer was kind and courteous and said, "Well, Son, you and your dad just follow me and we'll go check out an empty cell." When the jailer inserted a large steel key in the cell door, Mark heard a loud click, and then the squeaking of the heavy cell door being opened. Chuck led him into the cell and let him feel the cold cement walls and heavy metal bars. "Try the bed out if you'd like," said the jailer as Chuck led Mark to the metal cot with its thin cotton mattress.

Mark did, and he scrunched up his face and said, "It's not very comfortable!"

"That's right, Son," said the jailer. "This isn't like home. This place is for guys who are serving time for committing crimes."

"How do they go to the bathroom?" Mark asked.

"There's a little toilet in the back corner," said the jailer.

"I think we've taken enough of this kind gentleman's time," said Chuck after Mark had asked a dozen questions. "We'd better get on our way and let him get back to work. Thank you very much for showing us the cell," he said to the jailer.

"That was very interesting," said Mark as the jailer shook his hand. "Thanks for letting me see the cell!" he called back to the jailer as he and his dad walked down the hall.

"You're welcome, Son," the jailer replied warmly. He tracked Mark with his eyes as the duo walked away, and he wondered what it would be like to be blind. He was filled with admiration for Mark's enthusiastic curiosity.

It was just after 11:30 when they reached the parking lot. The short drive home would mean perfect timing for lunch and a slice of Mom's fresh-baked apple pie. Mark was loaded with more questions as they pulled onto the highway. "Dad, what's going to happen to the bad man who was in the courtroom today?"

"If he's found guilty, he's going to spend many years in jail, Mark, maybe the rest of his life. That's the penalty one has to pay for armed bank robbery and attempted murder, and when the crime is against a police officer, which it was, that's even worse. It's good the police officer didn't die, and it's also good there were other police officers outside the bank when the guy tried to get away."

"I think I would like to be a lawyer, Dad," Mark said as they pulled up in front of the house. "Wait until Mom and Michael hear all about our morning!"

As they walked hand-in-hand into the house, they were greeted by the sweet smell of pie. "Well, there are my two adventurers, home from their courthouse field trip!" said Marty enthusiastically. "How was it?"

Just then, the front door opened and Michael came in. "I'm starving!" he said as he walked into the kitchen.

"OK, OK, all of you go get washed up and we'll have some lunch while you tell me about your mornings," said Marty.

They were soon gathered around the table feasting on turkey sandwiches and potato salad, and of course, generous slices of apple pie for dessert. Mark had so much to say he felt near to bursting. "It smelled like pine trees in the courthouse, Mom," said Mark. "We had to climb three flights of stairs to get to the courtroom. There was a judge sitting in the front of the room. Me and dad sat in the back and listened."

"Were there any bad guys?" asked Michael.

"Yes!" said Mark. "They brought a man into the courtroom and he had chains on his ankles and hands so he couldn't run away! He was real bad!"

"What did he do?" he asked.

"He robbed a bank and shot a policeman!" said Mark. "Luckily, the policeman didn't die. The bad guy tried to get away from the bank, but they caught him!"

"I bet he'll be in jail for a long time!" Michael said.

"He will!" said Mark. "Dad said maybe for the rest of his life! Oh, and wait until I tell you this, Michael!" Mark said excitedly. "When we left the courtroom and went downstairs, we walked to the jail, and Dad asked if we could check out a cell, and the jailer let us go into one! It was way smaller than our bedroom! I got to lie down on the cot. It felt like a rock!"

"It sounds like you and Dad had quite an adventure!" said Marty.

"We sure did," said Chuck. "I think you would have liked it, Michael," he added. "Maybe we can go again sometime."

"OK, Dad, but I know I want to be a doctor like Dr. Schoeneberger," said Michael as he got up from the table. "I've got to get back to the school for more ice hockey," he said, heading to the door with his skates slung over his shoulder, stick in hand.

"Make sure you get home in time for supper," Marty called out.

"I will!" Michael called back.

"Mom," Mark asked after he'd had a chance to tell her all about the courthouse visit, "can we get the 'L' braille volume so I can learn more about lawyers?"

"Sure, Mark," she said. "I'll do that tomorrow."

"I have to run over to the school right now," said Chuck. "I'll pick it up while I'm there."

"Thanks, Dad!" said Mark enthusiastically.

Mark was playing with Tregnor when his dad came home with the volume, but the dog was given short shrift when Chuck placed the encyclopedia in Mark's hands. "Here you are, Son," he said smiling. "Now you can learn all about being a lawyer."

Mark didn't waste any time getting started, but before his fingers read '**Lawyer**,' they read '**Law**,' and he began reading that article first. When he read what criminal law was about—arson, bribery, burglary, extortion, forgery, kidnapping, larceny, manslaughter, murder, perjury, rape and robbery, he got excited and wanted to read those articles as well. "Mom," he said, "I have a lot of reading to do! I'm going to be a lawyer just like Grandpa Kirkwood!"

"I think you'd be a fantastic lawyer," said Marty as she gave him a kiss on top of the head and headed into the kitchen where she found Chuck nosing around.

"Something smells great! What's for dinner, honey?" he asked as he hugged his wife.

"I made a hot dish with the leftover Christmas ham and some scalloped potatoes," she said.

"I can hardly wait!" he said as he breathed in the tantalizing aroma wafting through the kitchen. "I sure do love my wife," he said as he hugged her again.

"You love food!" she laughed. "Now scoot on out of here. You might want to take Tregnor for a short walk," she said. "Michael should be home soon."

When Chuck peeked into the living room, he saw Mark with his nose buried in the volume he'd brought home. Chuck smiled and quietly walked away. "It sure would be interesting," he thought, "if Mark actually ended up being a lawyer."

WHEN CHRISTMAS VACATION WAS FINISHED AND THE KIDS WERE back in school, Marty and Chuck began thinking about going back to school themselves, Chuck to finish his Master's thesis at St. Cloud Teachers College, and Marty to begin working toward a degree in Physical Therapy. Of course, this didn't intrigue the boys in the least. All their focus was concentrated on the shiny new bicycles in the garage.

"Dad, when can we ride the bikes Grandma Kirkwood gave us?" Michael asked at supper that night.

"It's only January, Michael," he said smiling. "We'll have to wait until the snow melts."

It didn't take long for the piles of white to disappear that year. Spring came early, and by April the snow was gone. Kids have long memories, and Michael was back to asking his dad about riding the bikes. "Well, I think you're right; it's time!" Chuck said one sunny Saturday during the second week of April. "Let's get them out and get started!"

Chuck began with Michael on his single bike to see how he would do before having the two boys try the tandem. "Okay, Michael," he said after Michael hopped on the saddle, eager to ride. "I'm going to run behind you and hold onto the seat. Once you're pedaling and I think you've got your balance, I'm going to let go and you'll be on your own. Sound good?"

"Okay, Dad!" he yelled eagerly. "Let's go!" Some of the older kids from the neighborhood gathered around Michael with their bicycles to witness his maiden voyage. They were pretty sure they knew what was going to happen.

"Here we go, Michael!" Chuck yelled as he began running down the street alongside his beaming son. All the kids cheered, and after a short distance, Chuck let go and yelled, "You're on your own now!" Michael pedaled like crazy, but wobbled back and forth, lost his balance and slid sideways to the pavement.

That didn't stop him! "I'm OK!" he yelled as he bounced up, walked his bike to the curb, pushed off on his own and was soon out of sight.

"Where in heaven's name did you pedal to, Michael?" Marty asked when he finally showed up at home around lunchtime, hot and sweaty and breathing heavily.

"I rode all around Perham!" he said excitedly. "It was so much fun! I got everywhere real fast!"

"You're quite a rider," said Marty. "Have a sandwich and then I want you to rest up a bit."

"We'll all go for a ride tomorrow," Chuck said. "You can try out the tandem with your brother."

After Sunday Mass, Michael ran up to Father Donnay. "Guess what, Father?" he blurted.

"What's that, Michael?" he said.

"I rode my new bike yesterday," he said excitedly, "and today Mark and I are going to try riding our new tandem bike for the first time!"

"Well, good for you, Michael," he said. "Be careful out there! How about you, Mark?" he asked. "Are you ready to go pedaling with your brother?"

"I think so," said Mark. "We've been practicing sitting on it and getting on and off in the garage. I think it will be fun out on the street."

Michael was in for a big surprise. He would learn in a hurry that maintaining balance on a non-moving tandem with a kickstand in the garage was quite different from pedaling down the road with a back-seat passenger. "Okay, Mark, you get on first while I hold the bike," Chuck said, "and then I'll have Michael get on. This is going to be a little tricky compared to riding alone, Michael, but once you get the hang of it, you'll be fine; just pay attention and don't go too fast. I'll push you down the street like I did yesterday, and when I let go, you and Mark will be on your own, okay?"

"Okay, Dad!" Michael said enthusiastically as he straddled the top bar and stood balancing the bike, eager to depart on the maiden voyage with his brother.

Chuck helped guide Mark onto his saddle, and as soon as he found the pedals, Chuck whispered into his ear, "Are you ready to try this, Mark?"

"Yeah, Dad!" he said confidently.

"OK, your turn, Michael," said Chuck as he held the bike.

Michael proudly positioned himself in the captain position and looked back at his brother. "Ready, Mark?" he asked.

"Ready back here!" said Mark.

"Okay, Dad!" said Michael excitedly. Chuck began pushing the tandem down the street and ran alongside as the neighborhood kids clapped and cheered. They moved slowly at first, then picked up a bit of speed. "Faster, Dad!" Mark yelled. "Go faster!"

"I've got it, Dad," yelled Michael. "You can let go!"

It looked like all was well, so Chuck gave a final gentle push. "Okay, boys, you're on your own!" he yelled. "Mom and I won't be far behind." By the time Marty and he got on their bikes, the twins were already a good distance ahead, and it took them awhile before they caught up.

After they'd circled the block around their home a few times, one of the neighborhood boys joined them and yelled, "Do you want to race?"

"Sure!" Michael yelled as he pushed down onto the pedals with gusto. "Pedal as hard as you can, Mark!" he yelled. "We'll beat Danny home!"

When they had to make a sharp right turn a block from their house, Chuck and Marty were close behind. That's when it happened! The twins were speeding around the corner neck and neck with Danny, their bikes only about three feet apart, when KABOOM! Marty saw the twins' bike leaning too far over as they entered the turn and she yelled out, "Michael, be careful!" It was too late. They avoided Danny, but crashed to the pavement with a sickening screeching and scraping of metal.

Chuck and Marty leapt from their bikes and ran to the twins. When Chuck saw bleeding from the back of Michael's head, he told Danny to pedal home a few houses down and have his mother call for an ambulance. Mark was crying quietly as he lay on the ground, but no sound was coming from Michael, not so much as a whimper, and his eyes were closed. "Michael!" Chuck yelled as his son lay unmoving in the middle of the street. "Michael!" he said again. "Can you hear me, Son?" There was no response, no movement.

By the time the ambulance arrived, Michael was still unresponsive. A small crowd had gathered, but Chuck and Marty hadn't moved him for fear of causing him more harm. Marty stared at the back of Michael's head and began crying when she saw his hair was soaked with blood. It took time for the EMT's to gently ease Michael onto a bodyboard and into the ambulance. Mark was able to stand, but only with help. His pants and shirt were torn and his left-side knee and elbow were skinned and bleeding lightly. His lip and mouth were bleeding, too, and he had knocked out his two front upper teeth! Between sobs he asked, "Is Michael going to be okay, Dad?"

"They'll take very good care of him at the hospital," said Chuck, trying to conceal his deep concern. We'll know more after we talk to the doctor."

"I'm worried about you, Mark," said Marty. "You're pretty banged up. We'll have the doctor take a look at you at the hospital just to make sure nothing's broken."

"I'm okay, Mom," he said. "Everything hurts a little, but I'm mostly just scared about Michael."

When they got to the hospital, Sister Giovanni met them in the Emergency Department waiting area. "Michael's being prepped in the Operating Room for possible surgery," she said. "Dr. Schoeneberger and Doctor Bertelson have been contacted, and they'll be here shortly. We'll know more after the examination and x-rays."

Dr. Schoeneberger was the first to arrive. He lived just two blocks from the hospital and happened to be home when he received the urgent call. He walked briskly through the entry into the Emergency Room and saw a tattered and toothless Mark standing next to his parents. "What happened to you and your brother, Mark?" he gently asked.

"We were racing Danny Sullivan to our house on our new tandem bicycle and we crashed when we were going around the corner," said Mark soberly.

"I'm sorry that happened," Dr. Schoeneberger said consolingly. "That must have been very scary. I'll have a look at you after I see Michael. Meanwhile, Sister Giovanni will take you into a room and get you cleaned up. She'll bandage up your knees and elbows while I'm examining your brother."

Sister Giovanni took Mark by the hand, and as she led him out of the operating room, she saw Dr. Bertelson entering through the front door. It didn't take long before he was standing alongside Dr. Schoeneberger as they took a look at the back of Michael's head. About a half inch of skin was torn in the form of a star, and they decided it would be best to just clean and bandage the wound, no suturing. They also decided to give Michael penicillin to ward off any possible infection. What to do beyond that was the question. "Under the circumstances, I think it's best we just keep a close watch and see how things go," Dr. Bertelson said. "We'll get the wound cleaned up, give him the shot of penicillin and go from there."

"Sounds like a good plan," said Dr. Schoeneberger.

A short time later, Sister Giovanni quietly entered the operating room with Mark and brought him to his parents at Michael's side. "We've just finished bandaging your brother's head, Mark," said Dr. Schoeneberger. "He's not awake yet. Let's have a look at you now," he said as he led Mark to an adjacent examining room. "How are you feeling?" he asked as he checked Mark over from head to toe.

"My knee and elbow sting a little," he said, "and my lip hurts and so does my mouth where my teeth fell out, but I'll be all right," he said calmly. "Is Michael going to be okay? Can we go back and see him now?"

"Let's do that," said Dr. Schoeneberger as he led Mark from the room and over to Michael's bedside. "Your brother's still not awake," he said. "We'll just keep him resting and see how he's doing in a little while."

"Can I touch him?" Mark asked.

"Certainly," said Dr. Bertelson. "You can talk to him as well if you'd like. Because he hit his head pretty hard, his eyes are closed and he's not moving, but he can still hear you and understand what you're saying."

Mark gently slipped his hands under and over one of Michael's and whispered, "I'm sorry you got hurt, Brother, but it will be all right.

I guess we shouldn't have raced with Danny Sullivan, but don't worry, he's okay and I'm okay. You'll be better soon and we can go fishing at Big Pine Lake."

As soon as the word fishing left Mark's mouth, something clicked and Michael's eyes slowly opened. He blinked upward at the bright operating room lights shining into his face. "Hi, Mark," he said feebly as everyone in the room breathed an audible sigh of relief and broke into big smiles.

"He just woke up, Mark!" Chuck whispered. "His eyes are open! He woke up when he heard your voice!"

"Brother," Mark said softly as he leaned in close to Michael, "I'm glad you woke up. We had a bad fall on the tandem and had to come to the hospital."

"I don't remember," said Michael quietly, "but my head hurts. Are you OK?" He stared at his brother and blinked several times as his eyes focused. "Your teeth are gone," he said.

"They got knocked out," said Mark. "Mom said new ones will fill in. Don't worry, I'm OK." Michael managed a small smile, then closed his eyes and was soon fast asleep.

Dr. Bertelson turned to Marty and Chuck and said, "We'd like to keep him in the hospital under close watch and see how things progress. If all goes well, we'll have him home in a day or two."

"It's a huge relief that he woke up, doctor," Chuck said.

"It sure is," said Marty, her eyes filling with tears. "Thank you both so much for coming so quickly to see him," she said as Dr. Schoeneberger warmly embraced her, "and thank you, too, for checking Mark over."

"Certainly," said Dr. Schoeneberger. "Mark's a bit beat up, but he'll be fine. He's a stoic little trooper."

"That he is," said Chuck. "Thank you both; we so appreciate it," said Chuck as he shook the doctors' hands.

That night after supper, the family said the Rosary together and prayed for Michael to have a speedy recovery. When Chuck and Marty peeked into the boys' bedroom on their way to bed, they heard Mark talking aloud..."Well, God, you know Michael. He likes to go fast. This time he went a little too fast around a corner. He likes to race and he didn't want Danny to beat us, but he did anyway because we never made it home. Please help Michael to get well soon. I love him a lot and I miss him."

Mark's prayer wasn't answered right away. Michael started having trouble breathing and his joints started swelling. He was kept in the hospital for a whole week and continued to receive penicillin shots to ward off infection. "Are either of you allergic to penicillin?" asked Dr. Schoeneberger when he saw Chuck and Marty at the hospital the next day.

"I am," Chuck said. "I had a head injury when I was playing ice hockey at St. John's, and my joints began swelling up after they gave me a shot."

"That's it then," said Dr. Schoeneberger. "Your son is likely allergic to penicillin as well. I'm going to discontinue it. We'll have him stay another day and monitor his symptoms. If he doesn't have any further problems, he can go home tomorrow."

Michael was much improved by the next morning and was released from the hospital. The family was thrilled to have him home, and the kids at school were happy to see him when he returned to the classroom. Mark had told the students the tandem-crash saga many times over, but they wanted to hear Michael's version. And then the teasing began for both boys. "You look like a beat-up boxer with that swollen lip, Mark," his friend said, "and you look like a Q-tip swab with that bandage on your head, Michael," he added, grinning widely. The twins took the kidding in stride. What else could they do?

The recovery and rehabilitation progressed smoothly as the weeks rolled by, and before long, school was out, summer fun kicked in, and the family was out riding their bikes together once again. Chuck finished a listening comprehension project as partial fulfillment for his M.A. in Secondary Education, and he anticipated spending most of the summer writing up the results so as to complete his degree by the following summer. "Chuck," Marty said one hot afternoon late in July after spending the afternoon typing up his manuscript in triplicate on their trusty old Olympia typewriter, "I think I'd like to go back to school."

This took him by surprise. Since being married, Marty had never mentioned wanting to go back to college. He knew she'd completed a year at the University of North Dakota. He also knew she'd quit college after her first year and taken a job in Minneapolis as a medical stenographer because she didn't have the money to continue with her schooling. What Chuck didn't know is Marty had recently been researching different careers and was particularly interested in working in the medical field. "Back to school! That's great!" he said. "Any idea what you might like to do?"

"Well," she said, "I know I want to do something to help people, and I think I'd especially like working in a rehab environment. I've been thinking a lot about Physical Therapy," she said enthusiastically.

"Honey," he said, "I think that would be perfect for you, patient and caring as you are! You'd be a wonderful physical therapist. Let's bring it up with the boys over dinner tonight and see what they think about their mom going back to school!"

Mark was the first to give his opinion. "I think it would be real good, Mom," he said. "If you were a physical therapist you'd be able to help people all the time."

"Yeah, Mom!" Michael chimed in. "It would be great! When I'm a doctor, you can come and help my patients!"

"Well, I've done some investigating," said Marty enthusiastically, "and have looked into Physical Therapy programs in our area. They do offer a four-year degree at St. Cloud Teachers College. It would lead to a Bachelor of Science degree in Physical Therapy, but it would also mean we'd all have to pull together because I'd be away from home a lot over the next three years."

"That'd be okay, Mom," Mark said. "We'd all be busy in school!"

By the time they'd finished supper, it seemed a decision had been reached. All the men in the family were very much in favor of the woman they loved pursuing her dream!

THE NEXT THREE YEARS WERE ACTION PACKED. THE ENTIRE FAMILY was involved in either educating others or getting an education for themselves. Michael and Mark had Mrs. Irene Winkler as their sixth-grade teacher and loved being in her class because they learned so much! The same was true in grades seven and eight when Mr. Jerome Engleson was their Social Studies and Science teacher and their dad was their English teacher! The twins complained about all the work they were given from Mr. Engleson and their dad, but that didn't faze either teacher. Both had graduated from St. John's University in 1952 and were used to working hard and expected their students to do the same.

Marty had been studying like crazy, too! She had always been a bright, responsible student, and having a physical therapy career goal made her efforts all the more meaningful, but that didn't mean it wasn't work! During her last year, she had an internship in order to gain practical experience, and had the opportunity to do that at St. James Hospital in Perham. The nuns greeted her with open arms, especially Sister Giovanni, who had assisted Dr. Schoeneberger when he delivered the twins. In June of 1966, Marty graduated with honors from St. Cloud State Teachers College with a Bachelor of Science degree in Physical Therapy. She was fortunate to start right in working, accepting a morning-shift position at St. James Hospital where she had done her internship.

Chuck had his Master of Arts degree in Secondary Education in hand and was happy to be enjoying the summer with his sons. Never a dull moment! They went fishing, they went biking, they went swimming and they went walking! Whenever she had free time, Marty helped Mark master the geography of the neighborhood and downtown. They walked the blocks again and again, Mark with his white cane and Tregnor walking alongside. After Mark memorized the lay of the land and had had several weeks of practice with his mom, Marty stayed behind one day while he and Tregnor ventured out on their own. Treg had become quite the dependable guide dog, until one day early in the morning on the Fourth of July.

"Mom, I'd like to take Treg for a short walk, just the two of us. Is that okay?" Mark asked.

"That's fine, Mark," she said. "Be careful. You know what happened last year when someone starting shooting off fireworks in the morning." Mark remembered all right. No one could find Treg until Chuck looked in the garage and found him in the washing machine, crouched on the cold, metal bottom, shivering and terrified.

"I will," Mark said as he went out the door with Treg, cane in one hand, leash in the other. It was a warm and sunny July morning, and everything was peaceful as they headed towards town, Mark moving his cane methodically on the concrete sidewalk. Treg had learned to slow down and stop at street corners until all was good to go, but this was the Fourth of July. Anything could happen, and it did! When they were downtown and nearing an intersection, some thoughtless idiot lit a cherry bomb and tossed it near them just to see what would happen! Treg went wild and jerked at the leash until he pulled Mark straight into an iron lamppost! Mark banged his forehead hard, and stood there for a few seconds, stunned and seeing stars. His cane had fallen to the ground and the leash had been pulled from his hand. Mark bent down slowly and began feeling around until he found his cane. "Treg!" he said. "Come here, Treg!" Unbeknownst to Mark, his dog was long gone. "Treg! Come!" Mark said again, feeling increasingly anxious. He tapped his cane around slowly until he found the curb, and then did an about-face and began retracing his route home. He hadn't gotten far when one of the friendly Perham townspeople stopped him and asked what had happened and was he okay.

"I bumped into a lamppost," he said.

"Well, I'm afraid your forehead's bleeding," the man said as he handed him a handkerchief. "Looks like a pretty good welt developing. You know me, Mark," he added. "I'm Ted Meinhover, football coach and History teacher at Perham High School."

"Oh, yes, Coach Meinhover!" said Mark, feeling greatly relieved. "Thank you for stopping to help me. Do you see my Welsh Corgi anywhere? Someone threw a cherry bomb near us and it scared him. I lost my hold on the leash and I think he ran away!"

"I don't see him," he said, "but he probably ran home. I'd like to accompany you there if you don't mind," he said, "just to make sure you're all right."

"Sure," said Mark, smiling. "I'd appreciate it a lot. I got a little dizzy after I hit the post."

"Happy to do it," he said. "That's what friends are for."

Mark and Coach Meinhover talked about football as they made their way down the street, and Mark told him his brother planned on going out for the team his freshman year. "I think he'd do real well, fast as he is and as much as he likes to rough it up," said Coach Meinhover.

"I think you're right," said Mark, smiling. "I can make it on my own from here," he said as they reached the sidewalk in front of the house. Thanks so much for walking me home!"

"It was my pleasure," he said. "Say hi to your mom and dad for me."

"I will," Mark called back as he made his way to the front door. "Thanks again, Coach!"

"My heavens! What happened to you?" Marty exclaimed as Mark came inside.

"Someone threw a firecracker near me when I was walking downtown," said Mark. "Treg got scared and pulled me into a lamppost; then he ran off. Is he here?"

"He showed up a few minutes before you," said Marty. "I knew something wasn't right. I was just about to go out looking for you."

"Coach Meinhover saw me and walked me home," he said.

"That was sure nice of him," she said as she began cleaning his forehead.

"He said to say hi to you and Dad. I like Coach Meinhover a lot. I hope I get him for one of my classes in the fall."

"I hope so, too," she said, "We'll see. Meanwhile, you have a nice long summer to enjoy. I'm happy to say this is just a small cut," she added as she cleaned the wound and put a bandaid in place. "Not as bad as it looked with all that blood, but you're going to have a pretty good bump for a few days. I want you to take it easy this afternoon."

By the next morning, Mark was ready for action. After breakfast the boys gathered their fishing gear, hopped on the tandem and peddled out of town toward Big Pine Lake. It wasn't far and was an enjoyable ride. When they arrived, Michael helped Mark position himself on the shore and then walked about twenty feet away so they wouldn't get their lines tangled. They both began casting out into the fresh lake water lapping up along the shoreline. After his third cast, Mark's rod doubled over and he yelled, "I think I've got a big one, Michael!"

"Keep playing him!" Michael yelled. "When you get him close in, I'll come and help you."

It took a while before the fish tired. When Mark felt it swishing near the shore, he attempted to reel it straight in, but it made a quick turn and his rod doubled up again. He let his line out and kept playing it. "I think I'm going to need your help landing this one!" he yelled. "I almost had it, but he took off again!"

"Okay, hang on, I'm coming!" Michael yelled as he set down his rod and reel and jogged over to his brother. Mark again had the fish near shore, and when Michael saw a huge Northern Pike swishing back and forth in the water, he whispered fervently, "Brother, just take it slow. You've got a giant fish! Pull your line tight and back up! When you get him on the ground, I'll hold him and attach the stringer!"

This was all well and good, but when the Northern was dragged onto the shore, it began flopping all over the place. There was no way Michael was going to slide a stringer near its needle-like teeth. This was a monster! It looked like it was about three feet long and weighed about 15 pounds! After several minutes, the Northern gasped for air and finally stopped moving about. "Got it!" said Michael as he slid the stringer behind the gills and through the mouth. "What a great catch, Mark!"

The boys kept at it the rest of the morning, but neither got another strike. You'd think that after catching one fish, there would be others soon to follow. At least that's what they were hoping, but that was not to be the case on this day. They finally tired of their fruitless casting and reeling and decided they'd had enough. It was time for lunch and they were hungry! The only question was how they were going to get the big fish home. It was too heavy to hold and steer the tandem at the same time, so Michael decided to tie the stringer to the back of Mark's saddle. Not totally satisfactory with the tail of the fish dragging on the ground, but it sure garnered a lot of smiles and comments as the boys pedaled through town. A big grin filled Mark's face as well when he heard a man yell, "Whoa! Who caught that whopper?"

"I did!" Mark yelled as he sat straight and proud and they pedaled on.

Chuck was working in the yard and could hear the boys happily yelling from a long block away. When they rolled up to the front of the house, he understood why. "Wow! That's a beauty!" he said.

"I caught it, Dad!" said Mark gleefully, "and Michael got the stringer on it. It sure did put up a fight!"

"Neither of us had another strike all morning," Michael said as they got off the tandem, "so we called it quits."

"Well, you boys did real well," said their beaming dad. "I bet you're hungry after all that. Go get ready for lunch and I'll take the fish out back."

After they ate and Mark entertained a delighted Marty with his dramatic reenactment of the mighty catch, she shooed the boys outside to help their dad with the Northern. He had the fish laid out on a long, flat board and was getting ready to cut off its head when Michael yelled, "Dad! Wait a minute!" Then he ran back into the house and came racing out carrying the 'F' volume of *World Book*. "I want to see if I can identify the stuff inside him, Dad!" he said excitedly.

"Okay, here we go!" said Chuck as he cut off the head.

Michael picked it apart and examined it closely. "I think I see the brain, Dad!" he said. When Chuck slit open the belly, Michael was able to find the spinal cord, heart, esophagus, liver, stomach, intestines, kidneys and anus. "Wow!" said Michael. "A fish has just about everything we do!"

"You missed a part," Chuck said. "See that baggy thing right below the backbone?

"Yes, I see it," he said. "What is it?"

"What does the encyclopedia say?" he asked.

Michael found a section that talked about special organs and read aloud: "*Most bony fish have a swim bladder below the backbone. The bag-like organ is also called an air bladder. In most fish, the swim bladder provides buoyancy, which enables the fish to remain at a particular depth in the water. In lungfish and a few other fish, the swim bladder serves as an air-breathing lung. Still other fish, including many catfish, use their swim bladders to produce sounds as well as to provide buoyancy. Some species communicate by means of such sounds.*

A fish would sink to the bottom if it did not have a way of keeping buoyant. Most fish gain buoyancy by inflating their swim bladder with gases produced by their blood. Water pressure increases with depth, and as a fish swims deeper, the increased water pressure makes its swim bladder smaller and thus reduces the buoyancy of the fish. The amount of gas in the bladder must be increased so that the bladder remains large enough to maintain buoyancy. The nervous system of a fish automatically regulates the amount of gas in the bladder so that it is kept properly filled. Sharks and rays do not have a swim bladder. To maintain buoyancy, these fish must swim constantly. When they rest, they stop swimming and sink to the bottom. Many bottom-dwelling fish also lack a swim bladder."

"That's too technical for me!" Mark said as Michael finished.

"I think it's amazing," said Michael.

"I just want to eat the fish!" laughed Mark. He got up and made his way back into the house. He found Treg snuggled up in the corner of the sofa. He sat down next to him and began petting him and telling him all about the fish he caught. Treg was the best of listeners, so Mark kept talking, telling him what he thought high school was going to be like. "I'm taking Speech from Mrs. Pederson and am going to join the Debate Club since I want to be a lawyer," he said. Treg just lay there and took it all in. He was getting along in age, and although he didn't hear Mark say any of his favorite words such as 'go for a walk' or 'time for dinner,' he loved the attention.

Marty fried up a fish dinner fit for a king! The platter of aromatic Northern was prepared a crispy golden brown, just the way they liked it, accompanied by hash browns and garden-fresh steamed green beans. "This is as good as it gets!" said Chuck.

After supper the twins started talking about their future plans. "I can give you an aptitude test which might help you zero in on some career choices," said Chuck.

"Dad, I already know I want to be a doctor, a surgeon who operates on people and makes them better!" said Michael.

"Not me," Mark said. "I've wanted to be a lawyer ever since we went to the courthouse in Fergus Falls."

"It just amazes me how you two already know what you want to do," Marty said. "I don't think I ever thought of being a physical therapist until I'd worked as a medical stenographer for several years."

"Well, you boys definitely have your mother's brains," Chuck said. "I have no doubt you'll accomplish whatever you set out to do."

That evening after they were in bed, Chuck and Marty began talking about how much it might cost if the twins were serious about pursuing the career goals they'd mentioned. "With both of us working I think we could swing it," Chuck said, "but it's going to be expensive, especially with them entering college at the same time."

"Maybe they'll get scholarships," she said. "If not, we'll be eating a lot of fish from Big Pine Lake!" laughed Marty.

"That's fine with me!" said Chuck as he leaned over and kissed his wife tenderly.

"Who knows how it will all turn out? Time will tell," she murmured as they snuggled up and Chuck turned off the light.

———◆◆◆———

AND TIME DID TELL! BY THE TIME THEY WERE SENIORS, THE TWINS were carrying 'A' averages and the Perham High School administration was in a quandary about their choice for valedictorian and salutatorian. To simplify matters, they made the twins co-valedictorians, and let them decide for themselves how to divvy up the responsibilities.

It was a beautiful June day. The sun was shining down on more than one hundred graduates-to-be, all seated on folding chairs on the football field. Facing the students were rows of relatives and friends, all there to celebrate the moment when their loved ones would be declared bona fide graduates of Perham High School. After the band performed a rousing welcome and a few requisite introductions were given, Mark rose slowly and cane-tapped his way across the wooden floor to the podium. *"Good afternoon, ladies and gentlemen,"* he said. *"It's wonderful to have all of you here to recognize and celebrate the Perham High School graduating class of 1970. My name, for those of you who don't know me, is Mark Dowdle, and it's my pleasure this afternoon to say a few words, along with my twin brother, Michael, in honor of this momentous occasion."* A hush fell over the audience as Mark stood silent for a few seconds before beginning his address:

"Parents, teachers, friends and classmates. The time has come to say farewell, and I say to my fellow students and graduates-to-be, shoot for the moon! We've certainly been living during extraordinary times, have we not? Who would have thought that in 1968 the Apollo 8 astronauts would be flying ten orbits around the moon, that in 1969 the Apollo 11, with 12 astronauts, would be landing on the moon! They collected samples, took photographs and set up experiments, all from 239,000 miles away! It may be that none of us end up on a flight to the moon, but we have plenty-enough excitement ahead of us. The world is ours to explore, lives of continued learning and adventure are ours to go after! We all have reason to be inspired by the anticipation of what lies ahead! The loud response I just heard told me you agree!"

Mark paused for a moment as the crowd quieted, and then continued. *"Did you know that although the moon is the brightest object in the night sky, it doesn't give off any light of its own? It's only reflecting light from the sun. That's how I see us as we leave here and embark on our new paths. We are reflectors of light. We've gone through many phases of life since starting our schooling, and we've been fortunate to have our parents, teachers and friends encourage and support us along the way. Now it's our turn to stand proud, help ourselves and prepare to help others. My brother, Michael, and I intend to do just that when we enter St. John's University at Collegeville in the fall. Michael will be studying to be a medical doctor and I'll be studying law. It doesn't matter what career you choose as long as you're happy doing it. Whatever your work, make sure you feel passionate about it, because it will be a major chapter in your life. I'd like to close by reciting the beginning of one of my favorite stories from the Bible. It's about a man who was born blind, and Jesus helped him see: And as he was passing by, he saw a man blind from birth. And his disciples asked him, "Rabbi, who has sinned, this man or his parents, that he should be born blind?" Jesus answered, "Neither has this man sinned, nor his parents, but the works of God were to be made manifest to him. I must do the works of him who sent me while it is day; night is coming when no one can work. As long as I am in the world, I am the light of the world."*

A smile filled Mark's face. *"So, there you have it, my friends,"* he said enthusiastically. *"Shoot for the moon! Reflect your bright light wherever you go! Thank you for the love and kindness you've shown me over the years. I will never forget you or the inspiring and supportive teachers who were an integral part of my high school experience. Lastly, I'm especially grateful for my parents and brother, Michael. They are my eyes, my heart, and truly the bright lights of my life."* The audience was hushed, all eyes on Mark, and he could feel the emotional magnitude of this day and the moment welling up in him. He dropped his head and paused to compose himself for a few seconds. *"I'll turn the microphone over to Michael now so he can share a few words of wisdom,"* he said as he looked up.

The audience cheered and applauded as Mark finished. The applause continued as Michael approached him and they exchanged a warm embrace before Michael put an arm around his brother's shoulder and guided him back to his seat.

"*I don't know about wisdom, but thank you for your kind words, Mark,*" said Michael as he stood at the podium. "*And thank you for sharing your words of wisdom with all of us. Over the past 17 years I've learned so much from you about kindness, tolerance, respect, generosity…the list goes on. Needless to say, I feel exceedingly blessed to have you as my brother. To you, Mark, to my parents, my teachers, classmates and friends here today, whatever wisdom I may have is thanks to all of you. Each of you in your own way has helped me to be successful throughout this high school journey, and, like my brother, I couldn't have done it without your love and support. I'm sure all of my fellow seniors sitting out there feel the same way about their teachers, friends and families, filled with gratitude for those who've impacted their schooling and lives in such a positive way. It's difficult to say goodbye, but this chapter now ends and it's time to turn the page and start writing the next one! We did it! Time to spread our wings and fly!*"

Michael stood smiling as the students cheered and applauded, and then continued: "*What it all means is that we're going to be making some serious choices for our futures, including decisions about college and careers. Mark and I are lucky, as it was pretty easy for us to narrow down the options. I knew from a young age that I wanted to be a medical doctor and Mark long ago decided he was interested in becoming a lawyer. Choosing a college was pretty easy as well, as I'll be proudly attending St. John's University, our dad's alma mater.*" Michael zeroed in on his dad's beaming thumb's-up reaction in the audience and gave him a smile and wink before continuing: "*Some of you may find it challenging to choose a path. That's okay! It's okay to be uncertain! Yesterday you were a high school student and today you'll be a high school graduate! Take some time to kindle your passions and discover what it is that most speaks to your heart. Never give up, no matter how difficult the road ahead may be. All that matters is that you feel good about what you're doing or what you're studying, and that you take it on with determination and courage and 100% effort. If you do that, everything will fall into place and you will succeed.*"

Michael paused as he gazed out at the rows of smiling faces. "*My friends,*" he continued, "*I know I began by telling you I don't know about wisdom, but when I remember the inspiration of my grandmother, I'm reminded I carry with me her sage words: When a job is once begun, be the labor great or small, never leave it 'til it's done, do it well or not at all. My grandmother's words have as much truth for us today as they did for her many decades ago, true and simple words of wisdom. And so, I bid you farewell, my friends!"* said Michael enthusiastically. *"May your futures be filled with peace and happiness! Now let's get on with this show and graduate!"* he finished as the audience applauded exuberantly.

The principal handed out the diplomas, the band played, mortarboards sailed high into the air and the Perham High School class of 1970 was officially set free!

That night at supper as the family held hands to pray, Chuck squeezed his sons' hands and said, "Lord, thank you for letting our sons live! Thank you for guiding them and helping them to be successful in their education. And thank you for letting us be a part of their lives. We praise you, Lord, and ask that you remain a vital part of their lives as they continue with their schooling. Amen."

THE BOYS HAD EARNED SCHOLARSHIPS TO ST. JOHN'S UNIVERSITY and would soon be beginning what would become an exciting new phase of their life journey. Over the rest of the summer, they shared many a fishing day with their dad at Big Pine Lake and had a lot of time to sit and talk about their upcoming college adventure.

"Don't expect it to be easy," Chuck said seriously, "because it won't be. I worked my butt off at St. John's just to survive! You two are receiving scholarships, so even more will be expected from you."

"You worry too much, Dad," Michael said. "We'll be fine."

"Yeah, Dad, take it easy," Mark said as he cast out his line. "We're your brilliant offspring, remember?"

"Okay, okay," laughed Chuck. "That you are! I'm just glad I'm not you, Michael. All those science classes!"

"That's the best part, Dad!" said Michael. "Biology and chemistry? I can hardly wait! That's why I'm taking pre-med, why I'm going to be a doctor!"

"And no doubt a very good one," beamed Chuck.

They had a lucky day at the lake, and as a result enjoyed yet another delicious fish dinner. "Mom, we may be able to catch them," Michael said as he speared a golden-brown piece of walleyed pike with his fork, "but you sure know how to fry 'em up!"

"Nice of you to say so," she said. "Thank you, Michael."

"Yeah, Mom," Mark said. "We're really going to miss your cooking. And we're really going to miss you and Dad."

"It will be way too quiet around here," she said. "I know you'll do just fine away at college, and I'm so excited for both of you, but we sure will miss you two. By the way," she added, "I've been thinking about your upcoming birthday. Have you two thought about how you'd like to celebrate your 17th?"

"I know what I'd like," Mark said. "I'd like you to take a day off from cooking and we all go out to dinner."

"Great idea!" Chuck said enthusiastically.

"I'm sure not going to argue," laughed Marty.

"Sounds good to me!" said Michael. "And what's our favorite Perham restaurant?"

"Stoll's!" everyone shouted out in unison.

You'd think everyone would have been too stuffed to even think about dessert after downing a hearty Stoll's meal of roast beef, mashed potatoes and gravy, steamed beans and fresh-baked rolls, but they weren't! When they got home, Marty brought out not just one, but two birthday cakes!

"Wow, Marty!" said Chuck gleefully.

"Wow, Mom!" Michael said. "You didn't exactly take the day off! Two cakes! I'll describe them to you, Mark," he said. "One is our favorite double-layer devil's food cake covered with swirls of rich chocolate frosting and the other is a huge angel food cake covered with creamy light-blue frosting. And they each have seventeen candles blazing away!"

"I'll have a slab of each!" roared Chuck.

"Gee, Mom," Mark said, "thanks so much. I really appreciate it. I love you!"

Tears welled up in Marty's eyes. "I love you, too, Mark, and I love you, too, Michael," she said as she gave them each a big hug.

"Hey, what about me?" laughed Chuck as he got up and hugged Marty, then his sons. "I love you all," he said, "very much!"

Michael got up and went over to Mark, gave him a smacking kiss on top of the head. "Love you, Brother!" he said.

"Ditto," said Mark smiling. "Happy Birthday, Brother!"

"This night is turning into a real love-fest," laughed Chuck.

"I'm going to miss you boys so much," said Marty. "I knew the day would come when you'd be heading off to college, but I'll never be ready to say goodbye."

"OK, OK, enough talk," said Chuck. "Make your wishes and blow out the candles, boys, before these cakes go up in flames!"

With Michael's help, Mark moved toward the angel food cake, his face close enough that he could feel the heat from the burning candles, and with one big breath he blew them all out.

"Wow!" Chuck said. "Every last one! Go ahead, Michael, try and match that!" A smiling Michael positioned himself in front of the devil's food cake, took a long breath in, held it a second and let loose, extinguishing all seventeen candles.

"Good going, Michael!" said Chuck.

"I say let's serve these cakes up!" said Mark.

After eating their fill, the family gathered in the living room to say the Rosary and give thanks for the seventeen wonderful years they'd been blessed to be with one another. "Where's Treg?" asked Mark. "He's been around almost as long as we have and should be in here celebrating with us!"

"I'll call him," said Chuck. He let the screen door slam on his way out, and when he didn't see Treg heading towards him or lying in his favorite spot under the elm tree, he called out, "Treg! Come here, boy!" No dog ran from around the side of the house as sometimes happened. No dog barked in response to Chuck's beckoning. No sign whatsoever. Chuck looked in Treg's doghouse, thinking maybe he'd gone in there earlier to keep cool and had fallen asleep. After all, he was getting older and frequently napped; as a matter of fact, he was soon going to be seventeen, same as the twins, though that translated to 94 in human years! Chuck called again, and when Treg didn't appear, he began to panic a little. Treg couldn't get out of the backyard, as it was fenced all the way around. Could he have slipped out of the garage and no one noticed? Chuck walked around the side of the house, wondering if Treg had climbed the wooden steps to the above-ground pool, tried to drink and fallen in. He'd done that once before a few years back, had lost his balance and fallen in, but fortunately the family was there to pull him out.

Sadly, as Chuck would soon find out, this time he would not be so lucky. When Chuck peeked over the side of the pool, his heart sank to its lowest low. There was Treg, floating on top of the water. His rust-colored little body was motionless and bloated. He had obviously fallen in and drowned. Chuck was stunned and overwhelmed with sadness! He pulled Treg from the pool and held him for several minutes before wrapping him in a dry towel he pulled from the clothesline.

"Where's Treg?" asked Michael when Chuck walked back into the living room.

Marty could tell by the look on her husband's face that something was terribly wrong. "What is it, Chuck?" she said quietly, her heart pounding.

Mark could feel the heaviness in the room. "What's wrong, Dad?" he asked. "Is something wrong with Treg?"

Chuck sat down on the couch, his eyes welling up with tears. "I'm very sad to tell you that Treg is no longer with us," he said, his voice choked with emotion. "He fell into the pool and drowned."

"No!" yelled Michael as he jumped up and ran outside, Marty close behind.

"I'm sorry, Dad," said Mark, tears streaming down his face. "I'm sorry you had to find him like that."

"I'm sorry for you, too, Mark," he said. "I know Treg held a mighty place in all of our hearts, but especially yours."

"I can't imagine life without him," he said quietly.

"We'll bury him tomorrow," said Chuck when everyone was gathered back together in the living room. More tears were shed as the family shared their favorite Treg memories and began to talk about what happens to animals after they die.

"I think they have an afterlife," said Michael. "After all, God created them, too."

"I think you're right," said Marty. "And Treg will likely have quite a frisky one."

"He was such a good dog," said Mark with a sigh.

"That he was," said Chuck as he dropped his head, "that he was."

They finished the Rosary together and headed off to bed early, everyone emotionally spent from the exhaustive mix of birthday celebration and loss of their beloved Treg.

NEAR THE END OF AUGUST, WHEN THE TWINS WERE GETTING READY to leave home for St. John's, Michael was looking over the courses they'd be taking. "I'm going to love this, Mark," he said gleefully. "I'll be taking General Chemistry with labs, General Biology with labs, Organic Chemistry with labs, Physics, Biochemistry, Calculus...

"More fun than Disneyland," laughed Mark. "I'm with Dad. You can have every bit of that stuff! I prefer my courses in the Social Sciences and Humanities. Plus I'll have courses like Speech and Debate, participating in mock trials. I bet you'd like that, knowing how much you like to argue," he kidded.

"You know," Michael said, "I think we're both going to love what we're studying. Good thing since we're going to have to get good grades to keep our scholarships. Here's to us!" He slapped his brother on the back and bellowed, "Here's to the Dowdle twins! May they cruise through their courses at St. John's with straight A's!"

"I'll drink to that!" Mark said as he downed a swig of water from the glass he was holding.

The Saturday before they left for St. John's, Michael heard a knock on the door, and when he opened it, he was surprised to be greeted by Tom Schmitz, the Perham Ford dealer and Chuck's fellow Johnnie. "Tell your mom and dad their new car is sitting outside," he said enthusiastically.

"New car?" said Michael.

"Didn't they tell you?" said Tom. "They're giving you two boys the old car to take to St. John's and they bought a new one for themselves. There she sits!" he said as he pointed at the shiny silver sedan at the curb.

"Wow, that's great news for all of us!" said Michael.

"Well, I guess the cat came flying out of that bag!" laughed Chuck as he came to the door.

"I'm afraid it did, Charlie," he said. "I'm sorry about that. I thought the boys knew."

"That's okay," Chuck said. "We were getting ready to tell them. Now is as good a time as any."

Mark joined his brother and dad at the door to find out what was going on. When he heard Michael and he were going to take the old car to St. John's, he was overjoyed.

"Wow! What a great surprise! Thanks, Dad!" Mark said.

"Yeah, thanks, Dad!" gushed Michael as Chuck handed him the keys. He put his arm around his brother and said, "Now we're *really* going to have fun at college, Mark!"

When they drove off for school the next week, the joy of their wheels quickly turned sour. They hadn't gotten more than fifteen miles out of Perham when Mark felt a bump. "What was that?" he said worriedly.

"What was what?" said Michael as he drove down the highway unconcerned.

"Don't you feel it?" Mark asked. "Something's going on with the car. In the front, my side. I'd stop and check it out."

"I think you're worried about nothing," said Michael, "but I'll take a look just to make sure." He pulled over, got out of the car and let out a loud groan. "Damn! We've got a flat!" he yelled.

Fortunately, Chuck had shown Michael how to fix a flat tire the day before they left, just in case something like this happened. Michael knew what to do, but it meant unloading their college stuff to unbury the spare tire. It took some time and a little doing, but Michael moved quickly, and within an hour they were ready to roll. "Well," a sweaty Michael said as he hopped back into the driver's seat and eased the station wagon onto the highway, "no more tires to spare; hopefully that won't happen again!"

The miles rolled by, and they soon found themselves driving off the main highway and onto the blacktop road leading into St. John's University. "I can't believe we're actually at college!" gushed Mark.

On the way in, Michael described the beautiful scenery and buildings to his brother and told him they'd soon be settled in their dorm and sitting down for their first Johnnie meal. "I'm looking forward to that," Mark said. "I sure hope the food's good. I'm hungry!"

After unpacking and moving into their room in St. Mary's Hall, they heard bells ringing. "I know what that means," said Mark. "Supper in fifteen minutes!"

"This is pretty exciting," said Michael as they headed to the refectory. He tried to take it all in as he described the scene to his brother, students coming from all directions, black-robed monks and brothers filing down the path to the dining hall, freshmen looking lost in an exhilarated sort of way.

When they arrived, they soon discovered it was nothing like home. Rows of students were seated on benches at long rectangular tables. The monks were also seated at those tables. On the tabletop were plates, silverware, napkins, salt & pepper, thick slices of heavy dark "Johnnie Bread" and large bowls of peanut butter. "No butter," Michael whispered to Mark, "just peanut butter! I think they're expecting us to spread that on the bread!"

"Are you kidding me?" Mark said as everyone grew silent and a priest began praying: *Heavenly Father, bless us as we embark on a new school year, and bless this food which has been gracefully prepared for us by the sisters. We pray, Lord, that the freshmen students will make a smooth adjustment to their new living arrangements and college life and that they and all the students and faculty have an enriching and successful school year. Amen.*

It didn't take long to learn who the "other" students were. They were the first ones to go after the plates of Johnnie Bread and peanut butter. Michael was lucky to nab slices for himself and Mark before it was gone. "Not quite like home," he whispered to his brother. He eyed the rest of the supper being served, smoked liver sausage, sauerkraut and boiled potatoes. "I don't know if you're going to like the meal, Mark," he said as he described it to him, "but give it a try."

Over the next several days they adjusted to the food, and they liked the fact that their dorm was on the first floor of St. Mary's Hall. Mark had some difficulty at first making his way from class to class, but thanks to help from fellow Johnnies, he soon conquered the maze of pathways to his classrooms and began feeling right at home. Michael had it easy, spending the majority of his time in one science building.

The most enjoyable adjustment for the twins occurred near the end of September when all the freshmen were invited to a dance at St. Benedict's University, a Catholic women's school located just a few miles away in St. Joseph. The dance started at nine, and a caravan of Johnnie buses pulled up in front of St. John's at eight-thirty sharp to transport about three hundred eager freshmen to St. Ben's. The dance was held in the festively-decorated gym, where orange, yellow, brown and green foliage lined the walls and orange and black lanterns hung from the ceiling, creating an innocent, but seductive feel. "This is very interesting, Mark," Michael said as they slowly walked arm-in-arm around the dance floor. He was describing it to his brother when he stopped abruptly, causing Mark to stumble and almost fall. "What's going on?" said Mark. "I just about made a total fool of myself!"

"Sorry!" whispered Michael furtively. "I'm looking at the two-most-beautiful girls ever! Blond hair, gorgeous smiles, both wearing pink angora sweaters. They're about twenty feet from us, talking to each other. I think they're identical twins!"

"Well, don't just stand there, Michael! What are you waiting for?" said Mark, laughing. "Let's get them out on the dance floor before a couple of studs beat us to it!"

"Hi!" said Michael as he and Mark approached the girls. "Would you two care to dance?"

"Sure, we'd love to!" they said with easy smiles.

"You must be twins, the way you replied in perfect unison!" said Mark.

"Uh...we are. Pretty easy to tell, don't you think?" laughed one of the girls.

"Not so easy for him," said Michael grinning. "This is my twin brother, Mark, and he's blind. I'm Michael."

"Oh, I'm so sorry!" she said. "It's hard to tell anything in this dark gym. "I'm Linda, Linda Johnson, and this is my sister, Laurie.

"How crazy is this?" laughed Laurie. "Two sets of identical twins!"

"Michael's the energetic genius," said Mark, grinning. "He's taking pre-med and plans on being a surgeon."

"And Mark's the brilliant analytic," said Michael, smiling, his arm around his brother, "calm and confident. He's pre-law."

"How about you two?" asked Mark.

"You won't believe this," Linda said, "but I'm pre-law as well. We may be having some courses together because I understand St. John's and St. Ben's share classes on occasion. Laurie's studying to be a nurse."

"Wow, a nurse and a lawyer. That's great," said Mark.

"Where are you two from?" asked Michael.

"Coon Rapids, north of Minneapolis," Laurie said.

"We know where that is," Mark said. "We have cousins who live in Columbia Heights. Michael and I are from Perham."

As fate would have it, the next two songs were slow numbers. Linda and Mark moved gently and easily around the floor as if they'd danced together for years. "Would you like to sit this one out and have something to drink?" asked Mark when a fast tune came up.

"Sure, I'd love to," Linda said. The warmth in her voice melted Mark's heart. "Laurie and I chose St. Ben's because our mother went here," she said after they were seated at a table in a quiet corner. "Why did you and Michael choose St. John's?

"Our dad graduated from St. John's in 1952," he said, "and both Michael and I were lucky enough to get scholarships, so it was a pretty easy decision. So far, we love it, and being here at the dance meeting girls like you and your sister, well, that's a dream come true!" said Mark, grinning from ear to ear. "I hope we'll be able to see more of each other."

"I'd love that, Mark," she said, "and I think it's safe to say Laurie would as well. Let me just tell you she and Michael are looking pretty happy out on the dance floor!" she laughed.

After a few more songs there was a break in the music, and Laurie and Michael joined Linda and Mark at their table. "What are you two doing way back here?" Michael asked as Laurie and he sat down.

"The music was too fast for my two left feet," laughed Mark, "plus this breather has given us a chance to find out more about each other."

The four of them chatted through another couple of songs. "There's a nice slow one, Laurie!" said Michael. "Would you like to go back out?"

"You don't have to ask me twice!" laughed Laurie. "Let's go!"

"They seem to be genuinely enjoying each other," Linda said. "Would you like to try again with this slower song?"

"Sure," said Mark as they stood up and Linda linked her arm through his.

The evening rolled by as the happy duos danced away the hours, and the time to leave came way too soon. Michael couldn't conceal his excitement on the bus ride back to St. John's. "Brother!" he whispered emphatically, "I think I'm in love!"

Mark smiled and whispered quietly, "Well, you're not the only one! Love at first sight! And I couldn't even see Linda! But I sure could sense something special!"

"Those girls really got to us!" laughed Michael.

"I know," said Mark smiling. "My heart felt like it was leaping out of my chest! I can hardly wait to see Linda again!"

"I know what you mean. I already miss Laurie," laughed Michael as the bus rolled into St. John's.

That was all well and good, but this was college, and there was serious studying to be done and subject matter to be mastered. And, of course, letters to be written home.

September 30, 1970

Dear Mom and Dad,

I've just gotten back to my room after a night out and am sitting down to write this braille letter to you because something wonderful happened tonight! Michael and I went to a dance at St. Ben's and it seems we fell instantly in love with twin co-eds from Coon Rapids! I'm not kidding! The girls' names are Laurie and Linda Johnson. Michael couldn't stop talking about Laurie on the bus ride back to St. John's and I can't stop thinking about Linda. She's a pre-law student just like me! We'll probably have some courses together because Bennies and Johnnies share some of their classes. How sweet that would be!

Well, it's past midnight and I have a day of studying tomorrow, so I'd best be getting to bed. I just wanted to share our good news. I hope all's well back home!

—Love, Mark

When Monday morning arrived, reality set in and the twins began attacking their studies in earnest. That didn't mean they were thinking any less about Laurie and Linda, but they knew they had to maintain a 'B' or better average in all of their subjects to retain their scholarships, and that meant only one thing, work! Before the week ended, a letter arrived from their dad, and they were eager to hear what he had to say.

October 6, 1970

Dear Michael and Mark,

Your mom and I got a good chuckle out of Mark's letter, him telling us that the two of you were madly in love after meeting the twin Bennies at a dance. Well, all I can say is one never knows! You both seem to be adjusting well to life at St. John's and that's great. I still remember some of the many excellent professors I had. Rev. Boniface Axtman O.S.B. and Rev. Alexius Portz O.S.B. for Philosophy. I'd always come in late for Bonnie's class on Monday morning after taking the bus back from visiting Marty in Minneapolis over the weekend. Father Boniface would greet me with, "Well, Mr. Dowdle, it's nice of you to be with us this morning." Embarrassing, but worth it to be able to see her. Another professor I remember well was Rev. Arno Gustin O.S.B. I couldn't figure out what to write for a research paper in an Education class, and he suggested I define a liberal education. Believe me, that got me thinking. I remember writing how a liberal education is one most in accord with one's nature.

That was the thing about St. John's. It got me thinking more than any time in my life, and it sure was a joy. I had Rev. Bernardo Martinez, O.S.B. for Economics, and I loved the subject. I worked my tail off mastering the material. Father Bernardo was a great teacher and a truly nice person. The summer your mom and I lived in Minneapolis after we got married, before my senior year at St. John's, he paid us a visit. He was attending the University of Minnesota and was at a Minneapolis parish. He and I even went and played tennis against a couple of other guys. He was a much better player than I!

It was a long time ago, 1952, but I sometimes wonder if any of the men I remember are still teaching: Dr. J. Arthur Farley in Education, Mr. Stephen Humphrey, English, Mr. John Hiller, Physical Education, Mr. Emerson Hynes, Social Science. I took a Bible class from Rev. Gerald McMahan O.S.B. and a speech class from Rev. Dominic Keller O.S.B. Had to get up on the stage and give a prepared speech for the final. I was scared as hell! So many fond memories of my time at St. John's. I just wanted to share a few names in case you cross paths with any who are still there. They keep coming back to me: Rev. Lancelot Atsch O.S.B. for a 'Marriage & the Family' course, Mr. Francis Schoffman for Geology, Rev. Vincent

'Smiling Jack' Tegeder O.S.B. for History, Rev. Jeremy Murphy O.S.B. for Political Science. OK, enough of that, right?

I shouldn't be telling you boys this, but let's just say I didn't do too well in school before I was admitted to St. John's. I have Rev. Martin Schirber, O.S.B., to thank for my turnaround. When he admitted me, he changed my life, and I'll be forever grateful.

Enough of this reminiscing. If you ever meet any of the professors I've mentioned, please give them my best! Mom sends her love!

—Love, Dad

October 9, 1970

Dear Mom and Dad,

Mark said he doesn't have any of the professors Dad listed in his letter to us, nor do I. I'll say this, Dad, for going back eighteen years, you sure remember a lot of them. One you didn't mention is Rev. Matthew Kiess O.S.B. who was here during your time and is still here teaching Chemistry. He's a fixture in the chemistry lab, also leads the Chemistry Club, which I joined. Mark joined the Debate Club, obviously more in line with his pre-law courses. I'm going back over to St. Ben's with him next week for moral support, as his Debate Club will be debating the women of St. Ben's, and Mark's one of the debaters! Of course, I'm hoping to run into Laurie Johnson while I'm there and Mark the same with Linda!

That's the news for now. It's back to studying for me!

—Love, Michael

Well, Michael certainly got his wish regarding crossing paths with Laurie at the St. Ben's debates. There she was, sitting right across from him in the auditorium. And to his amazement and unbeknownst to Mark, there was Linda, sitting up on the stage directly across from his brother. She was going to be debating Mark! The audience grew silent as a neatly-dressed, middle-aged woman approached the microphone near the front of the stage. *"Good afternoon, ladies and gentlemen,"* she said in a clear and friendly voice. *"My name is Sister Mary Elizabeth Collins and I'm the Dean at St. Benedict's University. I'd like to extend a special welcome to the debaters from St. John's University. All of us are in for an exciting program this afternoon. As I'm sure you're aware, earlier this year the United States Supreme Court began hearing a case concerning the rights of women to have abortions. This case began after a Texas waitress who called herself 'Jane Roe' challenged a Texas law that made abortion a criminal offense. Roe had been denied an abortion under the law and sued Dallas County District Attorney Henry Wade. With this topic presently being debated nationally by citizens of our country, it seemed only natural that we include it as one of our debate topics today. We'll begin with the affirmative speaker, Linda Johnson."*

Mark could barely conceal his shock at hearing the introduction of his competitor, none other than his new love! Linda rose calmly from her chair and walked confidently to the microphone. *"Ladies and gentlemen, and my respected opponent,"* she began as Mark's face fell, *"I stand before you today to prove that every woman should have the right to have an abortion in the United States. First let us consider a woman's right to privacy. What could be more private to a woman than a fetus growing within her? Should the government be telling women what they can or cannot do with their own bodies? I should say not! Where does it end? Next they'll be telling women what they can or cannot do in their own bedrooms. Sounds crazy, but it could happen. It would be ridiculous and it would be wrong, just as is the thought of the government having control over choices a woman makes regarding her own body. That's a dictatorship, not a democracy!"*

Mark's face grew grim. He was listening intently and couldn't believe what he was hearing coming from the lips of the one with whom he was smitten!

"Have you ever researched women's rights in our country?" Linda continued. *"Did you know it wasn't until 1920 that the United States adopted the 19th Amendment to the Constitution, granting American women the right to vote? Did you know in the early 1900's the distribution of birth control information was illegal in the United States? Did you know that during World War II several million American women took factory production jobs to aid the war effort? When they were needed to help win the war, they sure were given the right to do the work of men. But after the war, these same women were encouraged to become full-time housewives.*

Perhaps you're wondering what all this has to do with abortion. Well, it has everything to do with abortion, because what women are asking for is the right to be treated as equals, not just when our country is threatened, but always.

"In 1963," she continued, "*the Equal Pay Act came to be, which required equal pay for men and women doing the same work. In 1964, Title VII of the Civil Rights Act prohibited job discrimination on the basis of sex as well as color, race, national origin and religion. And now it's 1970, and are you telling me that the United States government should have the right to tell me what I should or shouldn't do with my body? Absolutely not!*"

Linda paused and looked out solemnly over the audience for several seconds before continuing. "*What all of this boils down to, ladies and gentlemen, is not simply the invasion of a woman's privacy or the curtailing of her rights as a citizen of this country; it's the removal of freedom, the freedom of a woman to choose when and if she should give birth to a child. If this freedom is taken from her, she is no longer living in the 'land of the free.'*"

As Linda turned away from the microphone and headed back to her seat, Sister Mary Elizabeth Collins rose and walked toward Mark to help guide him to the microphone. "Our next speaker is Mr. Mark Dowdle from St. John's University," she said, "and Mark will be taking the negative position."

Mark stood motionless at the podium for a few moments, staring straight ahead, and then, in acknowledgement to Linda, he nodded in her direction before turning back to the audience. After hearing Linda's eloquent speech, he knew he was in for a fight, a real verbal battle, and he was ready to give it to her. "*Ladies and gentlemen,*" he said slowly and seriously, "*Miss Johnson has given us quite a history lesson today. I was happy to hear her closing remarks about choice, which is what I'd like to speak about this afternoon, freedom of choice, freedom to choose life or death for an unborn child.*

"*As I listened to Miss Johnson attempting to make her case for abortion, I was thinking about the precious gift of life. I'd like to begin my remarks by reviewing for you the beginnings of that life and its early development. Once pregnancy begins, the embryo develops rapidly. Within two months, all the tissues and organs of the body have begun to form. The central nervous system, which consists of the brain and spinal cord, starts to develop in the third week of pregnancy. The eyes and ears begin to develop in the fourth week. The structures of the mouth, such as the lips and palate, begin to form between the fourth and fifth weeks of pregnancy. The arms and legs appear as buds of tissue during the fifth week of pregnancy. After that, the fetus increases rapidly in size until the mother gives birth to her child, the same child whose potential termination of vibrant life is strongly supported by Miss Johnson's pro-abortion stance."*

Mark could feel the rapt attention of the audience as he continued. *"Does this mean there is never justification for terminating a pregnancy? No. In my opinion there are exceptions, such as when a woman is traumatically impregnated due to rape or when the mother is in danger of losing her life due to medical complications. The Roman Catholic Church teaches that a doctor should attempt to save both the life of the mother and the unborn child, but if this becomes impossible, I believe the mother's life becomes the priority. During abortion discussions, the question of when life begins often arises. I don't believe there's any question whatsoever. A male delivers sperm to a female's egg, a remarkable moment of fertilization occurs, and thus begins the miraculous journey of human development."*

It was difficult for Mark to gauge the audience reaction, Linda's as well for that matter, but he could definitely feel the tense silence in the room as he stopped speaking and turned toward Sister Mary Elizabeth. She quickly rose and guided him back to his seat before approaching the microphone. "Those are the affirmative statements from each debater, ladies and gentlemen. We'll take a 15-minute break before moving on to the rebuttals."

Linda would be up first. She sat in her seat, her head down and concentrated on her notes, flipping through pages and scribbling like crazy. Mark just sat quietly and seemed to be gazing contentedly into space without concern. When the break ended, Sister Mary Elizabeth once again approached the microphone. "Thank you once again, ladies and gentlemen, for being with us this afternoon. I told you it would be an exciting program and these two do not disappoint! It's now time for the rebuttals, and starting off is Linda Johnson."

"First," said Linda as she turned and smiled at Mark, *"I'd like to thank Mr. Dowdle for helping to make my point when he said he supported abortion in particular instances, believing it to be an appropriate procedure when a woman's life was at risk or she had been impregnated against her will. There are other times as well. I'd like to focus on just one of those since my opponent made such an effort to give us a textbook version on when life begins and how it develops. Thank you, Mr. Dowdle, for that lesson, but unfortunately you failed to distinguish between human life and personhood. Personhood implies both the capacity for self-conscious thought and acceptance as a member of a social community. Can a fetus do that? Fetuses are not persons, and they're not entitled to the rights normally given to persons. Birth represents the beginning of personhood, Mr. Dowdle, and therefore abortion should be legal from conception until birth."*

With that, Linda turned and walked briskly to her seat. Mark waited for her to continue speaking, but hearing nothing, he realized she was finished. She'd ended her rebuttal in the same abrupt manner he'd ended his affirmative speech, and it took him by surprise. Mark slowly rose from his chair as Sister Mary Elizabeth once again approached him and led him to the microphone.

"Well," he said, *"this is proving to be a very interesting afternoon."* One could hear whispers and quiet chuckling ripple through the college audience as he continued. *"Miss Johnson began today by making a plea for a woman's privacy, rights, equality and freedom. I've prepared mentally to address each of those terms, but now she's introduced a new term, 'personhood,' so I'll begin with that. Miss Johnson stated that personhood implies both the capacity for self-conscious thought and acceptance as a member of a social community. She went on to say fetuses are not persons and are therefore not entitled to the rights normally given to persons. Birth represents the beginning of personhood according to my opponent, and therefore, she reasoned, abortion should be legal from conception until birth."*

Mark paused and turned for a few seconds in Linda's direction. *"I hope I've accurately summed up your statements, Miss Johnson,"* he continued, *"because what you've said strikes me as quite illogical. First of all, I don't believe you have the right to tell anyone who is and isn't a person? God took charge of that when he created us. He created men and women and gave us the capacity to create other men and women. These other men and women didn't suddenly begin thinking as soon as they were born. It was a gradual process that began when a mother became impregnated and carried her child for nine months, then bore the child and began nurturing that child. In my opinion it's an insult to motherhood, Miss Johnson, to say that because a fetus hasn't been born that it doesn't qualify for personhood. That fact that a living, growing, developing fetus has the capacity for future life outside the womb is clearly enough to qualify it for personhood.*

"Now let's move onto some of Miss Johnson's other arguments," he continued. *"First, let's consider her plea for privacy. I'll be the first to agree that what's happening in a woman's body during pregnancy is very private. She's experiencing a symbiotic relationship with a fetus that's growing inside her, and what business is that of the government? I'll tell you what business it is of the government! When these two beings, mother and fetus, have entered into a mutually-beneficial relationship to produce life, then the government has the responsibility to protect that life, not help to destroy it! Does not our Constitution guarantee us the right to life, liberty and the pursuit of happiness?*

"Notice, Miss Johnson, that I said 'right to life' because I believe a fetus has rights, too. It's a living organism unable to speak for itself, thus the mother has the responsibility to speak on its behalf, and if she's unwilling, then the government has to step in and protect the rights of the unborn child. You folks will recall Miss Johnson spoke to the unfairness of women enduring far too many years of unequal rights compared to their male counterparts, and I certainly agree with that, but political, economic and social rights don't fall in the same category as biological rights. If one isn't given the right to live, then every other right becomes irrelevant, not even debatable if one doesn't exist to experience and enjoy them!

"In closing," Mark said as he gazed out towards the hushed audience, *"the mother's right to choose life, not death, for herself and her unborn child, that's a magnificent gift of freedom that comes with being a privileged citizen of this country, and I'm filled with appreciation and gratitude on behalf of every miraculous life in the making."*

Mark turned towards where Sister Mary Elizabeth Collins was sitting, signaling that he was finished, but just as she rose, Linda stood quickly from her chair and went to Mark at the podium. She put her hand on his shoulder and then did something rarely seen, if ever, at a debate. She leaned her head near his cheek and kissed him! Mark could feel his face burning as the college audience began hooting and whistling their approval. "Your show of concession?" he whispered to Linda as he grinned from ear to ear.

"Well," said a smiling Sister Mary Elizabeth as she reached the podium alongside the duo, "I told you this was going to be an exciting afternoon! In just a few minutes we'll have the judges' results and then we'll proceed with the next debate."

Linda linked her arm through Mark's as they exited the stage together and she escorted him down the three short steps. "I hope you understand this was just a debate, Mark, and that I actually agree with your side. You did great!" she whispered.

"Thanks, Linda," he said quietly as they took their seats, side by side, in the audience. "You were pretty impressive yourself!" Laurie and Michael had found one another and were sitting together as well.

The crowd hushed as Sister Mary Elizabeth approached the microphone. "Ladies and gentleman," she said, "our three judges have decided on a winner. Their decision is 2-1 in favor of Miss Johnson." Soft murmurings could be heard throughout the audience followed by short applause. "We'll now proceed with our next debate," said Sister Mary Elizabeth as the next two students took their places on the stage.

It was close to dinnertime at the conclusion of the afternoon's final debate and Sister Mary Elizabeth addressed the audience once again. "It was certainly a pleasure for all of us to hear these debaters in action," she said, "and I hope we'll have an opportunity to do it again in the near future. This completes the debates for today, and before you leave, I'd like to announce that the Saint John's University Debate Team and any other Johnnies in attendance are welcome to have dinner with us in the dining hall a half hour from now."

Michael nudged his brother and said, "Let's stay for dinner, Mark. Laurie told me the food is really good!"

Mark didn't need any encouragement. His mind was on the kiss Laurie had given him right after he'd finished his final remarks of their debate. As the foursome left the auditorium and headed toward the dining room, Linda took hold of Mark's hand. "I hope I didn't embarrass you when I kissed you," she said. "I was just so proud of you and I had the urge to do it, so I did!"

"I'm glad you did," he said as they walked onward. "At first I thought it was Sister Mary Elizabeth kissing me and I wondered what the heck was going on! When I realized it was you, I knew everything was right with the world, debate or no debate."

"That's so sweet," said Linda.

"And I realized another thing, too," said Mark.

"What's that?" she asked.

"That there *is* such a thing as love at first sight…or non-sight in this case," he said smiling. "I think I'm falling in love with you!"

Linda squeezed his hand and said nothing as they entered the dining hall. Many students were already seated at the large round tables. "It sure is different from St. John's, Mark," Michael said to his brother. "The tables are covered with white tablecloths and have place settings with shiny silverware and cloth napkins. Feels like a schnazzy restaurant!"

"You girls are treated like queens here!" said Mark.

"Of course!" laughed Laurie and Linda in unison.

After they were seated, Sister Mary Elizabeth and several other "Bennie" coeds joined them at their table. Everyone grew silent as Sister Mary Elizabeth stood and tinkled her glass with her knife. "Dear Lord," she began to pray, "thank you for blessing us with the many gifts we've been able to enjoy today and for the beautiful meal we now have the privilege of sharing with the visiting students from St. John's. In your name. Amen."

A bevy of Bennies came streaming from the kitchen carrying large white porcelain bowls brimming with mashed potatoes and green beans, followed by more coeds carrying platters piled high with steaming layers of sliced roast beef. "Let the feast begin!" said a jovial Sister Mary Elizabeth. "I sure hope you boys like roast beef!"

"So happens it's one of our favorite meals!" said Mark. "We used to have it quite often at home on Sundays. Our dad loves it and our mom is an exceptional cook!"

"Well, we probably can't compete with Mom's home-cooked version, but I'm glad it's a meal you enjoy!" she said. "I'll stop talking now and let you young people eat and visit."

A Bennie freshman sitting across from Linda smiled and asked, "Did you and Laurie know Michael and Mark before you came to St.

Benedict's? I noticed you leaving the debate together and you seemed like longtime close friends."

"Well, longtime, no," said Linda laughing. "but we did latch onto these two at the dance we hosted for the Johnnies in September."

"And we were happy to be latched onto!" Mark said enthusiastically as Michael laughed.

After everyone was finished eating the main meal and the empty dishes were removed, the servers again emerged from the kitchen, this time pushing rolling carts filled with dessert plates containing generous slices of pie topped with hefty scoops of vanilla ice cream. Michael nudged Mark and said, "Cherry pie and ice cream!"

"Did I somehow arrive in heaven?" asked Mark as everyone laughed.

When it came time to leave, the two couples stood outside waiting for the bus. It had grown dark, and the cool October air breezed against their faces.

"Linda," Mark whispered as he pulled her close to his side, "I'd like to return that kiss you gave me. I have the urge, just like you did!" he said smiling. Linda drew her face close to his, and their warm lips softly pressed together. Then a contagion set in. Michael and Laurie embraced and looked into each other's eyes, Laurie then closing hers as Michael gently kissed her.

"Darn, there's the bus," laughed Michael as it rounded the corner. Everyone said their good-byes and the twins were soon headed back to Saint John's.

"How long have you and your brother known those two gals?" asked a fellow Johnnie sitting across the aisle from Michael. "A bunch of us couldn't help but notice what good friends you are," he said with a wink.

"We met them at the September dance at St. Benedict's," Michael said.

"Good for you!" he laughed. "You two are a couple of fast workers."

"Twice as fast," said Michael smiling.

During the rest of the ride back to the university, everyone was content to sit quietly. Who wouldn't be after a hearty meal like that!

"Well, Mark," Michael said when they got off the bus and began walking in the dark towards Mary's Hall, "What do you think?"

"I think," he answered, "that I'm in love!"

Michael playfully nudged his brother. "Are you kidding?" he asked.

"Not at all!" Mark answered. "I think Linda is the girl for me!"

"Funny thing is," said Michael, "I feel the same way about Laurie."

------◆-◆-◆------

MICHAEL AND MARK WERE KEPT BUSY WITH THEIR STUDIES DURING the rest of October and November, as were Linda and Laurie. When December arrived and the twins learned St. John's would be hosting an all-class, pre-Christmas dance before vacation, they grew very excited.

"It's a by-invitation-only event!" said Mark. "Perfect opportunity to get together with Linda and Laurie before we head home for Christmas!"

"Couldn't be better timing!" Michael responded enthusiastically. "If it's all right with you, I'll call Laurie and ask if she and Linda would do us the honor of being our dates."

"Please do!" Mark said eagerly. "I can hardly wait!"

A light snow was falling the night of the dance, bright stars twinkling against an ebony sky and a full moon lighting the way as Michael and Mark left St. Benedict's with the girls and drove the short distance on the highway and onto the road through the woods to St. John's. "This is beautiful!" said Laurie.

"I'm so excited, Mark!" gushed Linda. "This is the first time I've seen your campus."

"I never have!" said Mark smiling, causing Michael and girls to break out in laughter. "I think you're going to like being here," he added. "Michael and I sure do."

The dance was held in the gym, cozily lit and festively decorated for Christmas. A large tableau of the Holy Family filled one corner and aromatic evergreens laced with golden lights were positioned strategically among tables lining the edges of the gym floor. "I love this, Mark!" Linda said as she reached for his hand. "I love the smell of those pine trees!"

All Mark heard was the word 'love' among the words Linda had just spoken, and that was all the encouragement he needed. They'd barely found a table and chairs when the band began playing "White Christmas," a holiday favorite.

"Aha! A nice slow number!" laughed Michael.

"Would you ladies like to dance?" asked Mark.

"Of course!" replied Linda and Laurie in unison as the two couples found their way to the dance floor. They moved slowly and sweetly, Linda resting her head on Mark's shoulder as he held her close, Laurie and Michael gazing into each other's eyes.

"Thank you for inviting us to the dance, Michael," whispered Laurie. "This is far more thrilling than studying!"

"I hope so," laughed Michael. "We jumped at the chance to invite you two. You can probably tell we're smitten!"

Laurie could feel herself blushing and was grateful for the darkened gym; Michael could feel the effect of his words as the band played on and she melted warmly into his arms.

On the drive back to St. Ben's, Michael and Mark both sensed that Laurie and Linda were very happy with the way the evening had unfolded. When they reached St. Ben's, the brothers walked the girls to their dormitory, embraced them, kissed them goodnight and headed on their way.

"Brother," Michael said when they were back in the car, "we're in trouble!"

"I'll say!" said Mark. "Double trouble!"

When they went home for Christmas vacation, they had a lot to tell their parents, but it wasn't so much about how their studies were going as it was about the special twin romance in their lives. Mark continued where he'd left off in his October letter, exuberantly expressing how Michael and he had without a doubt fallen in love with the Johnson twins, Michael enthusiastically confirming his every word.

"Well, boys, it won't be the first time a fellow has fallen hard for a beautiful female," laughed their dad. "Just look at your mom and me!"

When the boys arrived back at St. John's after Christmas vacation, their minds were still on the Johnson girls, but it was time to get serious about finals. That meant putting in a lot of extra hours studying. That they did and it paid off. They both received straight A's in their first semester classes, and they were two proud Johnnies! After the second semester began, time seemed to move at a slower pace, and when the snow melted in April and pink blossoms appeared on the trees in May, the boys experienced spring fever like never before, not to mention the fact that their male hormones were running rampant!

"We'd love to!" said Mark enthusiastically over the phone to Linda when she asked if Michael and he would like to visit Laurie and her at their parents' house over the summer.

"You don't have to ask me twice!" said Michael when Mark mentioned it to him.

What the boys didn't know is that they were going to be put to work as soon as they got home, and that the work was going to last the entire summer. While they'd been away at college, Marty had started working full time at St. James Hospital and Chuck had begun selling *World Book* to libraries, schools and parents in a wider geographical area, including the small towns around Perham and even some of the larger ones like Detroit Lakes, Fergus Falls and Wadena.

The summer proved to be quite a learning experience for Mark and Michael. They'd drive to one of the small towns such as New York Mills with their dad and begin knocking on doors, handing out cards and giving *World Book* sales demonstrations. At first Chuck did pretty much all of the talking, and gradually the twins added to his spiel by explaining just how useful *World Book* had been for them throughout their lives. Mark brought the braille 'A' volume along and clinched many a sale as he wowed prospective buyers with his advanced reading skills. Before the summer was over, the boys were knocking on doors by themselves and surprising Chuck with their many sales.

After celebrating their eighteenth birthday on August 9th, 1971, the twins asked their parents if they could take some time off to drive to Minneapolis to visit with the Johnson girls. "This must be getting serious!" said Marty as she smiled at her two beaming sons.

"It is serious, Mom!" Mark said. "Linda is a lot like you. She's bright and loving, soft-spoken and so compassionate. I just can't get enough of her!"

"And I can't stop thinking about Laurie!" said Michael. "A beautiful person through and through. I love that girl!"

"Well," Chuck said, "how would you feel about your mother and me driving down with you? We've been talking about visiting Aunt Pearl and Uncle Bill in Columbia Heights before school starts. We could all stay with them, and you two could have a good visit with your cousins at the same time."

"That would be great! We haven't seen our cousins in a long time," said Michael

"Patty, Linda, Terri, Connie, Mike!" rattled off Mark. "I'd love to catch up with all of them. Let's do it!"

Patty was nineteen and in her second year at the University of Minnesota, studying to be a teacher. Linda was seventeen and had just graduated from Columbia Heights High School. Terri was fifteen and had just completed tenth grade at the same school. Connie and little Mike were eight and five, respectively. The cousins always had a good time whenever they got together, as did the two sets of parents. Pearl and Marty got along like sisters, and Bill and Chuck had an especially-close relationship as brothers, just like Mark and Michael.

"Would it be okay if I called Linda and found out when would be a good couple of days for us to be there? Mark asked.

"Sure," Marty said, "just let us know and we'll call Pearl and Bill and let them know when we plan to be in town."

When Mark called and talked with Linda, she sounded thrilled to hear his voice again. After learning Mark's parents would be coming along to visit relatives in Columbia Heights, Linda mentioned it to her mother that evening, and she was quick to suggest a group gathering. "Why don't you invite them all over for Sunday dinner," she said enthusiastically, "the boys, their parents and the relatives! We can do it the last weekend of the month if that works for everyone." Walter Johnson was a contractor who built many homes in Coon Rapids, including a large home for his own family, one that could easily accommodate all the visiting Dowdles for a shared meal.

Linda called Mark the next morning to tell him about the proposed plan, Chuck called his brother, Bill, who talked to Pearl, and it was settled, everyone would be there. Perfect timing! One last precious week of fun and relaxation before fall classes started up for all the kids, including the Johnson girls at St. Benedict's and Mark and Michael at St. John's. Everyone was looking forward to the time together, especially dinner at the Johnson's. It was bound to be an entertaining Sunday meal with fifteen people of all ages from three families, including two sets of smitten twins!

The next couple of weeks rolled by and it was soon the end of August, time for Marty and Chuck and the boys to head to Minneapolis. The twins were giddy with anticipation, as they hadn't seen their girlfriends all summer. That was only part of the excitement, however. At ten o'clock in the morning, Chuck's friend from St. John's and Perham automobile dealer, Tom Schmitz, slowly drove up in a brand-new, four-door silver sedan. He parked in front of the house and just sat there.

"That's Tom Schmitz," said Michael as he glanced curiously out the kitchen window. "Looks like he came to show you some fancy new wheels, Dad."

"Why don't you run out and ask him what's up," said Chuck. "I'll be right there."

As Michael walked towards the shiny 1971 Ford, Tom got out and dangled the keys in his hand. "How do you like her?" he asked.

"That's one good-looking car," Michael said. "Is it yours?"

"No," said Tom smiling, "recent purchase by your mom and dad."

"You're kidding!" Michael laughed. "Why would they do that when they already have one just like it?"

"Because this baby belongs to you and Mark!" said Tom, grinning from ear to ear. "They bought it for the two of you since your station wagon's getting so old."

Michael couldn't believe his ears. He turned and ran towards the house just as his mom and dad and Mark opened the front door and stepped onto the porch.

"Well? What do you think?" asked Chuck.

"I can't believe it!" yelled Michael. "Mark, it's ours! A brand-new silver sedan!

"What?" said a stunned Mark. "Dad, Mom, why…"

"Questions later, Mark!" shouted Michael. "C'mon, check it out! Thank you, Dad! Thank-you, Mom!" they both yelled out as they rushed hand in hand down the walk to the car.

Mark moved his hands slowly along the outside of the warm metallic side before feeling for the handle and opening the front passenger door. "It smells wonderfully new," he said as he guided himself onto the seat.

Michael ran around to the driver's side and jumped in next to his brother. "Is this for real?" asked Mark incredulously as he ran his hands along the smooth dashboard.

"It sure is," gushed Michael. "I still can't believe it!"

"So generous of Mom and Dad," said Mark, shaking his head in disbelief. He paused and said, "I wonder if they'll let us drive it to Minneapolis."

"Let's find out," Michael said as he got out and walked to the house with his brother.

A beaming Marty and Chuck were standing on the porch, chatting with Tom Schmitz. "How do you like your new car?" asked Marty.

"We love it! Thank you! Thank you!" said the twins in unison as they hugged their parents.

"It sure will make for a sweet drive to St. John's compared to the old wagon," said Michael.

"And Linda and Laurie will think we're hot stuff!" said Mark smiling.

"Speaking of impressing our girlfriends, do you think we could drive it to Minneapolis today?" asked Michael.

"Of course," said Chuck. "That's the reason we wanted it delivered this morning. We'll hit the road as soon as we finish packing up."

They bid farewell to Tom and were soon gliding along Highway 78 in the shiny new sedan, a broadly-grinning Michael at the wheel. As was their custom whenever they traveled, the family said the Rosary together and then talked about this and that as the miles flew by. It seemed like no time at all before they pulled up in front of Bill and Pearl's house in Columbia Heights. Five year-old Michael was the first to see them. "Dad! They're here!" he yelled from the window.

Bill and Pearl came out to meet them at the curb, and after all the prerequisite hugs and kisses had taken place, Bill said, "I thought you bought a new car last year, Charlie."

"We did," he said.

"This baby is ours, Uncle Bill!" Michael blurted as Mark and he stepped out of the car. "Dad and Mom bought it for us so we wouldn't have to drive the old wreck anymore!"

"Wow! You're some pretty lucky guys," said Aunt Pearl.

"That we are," said Mark smiling

After greeting their cousins and learning the new car belonged to Michael and Mark, Bill's eldest daughter, Patty, put her arm around her dad and said, "Hey, Dad, doesn't this give you an idea for your great kids?"

Bill smiled and said, "We'll see."

As the clan headed for the house, the men opened the trunk and toted in the luggage. "All the girls sleep upstairs," Bill said. "Mike's been sleeping in the guest room downstairs, but while you're here, he'll sleep upstairs with his sisters so you and Marty can have the guest room."

"Can Mark and I sleep down in the basement again, Uncle Bill?" asked Michael.

"You don't have a choice; that's the only place left!" laughed Bill. Sleeping in the basement didn't bother Michael or Mark one bit. As a matter of fact, they preferred it for a number of reasons. It was cooler than the rest of the house, and there was a big tiled shower and a king-sized bed! Bill had finished off the basement with paneling and carpeted floors, so it was just like sleeping in any other room of the house, only better because it was private and quiet. The only drawback was one had to climb up and down the stairs to get to the main floor, but there was a railing, so no problem for Mark.

While everyone got settled in the living room, Marty went to the kitchen to visit with Pearl and help with dinner. "Sure smells good in here, Pearl," she said warmly as she slipped on her apron.

"Must be the ham!" she said. "I also made some potato salad and baked beans, nothing fancy. Does that sound okay, Marty?"

"It sounds delicious!" she said.

"Oh...and I baked a cake," she said smiling. "I hope the boys like chocolate!"

"Like is an understatement," laughed Marty. "I don't think there's any dessert they don't love, especially if chocolate's involved!"

Pearl beamed and said, "Well, they should be pretty happy then."

"What have you been doing with yourself all summer, Charlie," asked Bill as they sat together in the living room with the twins and their cousins. "Must be making some big bucks by the looks of that shiny new set of wheels out there!"

"We've been making a little," he laughed. "I'll let my salesmen tell you about that."

"Michael and I have worked all summer, Uncle Bill," Mark said. "Dad put us to work selling *World Book Encyclopedia* door-to-door as soon as we got home from college. It's been a good experience, not always easy, but definitely interesting."

"And now Dad's a regional manager for the company," added Michael.

"Well, that's a feather in your cap, Charlie. Congratulations!" Bill said.

"Thanks," Chuck said. "I sure am proud of Mark and Michael. They've done a great job, didn't get in as much fishing as they would have liked, but they made a little money and learned a lot about selling."

"And a lot about people," added Mark.

"The people learning is important and definitely valuable," Bill said, "regardless of what you both may go on to do in life."

"Well, with plans to be a doctor and a lawyer, they'll get to know a lot about people!" said Chuck. "How about you, Patty?" he asked. "How are things going at the University of Minnesota?"

"I love it!" she said. "I just finished my second year, so I haven't done any practice teaching yet. That will be coming up soon, and I'm really looking forward to it."

"That's great, Patty," Chuck said. "It'll be neat having another teacher in the family, and I know you'll be a good one."

"I hope so," she said.

"Come and set the table," Pearl called, and Patty, Linda, Terri and Connie immediately hopped up and headed to the kitchen.

"Those girls are really on the ball!" said Chuck.

"They just want to eat!" Bill laughed. "Let's go sit down."

Bill and Pearl put extra leaves in the table so it would seat eleven people, and once everyone found their place there wasn't an inch to spare! Before Bill began saying grace, Chuck said, "I didn't tell you this yet, but seeing all of us crowded around this table made me think of it. We're all invited to dinner this Sunday at Mark and Michael's girlfriends' house in Coon Rapids. Their parents want everyone to come!"

"If everybody goes, there will be fifteen people," said Michael. "Should be interesting!"

"Definitely not boring," laughed Mark.

"Okay, we'll talk more about it after dinner," Bill said. Everyone made the sign of the cross and began saying, "Bless us, O Lord, for these Thy gifts, which we are about to receive, from Thy bounty and goodness, through Christ, our Lord. Amen."

"The ham looks delicious, Aunt Pearl," Michael said as he served his brother a couple of slices.

"Smells so good!" said Mark.

"Don't hold back!" said Pearl. "The potato salad is the girls' favorite recipe."

"So, Charlie, tell us more about the two gals who are sweet on your boys," Bill said smiling.

"Suffice it to say, our sons have fallen for them, as well. They're two St. Benedict's coeds who live in Coon Rapids," Chuck said, "Laurie and Linda Johnson, and believe it or not, they're identical twins! Marty and I have never met them, but the boys are clearly smitten, so I guess it's about time we do! Their parents are Walter and Grace. Walter's a building contractor, and he's building houses in Coon Rapids."

"Identical twin girlfriends! Way to go, boys!" laughed Bill as everyone cheered and Mark and Michael beamed.

"It's so nice of their parents to include all of us in the invitation," said Pearl. "That's quite a crowd to feed!"

"I say let's accept," said Bill as everyone voiced their agreement. "It will be fun!"

While they were eating, Patty, Linda and Terri came at the twins with a barrage of questions. "Where did you meet them?" asked Patty.

"And what do they look like?" asked Linda.

"When are you getting married?" asked Terri. "A double-ring ceremony!" she said as everyone laughed.

"Hold on, hold on," said a smiling Mark. "Hang onto those questions and we'll tell all when everybody's together next Sunday."

After dinner, the girls talked nonstop while they shared the clean-up duties. "I can't wait to meet the twin girlfriends," Terri said as she wiped the dishes. "I wonder what they look like."

"Probably adorable as can be," Patty said. "You know Michael. He goes for cute!"

"It sure must be interesting for Mark," Linda said. "His first serious girlfriend and he's never actually seen her!

"It probably makes them that much closer," said Patty.

"And Mark's girlfriend shares your name, Linda!" said Terri. "I can hardly wait until Sunday!"

"I'm ready for dessert!" said Bill after the girls finished up in the kitchen and joined the group in the living room.

"I hear you boys like chocolate cake," said Pearl. "Is that true?" Her question was quickly answered as Mark and Michael flashed appreciative smiles her way.

"Do we ever, Aunt Pearl!" said Michael. "I'm stuffed after that dinner, but there's always room for chocolate cake."

"I agree!" said Mark enthusiastically. "Bring it on!"

They all chatted over dessert and discussed plans for the rest of the week. It was decided that the three older girls would shop to their hearts' content with Pearl and Marty on Thursday and Friday, and Bill, Chuck, Mark and Michael would take turns entertaining Connie and young Michael for the two days. Saturday they'd all go to the lake for swimming and a picnic. That left Sunday for a leisurely breakfast, morning Mass, a couple of hours to relax and get ready for dinner with the Johnsons in Coon Rapids.

Pearl, Marty and the girls were out the door just after nine o'clock on Thursday morning, excited about hitting the stores in downtown Minneapolis as soon they opened at ten. "I don't get this thing about women and shopping," said Bill as he and Chuck enjoyed their morning coffee. "It's not how I'd choose to spend a day off, that's for sure. They love it! The question is why?"

"I'm with you," laughed Chuck. "I hate shopping!"

"We'll probably never figure it out," said Bill, "but I do know one thing, it's time for breakfast! What would you like?"

"I'll have whatever you're having," he said.

"Okay. Ham & eggs with wheat toast and homemade jam coming right up. Sound good?" asked Bill.

"Perfect!" said Chuck.

"Well, Charlie," Bill said as he began frying the eggs with slices of savory ham left over from last night's dinner, "what should we do today?"

"I wouldn't mind if we visited a couple of the old Minneapolis haunts if that's all right with you," said Chuck.

"Sure. What did you have in mind?" he said.

"Oh, places like the Nordic Hotel, St. Olaf's, Gamble-Robinson and the Minneapolis Recreation Hall," he said. Chuck always seemed to want to go back to those places to see how they'd changed. In the summer of 1945, the summer World War II ended, he had roomed with his brother in the Nordic Hotel. It was catty corner from St. Olaf's Catholic Church, and both buildings were smack dab in the center of the city, only a couple of blocks from one of the main drags, Hennepin Avenue. Chuck had worked at Gamble-Robinson, a fruit and vegetable warehouse, and he played pool at the Minneapolis Recreation Center in the late afternoons and evenings. He got paid fifty cents an hour for being a "houseman," a guy who filled in whenever they needed a fourth player at a table. The convenient thing about living at the Nordic Hotel that summer was that he was able to walk to both work and church. Just a streetcar-ride away were Lake Calhoun and Lake Nokomis, two places he loved to swim after a sweaty day of warehouse work. How sweet it was!

It wasn't long before Bill and Chuck were done with breakfast and headed out for a fun-filled day of driving around Minneapolis and reminiscing about the old haunts, leaving Connie and young Michael to be entertained by their two uncles. The day passed quickly for everyone, and Bill and Chuck no sooner arrived home from sightseeing than the gaggle of gals pulled up from their day of shopping. There was chatter and ravenous appetites all the way around, and the gang was soon gathered around the table for a repeat of yesterday's dinner: ham, potato salad, rolls, chocolate cake and ice cream. As far as Michael and Mark were concerned, it didn't get any better than this!

The next morning the girls were up early and re-energized for another day of shopping. They all seemed just as excited to be doing it again, regardless of whether it was a repeat of the day before. "There are some stores we just didn't have time for," explained Pearl.

"Oh no! That's terrible!" said Bill kiddingly.

"I can't imagine!" said Chuck, both men finding themselves to be quite amused.

Michael and Mark were ready for some action of a different kind, and Connie, their eight year-old cousin, was up for that. "Let's go fishing!" she said excitedly after they'd finished breakfast. She'd uttered the golden words, words that both big Michael and little Michael were grateful to hear. "Yeah!" they yelled in unison.

"I say we head to Turtle Lake," said Mark as everyone voiced their approval. The summer months had passed quickly, not nearly enough free time for leisurely fishing days at the lake, and it was an excited group of six that was headed out the door by ten o'clock. It was a bit of a drive, but not too far, only about a half hour from Columbia Heights.

Guess who caught the biggest fish that day? Connie! And who caught the most fish? That would be little Michael! Only five years old, but he already knew how to cast out from the shore. "I've got one!" he yelled, as Bill dropped what he was doing and came jogging over.

"Good going, Michael," said his dad, proudly. "Take it easy, nice and slow; just keep reeling it in like I showed you. I'll help you when he gets close." It didn't take long, and Bill soon netted Michael's catch, the first fish of the day!

"I want to catch another one, Dad!" yelled Michael.

"Okay, you do that," said Bill with a smile as he took the hook out of the walleye's mouth and put it on a stringer.

Just then Connie let out a scream as her rod doubled over and just about snapped in half. "Uncle Chuck, I need help!" she yelled.

Chuck was closest to her, so he rushed over and got to her just as a huge northern pike shot from the water and tried shaking the hook from its mouth. Connie had never caught such a big fish, of that she was certain. "Just keep playing it," Chuck urged. "You're doing great! When it turns away, give it a little line, and when it feels slack, reel it in! You've got a big northern pike on that line, Connie, and it's going to get tired a lot faster than you." That was for sure. Connie was a determined young girl who didn't give up easily on anything.

"Uncle Chuck," she said, "what if the fish breaks my line?"

"It won't!" Bill yelled from a distance as he watched his daughter take on the big northern. "That line is a fifty-pound test!"

After five minutes or so, which must have seemed like an hour to Connie, she finally began reeling the exhausted fish to shore. No sooner had she done so when Mark got a strike on his line, and Michael rushed over to help him. It was great that Mark, Connie and little Michael were catching fish and that Bill, Chuck and big Michael were able to help them, but that didn't leave much time for them to catch fish of their own. That's life, and that's the way it went for most of the afternoon.

When it was time to call it a day, little Michael had caught more fish than anyone—three walleyes! Connie was skunked the rest of the afternoon, but her northern weighed in at fifteen pounds, impressive enough! Bill, Chuck and Michael had to leave empty-handed, but that's the way fishing goes sometimes. It didn't matter, because among all of them, they'd caught enough to anticipate quite a fish feast for supper, and everyone had thoroughly enjoyed their day at the lake.

When the fishing gang arrived home, they cleaned their catch, made a beautiful garden-fresh salad, set the table and had everything ready to go for the evening meal when the exhausted women returned from their marathon shopping day. "Mom! Mom! Wait until you hear about the fish I caught!" yelled Connie as Pearl and the gals came in the front door.

"Me, too, Mom!" yelled little Michael as he ran up to her. "I caught a whole bunch!"

"You can tell her all about it over dinner," said Bill, "which, I'm happy to tell you ladies, happens to be nearly all prepared. I just need a couple of minutes to fry up the fish."

"Wow! Thank you!" they all said in unison.

"I'm so hungry!" said Connie.

"I think we're all hungry and I know we're all pooped out!" said Pearl. "This is so appreciated!"

"From having shopped all day, it doesn't look like you bought that much," said Bill.

"That's right, dear," laughed Pearl as she winked at the others.

"There's a lot more out in the car, Dad," said Terri laughing, "bags and bags!"

"Did you have fun, honey?" Chuck asked Marty.

"I sure did!" she said. "Look what I bought!" She opened the package she was carrying and took out a one-piece aquamarine bathing suit. "How do you like it?" she asked as she held it up in front of herself.

"I like it! I like it!" said Chuck approvingly. "I can hardly wait to see you in it!"

"Well, you won't have to wait long," Pearl said. "We gals decided we'd like to go to Lake Calhoun for our picnic tomorrow." They opened their packages and showed the men the swimming suits each of them had purchased. "Big summer sale at Dayton's," Pearl said. "We couldn't resist!"

"Sounds like a successful day!" Chuck said. "We had a pretty good time ourselves, will tell you all about it when we sit down to eat. Get ready for some fresh-caught walleyed and northern pike!" The meal did not disappoint. Everyone shared their stories from the day as the platters of scrumptious fried fish and side dishes were devoured.

"I don't know about everyone else, but I'm tired, ready to call it an early night," said Bill after they'd eaten dessert and sat chatting around the table.

"I'm pretty tired myself," said Pearl.

"Me, too!" said little Michael as everyone laughed.

"Then it's settled!" said Bill. "Off to bed we go!"

Saturday turned out to be a lazy day, a much-needed day of rest. A couple of oversized blankets were spread out on the warm, white sand at Lake Calhoun, and the parents just relaxed and enjoyed the quiet time while the kids went swimming. After a bit, Marty and Pearl went and changed into their new suits, and the men definitely sat up and took notice when they returned and sat down next to them!

"It's going to be rough going back to work on Monday after taking this time off," said Bill. "It's been great having you here."

"It's been really good for us as well," said Chuck, "restful and a lot of fun."

"We sure appreciate you taking all the time you have with us and for letting us stay," said Marty.

"Yes, thank you!" said Chuck.

"Any time," said Bill. "We're always glad to see you and the boys!"

The kids continued to entertain themselves out in the water, swimming around and playing water games in the roped-off area of the lake. Little Michael created some mighty splashes, having not yet mastered the art of smooth strokes. Connie, on the other hand, moved like a fish. Her older sisters were avid swimmers as well, but today those three appeared more interested in talking to boys out in the water. Michael and Mark swam out beyond the ropes, moving through the water with powerful strokes and competing with one another as always.

"Brother," Mark said breathlessly as he glided alongside Michael through the choppy lake water, "is this great or what?"

"Sure beats selling encyclopedias!" Michael yelled. The twins always swam alongside one another at Big Pine Lake in Perham, so swimming together in Lake Calhoun was nothing new. It was much like when they ran tandem track, only now they were in water. They'd spent so much time together over the years, had done so many things as a twosome, they could easily sense their proximity to each other regardless of Mark's blindness, or Michael when his eyes were closed.

After the kids had been in the water for a couple of hours, they began coming ashore to join their parents. Fortunately, the adults had taken advantage of the quiet time to eat a light lunch and talk and relax. The kids were chatting up a storm and hungry! "Mom, why don't you and Dad and Aunt Marilyn and Uncle Chuck go swimming while we eat lunch," said Terri.

That was Terri, always thinking of others. "Sounds good to me," said Pearl. "Let's try out these new suits, Marilyn!" Are you ready for a swim?"

"I sure am!" she said. With that, the four adults made their way down to the lake and eased into the refreshing water. "Feels wonderful!" said Marty.

"Swim to your heart's content," said Bill. "We'll give the kids time to eat and visit."

"Sounds good to me," Chuck said. "It sure is nice to see how much they enjoy each other's company."

After a relaxed hour or so enjoying their swim in the lake, it was four o'clock and the foursome was ready to come ashore. Warmed by the sun, refreshed by the water and sated with a delicious picnic in the good company of family was a perfect day all in all!

The three older girls left first, as they had places to go other than home. Bill and Pearl left next with Connie and little Michael. Marty and Chuck left last because Mark and Michael wanted one more jump in the lake. Finally, around five o'clock, they were driving on Central Avenue towards Columbia Heights.

"That was a great afternoon," said Mark.

"And the food was fantastic!" Michael said. "I loved that potato salad! You and Pearl sure are great cooks, Mom."

"You're just saying that because eating's your first love, Michael," she joked.

"It used to be," laughed Michael. "I have a new one now and her name's Laurie!"

"Same for me," said Mark smiling, "only mine's named Linda!"

"Wow, if you two like these gals more than food, this is getting serious!" laughed Chuck.

When they pulled up in front of the house, the sun was starting to go down and it was beginning to cool off. Not a sound could be heard when they first opened the front door. It was like a tomb! Just then they heard something resembling a hibernating grizzly bear coming from the direction of Pearl and Bill's bedroom. Aha, naptime! Bill was sleeping, snoring up a storm in his usual house-rattling style.

"Hard to believe anyone else in the house can sleep with that racket, right?" laughed Pearl as she came down the stairs. "Connie and Michael are actually napping upstairs as well, must have been all that exercise and the big lunch."

"That's fine with us," Marty said. "I think we're all pretty tired and would just as soon take it easy and hit the hay early." By the time the three older sisters got home that evening, they found everyone had gone to bed!

Bill was the first one up the next morning, and he had bacon, scrambled eggs, sourdough toast and steaming mugs of black coffee ready to go as the family brigade trickled their way into the dining room, the girls and little Michael still in their pajamas. "Don't mind our informal attire," said a sleepy-faced Terri. "We always come to breakfast in our PJ's on Sunday mornings."

"Hey, no sense in breaking a relaxing habit just because of a little company," laughed Chuck, already dressed for church and sitting at the table with Marty.

After breakfast, everyone lolled around and chatted in the living room as they shared sections of the *Minneapolis Tribune*. This was the same Sunday paper Marty and Chuck had delivered to their doorstep in Perham, so everyone was happy. Michael knew which columns and articles most interested his brother, and he began reading aloud to him. That's when it happened. Connie watched Michael, and immediately wanted a chance to read aloud to her cousin. Michael, of course, was happy to oblige. Connie may have been only eight, but she could read like a whiz! Of course, when little Michael saw his sister reading aloud to Mark, he wanted to try, too, even though he didn't yet know how to read. When his turn came, he cuddled up next to Mark and pretended he was reading. Of course, he wasn't actually doing so, but it sure was entertaining listening to him make up stories to go along with what he imagined was happening on the comics page. Mark smiled from ear to ear as he sat with his arm around his thoughtful and exuberant young cousin.

At nine o'clock, everyone started getting ready for church, ten o'clock Mass at Immaculate Conception in Columbia Heights. It was a large church with long pews in the middle and shorter pews on each side. After they arrived, the eleven of them paraded down the main aisle to an empty row near the front of the church, filing in one by one and filling the pew to capacity!

After Mass, according to plan, they headed for Coon Rapids. Bill and Pearl wanted Chuck and Marty to see the Johnsons' beautiful church, the Church of the Epiphany. It was indeed a magnificent structure, but what most captured Marty and Chuck's attention was the mission statement which appeared in the parish bulletin. It read as follows:

"We, the people of Epiphany Parish, have built a growing community on Coon Rapids farmland since our beginning in 1964. We are a parish with educational priorities. We are a caring people who minister by reaching out to our brothers and sisters, responding to their physical and spiritual needs. We will manifest Christ through fostering spiritual growth and unity, and witnessing our faith." The words **'Lighting the Way to Christ'** appeared in bold black letters beneath the statement. Before leaving the church, one of the parishioners invited them to the chapel where the Rosary was usually said before noon. "Would you like to do that?" Bill asked.

"If we have time, I think it would be an excellent way to pray that all goes well with our dinner with the Johnsons," Chuck said.

When they left the church, it was one o'clock, perfect timing! The Johnsons had gone to the 7:30 a.m. Mass, so were home early to start in on dinner preparations. After all, cooking for fifteen people was no small chore!

The caravan of guests pulled up in front of their house right on schedule at 2:00. When Linda looked out the window and saw Mark and Michael arrive in a sleek new silver Ford sedan, she ran out of the house and down the walk to greet them, almost knocking Mark over with her hearty embrace as he stepped from the car. He was taken by surprise, and so was everyone else. "Wow!" Patty said as she and her sisters watched from their car, "She really likes him!"

When Laurie came out of the house and saw Michael, it was another hug fest. "Well," chuckled Mr. Johnson as he came out of the house and shook hands with Chuck, "seems my daughters are pretty overjoyed to see your sons!"

"So I see, Walter," Chuck said with a smile, "and as I'm sure you noticed, my boys are beaming from ear to ear!"

"C'mon in everybody!" said Mrs. Johnson enthusiastically as she met them at the front door. "It's going to be a bit before we eat. Let's all head to the living room, have some formal introductions and get to know each other!"

"Well," said Mark after everyone had settled into the cozy and welcoming space, "I don't know how Michael and I got so lucky. This gal by my side is the one I haven't been able to stop talking about, the lovely Linda Johnson." Bill's older girls had their eyes glued to Linda's blushing face.

"Lucky is right! We still can't believe it," said a smiling Michael as he put his arm around Laurie's shoulder and pulled her close to him. "I'm honored to have this beautiful gal in my life, the brilliant and amazing Laurie Johnson." The boys made their introductions with such enthusiastic fanfare that everyone couldn't help but clap and cheer in honor of young love.

After the families had been introduced and had had some relaxed time to talk, the Johnsons took everyone on a grand tour of the house. First up were all the bathrooms, a necessity with eleven guests! Many wows and words of wonder could be heard coming from Pearl and Marty as they admired the spacious, airy kitchen and elegant master bedroom. "This bedroom suite is as large as the whole first floor of our house!" Pearl said.

"It's roomy, no doubt about that," Mr. Johnson said. "If there's one thing Grace and I like in a house it's lots of space!"

"You've sure got that!" Bill said.

The afternoon rolled along, and at four o'clock Grace rang an old-fashioned dinner bell in the kitchen. "Time to eat! Everyone come to the dining room!" she hollered.

There was a very large rectangular wood table in the center of the room, elegantly set for fifteen people, with seven chairs on each side and one on the end for Mr. Johnson. "Feels like the Last Supper!" he said, smiling.

There wasn't any question as to who was going to sit where. The Johnson twins had gotten the first names of everyone and made placards to go with each place setting. On one side of the table was Grace Johnson sitting next to her husband, and then Marty, Chuck, Linda, Mark, Laurie and Michael, on the other side was Bill sitting next to Mr. Johnson, and then Pearl, Patty, Mike, Linda, Connie and Terri, the Minneapolis Dowdle clan occupying all of one side of the large table and the young lovers and their parents the other.

"This is a very special occasion," Mr. Johnson said, "and we've got a lot to be thankful for." Everyone held hands around the table and bowed their heads as he began to pray: *"Lord, we thank You for this beautiful meal and for letting us all be together in celebration of the end of summer, the start of a new school year for all these young people, and the beginning of new and lasting friendships."*

"And loves!" added Mrs. Johnson just before the enthusiastic chorus of "Amen!"

As if they'd been given a cue in a play, Linda and Laurie immediately hopped up from their chairs and headed to the kitchen. "Everyone stay seated," said Laurie, "we've got this!" Linda was the first to emerge with a large ivory platter filled with steaming golden-brown sliced turkey.

"Mmmm," Mark said as he inhaled deeply. "That smells like Thanksgiving in August!"

"And I smell ham!" said Michael as Laurie emerged with a second large ivory platter piled high with thick juicy slices.

"With a crowd such as we are, we thought we'd best have both!" laughed Mrs. Johnson. "Don't want anyone going away hungry."

"No worry!" said Chuck as the girls carried out an array of side dishes and placed them on the table.

"Laurie and Linda must have told you how much Mark and I enjoy eating!" said Michael to Mrs. Johnson.

"I'll have you know the girls fixed the entire meal," said Mrs. Johnson proudly. "Wouldn't let me do a thing."

"I think they wanted to impress you two!" laughed Walter.

"Consider it done," said Mark smiling.

"No question about that," said Michael.

This brought a big smile to the girls' faces. "And we made pumpkin and apple pies for dessert, so leave room!" said Linda.

After everyone had feasted on the turkey and ham dinner, Linda and Laurie cleared away the dishes and proceeded to carry out four pies and a bowl of fresh whipped cream to a chorus of oohs and aahs.

"Umm," little Michael said as he dipped his fork into the bowl of whipped cream for a taste, "this is delicious!"

"Even better with a piece of pie!" laughed Bill as he served himself a generous slice of apple.

"I think I need to try both of them!" said Michael as the pies made their way around the table.

"You girls outdid yourselves!" Mark said as he savored his first bite of pumpkin. "This is delicious!"

After everyone had finished dessert, Linda and Laurie jumped into action and soon had the table cleared and the dishes washed and put away. "Why don't we move the action to the living room where we can get comfortable and digest our meal while we chat," Mrs. Johnson said. The "chat" turned out to be mainly talk about Bill's work at Minneapolis Honeywell, Mr. Johnson's contracting business and the kids' schools and their futures. It didn't take long before little Michael and Connie were curled up with their heads on their mother's lap, both fast asleep.

"I hate to break up this wonderful gathering, but we really need to be heading home," Pearl said. "The kids have to get up early tomorrow morning for their first day back at school, and Chuck and Marty are driving back to Perham tonight since they both have to work in the morning."

"You're right, honey," said Bill. "I took a few days off from work this week, but it'll be back to the old grind early tomorrow."

"Walter and Grace, we really want to thank you for including us in the invitation," said Pearl. "And Linda and Laurie, that meal was delicious!"

"It sure was," Marty added. "Thank you, all of you, for everything! It was so special having all of us together!"

After several rounds of hugs and good-byes, the Dowdle caravan was soon back on the road and headed for Columbia Heights. When they arrived, Chuck, Marty and the twins packed up, said a fond farewell to Bill and Pearl and the family and headed back to Perham.

"You boys certainly have a couple of sweet girlfriends," Marty said as they drove along, "and I certainly enjoyed meeting Walter and Grace."

"I feel the same," Chuck said. "They're going to make some really neat in-laws!"

"I think you're rushing things a little, Chuck" said Marty laughing.

"Maybe not," said Mark coyly. "May be happening sooner than you think." Their parents exchanged smiling glances as they settled back into the seats of the Ford sedan for a quiet and restful ride home.

"We're here," Michael whispered softly to Mark as they pulled into the driveway. Marty and Chuck had dozed off, and it was little wonder. They'd eaten a mighty meal with new acquaintances, were nestled in a warm car, and had just enjoyed a week of nonstop action with Bill and Pearl and all the family.

The next morning everyone was up early and ready and rarin' to go, Marty to St. James Hospital, Chuck to Perham High School and the boys to St. John's. Before she left, Marty gave each of them a big hug. "Now you be careful driving that new car, Michael!" she said. "Not too fast!"

"Don't worry, I'll keep an eye on him!" joked Mark. He grinned at his mom and a smile crossed Michael's face. Both boys had heard her admonitions many times before, and they knew it was just her way of telling them how much she loved them.

The twins loved their mother as well, of course, but the love they had for her was different from the love they were feeling for Linda and Laurie. This was a man to woman love, a passionate love, and they could hardly wait to get back to school to take advantage of the first opportunity to spend time with them again.

WHEN THEY WEREN'T OCCUPIED WITH THEIR STUDIES, MARK AND Michael drove over to St. Ben's on the weekends, and during school vacations they made many a trip to Coon Rapids to visit Linda and Laurie. This dating pattern continued over the next two years as their relationships developed and deepened.

During their daughters' senior year at St. Ben's, the Johnsons invited the Dowdles back to their home in Coon Rapids for Christmas Eve supper and a Christmas Day celebration. Walter and Grace were feeling something important was soon to happen. Chuck and Marty hadn't visited since that first time in the summer of 1971, so it was going to be a fun and interesting renewal of their acquaintance, especially knowing their sons had grown ever closer to the Johnsons' daughters. This would be a more intimate visit as well, very different with just the two families present.

With an abundance of snow on the ground, it wasn't an easy drive to Coon Rapids, but it didn't seem to bother Michael or Mark. Their minds were elsewhere. Something was definitely happening between the twins, something about which Chuck and Marty didn't have a clue, but they could certainly sense mystery in the air.

When they pulled up to the Johnson house they were greeted by a magical scene, pine trees sparkling with holiday lights and a large tableau of Joseph, Mary and baby Jesus in a stable, complete with three wise men and an array of farm animals gathered round. It was lovely to behold and a reminder of the true meaning of Christmas.

Linda was on watch at the window and came dashing out of the house as the car pulled up, hugging Mark warmly the moment he stepped from the car. "I'm so happy to see you!" she exclaimed as she wrapped her arms around him. The two of them stood there in a tight embrace, oblivious to the snow on the ground and chill in the air. Next up was Laurie, who repeated the enthusiastic greeting with Michael. Chuck and Marty got out of the car just as Grace and Walter came out onto the front porch, and the round of welcome hugs soon repeated itself, fathers and mothers, daughters and sons.

"Those kids are in love!" Walter said as he shook Chuck's hand and ushered him into the warm house.

"Tell me about it!" he said. "Your daughters were the topic of conversation all the way here. I'm afraid my boys are smitten to the point of no return, Walter," laughed Chuck. "They couldn't have fallen for two nicer girls than Linda and Laurie."

"I heard that, Chuck," said Grace as she and Marty walked into the house behind the men. "I'm biased, but I agree wholeheartedly! And vice versa I might add!" she said smiling.

They all removed their winter coats in the entryway and Linda and Laurie took them down the hall to hang in a large walk-in closet. "The house smells like evergreens!" Mark said as he inhaled deeply. "I love it!"

"Let's go into the living room, Mark," said Linda as she led him gently by the arm. "The Christmas tree is in there." Everyone soon followed and settled into place in front of a blazing fire.

"Everything looks so beautiful in here!" said Marty. "Such a lovely tree!" "I love the sound of the crackling fire," said Mark. "I can feel the heat!"

"We won't be eating for a little while," said Grace, "so why don't we just catch up on what's been happening with everyone since you were here."

"Go ahead, Marty," said Chuck. "You can get us started."

"Well, let's see," Marty said. "The boys had finished their freshman year at St. John's in 1971 when we were here visiting you that summer, and I began working as a physical therapist at St. James Hospital in Perham. I'm still doing that and enjoying every day of it. The boys come home from college over holidays and summer vacation, though they're often here as you know! We thoroughly enjoy having them around, pretty much a full-time job just keeping them fed, as you also know!" she said as everyone laughed. "Other than that, I've been getting in some reading and long walks and fun bike rides with Chuck in the neighborhood and around town."

"It's been busy for me, I'll say that!" said Chuck. "There's never a dull moment with teaching, and now that I'm Chair of the English Department, I organize the curriculum and evaluate the staff. It all takes time, but it seems the bulk of my time during the school year is spent grading papers. The boys and I have been busy during the summers selling *World Book Encyclopedia* around Otter Tail County, and that's been a big help financially, especially with the expense of two kids in college. Michael and Mark enjoy the selling and boy are they good at it!"

"No complaints here," Michael said. "It's fun. Mark and I have learned how to sell books, and when we add the money we've earned doing that to our scholarships, we feel extremely fortunate. All eyes were on Michael as he paused for a moment, turning to smile at Laurie before continuing. "I know I speak for Mark as well when I tell you the best thing to happen to us by far has been falling in love with your beautiful daughters," he said to Walter and Grace.

"I couldn't have said it any better," said Mark. I would like to add a little something, though," he said as he rose slowly. All eyes were now on Mark as he gently pulled Linda to her feet. Michael and Mark had planned this moment many months before and the time had finally come! Mark slowly knelt down in front of Linda and looked up at her. He reached out for her hands, and she, wondering what was going on, willingly placed them in his. He very softly, very seriously and reverently said, "You are a beautiful person in every way and I love you with all my heart, Linda Johnson. I can't imagine not spending every day of the rest of my life with you. Will you do me the honor of becoming my wife?"

Linda was stunned speechless! The parents gasped with surprise, except for a beaming Walter, of course, as Michael and Mark had secretly sought his approval several weeks before. A flood of tears came streaming down Linda's cheeks as she stared down at Mark. "I don't know how long I'm supposed to wait to hopefully hear a yes," he said nervously as everyone laughed.

"Mark, you know I will!" exclaimed Linda. Mark smiled broadly, reached into his coat pocket, took out the ring and slowly placed it on Linda's outstretched finger. "Oh, Mark, it's beautiful!" gushed Linda as the parents and Michael and Laurie cheered and applauded. "I love you so much!"

"I'm so happy for both of you!" gushed Laurie, standing to exchange hugs with her sister and future brother-in-law.

"Congratulations, Brother!" said Michael as he and Mark shook hands and embraced. There were hugs all around and love was in the air! Laurie had barely recovered and was just settling back onto the couch next to

Michael when he stood and turned to her, pulling her gently to her feet and kneeling down in front of her. Their eyes met and Michael felt like his heart might burst from his chest. "I've been in love with you from the moment we met, and every day that love has grown stronger. You make me the happiest man on this earth, Laurie Johnson. Will you marry me?"

Without hesitation, Laurie enthusiastically said, "Yes, Michael! I will! I will! I love you!"

Another round of clapping and cheering ensued as Michael slipped a sparkling ring onto Laurie's outstretched finger. "Oh, Michael," it's so beautiful!" she said as her eyes welled up with tears.

"She said YES! She said YES!" yelled Michael as everyone laughed. The two sets of newly-engaged couples embraced and kissed, Walter and Chuck shook hands, Grace and Marty exchanged heartfelt hugs, and everyone carried on in joyful fashion, boisterous in their approval of the afternoon's happenings.

"Well," Grace said gleefully, "this certainly was a pleasant surprise! You boys did a good job of keeping it secret! You, too, Walter!" she said as he winked and smiled at his future son-in-laws. "I bet you had this planned for a while."

"Too long!" Mark said.

"Well, let's get ready to eat!" said Grace. "I don't know how much more excitement I can take on an empty stomach!" Everyone laughed and headed towards the dining room. Instead of sitting down, Marty followed Grace and the girls into the kitchen. Grace held out her arms towards Marty and the two women embraced as tears of joy streamed down both of their faces. Laurie and Linda soon joined in, and the scene turned into a real mother-daughter cry-fest.

"What's going on? We're starving out here!" hollered Walter jokingly.

The large table was lavishly set for eight people, with an Advent-wreath centerpiece formed with wire and freshly-cut evergreens. Four colorful candles, three purple and one pink, a foot tall and an inch in diameter, were nestled in the evergreens equidistant from one another. A large white candle, this one also a foot tall, but four inches in diameter, graced the center of the ring, and all five candles were lit. The four smaller candles symbolized faith, hope, joy and love, and the large white candle, which was lit on Christmas Eve, was known as Christ's candle. "I knew it was going to happen sometime soon," Walter said as he smiled at Mark and Michael, "I just didn't know when! Good job!"

"I knew you two were a little antsy about something on the drive down, but you certainly surprised us," said Chuck, "and you chose the perfect time to do it! I don't know how you kept it a secret!"

The kitchen door swung open and Grace and Marty entered first, each toting a bottle of fine white wine, one of which they positioned at each end of the table in front of Walter and Chuck. Linda and Laurie entered next with two large platters of slice ham. The procession continued as Grace and Marty returned with steaming bowls of candied yams and scalloped potatoes, then Linda and Laurie with peas & carrots and a festive red molded jello salad. The enticing aroma of food filled the air!

The Advent wreath was glowing and emitting a soft, warm light as the ladies took their seats. *"Lord, thank you for these kids of ours, as they sure are something special,"* said Walter as everyone held hands and he prayed. *"They could not have made us any happier than we are at this moment. We love them and hope their futures together will be filled with joy, joy such as Chuck and I are so grateful to have found with our beautiful wives. We thank you for blessing us with our children and for this splendid food before us. Amen."*

"Amen!" said everyone in unison.

"I'd like to propose a toast," added Walter. "To Linda and Mark, Laurie and Michael, may your futures together shine as brightly as the light from Christ's candle as you prepare for your lives together." Everyone tipped their glasses and sipped their wine, all realizing it was a toast in celebration of partnerships filled with faith, hope and love.

Walter's solemn words hadn't dampened the boys' appetites. As a matter of fact, it had only whetted them! They were young, they were hungry and they were ready to eat! Michael's eyes grew wide as the platters of food made their way around the table, juicy sliced ham, golden-brown scalloped potatoes, peas & carrots bursting with color… it was indeed a Christmas Eve feast! "I forgot the rolls!" yelled Grace as she ran to the kitchen. She was back in a flash with a dozen piled high in a basket, fresh creamery butter on the side.

"Mrs. Johnson," Michael said, "you sure know how to cook! This is spectacular!"

"Sure is!" said Mark. "I feel very fortunate to be here!"

"Well, I'm glad you two like my cooking," she said, smiling. "You'll hopefully be here often to enjoy a whole lot more of it!" After dinner, which included fresh-baked apple pie and vanilla ice cream for dessert, everyone was content and ready to plop down in the living room by the cozy fire.

There wasn't much talk before Walter and Chuck's heads dropped downward and they were snoring up a storm. Grace and Marty just shook their heads and smiled. It had been a wonderful, but long day for everyone, so they gently woke their husbands and headed off to bed.

After exchanging gifts and enjoying a delicious Christmas breakfast in the morning, everyone piled into their cars and drove to the Church of the Epiphany in Coon Rapids for noon Mass. The beautifully-decorated church was packed when they found their place in a pew, so it was good they'd left early. During Communion, everyone in the church received, and it took a long, long time.

As they were leaving the church, Marty and Grace walked together towards their cars. "Thank you so much for having us," said Marty. "Chuck and I have enjoyed this time with you and Walter and the girls immensely, and it's certainly turned out to be a memorable Christmas!"

"Marty," Grace said very seriously, "I think your sons did it right. We already loved them like they were our own sons, and now they'll be a permanent part of the family! I'm so happy!"

"I feel the same about your girls," said Marty as she hugged Grace.

"We're going to have a lot of talking to do once they decide when and where they're getting married! I'm guessing a double-ring ceremony, but who knows!"

"Whatever it is, whenever it is, I'll be looking forward to helping out however I can!" said Marty.

She didn't have to wait long. On the drive back to Perham, getting married was about all the boys wanted to talk about. They were definitely anticipating a two-for-one affair, and thought it would be a good idea to plan it for as soon as possible after graduation so they could have some honeymoon time during the summer, before they all started graduate school at the University of Minnesota. Now all they had to do was discuss it with their brides-to-be and see if they were on board.

Linda and Laurie more than agreed. "The sooner the better as far as we're concerned!" said Linda enthusiastically when they had an opportunity to discuss it. "Graduation is June 22nd at St. Benedict's."

"June 3rd at St. John's," said Michael.

"We could get married that next week on the 9th if that works out with our folks," said Laurie.

"I think it would be a perfect time," Mark said. "Dad will be out of school and Mom and he usually like to go someplace and do something fun after working all year."

"Your mom and dad can stay at our house the week before the wedding if they want to, Michael," said Laurie. "That would make it easy for our moms to be together for all the last-minute preparations. I'm sure they'd like that."

WELL, THAT'S WHAT HAPPENED. THE TWINS GRADUATED WITH honors, all four of them, and on June 5th, four days before the wedding, the Dowdles headed to Coon Rapids, but not before a bit of excitement at home! After the St. John's graduation ceremony on June 3rd, Chuck and Marty drove back to Perham to take care of a few things before packing up and heading to Coon Rapids for their week at the Johnsons. Part of that included having Tom Schmitz deliver a new 1975 silver, four-door Ford sedan, just like the one they'd bought for themselves the year before!

When Michael and Mark pulled up to the house the next day and Michael saw two identical silver sedans sitting at the curb, he mentioned it to Mark and they both wondered what was happening. Certainly their mom and dad wouldn't be trading in the car they'd just recently bought. Granted, Tom Schmitz was quite a salesman, but this wouldn't be like his parents. They usually kept their cars until they registered at least 100,000 miles or more!

"What's going on with the new car out in front?" he asked his dad.

"Well, that's something we'll talk over with you two after supper," he said.

Marty was unable to contain her excitement and was the first to speak up as they were finishing dinner. "Boys," she said, "that new car belongs to your dad and me. We just bought it from Tim Schmitz."

"Wow!" said Mark. "You just bought a new car last year. You're each going to have a car now?"

"No," Marty said smiling, "but you two are!"

"What?" exclaimed the twins in unison.

"Us? Mark and me?" asked Michael incredulously as Mark's mouth fell open.

"That's right," said Chuck. "We talked it over and decided that the car you already have and the one we bought for ourselves last year would make a couple of nice wedding presents for you and your gals. We're giving them to you and keeping the new one that's out front for ourselves. How does that sound?"

The boys were flabbergasted. "I can't believe it! Thank you!" gushed Michael as he got up and hugged his parents. "This is almost too much to handle!"

"I think I'll handle it just fine once it sinks in!" laughed Mark. "Thanks, Mom and Dad!" he said as he got up to hug them.

"Well, you certainly deserve it," said Marty, "and Linda and Laurie as well, hard as you've worked through all your schooling. Tomorrow we'll take all three cars to Coon Rapids so you have your two there."

"Boy is Linda ever going to be surprised!" said Mark. "We've been talking about how we could work out transportation to the university. Problem solved, thanks to you! You have no idea how much this gift is appreciated," he said sincerely. "Thank you both so much."

"Well, Mark," Chuck said, "you and Michael have absolutely earned it. I'm so proud of both of you and so happy that you're soon to marry two wonderful women. When we get to Coon Rapids tomorrow morning, you can walk Linda out to the front of the house and hand her the keys to her new car!"

"Right now we should think about finishing our packing and getting to bed before it gets to be too late," said Marty.

The Dowdle caravan of silver Fords left Perham bright and early the next morning, arriving in Coon Rapids just before noon. Linda was the first one out of the Johnson house, and she did a double… make that *triple* take when she saw the trio of matching sedans! Mark stepped out as she opened his front passenger door, and before anything else happened or was said, the two of them stood in a long embrace. Michael followed suit, stepping from the vehicle parked just behind Mark's and standing with open arms as Laurie ran down the front path to meet him.

"OK, you two," Walter called to his daughters, "let's remember Michael and Mark's parents are our honored guests as well!"

"And your future in-laws!" laughed Grace as she came out onto the porch and greeted Chuck and Marty as they stepped from their car.

The girls said their hellos to Chuck and Marty, and soon hearty hugs and greetings had been exchanged all around. "You made it down here in good time," Linda said.

"We wanted to be here to help out however we can," said Marty.

"We're so happy to have you," said Grace, "and not just to help!"

"I'm just wondering," said a smiling Walter as he looked down the line of sedans parked at the curb, "are my eyes playing tricks on me or did you just pull up in three identical cars?"

"Three it is," laughed Chuck.

"We'll let Mark explain," said Marty as she put her arm around her son and slipped the car keys into his hand.

"You're not going to believe this, Linda," Mark said as he held them out towards her, "but this car is now officially ours, yours and mine! It's a wedding gift from my mom and dad!"

"Seriously?" said Linda. "You're right, I *can't* believe it!" The couple embraced again, then hugged Marty and Chuck, their eyes flooded with tears of gratitude. "Thank you both so much!" gushed Linda.

"And guess who else gets a silver Ford sedan for a wedding gift?" Michael said to Laurie.

"No! You can't be serious!" said Laurie, looking stunned. "Two cars? Are you kidding?" she said looking at Chuck and Marty, her voice filled with emotion.

"It's true, Laurie," Chuck said. "Marty and I talked about what we thought you'd most appreciate before you start graduate school, and we decided the cars would probably be pretty high on your list."

"Pretty high?" laughed Laurie as she warmly embraced her future in-laws. "I'd say at the top! Thank you both so much! I can't think of anything we'll make better use of!"

"That's so generous of you," said Grace. "Thank you!"

"It certainly is a wonderful and thoughtful surprise!" Walter said. "Let's all go into the house and celebrate the good fortune!"

After everyone brought their things to their rooms and had a chance to wash up and relax, they sat at the long dining room table to enjoy tuna sandwiches and cottage cheese with fresh, sliced peaches. "God sure has been good to us!" said Mark as they settled into their places. "Besides getting first-class educations, Michael and I snared two beautiful women and now we've been given matching silver sedans! I feel like I love everything and everybody right now!" he gushed.

Everyone couldn't help but to applaud his short and heartfelt speech, and before the tears started rolling again, Walter commenced with a short prayer: *"Lord, we are so thankful for our beautiful children, filled with love and gratitude as they are. We wish them much happiness in their marriages and Godspeed in their future educations. And thank you for enabling all of us to be together for this special week of wedding preparation and time together. Thank you for this food, now let's eat! Amen,"* he said smiling.

"Amen!" said everyone in unison.

The thrill of receiving matching cars was only the first of two grand surprises taking place that day for the twin foursome. "How'd you all like to take a short drive to see a new subdivision I'm building in Coon Rapids?" said Walter after they'd finished lunch.

"I'd love it!" said Marty. She had a keen interest in house design, much more so than Chuck. Before anyone could object, Walter ushered them out the door to the vehicles, the parents taking a seat in Walter's roomy Buick and the four kids loading into one of the silver Ford sedans.

"Just follow me!" Walter called to Michael. "It's only a ten-minute drive from here." It wasn't even that, as Walter had driven the route many a time and knew the way well. They soon pulled up in front of a beautiful two-story house, two majestic old oak trees gracing the newly-sodded grass.

"This is a neat neighborhood," Chuck said as he got out of the car and looked around.

"It sure is," said Marty, "so peaceful."

"This house we're going to look at is beautifully furnished," Walter said, "so I expect you gals will be pretty excited about that."

"I'm eager to see it," Marty said as they approached the front door. "I've always been interested in interior design."

"Well, in that case I think you're going to be very intrigued by this one, Marty," Walter said as he winked at his wife discreetly. Grace wondered what her husband had up his sleeve, as he'd built a number of similar-looking houses. Why would this one be any more interesting? When she walked through the front door, she saw immediately. This house was indeed different!

"Oh my, Walter, these corded walls are wonderful!" Marty said when she stepped inside and noticed how they were all lined with strands of thin, twisted rope. "It's as though this house was built for a blind person."

"Guess what?" said Walter cheerily. "It was!" That immediately got Mark's full attention, and he asked Linda to lead him to one of the walls. She placed his fingertips on the cord and he began following it along the wall. When he came to a corner and was about to enter another room, he felt a metal plate. "It's in braille!" said Mark excitedly. "It tells where I am and where I'm headed! What a great house!"

"Can you picture yourself living here?" asked Walter.

"Sure, in my dreams, maybe," laughed Mark.

"Well, sometimes dreams do come true," said a beaming Walter as he put his arm around Mark.

"Dad! What are you saying?" said Linda excitedly.

"Well, I thought you and Mark and Michael and Laurie might like to live here rent free while you're going to graduate school at the University of Minnesota. If so, I'd love to extend the offer as a wedding gift, how about that?"

The announcement took everyone by surprise, including Grace, who had no inkling about the new house. It had two large master bedrooms and connecting studies, one upstairs, one down. A large great room led to a spacious kitchen, and informational braille was imbedded on plaques near each of the appliances and on the knobs.

"Really?" said the four kids in shocked unison as they slowly gazed around.

"Are you serious?" asked Laurie.

"Absolutely," said Walter. "What do you think, Mark?"

Mark didn't hesitate. "I think it's incredible!" he said. "Thank you!"

"I love it!" gushed Linda. "Wow! Thank you, Dad!"

"I love it as well!" said Michael. "I can't believe this is happening! First we get cars and then we get a place to live! Thank you!"

"It's so beautiful!" exclaimed Laurie. "Thank you, Dad!"

"You're a pretty thoughtful guy, you know that?" said a smiling Grace as she put her arm around her husband.

"Group hug!" said Laurie as everyone came together for a warm embrace.

On the drive home, all the twins could talk about was how fortunate and grateful they were to have parents like theirs. "Mark and I were just about to start looking for a place," Linda said. "All of us living together in Coon Rapids is just fine with me!"

"Same here," said Laurie. "It'll be fun being in the same house. We'll take the upstairs bedroom and study, you two can be down if that sounds good to you."

"That would make it easier for Mark," said Linda.

"Hey, I can slide down the banister!" he said as everyone laughed.

The week whizzed by, and when Saturday morning arrived, the Johnson house was abuzz with activity. The wedding was scheduled for 2:30 p.m. at the Church of the Epiphany in Coon Rapids, the Johnson's church and where Linda and Laurie had gone to school, so they felt right at home. It was a walk down memory lane for Marty and Chuck when they entered the church, as they'd also had a June wedding.

Before the Mass began, the organ began playing, Grace and Marty wiped away their tears and a beaming Walter walked down the aisle with a radiant bride on each arm. Linda and Laurie were all smiles, as were their beaming husbands-to-be standing proudly near the first pew. As they reached the front of the church, Walter kissed each of the girls and handed them off to Michael and Mark with a warm embrace before the young couples moved to four kneeling benches positioned in front of the altar. The Mass began, and a hush blanketed the large church until Holy Communion. The twins received, followed by their parents and the rest of the congregation. It took a long time, as the church was packed with guests, but at last the four "I do's" were done and the duos were pronounced husband and wife!

After the ceremony, everyone gathered in the reception hall for a delicious luncheon prepared by the women of the parish. It was all very elegant and the guests enjoyed themselves immensely, the last few not leaving until after 6:00 p.m. It had been a happy, but exhausting few days for the newlyweds, and they were tired and ready for a relaxing honeymoon at their beautiful new abode. You heard right! The newlyweds had decided to honeymoon at home, and they couldn't get there soon enough! They pulled up in front of the new house at seven o'clock and sat for a few minutes, admiring it from the outside and talking with one another. "Something tells me it's going to be real easy adjusting to these new digs," Mark said.

"Well, let's get started. Married life here we come!" said a boisterous Michael as he jaunted toward the house with his arm around his new bride.

"Ready or not!" laughed Laurie as he swooped her up and carried her into the house.

"I get the feeling this is going to be an interesting experience," Linda said quietly to Mark as she covered his hand with hers and the two of them slowly made their way up the walkway.

"Yes," he said softy. "I would agree. You know only too well that it takes a little getting used to Michael's bursts of energy."

"And Laurie's boundless energy," added Linda, "but I wouldn't have it any other way."

"Me neither," said Mark smiling. "Now my sweet bride, tell me when we've reached the threshold so your new husband can carry you over!"

Mark soon found himself exploring every nook of the big new house, room by room. While he was doing that, Michael, Laurie and Linda were in the kitchen uncorking a bottle of fine white wine. "Come join us, Mark!" Linda called. "It's time to celebrate!"

"Man, this place is cool!" said Mark as he rounded the corner to partake in the festivities. "I can find my way so easily. Your dad was thinking way, way ahead when he planned this house for us."

"Well, Mark," Michael said as he placed a glass of wine in his brother's hand, "you're going to be a 'man of words, Attorney Mark Dowdle,' so how about you making the toast?"

"More like man of few words," laughed Mark as he raised his goblet. "Lord, bless our marriages and fill our lives with peace and happiness. Amen."

"Amen!" said everyone in unison as they clinked their glasses and sipped their wine.

The couples sat in the living room and talked about the wonder of their new lives, in awe of the fact that they were now married and settling into a beautiful new home. "Well," said Linda after a few minutes of amiable chatter, "it's getting dark and it's my wedding night. I'm going to head to the bedroom and see if someone follows."

"Me, too," Laurie giggled as she skipped out of the kitchen and up the stairway. "Anyone coming after me?" she called back teasingly over her shoulder.

"Did you hear those two?" laughed Michael.

"Hey, I may be blind, but I'm not deaf!" said Mark as he put down his wine glass and began to feel his way along the wall to the downstairs master suite. When he reached it and opened the door and entered, the first thing he sensed was the aroma of sweet perfume. He followed his nose until he walked straight into the arms of his waiting wife at their bedside. She giggled, and he held her close and kissed her tenderly as she began to slowly undress him. As they climbed into bed together, he curled up next to her warm body and began caressing her before engaging in an act of mutual, unimaginable bliss!

Mark was the first one up in the morning, so he decided to make a test run to the kitchen, hoping to have breakfast ready for everyone by the time they got up. It would be easy, he thought. They usually had oatmeal with cinnamon, raisins and walnuts, and Linda had set everything out on the kitchen counter the night before. All he had to do was put the ingredients in the four bowls, fill them each with a cup of cold water and cook them in the microwave one at a time. It seemed like a simple-enough plan; however, in his over-confident haste he made a wrong turn and crashed straight into the large patio door!

Everyone was awakened by the sound of shattering glass. Linda was the first to make it to the kitchen. "Mark! What happened?" she screamed as she saw him standing among the shards of broken glass, blood streaming from his wrist and dripping onto the floor.

"I don't know," he said, looking shocked.

Just then Michael and Laurie ran into the room. "Oh man!" yelled Michael. "What happened?"

"He doesn't know!" Linda said.

Laurie quickly examined the gash on Mark's left wrist. "I think we'd better get you to the hospital," she said, wrapping the bloody wound with a hand towel and applying pressure.

Mark wasn't concerned about the bleeding, which, of course, he couldn't see. He was much more concerned about possibly having injured a nerve and not being able to type on his braille machine, not with his left hand at least. "Do you think I severed a nerve?" he kept asking nervously as they drove to the Emergency Room.

Fortunately, he hadn't, and within an hour they were leaving the hospital. "I made a bloody mess out of breakfast, didn't I?" laughed a sutured-up Mark after they'd returned home.

"I'll say!" said Michael. "You go relax and we'll bring breakfast to you!"

After they'd eaten, Linda called her parents and told them about Mark's mishap. When Walter informed Marty and Chuck, they were upset, but took it in stride. This wasn't the first time one of the boys had bloodied himself up. However, they did want to see the twins before heading back to Perham, so after breakfast they and the Johnsons headed over to the new house.

"How did it happen?" asked Marty when she saw Mark's bandaged wrist.

"I guess I was feeling a little too confident when I left the bedroom," said Mark. "Turned the wrong way and crashed into the patio door."

"We're just glad it wasn't a more serious injury," said Walter as he inspected the door. "I'll have my men come over and replace the glass today. It'll be just like new."

After their parents left, the newlyweds sat and talked about their exciting morning and the adjustment to their new lives. "What would you think about getting a service dog, Mark?" Michael asked. "Seems it would be a useful set of eyes, especially for the times when you're alone."

"Might not be a half-bad idea," said Mark.

"I think it would be fantastic," said Linda.

"Me, too!" said Laurie.

The foursome didn't waste any time pondering it further. Several days into Mark's recovery, they were off to the local pound in search of a dog, and as fate would have it, a beautiful, three-year-old Golden Retriever named Prince had been brought in just 24 hours before. He was "too much dog" for the family that had turned him in, but an exceedingly-attentive and friendly animal nonetheless, a breed well known for its high intelligence and loyalty. Within the next hour, Michael and Laurie found themselves driving home with sweet Prince sitting happily by the open window next to Mark and Linda in the back seat.

"My first job is going to be to acquaint Prince with our house and the neighborhood," Mark said enthusiastically, "and after that we can visit the university campus and let him check it out!"

"Excellent idea," Linda said. "We'll have about a month and a half to get used to him and him to us before school starts, so that will give us plenty of time to do some training and have some fun together before we start in on the long school haul."

Prince was well-behaved and alert on the drive home, taking in all the sights and sniffing constantly out the open window. "Ah, it's good to be here," said Mark, exhaling a long breath as they pulled up to the house. "I sure hope Prince likes it." When they stepped in the front door, he bent over to give his new companion a loving pat. "Welcome to your new home," he said as Prince looked up at him.

"He's smiling at you," said Linda.

"And wagging his tail!" said Laurie.

"I'm sure he'll love it here," said Michael as he stroked Prince's sturdy back. "How could he not?"

"Watch and see what he does when I set him free in the house," said Mark as he unclipped the leash from Prince's collar. Off he went, wandering from room to room and giving each a thorough sniff test before moving on.

It wasn't long after dinner that Linda and Mark snuggled into their comfortable bed. They were fast asleep in minutes, Prince as well, contentedly sprawled out on the furry rug alongside Mark's side of the bed. He was a snorer as it turned out, loud enough to be noticed by anyone who was a light sleeper, but not loud enough to awaken the exhausted newlyweds. It must have felt good for him to be out of the pound and in a warm and cozy space with new people who were showing him a whole lot of love.

Laurie and Michael were up early the next morning, and by the time Linda and Mark made their appearance, breakfast was ready. Prince was still sleeping soundly when they tiptoed out of their bedroom. "I've got a trick to show you that I learned from a volunteer at the pound," said Mark. He walked slowly from the kitchen straight toward the dining room wall as all three observants held their breath. Then he began making a clicking sound with his mouth and stopped abruptly about three feet before his face was about to make contact.

"How did you do that?" asked Michael.

"Well, the volunteer told me to press my tongue tight against the roof of my mouth and then snap it down hard so it makes a clicking sound. He told me if I listened to the echo of the snapping click, I'd be able to tell if there's an object in front of me. I've tried it and it really works!" he said enthusiastically. "Hopefully it will keep me from crashing into any more glass doors!"

"I hope so," Laurie said. "We don't need more thrills like that!"

"I think my first order of the day is to work on getting Prince settled in, feed him and get him ready to explore the neighborhood," said Mark as he downed his last bite of oatmeal. He stood and carefully made his way along the wall and into the bedroom, where he found Prince wide awake, but still sprawled comfortably on the rug. For one second that is. As soon as Prince spotted his new master, he leapt up and came to him, pushing gently against Mark's legs. "Looks like you're ready for a walk!" said Mark as he bent down to pet Prince. This was one energetic dog, one who would require brisk daily exercise, all the better for inspiring Mark and Linda to get in a workout for themselves as well.

After Prince had eaten a hearty breakfast, the foursome took him for a walk around the neighborhood. It was easy to tell how much he loved it, because when they arrived home after a couple of miles, he was eager for more. Michael suggested they take another walk to a nearby park he and Laurie had discovered, so they did that and it was wonderful! The trails at Coon Rapids Dam Regional Park were lined with big, beautiful trees and spacious grasslands that seemed to go on for miles and miles. They hiked for more than an hour, and by the time they made it back to the Visitor Center parking area, they were all ready for a rest. All except Prince, that is. He was an exuberant dog, a large, male Golden Retriever who seemed ready for anything. And friendly as well, eager to make friends with everyone, even strangers and their dogs.

"Anybody hungry?" Michael asked. "It's about time for lunch. How about if we drive home, have some sandwiches and then head over to the University with Prince?"

"Great idea," Linda said. "Mark and I haven't had a chance to walk around the campus. While we're there we can stop in at the Law School for our schedules and maybe pick up our books and class materials at the bookstore."

After lunch, everyone piled back into the car and headed to the University of Minnesota. Prince assumed his favorite spot at the backseat window next to Mark and appeared to take in every detail as they drove along. After they arrived on campus, the fivesome first stopped at the Law School, then the School of Medicine and School of Nursing. Prince seemed to be recording every step of the way with his eyes and nose as they made their way from building to building.

Driving home, Linda began reading the fall curriculum and noticed one of the first semester classes was a survey course designed to help students decide what branch of law they intended to practice. "When we were going to college, Mark and I talked about whether we wanted to go into private or public law, she said, "and we've both pretty much decided on public law since it includes criminal law."

"The good stuff!" laughed Mark.

"You're sure you want to deal with criminals?" asked Michael.

"I think so," said Mark. "I've been interested since way back when after Dad and I visited the Otter Tail County Courthouse in Fergus Falls and listened to the District Attorney questioning a guy in a murder case."

"It's not just murderers you deal with in criminal law," Linda said. "You also get to try people for arson, bribery, burglary and other serious crimes."

"Well, yippee to that!" laughed Laurie. "Sounds like an impressive clientele. I think I'd rather avoid those types!"

"But, Laurie," said Linda, "as a nurse you'll be caring for everyone, criminals and non-criminals alike. Anyone can be sick or injured." Laurie didn't have a response, and saw her sister was getting into her debate mode, so she just kept quiet.

"All of us are just starting out," said Mark diplomatically. "Who knows? We may all end up changing our minds."

As soon as they got home, Linda saw there was a message from her mom. She called her back, and Grace told her Marty and Chuck were going to drive down from Perham for a visit at the end of July. She wondered if the four of them could make it to a picnic at Turtle Lake on the last Sunday of that month. "Bill and Pearl are going to join us as well," she told Linda.

"Sounds like a good time!" said Linda. "Hold on, let me ask the others." In less than a minute she was back on the line, telling her mom they'd love to be there.

"We've never been to Turtle Lake," said Michael that night at dinner. "What's it like?"

"It's beautiful, real woodsy," said Laurie. "A lot of people go out there to swim and have picnics during the summer."

"We've been there many a time over the years with Mom and Dad," said Linda.

"I'm sure Prince will like it," Mark said. "We all know how happy he is outdoors."

What Mark said was certainly true. Their daily routine had been established, which included a brisk walk in the nearby park and around the neighborhood. It was obvious Prince loved every minute. One major change was substituting a leather harness with handle for his leash, but this didn't seem to bother him. He seemed to enjoy being just that much closer to Mark.

The warm July days passed rapidly, and in no time at all the Turtle Lake picnic date arrived. A lot of focused training had taken place with Prince, and Mark was eager to show everyone how well he meshed with and enhanced their lifestyle.

When the newlyweds arrived at Turtle Lake, their parents and Bill and Pearl were already there. "We thought we'd better get here early so we could nab a good spot," Walter said. He was right, as it was only noon and already most of the picnic tables were taken. The next order of business was hugs and kisses and meeting Prince, who seemed to revel in the spotlight of adoration.

"If you kids want to swim, now might be a good time while we get the food ready. We'll just relax and visit until you're tired out and ready to eat," said Grace.

It was a beautiful day at Turtle Lake, calm and serene and perfect for an afternoon of swimming and picnicking. The water's surface was like a sheet of glass, hardly a ripple. There must have been a couple hundred people splashing around as Mark and Prince approached its edge with Linda, Laurie and Michael. "Prince, sit!" Mark said. "Stay!" he commanded as he dropped the leather handle and walked out into the shallow water with the others. Prince began whining and pawing at the warm sand as Mark waded away from him into deeper water.

"It will be interesting to see if he stays put once we get further out," Michael said.

"We'll see," Mark said to his brother as the two of them began swimming side by side. "This is a first for him." When Michael looked back, he could see Prince still sitting, acutely alert in following Mark's every stroke.

"He's a good dog!" Michael yelled when they were about a hundred feet out and enjoying their swim. "He hasn't taken his eyes off you!"

Then it happened. The younger kids were splashing playfully in the shallow water near the shoreline, the teenagers and older adults swimming further out, when the sun suddenly disappeared behind a dense, dark cloud on the far side of the lake. No one paid much attention at first, then the wind kicked up and a small funnel of water began swirling over the surface of the lake. "Tornado!" yelled one of the swimmers as the funnel increased in size and began moving slowly in the direction of the swimmers in the deeper water. The scene rapidly became a state of tumultuous confusion as everyone began clamoring to leave the lake. Thunder rolled, flashes of lightning illuminated the darkened sky and heavy rain began to fall.

"We've got to swim to shore!" Michael yelled to Mark. "I'm headed your way!" Good-sized waves had formed and were lapping against them, and the fierce wind rendered his words inaudible. Just then a large wave hit Mark's back and head and covered him completely. Prince bolted into the water and began paddling furiously towards him, weaving in and out among the anxious swimmers who were making their way to shore. Prince got to Mark just before Michael, and as soon as Mark grabbed the leather handle, Prince turned and headed for the shore. Prince was a powerful swimmer, and it didn't take long for the two of them to get to shallow water. What had happened was a good example of what Mark had read about a dog's willful disobedience. Prince had disregarded Mark's previous command to sit and stay, and in doing so, had rescued his master from a dangerous situation.

"Good boy, Prince," said an exhausted and grateful Mark as he hugged his dog.

Laurie and Linda were anxiously waiting for their husbands when they finally made it to shore. "We've got to hurry, Mark," said Linda as she took hold of his free hand. "This looks real bad! Mom and Dad are loading all the picnic stuff back into their car. We're just going to eat at their house." It didn't take them long to gather their things, and in a few minutes everything was packed and they joined a long caravan of cars vacating the lake.

"Well, that certainly was a short and exciting hour at the lake!" Grace said as Walter eased their car into the line of traffic and began driving slowly down the dirt road leading to the highway.

"I've never seen a waterspout form over a lake like that," Marty said, "and I'm not too eager to ever see one again! It was frightening!"

"We all know about tornadoes, that's for sure," Walter said, "and we know how destructive they can be. I hope this one dies down before it reaches any neighborhoods."

It took a little over an hour before they got home. Amazingly, it was calm, quiet and peaceful in Coon Rapids. "Sure is nice here," Walter said as Chuck and Bill helped him unload the car and carry things to the patio.

"Go ahead and set everything out," said Grace, "as I'm sure the kids will be ready to eat whenever they get here."

They didn't have long to wait. The timing was perfect! When Michael pulled into the driveway, the luncheon feast was laid out on the back picnic table. "Right on time!" said Chuck. "You must have followed your noses!"

"As usual," laughed Michael. "You all were lucky you got out of there when you did. By the time we left, the dirt road from the lake to the highway was backed up with cars and hardly moving, and still a lot of people packing up and trying to get away."

"I'm glad we're all here safely!" said Grace. "Why don't you kids go change into dry clothes. We'll be ready to eat as soon as you are." It didn't take the boys long once Michael saw what was spread out on the large picnic table and described it to Mark. Within minutes, they were in the house and back out again. It took the girls a little longer.

"Let's pray before we eat," Walter said, "not only for this delicious-looking food the ladies have fixed, but also for the safety of those who weren't able to get away from the lake as fast as we did; *Lord, we give you thanks for this food and ask you to shower your blessings on those who prepared it. Please watch over all the families that were enjoying the lake today. Amen.*"

"Boy, Dad," Laurie teased, "that was a short prayer for you. You must be hungry."

"I am!" he said.

"Just one minute before we dig in. I'd like to describe this feast to Mark," said Michael as he put his arm around his brother who was seated next to him. "First, there's a big pot of Mom's old-fashioned baked beans, you know the ones, Mark."

"I can smell them," Mark said with a big smile. "How well I remember!"

"Next we have an impressive bowl of delicious-looking potato salad. Who takes the honors for that?" Michael asked.

"That would be me!" said Grace cheerfully. "It's an old favorite of Walter's, lots of good stuff in it."

"Sounds great!" Mark said enthusiastically.

"You can be the first tester, Mark," said Linda as she scooped up a small spoonful and held it near his lips.

Mark opened his mouth and Linda very gently fed him the sampling. He chewed slowly, savoring the flavors. "Fantastic!" he said as he swallowed the bite.

"We know about the beautiful ham sandwiches, as our lovely wives made them before we left home this morning," Michael said. "And there's more, a colorful fruit salad, potato chips, olives and pickles! And last but not least, two perfect-looking pies! Who made them?"

"I did," Pearl said shyly. "We had so much rhubarb growing in our garden, I thought I'd make a couple."

"That's my gal!" said Bill, beaming.

"Wow! One of my favorite desserts, Aunt Pearl!" Mark said, licking his lips. "Thank you for making it!"

"Bill likes it tart and tasty with a bit of cinnamon, so that's the way I do it. I hope you'll like it," she said.

"I already know I do!" Mark said grinning.

"Enough talk. Let's get down to business," laughed Bill.

"I'm with you, Bill," Walter said. "Let the feast begin."

With five hungry men, it didn't take long for the great disappearing act to take place. Grace, Marty, Pearl, Linda and Laurie looked on in amazement as the foods they'd spent hours preparing vanished in mere minutes.

"Are you guys sure you're not too full for pie?" Pearl asked facetiously as she began cutting generous slices.

Everyone laughed at such a silly question. "That's your answer, Aunt Pearl," said Mark. "You know us. We always save room for dessert!"

"And how many would like vanilla ice cream?" asked Pearl, knowing full well what the unanimous answer would be. Sure enough, a flurry of hands fanned the air.

In spite of having had to leave the lake early, everyone seemed to be having a great time, and it was easy to see why. It was a sunny, restful Sunday afternoon in Coon Rapids, peaceful and quiet in the Johnson's beautifully-landscaped back yard. The food was delicious and the joyful sounds of family filled the air. Even Prince seemed extra happy. After Mark fed him and removed his harness, he just lay on the grass and gnawed contentedly on a meaty bone Walter had bought especially for him.

Around six o'clock the sun began to set, and those who were leaving gathered their things in preparation for the trip home. Pearl and Bill had to drive to Columbia Heights, which wasn't far, but the traffic could get heavy on a Sunday afternoon, and Bill had to get up early on

Monday morning to go to work at Honeywell. Marty and Chuck were staying the night with Grace and Walter and would head to Perham the next morning, so they weren't in a hurry to go anywhere. The twins would be starting graduate school at the University of Minnesota in a month, but were free spirits for now and taking advantage of every minute of leisure.

When they all woke up Monday morning and read the headlines in the Minneapolis papers, they were startled and saddened by the news:

BOY KILLED
IN TURTLE LAKE TRAGEDY

Early Sunday afternoon, while hundreds of swimmers and picnickers were enjoying a pleasant day in the sun at Turtle Lake, the sky turned black, rain began to fall, and a monster tornado in the form of a waterspout began moving rapidly towards the children and adults who were scrambling from the lake. Sadly, twelve-year-old Tony Swanson, son of John and Edith Swanson, didn't survive. He had been swimming in deeper water and was sucked into the funnel of the waterspout before he could reach shore. His crushed body was found beneath a felled tree in a woodsy area near the picnic grounds. Tony was the eldest child of Mr. and Mrs. Swanson, one of six children. Needless to say, this is a devastating tragedy for the Coon Rapids family and the community. Tony was an eighth-grade student at Coon Rapids Middle School. Funeral arrangements are pending.

After breakfast the next morning, the twins drove over to their parents' house to say goodbye to Marty and Chuck before they left for Perham. Grace was busy in the kitchen when they arrived. They'd just finished eating and were talking about the tragedy that had taken place at Turtle Lake.

"We were lucky to get out of there as fast as we did," Walter said. "I sure feel for the Swanson family. Their son must have been pretty far out in the water. According to the paper, there were no other serious injuries. The waterspout veered way left of the picnic grounds and into the wooded area when it reached land."

"I sort of panicked," Mark said. "Michael yelled for me to swim to shore just as a big wave slammed against my back. When I surfaced, I'd lost all sense of direction, and before I knew it, Prince was right there by my side." Prince heard his name, and nuzzled up against Mark's leg as he petted him fondly. "Isn't that something?" Mark said. "The last command I gave him before I went into the lake was to sit and stay, but when he saw I was in trouble, he overrode the order and was right there to help me. I love this dog!"

"Well, Prince certainly loves you, no question about that," Marty said. "He may well have saved your life!"

While everyone was enjoying some morning coffee, Chuck said, "Marty and I usually say our Rosary in the car whenever we begin traveling somewhere, but would you mind if we all prayed it together now for the Swanson child and his family?"

"That's an excellent idea, Chuck," Grace said. "Just give us a minute to get our rosaries and we can begin."

When everyone was settled, Chuck made the sign of the cross and began, "In the name of the Father, and of the Son, and of the Holy Spirit…" After the Rosary was finished, everyone said their goodbyes and the Johnson home was once again their own.

"That was really an enjoyable weekend," Marty said as she eased her body against the car's plush upholstery and closed her eyes. Chuck smiled over at her as he drove towards Perham, knowing she was tired and would soon dose off.

This gave him some pondering time before they reached home. He thought about life, what it had been like when Marty and he were first married, how it had changed when the twins came along. Oh, how it had changed! Those "preemies" were a handful, but they sure grew in a hurry, and Mark, in spite of his blindness, thrived no less than his sighted brother. Chuck thought about how the twins used to run the school track together, how the world had opened for Mark when he learned to read from the braille *World Book Encyclopedia*.

About a half hour from Perham, Marty opened her eyes and stretched. "I think I nodded off," she said.

"You did, honey," he said. "While you were sleeping, your lips began moving. It was like you were carrying on a conversation with someone."

"I was!" laughed Marty. "I dreamed I was giving birth to the boys, was trying to talk to Sister Giovanni as she was telling Dr. Schoeneberger she thought there was a second baby."

"How right she was!" said Chuck smiling.

"It's hard to believe they're going to be twenty-one this month!" said Marty.

Later that evening, Laurie, Linda, Michael and Mark were sitting in their living room, planning how they intended to spend August before school began. "You two are going to laugh at this after what Mark and I told you about our wanting to be criminal lawyers," Linda said.

"Uh oh, what now?" Laurie asked as she smiled at her sister. "Don't tell me you've changed your minds about law school!"

"No," she said, "but we recently read about providing legal services to low-income people in civil matters, and it sounds like something we'd like to investigate."

"What's the next step?" Michael asked.

"Well, we want to take a drive to St. Paul tomorrow and learn more about it," said Mark.

"We can all go," said Laurie cheerfully, "make a fun day out of it!"

"Sounds good to me," said Linda.

"I'm in," said Michael. "Let's do it."

"I have a feeling these August days are going to fly by," said Laurie. "It's a big month."

"Big month?" said Michael curiously. "Why do you say that?"

"My sweet husband," she said dramatically, "have you forgotten what happens in August?"

A smile broke over Mark's face as he looked Michael's way. "We're going to be twenty-one, Brother!"

"Wow! I actually haven't had time to think about it," laughed Michael. "So much has been happening around here that planning for a birthday has been the least of my concerns."

"Well, no need to worry about a thing," Laurie said. "My parents have invited us all over to their house for a grand celebration. My mom wants to make the cake and I told her to go for it!"

On Monday morning, everyone piled into the car and drove to St. Paul to learn more about the legal needs of low-income people. The more Linda and Mark discovered about that category of law, the more they began leaning in that direction.

"You know, Linda," he said, "it sure seems we'd be doing a lot more for humanity by helping poor people receive justice than by spending time trying to put criminals behind bars."

"I'm inclined to agree with you," she said, "but there's a lot to consider before we make up our minds. We've got some time before we have to do so. Do you want me to keep reading?"

"Yes, do," he said, as Linda continued: "*The harm resulting from an unfavorable outcome of a legal dispute is frequently more severe for the poor than for others. The ability to resist a loss of welfare eligibility or an eviction often literally means the difference between having adequate food, clothing, shelter, and doing without the essentials of a modern society. In most disputes, the opposing party likely will have aggressive legal representation available. Bureaucracies, merchants, collection agencies and the rest of the non-poor society with which the poor must deal all have their lawyers. To leave the poor to confront such parties without legal representation is to invite their victimization.*"

"Wow, sounds pretty dire," Mark said.

"Want me to continue?" she asked.

"Yes, please do," he said.

"Okay," said Linda as she read on: "*Because the need for legal advice may arise in any area of governmental regulation or private conduct affecting the poor and their essential life needs, legal services for the poor have a breadth of impact which may make them more critical for the poor than any one specific substantive aid program. A lawyer is the key to access to the legal system, and without such access, few rights are granted and none is secure.*"

"That's it," she said. "What do you think?"

"Very interesting," said Mark. "A lot to consider before we make up our minds. I think I'll write to my mom and dad and see what they think."

"Good idea," said Linda, "and we'll have a chance to talk it over with my folks when we see them Sunday."

That evening, Mark sat down at his braille machine and tapped out a letter to his parents:

August 3, 1974

Dear Mom & Dad,

This may come as a surprise to you, but after investigating what legal aid attorneys do for their clients, and after visiting the administrative offices of the Southern Minnesota Regional Legal Services in St. Paul today, Linda and I have become interested in the work they do. We'd like your opinion about our doing that kind of civil law. Of course, we've got three years before we make up our minds, but it doesn't hurt to examine all the possibilities before we do.

There's been so much going on recently that Michael and I completely forgot we'd be turning twenty-one this Sunday! Laurie and Linda's parents have invited us to their house for a birthday celebration. I wish you could be there to share in the festivities. We'll make up for it the next time we're together! I know you'll be with us in spirit!

We'll be looking forward to hearing from you.

—Love, Mark

During the rest of the week, the twins just kicked back and relaxed, took Prince on long walks at the Coon Rapids Dam Regional Park, and enjoyed their freedom, especially freedom from studying and sitting through examinations. It would all start up again soon enough, so they were going to enjoy August!

Grace outdid herself for the birthday supper. "Smells like turkey in here!" said Mark as soon as the foursome walked in the front door.

"It's not November," said Grace cheerily as they met at the entry, "but I'm so thankful to have you two as my sons that I wanted to make something special for this special day."

"And that she did!" said Walter as he welcomed the company. "Thanksgiving dinner with all the trimmings!"

Mark moved in Grace's direction with outstretched arms. As the two of them embraced, he said softly, "Mom, you know you've won our hearts and we love you like our own mother." This was the first time either of the boys had called Grace "Mom." Tears formed in her eyes as Michael moved in and gave her a big hug as well.

"I second Mark's words," said Michael. "We sure do love you."

When they sat down to eat, Walter began with a prayer: *Father, we thank You for all the blessings you've given us. Please guide our daughters and sons in their futures. And thank You for my thoughtful and caring wife, who has prepared this beautiful birthday supper. Amen."*

"We're a couple of lucky guys," Mark said. "Michael and I sure do love your daughters!"

Laurie and Linda beamed. "We drove to St. Paul on Monday to learn more about legal aid lawyers," said Linda. "It was so interesting. What would you think about us considering civil law, Dad?"

"That's entirely up to you," he said. "It certainly would be different from criminal law. Not as exciting, I suspect, since you'd be dealing mainly with government programs, landlord/tenant issues, consumer problems, family problems, that sort of thing. There's no hurry for you to make up your minds since you're just starting law school."

"That's right," said Grace. "Take the time you need to figure it out."

For the next fifteen minutes, the talk stopped and the serious eating commenced. "You outdid yourself once again, Mom," Michael said between mouthfuls. "This is delicious!"

Grace topped off the feast with brown-butter-frosted pumpkin spice cake and creamy vanilla ice cream. There were forty-two candles, twenty-one on each side of the cake. With Mark seated on one side of the table and Michael on the other, Grace positioned the glowing cake between them. "When I say blow, give it all you've got, Mark!" said Michael. "We're going to extinguish this beauty with one breath, okay?"

"Okay," he said, "I'm ready! Count of three!"

"Okay," said Michael. "One, two, three, BLOW!" Both boys blasted the cake with mighty air from their young lungs, creating so much smoke they set off the fire alarm! That in turn set off Prince, who began barking and didn't stop until the smoke had cleared from the room. Everyone had a good laugh and it was a birthday to be remembered!

———— ◆ · ◆ ————

August 17, 1974

Dear Mark,

I realize it's been two weeks since you wrote and asked about pursuing the practice of law with a focus on legal aid services. Sorry for the delay in responding. I've been real busy preparing for my classes, also selling encyclopedias like crazy. It seems like the schools and a lot of parents tend to wait until the last minute to place orders, and then they want them right now! Of course, you know that all too well from your selling days, always busier near the start of the school year.

Another reason it took me some time to reply is that I wrote to a former student who is now a practicing attorney, asked for her thoughts on pursuing law in the direction of legal aid services. She kindly wrote back, and here's what she had to say on the subject:

'In response to your question about the pursuit of law with a focus on legal aid services, if a lawyer stays in a legal aid setting after finishing law school, it's pure dedication. There's no money in it, that's for sure. I'd liken it to going to work for the Sierra Club or some other cause. You really have to believe in what you're doing, you have to want to be there. Your daughter-in-law and son might try it as students and stay with it or there might be a pivotal "crusaders" moment where they witness something unfair happening to a powerless client and feel called to get involved. One thing they might consider is that legal aid is often something law students do during the second and third years of law school to get them into the actual practice of law, working with real people. Law school doesn't really teach you how to practice law. It gives you knowledge of the law, but being able to apply it to real world situations is a long process. I'd also say learning to be a good lawyer is in part apprenticing yourself to someone who will teach you. It's very traditional that way. Your daughter-in-law and son might decide to work in a prestigious firm for a while and get training in some aspect of law, corporate transactions or civil litigation being two obvious tracks, and then realize their ideals are being squandered in a world where all they're doing is helping corporations wage battles over money. People with ideals typically find that working in a large firm isn't satisfying because they're so far removed from the problems of real people.'

Well, there you have it, kids, right from the horse's mouth. I hope this information is helpful. A lot to think about before you make up your minds, no doubt about that.

All's well here with Mom and me. We look forward to seeing you again and hope you had a grand birthday celebration with Grace and Walter and your lovely brides.

—Love, Dad

OVER THE NEXT FEW DAYS, LINDA AND MARK DIDN'T HAVE TIME TO concern themselves over whether they were going to practice criminal or civil law. Shortly after breakfast on Monday morning, a large box and separate package appeared at their front door from the University of Minnesota School of Law. The box contained all of the very expensive case books on torts, contracts, civil procedure, real property and criminal law, with a second set in braille and on compact discs for Mark. The smaller package contained their assignments.

The first assignment was an essay known as "The Timothy Problem." It was designed to see how well students dealt with a complex situation and to determine how ably they analyzed and reached a logical conclusion. When Mark and Linda were finished with the assignment and compared notes, they felt the essay wasn't too difficult and that they had done well, and this bolstered their confidence.

The second assignment was something else again, much more difficult and very confusing. They were asked to *brief* several cases, and neither of them had any idea how to go about doing that. That's when the heavy reading began. Fortunately, their packet contained samples, and it didn't take them long to get the hang of it, especially with each other's assistance. It did take them an ungodly amount of time, though, to complete each brief. Doing so consisted of reading a complicated court case and then attempting to make out the meaning of the relevant "Facts, Issue, Rule of Law, Analysis of Law and Conclusion." The books were designed to help students read cases and to understand the origin of current laws. Well, they helped, but by the time Linda and Mark finished their briefing assignment, they realized Law School at the University of Minnesota was not going to be a walk in the park.

That fact was driven home on the first day of school when they got to meet upper-classmen, several visiting attorneys who had graduated from the University of Minnesota, and their professors. The upper-classmen and visiting attorneys shared a unanimous warning: Law school will be difficult, different and challenging, regardless of one's previous academic prowess. When Linda and Mark spoke to some of the first-year students who'd made it through, they described it as grueling, with a number of students not moving on to the second year.

When the foursome got together for supper that night, they had a lot to share. "I think Law School's going to be a four-year course in survival tactics," said Mark.

"It was scary talking to the upper classmen," said Linda. "They sure didn't offer much encouragement. Sounds like it's going to be brutally hard."

"Just the opposite for me," said Michael smiling. "The semester starts with anatomy, histology, embryology, genetics, molecular biology and biochemistry. Easy peasey."

"Wow. Impressive!" said Linda.

"How'd your first day go, Laurie?" asked Michael.

"Not as intense as any of yours, thankfully!" laughed Laurie. "I'll be studying aspects of nursing that aim to improve people's health, will also be doing a lot of hands-on learning when I'm not in the classroom."

"We've all got our work cut out for us," said Linda. "Ready or not, here we come!"

"You kids must be very busy," said Grace when she called in October and Linda picked up the phone. "Haven't heard from you for way too long. How's school going?"

"It's been challenging for all of us," said Linda. "The amount of work they're giving us is exhausting."

Linda sounded tired, and it concerned Grace, so she just chatted casually with her for a while and then asked, "Do you remember what's coming up on November 1st?"

After a long hesitation, Linda answered. "We've been so busy I completely forgot. Our 21st birthday! Haven't had a minute to think about it."

"It's also All Saints Day," Grace said. "Anyway, your dad and I would love to take you all out for a smorgasbord dinner at the Radisson Hotel in Minneapolis. We hoped if we called enough in advance that you'd reserve the date for us, unless of course you'd like to spend the day with your husbands, which would be totally understandable!"

"It sounds great, Mom," said Linda. "Thank you! I'll ask the gang, but I'm sure Laurie and the guys would love to go. And, Mom, there's something I have to tell you, big news, but it's a secret. Don't say anything to Dad yet."

"You've got me curious," said Grace. "Whatever could it be?"

"I hope you're sitting down," laughed Linda. "You're not going to believe this, but Laurie and I missed our periods this month! We think we might be pregnant! Both of us!"

"Oh my!" said Grace after an audible gasp. "Pregnant? Both of you? That *is* big news! You're right, I can't believe it! Linda could hear her mother breathing heavily. "I'm stunned," she said, "and very happy at the same time!"

"We haven't said anything to Mark or Michael yet, so keep it a secret," Linda cautioned, "not a word to them or Dad. We'll soon know for sure, and if so, we plan to announce it at our birthday dinner."

"Oh, Linda, I'm so excited for all of you," said Grace. "I know Walter and the boys will be as well! Quite a surprise, I'll say that. We figured you were going to complete your schooling before starting a family."

"As did we!" laughed Linda. "So much for natural birth control. Turns out the rhythm method didn't work so well for either of us. I think your two daughters are soon to be two moms!"

"Well, this mom's pretty thrilled about becoming a grandmother and I know Grandpa Walter will be thrilled as well!"

"Okay, Mom, I've got to run," Linda said. "Remember, hush, hush. It's a big secret until we announce it at dinner."

"My lips are sealed," Grace said.

Halloween arrived and Walter and Grace were kept busy greeting the multitude of neighborhood trick-or-treaters at their door. Grace couldn't get the baby news from her mind as she dropped money and candy into the open bags. She was itching to tell Walter the good news, but true to her word, didn't say a thing.

The next day they all met at the Radisson in downtown Minneapolis. Walter and Grace greeted the kids with warm hugs at the front door of the hotel and escorted them to the dining room. It was a huge space with elegant table settings and glittering chandeliers. Linda relayed the scene in detail to Mark as they made their way to their table.

"The food looks great, Mark!" said Michael as he described the array of offerings to his brother. "There are hot and cold hors d'oeuvres, a dozen different kinds of cheeses, salads, side dishes, casseroles, roast beef, ham, turkey. You name it, it's here for the taking!"

None of the kids had ever been to a smorgasbord at the Radisson, and they were impressed. "I'm salivating," said Mark, "ready for round one!"

"Well," Walter said after they were seated, "it's really good to see you kids again. Grace tells me you've all been studying so hard you've lost track of time, you girls almost forgetting your birthday! Tonight, we'll just relax and celebrate, so let's begin with a prayer." Everyone bowed their heads as Walter began: "*Dear Lord, You have been so good to us, blessing us with two precious babies twenty-one years ago. We honor you! We thank you for letting our daughters meet and fall in love with two wonderful young men. And we thank you for this bounty of food which we are about to receive. Amen.*"

"OK, let's get this feast started!" said Grace as everyone headed up to the smorgasbord.

And what a feast it was! The men went for the ham and sweet potato casserole dish, Linda and Laurie had roast beef and Grace had turkey. The conversation was lively and they were all enjoying themselves immensely, even Prince, who was lying quietly under Mark's chair in hopeful anticipation of a dropped morsel. When they'd all had their fill, a waiter came and cleared the table of dishes.

"I'm so stuffed!" said Laurie.

"Me, too, but I saw a lot of good-looking desserts," said Michael.

"Wait just a minute!" Walter said. "You didn't think we were going to let this celebration pass without a special cake, did you?"

At that moment Walter signaled to one of the waiters standing near closed double doors leading to the kitchen, and when they opened, another waiter came through with a large pink-frosted angel food cake held high over his head, the crystal platter deftly balanced on one hand. When he set it down in the middle of the table, everyone was in awe. Adorned with edible flowers and an elegant HAPPY 21st BIRTHDAY inscription, the glowing cake was a beautiful sight to behold.

"It's beautiful, Mom and Dad!" Linda said after describing it to Mark. "Thank you!"

"Wow! It sure is! Thank you!" Laurie said.

"Seems like the perfect time to share another reason for celebration, don't you think, Laurie?" said Linda as she smiled at her sister.

"I think you're right," she said.

"You do the honors," Linda said.

Laurie cleared her throat in intentionally-dramatic fashion. "OK, before we blow out these candles, Linda and I have special news to share," said Laurie, "something big to celebrate in addition to our birthdays!"

"Tell us before the cake burns up!" laughed Michael.

"Well," said Laurie, "We just found out we're pregnant, both of us!"

"Wha…???" said a stunned Michael as Mark's mouth fell open.

"You're not kidding, are you?" said Walter.

"Really? Seriously?" said Michael, disbelief etched on his face

"It's true," said Linda as she reached for Mark's hand and placed it on her belly. "Both of us, pregnant!"

"Wow!" said Mark as he kissed her softly on the cheek. "Not what I was expecting to hear, that's for sure. I can't believe it!"

"Wow! Wow! Wow! That's a real stunner!" Michael said as he wiped the back of his hand across his brow. "Shocked as I am, I'm very happy!" he said as he hugged Laurie.

"Certainly not what you'd anticipated for this year, but it's wonderful news, and I'm so happy for all of you!" said Grace.

"Needless to say, the year won't play out quite as planned," said Laurie. "We've all got some serious talking to do."

"Don't worry, honey," Walter said. "You're in good hands and always will be. Having a baby is a grand adventure, just take things one day at a time. Congratulations to all four of you! Now why don't you take care of those candles before we're eating a pile of wax!"

The birthday sisters inhaled deeply, made their wishes and blew with gusto. Grace did the honors of serving everyone, things feeling a little déjà vu with the boys' birthday having been just three months earlier, but it was very different as well. All of their lives would soon be dramatically different!

After they left the hotel and drove home, Walter and Grace stayed up and talked about the upcoming changes for their girls and Michael and Mark. They had noted the concern on both boys' faces when Laurie made the big announcement. "It will be all right," said Walter proudly. "They'll have to make some adjustments, just as we did. And things have turned out pretty darn perfect with our babies!"

"Can't argue with that," said Grace. "Beautiful girls, inside and out. And I love our sons-in-law. We're very lucky. They'll all be wonderful parents, I know that."

"Do you remember how little we had when we were newlyweds and you announced you were pregnant?"

"I sure do," Grace said, "and we didn't have an education or a nice place to live. We eked out a living, you became a successful builder and here we are!"

"I think everyone struggles over this or that when they're starting out, that's just life," said Walter.

"Parents just don't like to see their kids suffer along the journey," said Grace with a sigh, "but it's inevitable, makes the easier times all the more appreciated. Best not to meddle, we'll just wait and watch and be there for them as need be, see how it all comes out."

"I agree. You lifted the thought right out of my head," he said with a chuckle.

There wasn't quite so much chuckling going on when the twins got home and sat down to talk. Even Prince was affected by the palpable tension. He moved around nervously after he'd eaten, unsettled, not lying quietly in the living room and dozing off as usual. "Why don't we say the Rosary before we get to talking about all this," suggested Mark.

"That's a good idea," Michael said. "The four of us have some important decisions to make, and I'm all for praying before every one.

So, I'll begin: *In the name of the Father, and of the Son, and of the Holy Spirit. I believe in God the Father almighty…"*

It was getting late by the time they finished the Rosary and everyone was exhausted, especially Linda and Laurie, not only from the fanfare of their birthdays, but also from the whirlwind of emotion surrounding their new status as mothers-to-be. And they couldn't help but notice the serious attitudes their husbands had developed since learning they were going to be fathers. "Why don't we all just go to bed and get a good night's sleep before we start discussing all this," said Laurie. "I'm pretty tired."

"Good idea," Linda said. "I'm tired, too. We'll all be able to think more clearly tomorrow."

"Well," Mark said softly as he reached for Linda's hand, "let's call it a day." As they got up and headed for their bedroom, Prince rose and followed close behind. He sensed something different had taken place. Life didn't feel quite as happy and relaxed as it had been, and he didn't want to miss anything or risk being left behind.

When they all sat together the next morning for breakfast, it seemed a lot of talk had already taken place between Laurie and Michael. They were in a decision-making mode. "Laurie and I talked well into the night before we finally got to sleep," Michael said, "and we've decided what we're going to do." This startled Mark. He was used to talking things over with his brother before they made major decisions. Not anymore. Now they talked things over with their wives! "We've decided it would be best for us if I quit med school at the end of the first semester and got a job," Michael said. "With a baby, we're going to need more money just to get by, and we need to face reality now before we get any deeper in debt."

At first neither Mark nor Linda knew what to say. After a long hesitation, Linda said, "We share your concerns, Michael. Mark and I did a lot of talking last night as well. We're all in the same boat. We coasted through St. Ben's and St. John's with scholarships and the help of our folks, but now it's a different story. We've been mulling over the idea of dropping out of graduate school at the end of the semester and getting jobs, and now that we know your plan is to do so, it seems like a wise choice for us as well."

"I agree," said a somber-faced Mark as he reached out to hold Linda's hand. "Have to face the fact that additional income will be a necessity nine months from now."

"Mom and Dad aren't going to believe all we have to tell them," said Michael.

"I'll write them a letter this afternoon," said Mark."

November 3, 1974

Dear Mom & Dad,

Walter and Grace took us all out to the Radisson Hotel in Minneapolis last Friday for Laurie and Linda's 21st birthday celebration. It was a smorgasbord and the food was great! But the magnificent dinner and cake weren't even close to the highlight of the night. That came when Linda and Laurie announced—better sit down for this one—they are both pregnant! It's true! The only one they'd told ahead of time was Grace, and she had somehow managed to keep it a secret.

Needless to say, Michael and I were stunned. So much for the rhythm method of birth control. We had of course planned on getting a good start in graduate school before starting a family. Not anymore! We prayed on it Friday night when we got home and talked about it into the wee hours of the morning. We've made some major decisions and they're going to result in major changes in our lives.

Michael and Laurie have decided she'll continue with her nursing program until she receives her R.N. degree in June, and Michael will drop out of medical school at the end of the first semester and look for work in Minneapolis, hopefully with a pharmaceutical company. Linda and I are going to drop out of Law School at the end of the first semester and will start looking for work as well. It looks like the only one staying in graduate school will be Laurie. The timing is good for her, as the babies aren't due until late July. She should be able to finish with school and get her degree before she delivers. Linda and I have talked about what kind of work we'll be looking for, but the success of that will depend on what's available.

That's what's been happening in our lives. Big surprise, I know. It's our new reality and we're dealing with it as best we can, leaning on each

*other and taking things one day at a time. We love you and will keep
you posted as the weeks roll along.*

—Love, Mark

November turned out to be an interesting month. Laurie was
saddened about the fact she would be the only one continuing with
graduate school, but happy as well because Michael had already secured
a position with a pharmaceutical company and would be starting work
at the end of the semester. When the company learned he had previous
selling experience with *World Book Encyclopedia*, their eyes lit up.
That experience, plus his focused science background from St. John's
University, made him a perfect candidate for contacting doctors and
introducing them to new drugs.

The job market wasn't quite so rosy for Linda or Mark. They
considered going to work for an insurance company, even went so far
as to take tests to be licensed to sell health, life and auto insurance,
but the more they talked about it and explored the field, the more
they knew selling insurance was not for them. Things were looking a
little dire until the end of the month when they received a letter from
Mark's parents.

November 15, 1974

Dear Linda and Mark,

*To say your letter was full of surprises is putting it mildly! We apologize for
the delay in getting back to you, as Marty and I had a lot to talk over. I'll
cut right to the chase. We're wondering if you'd consider coming to live with
us until you get on your feet financially, can zero in on your careers and
have the baby. We have plenty of room as you know, and we'd love to have
you here. Prince, too!*

*Before I left school today, I had a talk with Mr. Pfenninger, our
Principal, and told him about your decision to drop out of Law School,
at least for now. He said, "Tell Mark and Linda we'll have openings in
English, World History and Business Law next year, and if they want to
get teaching credentials and come back here and work, we'd love to have*

them!" He also said they'd create an elective course in Braille if you'd like to teach that, Mark. I don't know if you two have ever thought about teaching as a career, but it might be something to consider. I know I've loved it. In any event, I know you have a lot of thinking to do and some big decisions to make.

We invited Grace and Walter to our house for Thanksgiving. We'd love for Laurie and Michael and you two to come as well, if you can. It would give us a chance to all be together again, to visit and talk about your plans. I know it's a bit of a drive, but it you think you can take a break from your studies, we'd love to see you!

Your news was quite a surprise, as I said, but Marty and I are so very happy for all of you. We can't wait to be Grandma & Grandpa two times over and would love to congratulate you in person if you can make it here for Thanksgiving.

—Love, Dad

<hr />

WHEN THANKSGIVING DAY ARRIVED, SO DID ALL THE COMPANY! Grace and Walter showed up first, Grace enthusiastically jumping in to help Marty prepare the turkey and all the fixings. The four parents were looking forward to some time to relax and visit, as Walter set his own work hours and the four students didn't have to be back to school until Monday.

"What do you think is going to happen with those kids of ours?" Grace asked Marty as the two of them worked busily in the kitchen.

"You know, I think it will all be OK. They'll work it out," Marty said assuredly. "I'll admit, it was quite a struggle for Chuck and me to move to Karlsruhe, North Dakota, and eke out a living during his first year of teaching, but we did it. We moved to Perham during his second year and we've been happy here ever since. Oh, and by the way, Grace, I don't know if Linda mentioned it to you, but we invited her and Mark to come and live with us until after the baby's born and they've had a chance to get back on their feet."

"Oh, my!" said Grace in surprise. "I didn't know! That's very kind of you!"

The Thanksgiving feast went off without a hitch. There was a lot of laughter and talk about school and work and babies—and the very real possibility of twins given the double-sided family history. Marty and Chuck were delighted when Mark and Linda told them they'd decided to take them up on the generous offer to share their home.

Friday morning as they were getting ready to drive back to Coon Rapids, Walter said to Chuck and Marty, "What would you think about coming to our house for Christmas? By that time the kids will be wrapping up their first semester and we can all celebrate the new paths ahead."

"Sounds great to me," said Chuck.

"It would be lovely," said Marty. "Thank you for the invitation!"

Christmas would fall on a Tuesday, and everyone except Laurie would be finished with school. Except for Laurie, they'd all be selling their books back at the bookstore, especially the expensive law books Linda and Mark had purchased. Every penny saved would make a difference from this point on.

It didn't take the kids long to forget about school when Christmas Eve arrived and they pulled up in front of the festively-decorated Johnson home, hiking through a foot of snow to reach the front door. Marty and Chuck had arrived early from Perham and had been helping Walter and Grace prepare the holiday dinner. Walter had a blazing fire going and it was comfortable and warm in the house, and cheery, too. "Welcome! Welcome!" he said jovially as the kids came in, "and Merry Christmas to all of you!" After a round of hugs and kisses, everyone settled in the living room by the fire and glittering tree to relax and chat and appreciate the array of delicious aromas emanating from the kitchen.

The mid-day hours rolled by and the festive dinner was soon served. Table conversation centered on Linda and Laurie and how they'd been doing with their pregnancies. The radiant mothers-to-be said they felt fine, and judging by the way Laurie packed in the food, she was most certainly eating for two! "Every time I sit down for a meal I feel like I haven't eaten for days!" she said as she reached for a second helping of mashed potatoes. "Could be a problem if it keeps up for nine months!" Linda laughed. She didn't have the same voracious appetite as her sister, but she was enjoying every bite nonetheless.

"You girls both look very healthy," Grace said. "I suppose you're taking vitamins and have already seen a doctor."

"I haven't yet, Mom," said Linda. "I figured I'd wait until I get to Perham."

"Maybe you can get the same one who delivered the boys," Marty said smiling. "He's wonderful, Dr. Schoeneberger. After all these years he still has his practice here."

"That would be pretty special, to have the same doctor who delivered my husband," said Linda as she leaned over and kissed a beaming Mark on the cheek.

"I know you'd love him," said Marty. "Chuck and I sure do."

After feasting on the delicious Christmas Eve supper, everyone gathered once again in the living room and began opening presents. The highlight of the evening was when Linda and Laurie opened theirs. They were each handed a small envelope from their dad, but what it contained was huge! The girls opened them at the same time and each unfolded the notes within. Linda read hers aloud: *"To the Children We Love - Walter and I talked about what to get the four of you for Christmas, thought a lot about what life was like for us when we were just starting out. We decided that more than anything, you'd probably most appreciate having some extra money just for living. Enjoy! Much love, Mom & Dad."* In each of the girls' two envelopes was an even smaller envelope, and the girls opened them slowly together. Within each was a $5,000 check!

"Oh my gosh! Thank you!" said Linda as her mouth fell open. "Mark, it's a check for $5,000!"

"Dad! Mom! I can't believe this! Thank you!" said Laurie as she looked at her check. "It's $5,000 for us as well!" said Laurie to Michael as she hugged him. Tears streamed down the girls' faces as they got up to embrace their parents.

"That is so generous of you!" said Michael. "Thank you!"

"Yes, thank you so much! We sure can use it." said a stunned Mark as the boys stood and embraced Grace and Walter.

"Mark and I will definitely put this money to good use," said Laurie.

"The same goes for me and Michael," Linda said. "With our new lives in Perham and a baby on the way, there's no better gift!"

Chuck and Marty joined in the hugs of appreciation and gratitude and the Christmas Eve festivities carried on into the evening hours, with more gifts to be opened and platters of Grace and Marty's home-baked goodies to be enjoyed!

◆ • ◆

BY EARLY JANUARY, MARK AND LINDA HAD MOVED AND WERE settling into life in Perham. They made an appointment with Mr. Pfenninger to find out more about the possibility of becoming teachers, and he was very helpful in laying out a plan. This involved attending Moorhead State Teacher's College during the spring semester to pick up the required education units and do their practice teaching. It was a plan made in heaven, because the college was only sixty miles from Perham, and the education courses turned out to be extremely helpful.

During their practice hours, Linda taught a World History class to seniors and Mark taught a 7th grade English class. They were both very nervous the first day they entered their classrooms, especially Linda, who was just a couple of years older than her students. She later told Mark she had a difficult time just taking roll! In spite of their first-day jitters, both new teachers adjusted rapidly and very much enjoyed the interactions they had with their students. Mark's 7th graders were surprised when he entered the classroom for the first time. Not only was their teacher blind, but he also had a big hairy dog at his side! It didn't take the kids long to love and respect both their teacher and Prince.

The school year moved along nicely. Linda and Mark experienced a couple of hazardous drives to Moorhead State College in blinding snow in January and February, but when spring arrived and the snow started melting, they could see that what they had set out to accomplish was going to be a very satisfying experience, and they were feeling upbeat and optimistic. Then Linda got a newsy letter from her sister, an exciting letter that sent her into a tailspin!

April 1, 1975

Dear Linda,

I wish I could say April Fools about what I'm going to tell you, but I can't. It's a fact, it's true, and I'm not kidding. Are you sitting down? My belly's been getting big, like a balloon. I thought it was maybe because I've been eating so much! I saw my obstetrician today, Dr. Norman, and after he examined me, he smiled and asked, "Are you sure you don't want to know what's going on in there?" Of course that aroused my curiosity. I told him I didn't know if I wanted to know! Then he said, "I think being made aware of what's coming will help you and Michael to better plan." That was it! I was big, I was tired and the suspense was killing me. So I said to him, "OK, tell me! What's coming?" Dr. Norman could tell I was anxious, so he held my hands, looked straight at me with his caring brown eyes and said, "Laurie, you're pregnant with TRIPLETS, two boys and a girl!" That's right, I'm not kidding, Linda. THREE BABIES!

Dr. Norman said we misjudged the delivery date, thinks I'll be delivering near the beginning of July instead of near the end of the month like you. Wouldn't it be amusing if they were born on the Fourth of July? It may strike me as funny now, but the real fireworks will begin tonight when I break the news to Michael. He may just faint. By the way, he finished his training with the pharmaceutical company and will begin calling on local doctors in the very near future. I'm on schedule to graduate in early June, so I guess everything will work out. Needless to say, I'll be practicing my nursing profession at home for quite some time with three newborns!

Well, sister, that's the big news from Coon Rapids. I hope you're feeling good and that school's going well for you and Mark. Write back when you have a chance and tell us how things are going in Perham. Give my love to Mark and "Mom & Dad."

—Love, Laurie

April 4, 1975

Dear Laurie,

WOW! We can't believe it! Triplets! I haven't adjusted to the fact that I'm even pregnant! After we received your letter, although I'm still pretty small, Mark and I decided we'd like to know more as well. We saw Dr. Schoeneberger yesterday. He sure did get a kick out of your triplet news, reassured me that I'm carrying just one baby! And guess what? It's a boy! Mark's thrilled. He said as long as the baby's healthy, that's all that matters, but I think he was secretly hoping for a son. Triplets for you and Michael! I still can't believe it!

We've really been enjoying our classes at Moorhead State Teacher's College and our student teaching at Perham High School. It'll soon be ending, and then Mark and I will be sitting down with Mr. Pfenninger and talking about teaching jobs in the fall. I doubt I'll be able to work at that time due to the new baby. We'll see. Mark is hoping Mr. Pfenninger liked what he observed when he visited his classroom. Mark really likes working with young kids, loves their enthusiasm. At night I find him reading the braille transcriptions of his students' compositions and he seems totally immersed. He recently asked his 7th graders to write a short history about their junior high experiences up to the present time, and I want to share one with you, one he shared with me. It will show you why he enjoys teaching young kids so much:

Junior High and I
Jack Deibert

I changed the most in my life so far during this school year. I matured, and more and more responsibilities were put on me. There was more work and more learning happening than before. Even with the added work, 7th grade has been the most interesting and exciting year of my life.

I changed the most this year because of this school. The teachers expected more out of me, and they expected me to act better. During the first quarter, teachers took it easy on me, but for the rest of the year they really cracked down, and I learned a lot.

In this process I grew both physically and mentally. I can see now, looking back at 6th grade, how childish things were. I played silly tricks on substitutes and beat up little kids. The teachers didn't help me to grow. They let me go after I did something wrong. They gave me too much freedom and then expected me to use it wisely. If they had wanted me to learn more, they should have cracked down with more discipline. When I came to 7th grade, I got to play games like killer ball, caveman basketball and soccer, and to wrestle in P.E. Our 6th grade principal wouldn't let us play ball tag because we threw the ball too hard. The reason I think I changed so much was because of discipline.

I can easily see how I changed during the first semester of this school year. I can remember when there used to be a fight on our block, how I used to go see it to see who won. Now, I go to a fight to break it up. I do this by asking questions like, "Why are you fighting?" One of the fighters usually says, "He threw the ball at me" and the other fighter says, "He did not!" I say, "Big deal! It was an accident. Shake hands and play some more baseball."

In the second semester I changed even more. I began seeing why I should like girls. Girls were not cootie freaks anymore. I learned about love! I began to feel the creativeness about writing and how to make math fun. I began opening my mind, seeing what was happening in this world. I began opening myself to other people and telling them what was inside me. I also discovered what was happening with other people. The average and below-average people were like outsiders, so they joined a group of people. To stay in their group, they had to do what the group did, and that was smoke, take drugs, and that stuff. I began to see what was happening to those people. They started rebelling about learning, they hated school, and they couldn't wait to get out. I can see in the future what's going to happen to them. It makes me sad to see what they're missing.

During 7th grade, many responsibilities were put on me. Around the second quarter, I could feel the pressure from what was expected of me. I also felt the pressure of getting good grades. At first I asked myself, "Is this what it's like to grow up?" By the third quarter, I began to enjoy life more because what my parents hadn't let me do before, they began letting me do now. I've discovered how much responsibility will be on me as I grow up.

In the past year I've learned a lot and changed a lot. I've changed from the first day of school this year 'til right now. It's been a short time, a year, but I've changed a lot. I've never before thought about or written so much about what's inside of me. I've never before let myself go like this, but it feels good. See that? I changed right there! I think I'm going to open myself up like this again soon.

Isn't that something, Laurie? Can you believe a 7th grade boy wrote that? How times have changed! Well, my sister, that's about it from Perham. Please keep us posted on how you're doing and give my love to Michael.

—Love, Linda

Mark came home from school later than usual on Friday, and when he and Prince entered the house, their noses began sniffing the aromas, which led them to the kitchen where Linda had started fixing supper.

"Something smells fishy in here!" laughed Mark as he breathed in deeply and began removing Prince's harness.

"I thought we'd celebrate!" said Linda. "After I got home from school, Bruno Zanoni stopped by and dropped off some fresh-caught walleyed pike. We'll have it with fried potatoes and steamed green beans. How does that sound?"

"I love my wife. One of my favorite meals!" said Mark smiling. "By the way, what are we celebrating?"

"Two things," she said as she moved towards him and brushed her tummy up against him. "One, we know we're going to have a beautiful baby boy in the very near future, and two, Mr. Pfenninger stopped me as I was leaving the building this afternoon and said he'd like to talk to us about next year when we have some time."

"When we have some time? He put it that way?" Mark said.

"He did," Linda said.

"Well, I think we'll have time as soon as he does," Mark said. "I want to learn what he has to say!"

They didn't have long to wait for an appointment, and when they made it, it wasn't to meet with Mr. Pfenninger in his office. It was to have supper with his wife and him at their home. Why would he want to see them outside of school? Was it a test to see how they acted in a social setting? Was he curious to see how Mark got along with Prince when he wasn't at school? A lot of questions were going through Mark and Linda's minds when they arrived at the Pfenninger house for supper, but the atmosphere was relaxed, and Phil and his wife couldn't have been more hospitable. After enjoying a delicious meal, they all sat in the living room and talked about books and different topics, and Mark thought, "If this was some kind of intelligence test to determine whether we're qualified to teach, I sure hope we passed!"

Well, of course it wasn't. Before they left, Phil said he'd like to see them in his office Monday morning before their classes. It made for a nerve-wracking weekend, both of them wondering what Phil would have to say. When they walked in and sat down, he immediately put them at ease. On his desk were two contracts, one for each of them. I've certainly been happy with your work," he said, "and the District would like to offer you both teaching contracts for next year. Linda, you'd be teaching World History and Business Law, and Mark, you'd be teaching 7th, 8th and 9th grade English and two classes of Braille. Pretty much all of the kids you had in your 7th grade class this year asked if they could have you again in the 8th grade. We've already gotten back sign-ups for the Braille elective I said I'd offer and we have enough for two classes. So, what do you think?"

"I think it's a great opportunity to start a career doing something I love doing," Mark said enthusiastically. "Would I still have an aide from the County to transcribe student writing?"

"You sure would," he said, "and that person would be working closely with you in your Braille classes. This is something new for all of us, and the County sees it as an opportunity to get young people interested in working with and for the blind. How about you, Linda?" he added. "Have you made up your mind or do you need more time to think about it?"

"Well, I feel really good with my pregnancy right now, and I'd welcome the opportunity to teach World History and Business Law, but I think I should hold off a bit before I make my decision," Linda said. "How long will you be able to keep the position open?"

"I can hold it until the middle of July," he said. "We'll have to know by then."

"That's very generous of you," she said. "I appreciate the extra time and I'll certainly let you know before then."

That night at supper, Mark, Linda, Chuck and Marty discussed the pros and cons of having a baby and trying to hold down a teaching job at the same time. "I don't see how you could do it," Chuck said. "If you have the baby in July as predicted, you'll still be nursing. That's not so easy to work out when you're obligated to a classroom. And you'd have to hire someone to take care of the baby while you're in school. I don't know if you'll want to do that."

"I think Chuck is right, Linda," Marty said. "It'd be pretty challenging. Believe me, it's hard enough to take care of a newborn when you're *not* working. And childcare is expensive. My opinion is you'd be better off being at home, but that's for you and Mark to decide."

"Thanks for talking about it with us. I really appreciate it. What do you think, honey?" she said as she reached out to hold Mark's hand.

"I don't want you to feel like we're ganging up on you or anything, but I can tell you as of right now I agree with Mom and Dad," said Mark. "I'll be on board with whatever you decide, will go along with whatever makes you happy."

"OK. Three for three, the votes are in," Linda said laughing. "Make that four for four! I'm with all of you. This mama is going to stay home with her baby! I'll tell Mr. Pfenninger tomorrow so he can make the position available to someone else."

Mr. Pfenninger was surprised to see them back so soon when they entered his office the next morning. Mark handed him his signed contract, and Mr. Pfenninger clasped his arm and said cheerfully, "Welcome aboard, Mark!" Linda told him of her decision to hold off on teaching, at least for now. "I totally understand," he said. "I think it's a wise choice. Maybe after the baby's born and you've developed a routine you'll be able to substitute once in a while. If that works out, I'm sure we'll be able to offer you a permanent job down the road."

THE SCHOOL YEAR ENDED ON FRIDAY, JUNE 6TH, AND THE KIDS WERE eager to get out and start vacationing. Summer had arrived! There was swimming, water skiing and boating to look forward to, and northern pike and walleyed pike to be caught on Big Pine Lake! Chuck and Mark were going fishing Saturday, but their outing was cancelled when Mark got a call from his brother Friday night.

"Guess what?" he said. "We're having the babies sooner than we thought. Laurie went in to see her obstetrician today and he said he didn't want to wait any longer. She was already dilated one centimeter, so she's going to be induced on Monday! This Monday! I know this is short notice, but do you think you and Linda could make it down for the big event with Mom and Dad?"

"Wow! Brother! This is amazing! Of course, we'll all be there!" Mark said enthusiastically. "I'll talk to everyone as soon as we hang up, but I expect we'll drive down together tomorrow and be there in time for supper!"

"Sounds great!" Michael said. "We'll have your rooms ready! We can't wait to see you. Tell Dad to drive carefully. It's a zoo down here with the teenagers out of school and everyone on vacation."

Marty, Chuck, Linda, Mark and Prince left Perham after breakfast late Saturday morning, and when they arrived in Coon Rapids, a flushed Michael greeted them at the door. "Boy, am I glad you're here!" he said as they exchanged hugs. "Laurie's lying down in the bedroom. Her water broke about ten minutes ago and I think she's beginning to have labor pains! Mom, can you go talk with her and see what you think?"

"Sure," said Marty. A few short minutes later, she was back out. "Michael, it's time to head to the hospital," she said calmly. "Call the doctor and tell him you're on your way. While you and Linda are helping Laurie, I'll call Grace and Walter and tell them to meet us there."

When they got to the hospital, Grace and Walter were already there and were able to talk to their daughter briefly before the nurses whisked her away to be prepped for delivery. About an hour later, everyone gathered in her room, as she and Michael wanted all the family there for the birth of the triplets. This was going to be a new experience for the men, as none of them had ever been present for a live birth. When the twins were born in 1953, expectant fathers were typically shuttled to a waiting area where they sat it out while talking with other expectant fathers. After a baby was born, they met their child through the glass window of a viewing room amidst an exuberant handout of cigars, blue-banded for a boy, pink-banded for a girl. How times had changed!

Later that afternoon, around three o'clock, Laurie began having strong contractions. "Well, Laurie," said Dr. Nelson after examining her, "We're certainly not going to have to induce you. It looks like it won't be long at all." Beads of perspiration formed on Laurie's forehead as she breathed heavily and her contractions grew stronger. Michael sat nervously at her bedside, holding her hand and intermittently wiping her face with a cool cloth. "I'm going to see a couple of other patients," said Dr. Nelson as he headed out of the room. "I'll check on you again in a bit."

It was out of character for Laurie to do this, but she called out after him, "I wouldn't go far, Doctor!" The nurse smiled, as did everyone else, but Laurie meant business! She was serious! About ten minutes after Dr. Nelson left, Laurie's contractions grew more intense than ever, and she told the nurse it was definitely time to call the doctor.

"You're right, Laurie," he said as he came back to the room and did a quick exam. "You're very close!"

With the delivery team in place, Dr. Nelson injected a local anesthetic. "I'm going to do an episiotomy just before the first baby arrives, Laurie. That will widen your vagina and cause less damage to the tissues." Laurie looked at him like he was an alien from space. She was having a major contraction, and was experiencing pain like never before in her life. "Keep breathing the way you have been, and push real hard during the next one," he said.

Everyone in the room was focused on the drama and excitement of what was about to take place. Three babies! Linda began to feel woozy as she watched, and had to leave the room, a concerned Mark by her side. Grace and Marty stood holding hands near the bedside, Walter and Chuck standing side-by-side a short distance away. They all stared wide-eyed at the scene before them, feeling Laurie's obvious agony and watching the doctor's every move.

"Okay," Dr. Nelson said, "I'm going to make a small incision now. You won't feel anything." Shortly after the cut was made, Laurie made a strong, gasping push and the baby's head emerged, soon followed by the shoulders, trunk, legs, feet and ten little toes! If you think that didn't get everyone's attention, you have another guess coming! They all started clapping when Dr. Nelson held up the precious baby boy in his hands for Laurie to see. Her eyes welled up with tears as the doctor handed John Christian to the nurse and everyone readied for baby number two. "You have a beautiful little girl!" said Dr. Nelson as Gretchen Marie was born. Laurie was overwhelmed, tears now streaming down her face.

The third baby didn't come right away. Was something wrong? Were there only two? Did the doctor miscalculate? Not at all! After several minutes, Joseph Christopher's head began crowning and he was welcomed into the world with his brother and sister. "Congratulations, Laurie and Michael! Congratulations to all the family!" said Dr. Nelson jubilantly. Everyone in the room cheered and applauded, hugs and handshakes all around. "You may experience a bit of pain for a couple of days," he said as he began suturing up Laurie's incision. "It can be relieved with a warm bath or ice packs. I'll give you pain medication to take home in case you need it."

As he left, Dr. Nelson met Linda and Mark in the hall just outside the delivery room and told them the three healthy babies had been born. "I'm not feeling nearly so dizzy now," said Linda. "I'd like to go in!" When they entered the room, they saw everyone crowded around Laurie, congratulating her and Michael on the birth of their daughter and two sons.

"Oh, honey, Laurie did so well!" said Grace as she hugged her daughter. "The babies are small, but healthy and beautiful!"

Everyone stepped aside so Linda could get close to her sister. "I'm sorry I wasn't able to hang in there," she said to Laurie. "It just became too overwhelming. I thought I was going to faint!"

"Please don't feel bad at all. I totally understand," whispered Laurie lovingly to her sister. "I think there were about 20 people in the room counting all the delivery team. I had plenty of attention! Are you feeling OK now?"

"Much better," said Linda. "I can't wait to see the babies!"

"The nurse said she'd be bringing them back soon," said Laurie, just as the door to the room opened and not one, not two, but three nurses entered, each carrying a rosy-cheeked newborn swaddled in a nursing blanket.

Linda's mouth fell open in awe as her eyes welled up with tears. "Oh, Mark," she said, "there really are three babies and they're absolutely perfect!"

The first nurse approached Laurie's bedside and very gently placed a little bundle into her open arms. "Here's sweet Gretchen Marie," she said. "She weighed in at five pounds, three ounces, both boys at just over five pounds as well. Laurie cradled Gretchen as the second nurse handed

John Christian to Michael. He looked down at his newborn son with the radiant pride of first-time fatherhood, and then at Laurie lovingly as she smiled up at him, both barely able to comprehend the thrill and joy of their three beautiful children.

"Are you willing to hold this little one?" said the third nurse facetiously as she carefully placed Joseph Christopher into Grace's eagerly-outstretched arms.

"Uncle Mark, come closer and meet Gretchen Marie," said Laurie. As Mark reached out his hands, Laurie guided them to the top of the baby's small head. He slid his fingertips ever so gently over the soft fuzz and down the sides of Gretchen's face, experiencing with his touch what everyone else was experiencing with their eyes.

"Thank you for letting me do that, Laurie," he said as he slowly withdrew his hands and backed away. "She's beautiful, and I can tell you're a natural mother."

After everyone had spent a bit of time with the three babies, they left the room so as to give Michael and Laurie time to rest and be alone with their new family. It had been a memorable and emotional day, and both were understandably exhausted.

"Why don't you all drive over to our place for supper," Walter said as they walked to the parking lot together. "Grace has been planning for this day and we have plenty of food awaiting a celebration!" No one had to be asked twice to accept that invitation.

"I'm starving as usual," Linda said as they approached Walter and Grace's block. "Good thing we're here and not at our place!"

"She's right on that," laughed Mark as they pulled into the driveway. "There's not much in our fridge. We've been too busy to make it to the grocery store for days! Plus, you don't want me near the kitchen," he laughed. "I'm like Michael, big eater, but can barely boil water."

After everyone was in the Johnson house, they sat in the living room and munched on hors d'oeuvres, reliving the excitement of the day. As soon as Michael arrived from the hospital, Walter uncorked a bottle of chilled champagne and poured a glass for everyone except pregnant Linda, who had orange juice. "Here's to our three new beautiful grandchildren!" he said proudly. "Saturday, June 7th, 1975, a day of miracles, one we'll remember fondly and never forget!"

"Cheers to that!" said everyone in unison as they raised their drinks. "There's another important date coming up," said Mark as they sipped their champagne. Everyone looked at him quizzically, except Marty and Chuck, who had an idea of what he was going to say. "June 9th, this coming Monday, Mom & Dad's twenty-fourth wedding anniversary!"

"You're kidding!" Waltered bellowed. "Well, we're going to have to celebrate that, too!" Before anyone could interject, Walter began planning the festivities.

"Not so fast, dear," said Grace smiling. "Perhaps Marty and Chuck already have something in mind that involves just the two of them!"

"We certainly don't want to wear out our welcome here," said Marty smiling. "We were planning to stay until after the babies were born and then head home."

"I'm guessing Laurie will be coming home with the babies on Monday," Grace said. "Maybe you'd like to celebrate your anniversary with your new grandchildren. We'd love to have you stay with us an extra couple of days if you can!"

Marty and Chuck talked it over, and they agreed there was probably no better way to celebrate their wedding anniversary than to share it with family, so they decided to stay. After a delicious supper of cold chicken, potato salad, hot buns, dill pickles and fresh tomatoes from the garden, Grace went to the kitchen and returned with a beautiful pie. "You're going to love the dessert Grace made," Michael said to his brother. "It's a lemon meringue pie, and the peaks of meringue are slightly browned just like Mom makes!"

A big smile broke over Mark's face. "I can already taste it!" he said. After everyone had their fill and the dishes were done, they gathered in the living room and said the Joyful Mysteries of the Rosary in thanksgiving for all the gifts God had given them. Even Prince seemed thankful. He was happy to just lie there during the hubbub and gnaw on a large bone Walter had given him.

The next morning everyone met at the Church of the Epiphany in Coon Rapids for Sunday Mass, and after Mass they all drove to the hospital to see Laurie and the triplets. The new mom and babies were all doing fine, and Laurie announced she'd be coming home with them the next day. "That's great!" Grace said. "We're all so thankful everything went so well. We'll have everything ready and you'll have extra hands to help as well, experienced hands! Marty and Chuck are staying an extra day so we can all celebrate your homecoming on their 24th wedding anniversary, which happens to be tomorrow!"

Laurie was discharged from the hospital early Monday morning, and Michael took the day off from work so he could be home. Laurie started breastfeeding the triplets in the hospital, but wasn't sure how long she could keep it up. "It's quite a challenge, Michael," she said as they were driving home, "and draining in more ways than one!"

Michael laughed, knowing then that Laurie had definitely retained her sense of humor, and that was going to be very important in her attempts to nurse three babies over many months to come.

When they arrived home, everyone was waiting and the nursery was ready! Three cribs were positioned side by side, two blue and one pink. No sooner had Laurie settled the triplets in place than the boys started crying. They were hungry! But they had to wait. The feeding pattern had already been established in the hospital, and that pattern dictated that it was going to be "ladies first," whether the boys were crying or not, as Gretchen didn't take as much milk as did they. When their sister was finished, John Christian clamped onto one breast and Joseph Christopher the other. For some reason, Joseph had the healthiest appetite of the three. It was comical watching the two boys sucking away simultaneously, not quite so funny for Laurie. By the time all three babies had finished nursing, she was worn out and ready to rest!

"I think you may want to supplement what you're giving them with bottles," said Grace. Exhausted as Laurie was, all she could do was nod in agreement as she leaned back in the rocker and closed her eyes. Bottles it was! Shortly after Marty and Chuck left with Linda and Mark for Perham on Tuesday morning, the "bottle brigade" began in earnest. The triplets were demanding milk every three hours, and they wanted more each day. Even Gretchen was beginning to eat more, just like her brothers.

"I don't know about this!" Laurie said exhaustedly to her mother one day after they'd finished the diaper routine and were feeding the triplets. "There is just no way I could be handling all this without your help, Mom. Thank you!"

"Oh, you're welcome!" gushed Grace. "I love doing it!" And she must have, because she showed up promptly at 7:00 every morning.

The triplets were thriving. They had put on weight, they were cooing happily to one another, and they were on a regular feeding and sleeping schedule. Near the end of July, Grace decided it was time to back off from her daily role and let her daughter and Michael handle the triplet challenge. It was about that time a letter arrived from Linda.

July 31, 1975

Dear Laurie,

I guess we're both in a fix, you with the triplets and me with an overdue baby! I keep getting bigger and bigger, but otherwise nothing seems to be happening. The doctor says he'll give me another week and then he'll have to induce labor. We'll see! I have a hearty appetite and I feel good, but I sure am ready!

Chuck and Mark are out the door early each morning, busy selling encyclopedias. Their working together is paying off in more ways than one. They have some good father/son talks when they're traveling and also get to share teaching techniques they'll be trying next year.

It's so interesting how we all entered graduate school without a thought about having babies. How naïve could we get! And here we are, three already born and another on the way. It sure is different from St. Benedict's and our courting days!

Drop me a line when you have some free time. Ha! I can't imagine how busy you must be. I would love to know how it's all going and how Michael's doing. Such a big adjustment for both of you! If either of you have any tips for me and Mark before William Francis is born, please send them along.

—Love, Linda

She didn't have to wait much longer. William Francis Dowdle arrived early Friday morning on August 8th, 1975. He was a big baby, eight pounds, six ounces! Mark didn't go to work that day and the proud grandparents were at the hospital as well, eager to relish the birth of their fourth grandchild and wondering how their son would respond to fatherhood.

Mark didn't keep them in suspense. When William Francis was all cleaned up and brought to Linda, she cuddled him while he breastfed, and while he was suckling as though his life depended on it, Mark leaned down to kiss his son's fuzzy little head. It was precious to behold, a newborn son intent on his mother's milk and a new father intent on loving his son.

———◆·◆———

By early September, Mark and Linda had established a smooth routine in caring for their newborn son, and on Monday, September 8th, school began. Mark's first two classes were Braille, third period was his Prep, and after lunch he had 7th, 8th and 9th grade English. His classroom was like all the others, high ceilinged, large square iron radiators along one wall and room enough to accommodate forty desks. The space was painted a very bright pink, which of course didn't make any difference to Mark.

When the bell rang and the kids entered the room, Mark stood near the door to greet them, Prince by his side. When it rang the second time, Mark entered the room and sat at his desk with Prince alongside him on the floor, facing the students. "Good morning, class," he said. "My name is Mr. Dowdle, and I'm guessing some of you have seen me around town before. I was born in Perham and went to elementary school and high school here. It's good to be back, and I'm glad so many of you signed up to learn braille. I'm excited to be your teacher. Before we begin, you'll notice there are two rectangular cards on each desk. They each have your first and last names, and one of them is in braille. Please move around until you're seated in the desk that has your printed name on the card. That's the seating chart I'll be using, and it will be a big help in getting to know all twenty of you! It may seem a little unusual for you to see a dog in the classroom, but Prince here is my partner and friend, and in no time at all I'm sure he'll be your friend as well. So, let's begin by my answering any questions you may have. Just speak right up, and tell me your name before you speak so I can begin recognizing your voice. This will obviously be different than other classes where you're required to raise your hand before speaking. OK, any questions?"

"Mr. Dowdle, my name is Ken Anderson," a boy near the front of the room said. "I was wondering if you'd mind telling us a little more about yourself so those of us who don't know you or didn't know you when you were living in Perham can get to know you better."

"I think that's a good idea, Ken. Thanks for asking," Mark said. "I'll make it brief, and then each of you can tell me about yourselves. I think it will be an excellent way to spend our first class together. So, I was born in Perham in 1953 and I have an identical twin brother. I'm Mark and he's Michael. We both graduated from Perham High School and St. John's University and are married to identical twin sisters! My wife and I have a new baby boy at home, William Francis Dowdle, born just four weeks ago."

"My brother and I were born prematurely and were very small. We were given oxygen in the hospital to help us survive, and unfortunately that caused me to develop a condition called retinopathy of prematurity, which caused total blindness when I was just a toddler. It has never held me back in any way. My brother and I did pretty much everything together when we lived in Perham, including running track and riding our tandem bicycle all around town. Shortly after I got married, I had the good fortune of adopting Prince from a dog pound in Minneapolis, and he's been my eyes and loyal companion every moment since," said Mark as he reached down to pat his dog. "That's the short version of my tale, now it's your turn. How about starting us out, Ken?"

Ken stood and wasn't shy at all in telling about himself, and when he was finished, the other nineteen students did likewise.

"Thank you for that," said Mark smiling. "I really appreciate knowing more about each of you." Prince let out a big yawn and the whole class laughed.

"This is Ken. Your dog just gave us a huge yawn," he explained to Mark.

"I guess Prince didn't appreciate what you had to tell me about yourselves as much as I did," Mark said laughing. "Before the bell rings, let me give you your homework assignment. I want you to run your fingertips over the raised dots on the card on your desk. That's your name spelled in braille. See if you can recognize those letters in any order with your eyes closed by the time you come to class tomorrow."

The bell rang and Mark's room was soon empty as the students moved on to their next class. He walked between the rows, placing name cards on the desks of each of his next twenty braille students. Everything went smoothly during his second class, just as it had with the first. When he asked if they had any questions, a boy sitting in the back of the first row smiled mischievously and said, "My name is Alan Arvig, Mr. Dowdle, and I was wondering if you'd mind telling us how your brother and you met your wives."

The class broke into gentle laughter and wondered if their teacher would volunteer this personal information. Mark didn't hesitate a moment. "I understand your curiosity about that, Alan," he said, "because how often do identical twin men meet and marry identical twin women? Not very often at all! So, when Michael and I were freshmen at St. John's University, we were invited to a Christmas dance for all freshmen at St. Benedict's University, a women's school a few short miles from St. John's in St. Joseph, Minnesota. The dance was held in the gym, a festive atmosphere with lots of Christmas trees strung with colorful lights. I, of course, couldn't see the lights, but I sure could smell the fir trees! The dance music began playing a slow fox trot, and my brother pulled me toward two blond coeds he'd spotted standing a short distance from us. It was pretty dark in the gym, and he had no idea they were twins, and, of course, I didn't either. Long story short, we danced the hours away, and by the time I got back to St. John's that night, we were madly in love! The rest is history!" said Mark with a smile. "Now, Allen, why don't you tell all of us a little about yourself, and then the rest of the class can follow."

After the last student spoke, Mark had just enough time to give the class the same assignment he'd given his first period group. The bell rang and the kids headed off to their third period classes, saying their good-byes to Mark and Prince as they passed by. Mark stood and grasped Prince's leather handle. "Well, boy," he said with a sigh of relief, "two down, three to go. It's our prep period. Let's you and me head out for a walk and bathroom break."

On their way down the hall, Mark met Mr. Pfenninger, who stopped him and identified himself. "Well, Mark," he said, "how's it going so far?"

"I think I'm going to like teaching," Mark said. "Prince and I got off to a great start with my first two Braille classes. We're off for a walk before lunch and my afternoon English classes."

"Good for both of you! We're lucky to have you here!" said Mr. Pfenninger as he headed off to the cafeteria.

Lunch break was an hour, and Mark had time to walk home with his dad. "How'd it go, Mark?" Chuck asked as they headed down the street.

"I feel like it went really well," he said. "At least from what I could hear. I think they're going to enjoy learning braille, and if my first two classes are any indication, I think I'm going to like working with students. I hope my afternoon English classes go as smoothly as did my morning."

"I'm sure they will," said Chuck. "Just be yourself. That's what the kids want. You respect them and they'll respect you. Don't think for a minute they can't sense if you enjoy teaching and like being around them. They can! Now let's pick up the pace and get home to lunch!"

Linda was on the couch cuddled with William Francis when they came in. "How'd it go?" she asked as she greeted them enthusiastically. Mark reeled off the same story he'd just finished telling his dad.

"I'm listening!" Marty called out from the kitchen. "Just getting some food together." Monday's lunch was often made from Sunday-dinner leftovers, in this case sandwiches with thinly-sliced roast beef on white bread with iceberg lettuce and a lot of mustard, just the way Chuck and Mark liked them.

"I don't see how you two can even taste the roast beef!" said Linda as the two hungry men laughed and kept eating.

On the way back to school, Chuck told Mark to expect quite a difference between the 7th, 8th and 9th grade classes he was about to meet. "Just listen closely," he said, "and you'll soon see what I mean."

As the 7th graders made their way into the classroom and walked past Prince, Mark noticed most of their voices were high pitched, boys and girls alike, especially compared to the voices of his morning classes. Of course, that was because the Braille students were 9th graders. After the bell rang, Mark rose from his desk and faced the students. "Good afternoon, class," he said with a smile. "My name is Mark Dowdle and I'm happy to be your English teacher this year." No sooner had Mark finished introducing himself and Prince than the door opened and a flushed and sweaty, out-of-breath young boy rushed into the room. The students started chuckling and Mark immediately sensed what was happening. He looked towards the door and said, "Welcome, my friend. I'm Mr. Dowdle and this is my dog, Prince. It's the first day, don't worry about being a little late. Your name is on a card on your desk, so if you can find it and take a seat, I'll begin class."

It didn't take the boy long. There was only one empty desk among the thirty-six in the room. Mark was able to discern when the student was seated and he began speaking. "We're going to learn about language, literature and composition in this class, and I'm going to help you develop your listening, speaking, reading and writing skills. Believe me, class, when you're blind, you learn to listen. Sometimes your life depends on your ability to listen, blind or not, and so to help you become better listeners, I'm telling you right now that when I give directions, you're going to have to get them the first time. They won't be repeated," said Mark in a serious tone. He could hear murmurs of surprised concern around the room. "Don't be worried," he said, smiling. "All you have to do is listen. Okay, so let's start with a short language lesson first, the parts of speech. There are eight of them. Let's start with nouns. Can anyone tell me what a noun is?"

A voice from the back of the room said, "I can, Mr. Dowdle."

"Excellent," Mark said. "If you can tell me your name when you volunteer an answer, I'll try to remember it. For the next week or so, I'd appreciate it if all of you would identify yourself before speaking."

"My name is Jean Wendt," the girl said confidently, "and a noun is the name of a person, place or thing."

"That's right, Jean," he said, "and it can also be the name of an activity, a quality or an idea. Now, what I'd like you all to do is take out a piece of paper." Mark waited a few moments until the rustling had quieted. "Across the top write the following words: Person, Place, Thing, Activity, Quality and Idea," Mark said slowly, "and draw a line under each word. Now we're going to see how many nouns you can come up with for each of those words. Let's see who can fill their columns to the bottom of the page. OK, write!" The eager seventh graders dropped their heads and started scribbling like crazy. Mark and Prince walked up and down between the rows of desks, and whenever Prince brushed against one of them, they giggled and just kept on writing. After about ten minutes, Mark asked, "How's it going?"

A girl spoke up and said, "My name is Ann Schatschneider, Mr. Dowdle. I've filled all the lines for person, place, thing and activities, but it's hard to think of that many for qualities and ideas."

"She's right," the class chorused.

Mark paused for a moment and everyone was silent, waiting for what he was going to say. "First, thank you for saying your names before you spoke, Jean and Ann. Yours are the first two voices I'm going to work on remembering. Second, since you're all having a little trouble coming up with nouns for qualities and ideas, that will be your homework for tonight. I want you to fill every column to the bottom of the page. And while we still have some time before the period ends, I'd like to tell you about a book we're going to be reading, and I'll have a few of you take turns reading aloud. Be sure to say your name if you volunteer. The book is called *A Long Way to Go*. Has anyone read it?" Mark asked. No one answered, so Mark continued. "It's the story of three kids on vacation with their parents. They're 6, 8 and 10 years old, and are spending the day in a supervised childcare program at a Florida resort hotel. At the end of the day their parents don't come to pick them up. What would you do if you were one of those kids?"

A boy in the back of the room said, "My name is Leroy Rosenthal, Mr. Dowdle. I'd go look for my parents."

"Remember, Leroy," Mark said, "the kids are pretty young."

"I'd go anyway," Leroy said.

"Well, Leroy," Mark said, "we'll just have to see what happens with those kids. If you and a couple of other students back there will take those books from the shelf and pass them out, we'll begin reading." After all the students had a book, Mark said, "OK, who'd like to start us out?"

"I will, Mr. Dowdle. My name is Cleo Schmidt."

"Thanks, Cleo," Mark said, and the girl began reading aloud. Mark was immediately impressed, as Cleo read extremely well. Before the period ended, Dennis Schave, Marvin Schmidt and Eileen Wallace had each taken a turn. "Excellent reading, all of you," praised Mark after the students had returned their books to the shelf. "It's going to be interesting to find out how things go for those three kids. We now know they're afraid of what the hotel people might do and we know they've decided to try and walk the 600 miles back home, but we'll have to wait until tomorrow to find out more." The bell rang and the 7th graders rushed out of the classroom so they wouldn't be late for their fifth period class.

The five minutes between classes flew by, and before Mark and Prince were able to make it to the door to greet the students, the 8th graders were streaming into the room and finding their desks. The bell rang and Mark said, "Good afternoon, class. My name is Mr. Dowdle, and most of you have probably heard that name before. My dad teaches 10th, 11th and 12th grade English at the high school. I just finished teaching my 7th grade class, and we started with parts of speech." When Mark said parts of speech, there were audible groans from his 8th graders. They had been down this road before. "I know you had them last year," Mark said smiling, "so we'll just spend a short time reviewing. If you can show me that you have them mastered, that'll be it. To begin, I'm going to need eight of you to stand in a row at the back of the room, facing me." Mark didn't hear any movement. "C'mon, class! The sooner we do this, the sooner we'll be finished."

Eight students got up and made their way to the back of the room. "Are we all there?" asked Mark.

"Yes, Mr. Dowdle," they said in unison.

"OK. Starting with the person on my far left, each of you tell me your name and I'll try to remember. Since I'm not able to see you, hearing your voices is the only way I have of knowing who you are, so let's begin."

One at a time, the students began saying their names. After the last of the eight had spoken, Mark said, "Thank you very much. Now we're going to have a little fun with parts of speech." More groans.

"How can you have fun with parts of speech, Mr. Dowdle?" asked one of the boys standing in the back of the room as the class laughed. They'd all studied the parts of speech in the 7th grade and were not looking forward to repeating the experience.

"Just give me a chance to show you, Eugene," Mark said. Everyone looked at Eugene Klinnert with surprise, and then back at Mr. Dowdle. He had just heard eight different students speak their names, and could already identify which voice was Eugene's! "Before we begin, I'd like to introduce my dog, Prince. He's my eyes, you understand, and we're a team." Prince was standing alongside Mark, also facing the students standing at the back of the room. "OK, Mark said, "let's get started. The way this little game works is each one of you becomes a different part of speech. I'll call out your name and tell you what part of speech you are: Eugene Klinnert, noun; Judy Mondt, verb; Charles Meyers, adjective; Eugene Nibbe, adverb; Lorraine Lueders, pronoun; Donald Matz, preposition; Sharon Rosen, conjunction; Robert Przybylski, interjection. Again, everyone looked around the classroom at one another, wide-eyed, in awe that Mr. Dowdle had heard eight names spoken only once, and he already knew who they were. Amazing! They were lined up when they gave their names and hadn't changed their order, but nevertheless, it was eerie how he remembered them all! "What I'd like you to do," continued Mark, "is create sentences, but each person only gets to use his assigned part of speech. I'll be the period and comma and speak them out whenever I think they're needed. Are you ready?"

"Prepositions are used quite a bit," Mr. Dowdle," Donald Matz said, "so can each of us speak more than once while we're building the sentences if it's necessary?"

"Definitely, Donald," Mark answered. Again the students looked around at each other, amazed. Mr. Dowdle had remembered Donald Matz's voice with ease. "Let's just begin and see where it takes us. Ready, set, go."

"Whew!" Robert Przybylski said enthusiastically as the class chuckled. Eugene Klinnert followed with, "Mr. Dowdle." Judy Mondt said, "expects," Lorraine Lueders added, "us," Donald Matz said, "to,"… and so it moved along through that sentence and several more to follow, albeit slowly, but with plenty of humorous moments interspersed.

"Now that was fun, right?" said Mark smiling as the eight volunteers returned to their seats. "For your homework tonight, I'd like you all to write a five-sentence paragraph on the subject of your choice and identify the part of speech for every word you use. I know you studied this last year, but a little review won't hurt. And now, we only have about 20 minutes before the bell, so why don't we start reading our first book for this year. Copies are on the shelf under the windows, and if a couple of you would pass them out, I'd appreciate it. The book is called *The Diary of a Young Girl*. Have any of you read it?"

No one spoke up, so Mark continued. "It's about Anne Frank, a 13 year-old Jewish girl who fled with her family from their home and hid in a small attic apartment behind her dad's business for two years to avoid being taken to a concentration camp by the Nazis, a terrifying experience and certainly challenging to hide for so long in a small space with a family, but they had no choice, as their lives depended on it. How many of you think you could survive such a thing for two years?"

Again, no one said a word. Not a whisper could be heard. Mark sensed this was an important teaching moment, so he continued with his explanation of the book before he began having the class read aloud. "One of the interesting things about the book is that it's an actual diary," he said, "a true account. Anne was given the diary for her thirteenth birthday, and in it she wrote her innermost thoughts and feelings during the entire time she was in hiding with her family. Another interesting thing about the book is that another family, the Van Danns, were in hiding with the Franks. The Van Danns had a 16-year-old son." When Mark said that, he could hear some of the girls whisper to one another. "I think you're going to find the book not only fascinating, but very informative about what happened during World War II. The last thing I'd like to say about it before we get started reading is that Anne called her diary Kitty. We don't know why, but Kitty is the "audience" she created, the one to whom she revealed the thoughts and feelings closest to her heart during the two long years in hiding. So, let's get started. I'd like the same eight volunteers to read aloud. That way I'll hear your voices again and it will help me to remember you. Would you mind beginning, Eugene?"

"Which Eugene, Mr. Dowdle?" Eugene Klinnert asked.

"You, Eugene Klinnert," Mark said. The students looked at their teacher in awe, mighty impressed by his keen ability to "see" with his ears. Eugene began, and it didn't take long for the class to get drawn into the book. You could have heard a pin drop, all eyes on the pages as the designated readers took their turns. The minutes rolled by, the bell rang, and just like that, the 8th graders were headed to their last class of the day and the 9th graders were filing in.

The first thing Mark noticed was the difference in how his 8th graders had entered the room versus these 9th graders. No one was talking, whispering maybe, but no noticeable chatting or unnecessary sounds as the students observed the name cards on each desk and sat as designated. Mark had the feeling he and Prince were being observed very closely. "Good afternoon, class," he said warmly. Aside from a few low-voiced responses, the room was quiet. Mark could definitely feel all eyes on him. "My name is Mr. Dowdle," he said, "and if 9th grade English is not where you're expecting to be right now, you'd best be heading out of here." That seemed to break the ice a bit, and Mark could hear chuckles from around the room. "I'd first like to introduce my dog, Prince, and, of course, he wants to say hello. Prince, speak!" Mark commanded, and when Prince barked at the class, they all laughed. "The poor guy wants to get outside as much as I know you do after spending a long, hot day in school, but he seems to be holding up okay, and I hope you all are as well.

"As many of you know," Mark continued, "my dad teaches English at Perham High School. What I'll be teaching this year will fit right in with what's going to be expected of you when you become 10th graders. One thing my dad emphasized for 9th grade learning is a solid command of the parts of speech, so that's where we're going to begin. As you remember, there are eight of them. Would anyone like to describe what they are?"

"I will," Mr. Dowdle, said a girl sitting near the middle of the room.

"Thank you," said Mark, "and for all of you, please identify yourself before speaking so I can start to associate your voice with your name."

"I am Joyce Frank, Mr. Dowdle," said the girl, and then proceeded to not only give a detailed explanation of each part of speech, but to also use examples to illustrate the meaning of each. Who was this girl? Mark was impressed!

"If everyone in the class knows the parts of speech as well as you've just demonstrated, Joyce, we won't be needing to spend much time on them," said Mark. "That was an exceptional description of each, one of the best I've heard. Now let's see if the rest of you can do as well."

Mark spent the next fifteen minutes reviewing nouns, verbs, pronouns, adjectives, adverbs, prepositions, conjunctions and interjections with his students. "Okay, that's enough of that," he said after they'd gone through them all. "You'll be happy to know I'm *almost* satisfied! For your homework tonight I'd like you to write a short descriptive paragraph about yourself, three or four sentences, and identify the part of speech for each word. Now, in the time we have left today, I'd like us to begin reading the first novel we're going to be studying. If a couple of you can hand out copies of *To Kill a Mockingbird* from the back shelves, I'd appreciate it."

Mark waited until the bustle of the book handout had quieted before he spoke. "I think you're going to enjoy this book," he said. "It's a serious novel, compassionate, dramatic and deep. Has anyone in here read it before?" Not a voice was heard, so Mark continued. "Okay, let me tell you a little about it, and then you can spend the rest of the class time reading. *To Kill a Mockingbird* is about accepting others in spite of their differences. What happens when racism raises its ugly head in a small, sleepy Southern town is one of the questions you're going to have answered by the time you finish this book, and perhaps you'll have a few other questions answered as well. So, let's get started. It's nice and hot this afternoon, just the way it was in the Alabama town where this story begins. You can use the rest of the hour to read silently."

Mark could hear the fluttering of turning pages as his 9th graders delved into the story. Once again the minutes passed quickly. "Would you like to take the book home today?" asked Mark just before the final bell.

A chorus of "yesses," answered his question, and Mark couldn't see it, but some of the students were holding their books open and reading as they left the room.

That night at supper, the table talk wasn't about how Marty's day had gone at the hospital nor how Linda had cared for little William Francis all day at home, and not about how Chuck's day had gone at school with his 10th, 11th and 12th grade English classes. It was about how Mark had fared with his classes. "Boy! I have a whole new appreciation for your work, Dad," he said as they all sat down to eat.

"It's pretty neat you recognize that so early on, Mark," Chuck said, "and I'm sure you'll gain an even fuller appreciation the longer you teach. I'd say we all have important jobs, especially our gals. It looks like they're ready for us to chow down, so let's pray."

"If it's okay with you, I'd like to say grace tonight, Dad," Mark said.

"Please do," Chuck said.

"Father in heaven," he began, "thank you for showering our families with your many gifts. Thank you for your love and care of Mom & Dad and Linda. Thank you for our beautiful son and thank you for letting my first day of teaching be a success. And thank you for this food! Amen."

"Amen!" chorused everyone as Linda leaned over and kissed him on the cheek.

"Very nice, Mark," Marty said.

"Way to keep it short," said a smiling Chuck. "The aroma of fried chicken is making me delirious." Marty and Linda laughed and some serious eating began!

"So, Mark," said Linda in between bites, "tell us more. How did it go?"

"It all felt pretty great," said Mark. "The students in my two morning Braille classes are enthusiastic and ready to learn. In the afternoon it's all English, three in a row, 7th, 8th and 9th graders. I'm getting to experience the whole range of junior high kids. It feels rewarding already and it's only the first day! And Dad, you'll be happy to know I started each English class by reviewing the parts of speech."

"Good work!" said Chuck.

"I bet that went over like a lead balloon," said Linda as she gave Mark a playful jab.

"Hey, it wasn't so bad," said Mark laughing. "The kids were friendly and attentive, even indulged me by participating in some dramatic exercises related to the parts of speech. And I introduced our first reading book in each of my afternoon classes, *To Kill a Mockingbird* for the 9th graders, and they didn't want to put it down, even when the bell rang."

"Sounds like everything went really well," said Marty. "They sure are lucky to have you."

"Thanks, Mom, and I feel lucky to have them!" said Mark.

"How did Prince do?" asked Linda.

"The perfect teacher's assistant, happily soaked up a whole lot of affection," said Mark as he reached down and scratched the head of his loyal companion. "It was quite a first day for both of us. How about you, Mom? Tell us about your day."

"Enjoyable as always, but not nearly as exciting as yours," she said. "You all know how I spend mine. Let's hear how your wife's day went with our adorable grandson."

"It was wonderful!" Linda said. "William Francis is such a good little baby! A day of eating and sleeping and a whole lot of cooing. The hours flew by. I sure am enjoying being a mother."

"And you two mothers don't come any better," Mark said as he smiled at his mom and reached out to hold Linda's hand.

The peace was broken when a demanding cry was heard from down the hall. "Could be a dirty diaper or a hunger call," Linda said as she rose from her chair.

"Or both!" laughed Mark as he stood up. "We'd better double-team this one."

"I bet that makes you think of old times," Chuck said as Marty and he remained seated and kept eating.

"It sure does," she said, "although we were living in a basement apartment, not in a big bright house like this."

"It sure is nice we're able to help the kids get off to an easier start," he said.

"I'll say," she said. "The basement apartment was comfortable, and memorable to say the least, but if I'd had a choice, I would have much preferred to live above ground with the twins."

Linda came out with the nursing baby cuddled in her arms, Mark close behind. "Double whammy," she laughed as she smiled down at William Francis, sucking as if his life depended on it. "This boy likes to eat as much as his dad does, and he definitely had dirty diapers!"

"He sure did!" Mark said as he threw his head back and theatrically sniffed in a large draught of fresh air.

After the dishes were done, everyone relaxed out on the back patio. It was still warm in the house, and a welcoming breeze caused the leaves on the trees to flutter. As the sunlight filtered through, William Francis seemed hypnotized by their movement. He cooed constantly while Mark held him in his arms and gently rocked him. "Best time to hold my son," Mark said smiling. "He's clean, fed and happy!"

Tuesday morning arrived and Mark was ready. How could he not be? He'd thought a lot about his approach to day two of classes. When he met with his first period Braille class, he wondered how one of his students had fared in trying to read her name in braille. She had a long last name, Boedigheimer. When she entered the room and said, "Good morning, Mr. Dowdle," Mark recognized her voice and greeted her. "Good morning, Ruth," he said, and this surprised her. As far as she knew, he had only heard her name spoken once, and that was yesterday in his 9th grade English class. "How did you do reading your name in braille?" he asked.

"It was fun!" she said enthusiastically. "My last name has three e's and two i's, so that made it easier."

"Good for you!" he said. "Yours is the longest name in the class. It will be interesting to see how everyone else did."

As his students entered the room, each of them greeted Mark and said their names. "Good morning, Mr. Dowdle, Allen Arvig here," Allen said. "Good morning, Mr. Dowdle, it's Barbara Bahls," said Barbara. "Hi, Mr. Dowdle, Laurie Hertel here," said Laurie, and that's the way it went until all twenty had entered the room. Mark wasn't the only one who was greeted by the students. Prince was lying quietly by Mark's desk, and each student said good morning to him as well, some venturing to give him a gentle stroke on his back or pat on the head before taking their seats. This seemed more than fine with Prince, who stretched out and relaxed with the show of affection. Mark asked Laurie if she would take roll, and she said she'd be happy to do so. Just like that, day two of class was off to a rapid start.

"Well," Mark began, "how many of you were able to learn your name in braille last night?" All twenty hands shot up, but when Mark didn't hear a response he asked, "Was it that hard?"

"Colleen Belka, Mr. Dowdle. All of us just raised our hands. We forgot that you can't see!"

"Thanks, Colleen," Mark said smiling. "I know this form of interacting takes some getting used to. Let me ask that question a different way. Was anyone not able to read their name in braille?" Silence filled the room. "Great!" said Mark. "Let's get started on our next assignment. The first thing I'd like you to do is exchange your braille name card with that of another student. Once you've done that, close your eyes and run your fingers over the raised dots and practice reading your fellow student's name in braille. Everyone exchanged name cards and the room soon quieted down as the students went to work. Mark leaned forward and gave Prince a gentle, loving stroke. "This teaching is going to be okay," he thought to himself.

After about 15 minutes, Mark heard his students beginning to talk quietly with one another. "How did that go?" he asked.

"Colleen Belka, Mr. Dowdle. I had Laurie Hertel's name, and it was pretty easy. Our names have some of the same letters, so I had a head start."

"That's what you're going to find," Mark said. "You'll often be encountering repeated letters, so the more you practice, the easier braille will become. One of the things we'll be doing in this class is reading from the Braille edition of the *World Book Encyclopedia*. Of course, I've been doing this since I was young," he said as he reached for the 'B' volume sitting on his desk. "When I demonstrate, you'll see my fingers moving very quickly. It takes time to learn; the important thing is to be patient and not give up." The students watched Mark's every move as he navigated his way to the **Braille** article and began to read aloud: *"Braille is a code consisting of small raised dots on paper, dots that can be read by touch. Louis Braille, a 15-year-old blind French student, developed a raised-dot reading system in 1824. The idea came to him from the dot code punched on cardboard used by Captain Charles Barbier to send night messages to his soldiers.*

"In 1829, Braille published a dot system based on a 'cell' of six dots. From the 63 possible dot arrangements, Braille worked out a complete alphabet, punctuation marks, numerals, and, later, a system of writing music. His code was at first not officially accepted, but eventually won universal acceptance for all written languages and for mathematics, science and computer notation.

"People who are blind read braille by running their fingers along the dots. They can write braille on a six-key machine called a Braillewriter, or with a stylus on a pocket-sized metal or plastic slate. Braille books are pressed from metal plates. The characters are stamped on both sides of the paper by a method called interpointing. Dots on one side of the page do not interfere with those printed on the other. In the early 1960's, publishers began using computers to speed up production of braille books. Text typed into the computer is automatically translated to braille. The computer transfers

the raised braille figures onto paper or metal plates for use in a press. By an alternative method, a vacuum braille-former duplicates hand-transcribed braille pages onto plastic sheets which are then bound in volumes."

Mark closed the book with a flourish. "There you have it," he said. "Reading about braille from a Braille encyclopedia." He smiled as he heard the students sharing their enthusiastic reactions.

"This is Joyce Frank, Mr. Dowdle. Where did you get that braille volume of World Book?"

"I'm glad you asked, Joyce," said Mark. "Perham High School has a complete set in a special room in their library. I've been using them for as long as I can remember."

"David Buendiger, Mr. Dowdle. Can any of us go into that room and use the books?"

"You sure can, David," Mark said. The students turned and smiled at one another. It was going to be fun trying to read so many things in braille! "During the time that remains, I'm going to ask Rose Hammers to hand out paper copies of the braille alphabet. Close your eyes and let your fingers work their way through each letter." Rose passed out the sheets, and after a cursory examination of the dotted configurations and printed letters, Mark could feel the intensity of his students as they sat quietly, moving their fingers slowly from one letter to the next.

Their concentration was interrupted by the ringing bell, and just like that, the students were on their way out the door and Mark was greeting his second-period Braille class.

"Good morning, Mr. Dowdle. Linda Hertel," said the first student to enter the room.

Mark turned his head in her direction and said, "Just a minute, Linda. That name's familiar. I believe I have a Hertel student in my first-period Braille class as well."

"You do!" Linda said exuberantly. "That's my identical twin sister, Laurie."

"You're kidding!" said Mark. "Laurie and Linda? Those are the names of the identical twin gals my twin brother and I are married to!"

"Really?" said Linda. "Wow! What are the odds of that?"

"I'd say pretty slim!" said Mark laughing. "Say, Linda," he added, "would you mind taking roll for me today? So happens your sister did it for my first period class."

"Of course," she said. It was an easy task, as each of the twenty desks was filled and she simply had to write, 'All Present,' on the attendance slip and attach it to the clip outside the door.

"Well, class," Mark said with a smile, "I just became aware of the fact that I'm not the only identical twin at this school. Linda Hertel is here with us, and her twin, Laurie, is in my first-period Braille class. Not only that, but amazingly enough, my twin brother and I are married to identical twins who happen to be named Laurie and Linda!"

"Wow, Mr. Dowdle! Ken Anderson here. That's pretty wild. And I just want to tell you the Hertel twins are two beautiful blondes!"

"All right," said Mark smiling, "time to get down to business. I presume you all did your homework and are making progress at memorizing the letters of your name. The first thing I'd like you to do today is exchange your braille name card with that of another student. Close your eyes and practice the raised-dot pattern for each letter of their name." The students exchanged cards, and twenty heads bowed in silence as fingertips moved slowly across the raised surfaces.

While they were all hard at work, Mark reached down and removed Prince's bulky harness, after which Prince stretched out contentedly alongside the desk. When Mark reached down to pet him a few minutes later, he wasn't there. "I'm sorry to interrupt your concentration," said Mark with a slight note of panic in his voice, "but is Prince still in the room?"

"This is Evalin Cavalier, Mr. Dowdle. He's right here by me. He's been going up and down the rows of desks and everyone's been petting him."

"Well, it sure didn't take him long to feel at home with all of you," laughed Mark. When Prince heard Mark's voice, he returned to the front of the room and sat by Mark's side, looking up at him with adoration. "Good boy, Prince," said Mark as he patted his dog's head.

After another ten minutes, Mark could sense the students were ready to move on. "How did everyone do with that?" he asked.

"Good!" came the chorus of responses.

Janice Lillis spoke up and said, "Janice Lillis, Mr. Dowdle. I exchanged with Robert Fellerer. His first and last names combined have four r's and four e's and two l's, so the repetition helped a lot."

"Excellent observation, Janice," Mark said. "My first-period class found the same thing to be true. What I'd like to do now is give you the opportunity to watch my fingers in action as I read a short article from the Braille edition of the *World Book Encyclopedia*. I have the 'B' volume here and am going to read the article on braille so you can learn how the braille code came to be." As soon as Mark began reading, twenty pairs of eyes focused intently on his deft fingertips moving across the page. When they heard it was a 15-year-old blind French student, Louis Braille, who created the braille code, their faces registered complete amazement. Fifteen was how old many of them were now or would be this year! What an accomplishment!

Mark finished the article and asked the class if there were any questions. "Mr. Dowdle, it's Carol Fisk," she said. "How long have you been reading braille?"

"Many, many years, Carol," said Mark smiling. "It all started when my dad was teaching at Perham High School and began selling *World Book* during the summers. *World Book* began publishing their encyclopedia in braille, and my dad was lucky enough to acquire a set for the high school. I was just a young kid at the time, and took to reading braille like a fish to water. The complete set is still around, is kept in a special room in the high school library. Any of you are welcome to use it whenever you'd like."

"Thanks, Mr. Dowdle," said Carol. "I'll definitely do that!"

"Of course," said Mark. "Now I'm going to ask Virginia Benke to give each of you a copy of the braille alphabet. Take good care of these. You can bring them home if you'd like and study to your heart's content, just be sure to have them with you in class every day. Remember, it takes time and patience to memorize the raised patterns, so don't expect to master the entire alphabet in a day or two. Thank you, Virginia," Mark said as the last student received their handout. "For the rest of the class time, I'd like you each to choose a word, any word, and study its braille spelling. See how close you can get to memorizing every letter."

It seems they'd barely gotten started when the bell rang, and the students were up and moving on to their third-period classes. "Wow," said Mark aloud after the room had emptied. "Where did the minutes go, Prince? I need better time-management skills! And you deserve a breather. Time for a walk!" He could sense Prince's joyful anticipation as he attached his harness and they headed out the door.

"Ahhh," Mark said as the two companions stepped into the bright mid-morning sun and Prince sniffed the crisp, fall air. "We need this! Let's go!" Both were smiling from ear to ear as they picked up their pace, happy as always to be outdoors together and headed home for lunch.

"Why is it that time flies so rapidly when one wants it to slow down?" Mark asked himself on his way back to school after a too-quick stop at home. Before he knew it, he was standing in front of his fourth period 7th grade English class. "Well, students, let's get started with a quick review of your homework," he said. "Was anyone able to write a complete list to the bottom of the page for each noun?" After an extended moment of silence, he could hear giggles from around the room. "Hmmm, I'm taking that response to be a big negative," said Mark smiling. "I'm guessing you struggled a bit with "ideas" and "qualities. Am I right?" he asked as the class voiced their agreement.

"Ruth Silbernagel, Mr. Dowdle. My columns are almost full, but it was hard, even with my mom helping me."

"As long as you did your best, Ruth, that's what matters," he said, "and that's true for all of you. A determined effort is what matters. To sum up the point of the exercise, what we've learned is that a noun can be more than just a person, place or thing. We'll move on for now. I'd like you to select a noun from each of your six lists and write those on a piece of paper in a vertical row of six."

"Janice Stollenwerk, Mr. Dowdle. Everyone's finished," she said after a couple of minutes.

"Thanks, Janice," he said. "Now let's talk about action in a sentence, verbs that is, because names don't tell us much all by themselves."

"It's Janice again. Just so you know, we learned about verbs in the 6th grade, Mr. Dowdle."

"That's great, Janice," said Mark. "You already know then that all it takes is a verb added to a noun to make a sentence."

"Yes," said Janice as the 7th graders' heads nodded in agreement. Mark didn't see them, of course, and had he been able to note their expressions, he would have been aware that boredom was making its way into the lesson.

"Okay," he said, 'the next thing I'd like you to do is add any verb to each of the six nouns you've selected, and Janice, I'll ask you to tell me when everyone is finished."

This just took the students a minute or two. "All finished, Mr. Dowdle," said Janice.

"Thanks again, Janice," Mark said. "As you can see, the nouns and verbs are just the who and the what. The most interesting aspects of a sentence happen when more words are added, words that answer the why, when, where and how questions. I'd like you to start adding other words to your noun-verb sentences and see how detailed you can make them." After about fifteen minutes, Mark said, "It looks like you're all still working on it. Finish your sentences at home tonight and be prepared to read a couple of examples aloud in class tomorrow. We're going to spend the rest of the hour reading from *A Long Way to Go*. Janice, if you'd pass out the books, I'd like you to begin reading aloud where we left off yesterday. Jerry Theodorson and Dale Witzke will follow. When one reader gets tired, just make eye contact with the next reader and they can take over."

Once she started reading, there was no stopping Janice. Mark finally found his chance to break in. "Thanks, Janice. Well done. Let's have Jerry read for a while."

The minutes rolled by as the students found themselves engrossed in the tale. "A lot has happened in the story since yesterday," said Mark as they wound up their reading for the hour. Who would have thought those kids would take off like that?"

"Leroy Rosenthal, Mr. Dowdle. I would have done the same thing!"

"Well, kids are curious, that's for sure!" said Mark. "They're only going to sit in a hotel room for so long. To sum it up, the two older children, Ashley and Brett, are wondering why their parents haven't returned, and six-year-old Shane is shocked when she learns her mom and dad are still gone. The kids are afraid of what the hotel people are going to do with them once they find out, and thus decide to leave. As you've learned, their initial plan is foiled when they're spotted by the hotel manager as they're headed down the beach.

He brings them back to their parents' room, where they find their mother's pocketbook with $23.00 in it, nothing more. As you read, the kids stayed in the hotel room all morning and then slipped out once again."

"Mr. Dowdle, Jean Wendt. I wondered if they were going to be harmed when they met that Birdwoman. She was really weird. I thought she was going to call the police and turn the kids in, but when she encouraged them to go home and not let people stop them no matter what, I knew she was in favor of what they were trying to do and was going to help them."

"I can see you're really enjoying the story, Jean," he said. "How about the rest of you?" he asked, and a chorus of yesses answered back.

"Ann Schatschneider, Mr Dowdle. We know the kids stayed with the Birdwoman for two days and have now traveled 100 miles. I can't wait to find out what happens next! Can we take the books home?"

Mark heard shared enthusiasm coming from his 7th graders. "OK," he said, "and remember, you also have your six sentences for homework." No sooner had he spoken when the bell rang and the students were out the door and headed to their next class. "Wow! Do you think we can keep up this pace, Prince?" he said as he reached down and gave him a scratch. He could hear Prince's tail thumping exuberantly on the floor. "You're right. Of course we can!" he said laughing.

And that they did! The first half of the next period rolled by with a review of the parts of speech. "I'd like to go around the room and have each of you read one of the sentences you've written from your homework assignment, and then read it again slowly, identifying the part of speech for each word as you go.

"Eugene Klinnert, Mr. Dowdle. I'll start if you'd like," he said.

"Thanks, Eugene, I appreciate that," said Mark. "Whenever you're ready."

Eugene read a lengthy sentence and proceeded to correctly identify the part of speech for each word. "Well done!" said Mark when he'd finished. "I'm impressed! Who's next?"

And so it went, up and down the rows of students eager to demonstrate their parts-of-speech prowess and be done with it! The sooner they moved on from this less-than-enthralling subject, the happier they'd be. "Very good, all of you," said Mark when they'd finished, "and kudos to your 7th grade English teacher, whomever that was, obviously did an excellent job!"

Mrs. Winkler is the name they called out. "Oh, yes, I've met her," said Mark. "You're very fortunate. I'll have you pass your papers to the front and I'll look them over tonight with my father's help. For the rest of the class time we're going to continue reading from *The Diary of a Young Girl*. A couple of you in the back can go ahead and hand out the books."

"Mr. Dowdle, can we read to ourselves today?" asked one of the students.

Mark recognized Lorraine Leuders' voice. "Why's that, Lorraine?"

"The reading aloud is a bit boring," she said as the class chuckled, "and besides, we can read faster if we read to ourselves."

Mark was amused by Lorraine. He appreciated she wasn't afraid to let him know just what she thought. "I can understand how you feel," said Mark. "How do the rest of you feel about reading to yourselves?" He heard murmurs of support from around the room. "OK, you've convinced me," he said smiling. "Carry on." The room fell silent as the students found their place in the book and began reading.

It seemed in no time at all the bell rang, the 8th graders were gone and the 9th graders were in their seats. "This is only my second day of teaching," said Mark as he stood before his class, "and I've already learned a lot. Number one is students don't like repetition, such as going over the parts of speech. Number two is students prefer to read to themselves such as you did yesterday. So, I'll ask the Hertel twins to pick up the descriptive paragraphs you wrote for homework and you can have the rest of the hour to read." Everyone seemed happy with that, because once the papers were collected and on his desk, a tranquil silence filled the room.

Wednesday, Thursday and Friday zipped by, with Mark barely moving a muscle. His students simply seemed to enter the classroom, sit down and go to work on the day's assignment. They didn't even mind when he interrupted them occasionally to teach them more about adding modification to their sentences. Mark wondered, could it be that teaching was going to be this easy? He soon found out that was not the case.

Early Monday morning during the second week of school, Prince and Mark were in the classroom getting ready for the first period Braille class. Ninth grader Joey Gentilli, who was in two of Mark's classes, entered the room. "Good morning, Mr. Dowdle," he said in a soft voice. "It's Joey Gentilli. I'm in your first-period Braille class and last-period English class.

Mark was a little surprised. A whole week had gone by and he'd rarely heard Joey's voice. "Good morning, Joey," he said warmly. "What brings you here so early?"

"I wanted to talk to you about what happened in that book we're reading," he said.

"Of course," said Mark.

"Well, it really bothered me the way Boo Radley was treated just because he was different," said Joey. Why does that have to happen to people, Mr. Dowdle?"

"I don't know, Joey" said Mark, shaking his head. "That's a hard question to answer and a good one to ask. It would be an interesting subject for all of us to discuss in class this afternoon."

"Please don't mention I was the one who brought it up, Mr. Dowdle," he said quietly.

"I won't," Mark said as Joey headed to his seat.

While the rest of the students filed in for first-period Braille, Mark couldn't help but wonder why Joey was so sensitive about the way Boo Radley was treated. Was Joey different, too? The only thing Mark had noticed is that Joey spoke with a lisp. Time will tell, he thought as the bell rang and class began.

"Good morning!" he said enthusiastically. "Week two! After last week, I wasn't sure if you were going to show up today."

Joyce Frank laughed and said, "We're all here, Mr. Dowdle."

"Thank you, Joyce," Mark said as members of the class looked her way and then at one another, wondering if their teacher would remember all the names from last week. "We began memorizing the braille alphabet last week. How has that been going for you?" he asked.

Mark was surprised to hear Joey speak out. "Joey Gentilli, Mr. Dowdle. I think learning the alphabet is really hard."

Mark recognized the voice immediately. "Well, that's to be expected, Joey. Learning to read braille isn't easy. It takes determination and a lot of practice. You'll all catch on over time, not likely as fast as someone who's blind since they don't have any visual distractions. I think you'll find it helpful to close your eyes while you're learning."

"Thanks, Mr. Dowdle," said Joey.

"Okay, let's get started," he said. "This week we're going to start learning the Dolch Basic Sight Words. These 220 words are the most commonly used in our language, words like the, a, an, etc. This will be our focus for the week. I want you to start at the top and work your way down the list. Next week we'll begin typing some short sentences in braille."

"Alan Arvig, Mr. Dowdle. How will we do that?"

"I'm glad you asked, Alan," he said. "I'm happy to tell you we'll be getting Braille machines in the classroom, ten of them. Instead of having a key for every letter of the alphabet, they have a key corresponding to each of the six dots of the braille code. They're very special typewriters as you'll soon find out." Mark smiled as he heard the excited whispers of anticipation among his students. "For now, let's get started on our 220 words!" he said. He took a stack of the Dolch Basic Sight Word cards from his desk and walked up and down the rows of students with Prince, handing a card to each of them.

Mark followed the same procedure with his second-period Braille class, and before he knew it, he and Prince were outside, enjoying the brisk fall air on their walk home for lunch. Other teachers weren't allowed to leave the school during their third-period prep, but the principal made an exception in Mark's case. After a hearty turkey sandwich and a generous slice of homemade chocolate cake, Mark was back at school and ready to take on his three afternoon English classes.

"I'm handing back the six sentences you turned in last Friday," he said to his 7th graders as he beckoned a student for assistance. "With my dad's assistance, they've been graded and have comments for improvements. You'll remember we talked last week about writing detailed sentences. We're going to continue with that today, but first I'd like you to complete an exercise. Take out your notebooks and write down the following twelve sentences as I say them. You can write them as one paragraph or on twelve separate lines, your choice," said Mark as he slowly began reciting…"The river was treacherous. It was swift. It devoured property along its banks. The devouring was merciless. The property was expensive. The river raged out of control. It chewed earth away. It chewed away trees. It chewed away houses. It spewed the earth, trees and houses into the current. The current was dark. The current was swirling."

"Does everybody have those written down?" asked Mark when he'd finished.

"Yes," the class chorused.

"Mr. Dowdle, it's Ruth Silbernagel. I'm wondering why the sentences are so short."

"That's exactly the point in having you do this exercise, Ruth," he said. "The task now is for each of you to combine all of the points in those twelve short sentences into one long descriptive sentence. I hear those moans and groans," he said smiling. "I know you can do it, so let's get started. You can omit some words, but you have to stick with the main thought of each sentence."

"Sounds like everyone's still working on it. Am I right" said Mark a few minutes before the bell rang.

"Yes," said the students in unison. "We need more time!"

"Finish it tonight for homework and bring it in tomorrow," he said. "I'd also like any of you who haven't yet finished *A Long Way to Go* to try and do that by tomorrow so we can talk about it together in class."

The 7th graders were soon on their way and the 8th graders made their way in the door. Mark gave them the same sentence assignment he'd given the 7th graders, but they finished early, so he collected their papers and began discussing *The Diary of a Young Girl*. "Any thoughts you'd like to share on the book?" he asked.

"Sharon Rosen, Mr. Dowdle. I would hate to be cooped up like that with grown-ups for two years," she said as the class laughed. "I guess if my life depended on it I'd be able to do it."

"That was certainly true for Anne," said Mark. "She had no choice. Would anyone else like to share their thoughts?"

"Judy Mondt, Mr. Dowdle. It was so interesting the way Anne revealed all her personal confidences to Kitty, everything that was on her mind and in her heart. It's fascinating, especially since she was thirteen like me." The other girls in the class nodded their heads in agreement.

"I can sure understand how that would make it even more intriguing," said Mark. "How about you boys? Any thoughts to share?"

"Charles Meyer, Mr. Dowdle."

"Yes, Charles. What do you think?"

"It was interesting how the Franks and all those other people went into hiding to escape from the Nazis. It made me think about how much families had to deal with during the war," he said.

"You're right on that, Charles," Mark said. "Just think how terrifying it must have been. They had to tolerate an extraordinary amount just to survive, and of course there were a large number who didn't make it."

The class rolled by as the students asked more questions and shared their thoughts. Mark was enjoying every minute of the lively, impromptu discussion, impressed as he was by his well-spoken 8th graders. "For your homework tonight," he said, "I'd like you to write a page comparing your family life with that of the Frank family." The students moaned, the bell rang, the 9th graders filed in, and just like that, his last class of the day was seated and ready to go.

Since each of the three books he'd assigned his English classes had a strong focus on family, Mark decided he'd simplify things by assigning his 9th graders the same homework he'd given his 8th graders and would soon be giving his 7th graders. He started the class with the sentence-combining exercise he'd given the other two classes, after which the students read silently from *To Kill a Mockingbird*. "I hate to interrupt," said Mark a few minutes before the end of the hour. "I can feel how you've been drawn into the story. For your homework tonight, I'd like you to write a page comparing your family life with that of the Finch family."

The 9th graders looked around at one another, reactions ranging from smiling to frowning. They were being asked to reveal something not only about themselves, but about members of their families. Mark was surprised to hear Joey Gentilli speak out in class once again. "Won't that get a little personal, Mr. Dowdle?" he asked.

Mark recognized Joey's voice from their earlier conversation. "How much you choose to share is totally up to you, Joey," he said. "It's a good way for me to get to know all of you better, but I don't want anyone to feel uncomfortable. Your family comparison, regardless of the level of depth you choose, will also help to demonstrate your understanding of the role Atticus, Scout and Jem played in the book." Had Mark been able to see Joey's face, he would have realized his explanation provided little reassurance. Remembering Joey's concern for how Boo Radley was treated, Mark asked the class, "How about Boo Radley? What do you all think about him?"

"Ruth Boedigheimer, Mr. Dowdle. I think Boo was a very lonely man. He wasn't accepted by others in the town just because he was different, and I think that's very sad."

"Well," Mark said, "what are we to think about those who are unlike us?" No one answered, so he continued. "I think Jean Louise or 'Scout' possessed the answer. She accepted Boo Radley just the way he was, and she understood and liked him in spite of his being different. Boo felt the same way about Scout, and that's why you see him protecting her from Bob Ewell and walking home with her near the end of the book."

The deep-felt class discussion continued, and when the bell rang the 9th graders didn't rush from the room, even though it was the last class of the day. They filed out slowly, still pondering all that had been talked about.

Before Mark knew it, it was Tuesday afternoon and he was standing before his 7th graders. "Okay," he said, "let's see what you came up with for the combined-sentences assignment. I'd like each of you to read your sentence aloud."

Up and down the rows of desks they went, everyone listening patiently as one student after another shared their completed sentence. "Well, done," said Mark after each had had their turn. "You can see how all of you came up with a unique way of combining the same facts. It just shows how much flexibility is permitted within the structure of an English sentence."

"How would you have written it, Mr. Dowdle?" a student asked.

Mark recognized Marvin Schmidt's voice. "Well, I can answer that right now, Marvin," he said smiling. Mark reached for a sheet on his desk and began moving his fingers across the raised dots as he read out loud: "The swift, treacherous river, which mercilessly devoured the expensive property along its banks, raged out of control, chewing away earth, trees and houses, and spewing them into its dark, swelling current!" said Mark as he finished with a flourish. The class spontaneously applauded. They sure were impressed with their 'Mr. Dowdle.' Not only was he a fun and enthusiastic teacher, he completed his own assignments! And he was blind and read braille!

For the rest of the period, the class talked about *A Long Way to Go.* "I'd like you to finish the book at home tonight," said Mark right before the end of class. "Tomorrow we'll begin working on a writing assignment having to do with the book and family life." He didn't have time to elaborate, as the bell rang and the students were out the door.

The only thing the next class wanted to talk about was the Frank family and all the people who were hiding with them and how difficult it must have been. Robert Przybylski said, "I'm sure glad I've never had to go through anything like that, Mr. Dowdle. I don't think I would have made it."

"You'd be surprised how much you can tolerate when you have no choice, Robert," said Mark. "The human spirit is very strong." The students looked at their teacher admiringly, realizing he was likely referring to his lifelong blindness. The minutes rolled by as the discussion carried on, and it seemed to Mark that everyone in the class was interested and involved. As all bells are destined to do, it rang, and the 8th graders headed off to their last class of the day.

When Mark's 9th graders entered the room, they first talked about Boo Radley, and then about the warm relationship Scout and Jem had with their father, Atticus, and how proud they were of him for fighting for justice for Tom Robinson. Mark wasn't able to see Joey Gentilli's face, but had he been able to do so, he would have realized Joey was a deeply-bothered boy.

The rest of the week passed quickly. Mark's two Braille classes continued mastering the braille alphabet and Dolch Basic Sight Words, and his three English classes began their writing assignments.

As soon as his afternoon 7th graders were settled in, Mark said, "Well, are we all ready to write about our families?" The students moaned. "It isn't as bad as all that, believe me," said Mark reassuringly. "Before we begin, I want to say something about a specific writing process we'll be following for the rest of the week: When you think, you're involved in the first step of the writing process called 'pre-writing.' What you're going to be thinking about in today's assignment is how your family compares to that in *A Long Way to Go*. After you've gotten your thoughts down on paper and have finished your comparison, you'll find out how clearly you've communicated. You'll do this by sharing your writing with one or more students in the class and listening to their ideas for possible changes and improvements. This is called the 'response-group' step. Any revising you choose to do based on their feedback is completely up to you."

Mark was beginning to wonder if there'd been a student mutiny, quiet as it was. "I hope everyone's awake, or still here for that matter," he said smiling. "Any questions before we begin?" Hearing a smattering of no's, Mark said, "OK, you'll have the rest of the period to get started. I'll collect your papers at the end of class and hand them back to you tomorrow. You'll be able to finish your first draft and ask your fellow students for input. I'll collect your papers again tomorrow and hand them back on Friday. You'll write a finished paper and hand it in for a grade. And, remember, I'll be looking for detailed, descriptive sentences."

It didn't take the 7th graders long to get rolling. Nor did it take the 8th and 9th graders long to begin comparing their families to those in *The Diary of Anne Frank* and *To Kill a Mockingbird*. What Mark could feel, but not see, was the intensity with which they approached the assignment, especially Joey Gentilli, who never once raised his head as he wrote.

Thursday afternoon during sixth period, when Mark handed the 9th graders back their papers and asked them to exchange with another student, Rose Hammers, a quiet student who sat near Joey, asked him if he'd like to exchange with her. Joey hesitated at first, but then nodded and handed Rose his paper, and she hers. All seemed smooth enough with the overall process, and Mark collected all the papers once again at the end of the period. "Very good," he said. "I'll hand these back tomorrow and you can make any changes and write out your final copy."

As far as Mark was concerned, his second week of school was successful. Challenging as well, but nothing he couldn't handle. He was feeling upbeat as he and Prince headed for home, looking forward to a relaxing weekend.

What Mark didn't know was that he was about to be deeply affected, his confidence shaken, as the result of a tragic headline in the upcoming Sunday paper. "I can't believe it," Chuck said, shaking his head and looking down as he walked in the door, open newspaper in hand.

"What is it?" asked Marty.

"PERHAM HIGH SCHOOL STUDENT COMMITS SUICIDE," read Chuck.

"Oh no!" gasped Marty, Linda and Mark in unison.

"School has barely started and something like this happens," said Chuck, somberly. "The student was Joey Gentilli," he said as he scanned farther. "Do you recognize the name?"

Mark felt like he'd been hit with a sledgehammer. He crumpled forward in his chair, bent over with his head in his hands and began sobbing uncontrollably. Linda put her arm around his shoulder and everyone remained silent for several minutes until Mark raised his head. "I had him in Braille and English," said Mark numbly. "Just this week, early Monday morning before class started, he came into my room and began telling me how upsetting it was for him to read about the way Boo Radley was treated in *To Kill a Mockingbird* just because he was different. I told him it was a topic worth discussing in class, which we did that afternoon. I gave the students a writing assignment, which was to compare the Finch family to their own. I remember Joey questioning whether that might get a bit personal."

Mark didn't realize just how personal reading the book was for Joey until Chuck read Joey's paper aloud:

Dear Mr. Dowdle,

I've enjoyed being in both your Braille and English classes these past two weeks and having been able to talk with you. You listened to me with your heart, it seemed, and treated me with respect, and I appreciate that more than anything. I don't get much of that at home from my mother or older sister. My dad died in an auto accident when I was just a kid, and I don't remember much about him.

Life has been pretty tough at home. My mother and sister have teased me about my cleft palate and lisp for as long as I can remember. Believe me, my life has not been anything like Scout's in 'To Kill a Mockingbird.' Scout's father, Atticus, loved and respected her. In a way, I envied her and wished he could have been my father.

When you and I were talking, I mentioned I thought it was unfair the way Boo Radley was treated. After the class discussion, I began thinking about how I've long been mistreated by my mother and sister, just as were Boo Radley and Tom Robinson, all of us simply because we're different. Tom was innocent of any wrongdoing, just like Boo, and a jury convicted him.

Mr. Dowdle, I'm tired of not being accepted by my mother and sister. Being taunted by them every day has been like living in a prison. I do not feel respected or loved at home. I'm ready to break out, sooner rather than later.

—Your friend, Joey Gentilli

Monday morning during Mark's first period Braille class, you could have heard a pin drop as the solemn students took their seats and went to work. Mark heard a light knock at the door, and Mr. Pfenninger, the principal, opened it quietly and walked over to Mark's desk. He bent his head near him and whispered in his ear, "Mr. Pfenninger, Mark. I have Joey Gentilli's mother outside in the hallway. She's come to the school to gather his things and to have a word with his teachers if possible. Would you have time to speak with her if I sit in with your class?"

"Of course," Mark said as he reached for his briefcase with one hand and Prince's leather handle with the other. As he walked out of the room, Mrs. Gentilli approached Mark and thanked him for taking the time to speak with her. "It's heartbreaking," said Mark. "I'm so very sorry. Let's head down the hall to Mr. Pfenninger's office where we can talk in private."

Mr. Pfenninger, meanwhile, sat at Mark's desk and just observed. He couldn't help but notice the one conspicuously-empty desk, Joey Gentilli's. The second thing he saw was how industriously the Braille students went about their assignment, concentrated on their work, eyes closed. The principal was impressed as he watched their fingers patiently work their way across the rows of raised-dot letters.

"Mrs. Gentilli," Mark said somberly after they were seated in the principal's office, "I was completely crushed when my father read the news to me about Joey's death. Again, I am so sorry for your loss. As you know, I had Joey for Braille and English." Mrs. Gentilli sat quietly and nodded, not thinking about Mark's blindness. "The only thing I have to give you is a composition I had the 9th graders write last week. I was going to hand them back today, and you're certainly welcome to have Joey's."

"That would mean a lot to me, Mr. Dowdle," she said.

Mark reached into his briefcase and fingered through the contents. He handed the stack of compositions to Joey's mother and said, "Would you mind looking through these and finding Joey's for me, Mrs. Gentilli?"

"Of course," she said as she leafed through the pages and found her son's paper.

"I could tell from Joey's composition that he was an extremely-sensitive boy, Mrs. Gentilli. It seems he was hurting, and at some level, crying for help. I think you'll see what I mean when you read it."

"Well, Mr. Dowdle," she said as she rose to leave, "I won't take any more of your time. Thank you very much for seeing me."

Mark and Prince walked slowly back to the classroom. Mr. Pfenninger got up from the desk and walked toward him as he came in the door. "I'm really impressed with these kids," he whispered in Mark's ear. "They haven't stopped working for a second. How did it go?"

"It was OK," said Mark quietly. "I think she's in a state of shock, as are we all. I gave her a composition Joey wrote last week; so happens it was about some of his struggles at home. I expect it will be a very difficult read for her."

"I really appreciate you taking the time to talk with her. I know it wasn't easy," said Mr. Pfenninger as he put his hand on Mark's shoulder and sighed deeply.

"I appreciate you giving me the opportunity," said Mark. "This is a rough time for all of us. Thanks again for sitting in."

When Mark met with his 9th grade English class, it was much like his Braille classes. The students were clearly subdued. He passed their papers back and gave them time to read the written remarks. "I certainly know more about you and your families now than when we first met two weeks ago," said Mark. "I want to thank you for sharing the things you did with me." Mark paused and looked down for a few moments. "I know we're all feeling stunned and saddened by the news of Joey Gentilli," he said somberly as he raised his head. "If he were here to share his composition with you today, you'd be able to see a bit into his heart. You'd hear him say how unfair it was for Boo Radley and Tom Robinson to be mistreated just because they were different. Joey thought of himself as different, too, because of his lisp, and he yearned to be accepted in spite of it.

While most of the students remained quiet, the conversation continued as several spoke up and talked about their feelings over the loss of their classmate. "It's a lesson for all of us," said Mark just before the period ended, "the importance of kindness."

The rest of the week flew by. Mark attended Joey's funeral with Chuck on Saturday. At the end of the service, Mrs. Gentilli approached Mark and thanked him for being there. "The things Joey wrote in his composition were very difficult for me to take in," she said, "and for my daughter, Gloria, as well. I was wondering if we might be able to meet at my home soon and talk about it."

"Yes, of course, Mrs. Gentilli," said Mark.

"I know this is short notice, but would you have any time tomorrow?" she said.

"Tomorrow would be fine," he said. "If 3:00 is OK, I'll have my father drive me."

"That would be fine, Mr. Dowdle," she said. "I'll see you then. Thank you."

On their way home, Mark and his dad talked about Mrs. Gentilli wanting to see him. "I'm sure it's about the notes I wrote on Joey's final composition," said Mark in recollecting what he'd had his dad write on his behalf:

Joey, I enjoy having you in both classes and appreciate my conversations with you just as you kindly say the same. I'm sorry to learn your mother and sister don't treat you with respect. One would hope and expect those to be the people who would most love and respect you. I'm very sorry to learn your father was tragically killed in an auto accident when you were young.

I've always had respect and love from my parents and twin brother, may have even received extra because of my blindness. I won't say I was never teased by them, but sometimes, as in your case, it can be taken too far. I want you to know I respect you and care very much about you.

You did an excellent job of bringing out the fact that Boo Radley and Tom Robinson didn't deserve to be mistreated, just as you should never have to tolerate being disrespected or bullied. We all want and deserve to be accepted the way we are, Joey. You, me, everyone. I'll be looking forward to seeing you in class on Monday. Good job on your first paper.

"I'll wait for you here, Mark," Chuck said as they pulled up to the Gentilli home.

"Okay, Dad," he said. "I don't expect I'll be too long." Mark felt a chill in the air as he stepped from the car with Prince. It was a bit of a walk from the street to the house, and Mrs. Gentilli opened the door as they approached.

"Hello, Mr. Dowdle," she said. "I so appreciate you coming. Thank you."

"Thank you for having me," said Mark, "and as well my sidekick, Prince."

"You and Prince come right in," she said.

After they were comfortably settled in the living room, Mrs. Gentilli said, "Mr. Dowdle, I'd like to have my daughter, Gloria, join us if that's all right."

"Of course," said Mark. Gloria entered the room, eyes downcast, and sat next to her mother on the sofa, across from Mark. He was sitting in a large easy chair, Prince lying on the carpet by his side.

"Gloria graduated from Perham High School two years ago," said Mrs. Gentilli.

"I'm glad to meet you, Gloria," Mark said. She nodded slightly, but didn't raise her head.

"The reason I asked to meet with you," Mrs. Gentilli began, "is that Gloria and I were very upset when we read Joey's composition and your notes. We always thought we were treating him with respect, and, of course, we loved him. We did tease him every now and then, but I'm sure that happens in all families."

"We all encounter a bit of friendly teasing here and there," said Mark. "For Joey, it felt like the teasing he was enduring at home because of his cleft palate and lisp was not a form of affection. To him it felt like bullying. He just wanted to feel loved instead of constantly struggling to be accepted and respected. Sadly, he eventually gave up."

Tears began forming in Gloria's eyes and Mrs. Gentilli's face was reddened and strained. "I'm extremely sorry to hear you say that, Mr. Dowdle," said Joey's mother. "I guess we developed a habit of teasing Joey and didn't think anything of it. Just got used to talking that way. I never realized…" she said, her voice breaking off.

"I'll be straightforward and tell you words are very powerful," said Mark. "We can easily underestimate the impact of things we say, especially negative things said from a parent to a child. It's worse yet when a child is already feeling unaccepted and is hungering for love. Some very sensitive kids, like Joey, experience things more deeply than the average child. He internalized things that felt hurtful, to the point, I believe, where the pain became unbearable."

Gloria sat unmoving, tears streaming down her face. "Well, Mr. Dowdle," said Mrs. Gentilli as she rose from the sofa, "I don't want to take any more of your time. I know your father is waiting. I appreciate you coming here and sharing your insights. One last thing. The paper didn't report this detail, but I will tell you that Joey hung himself in the garage."

Mark grimaced when he heard those words. "I'm very sorry, Mrs. Gentilli, and I'm very sorry for the loss of your brother, Gloria. I can't imagine how difficult this must be for both of you." Hearing nothing, he followed Joey's mother to the front door as Prince guided his way. "I appreciate having had this time to talk," he said as he stepped onto the walkway. "Thank you." Hearing nothing, Mark paused and held his focus on Mrs. Gentilli. "Your son was very special to me," he said somberly before he turned and headed to the car.

"I hope that went OK," said his dad after driving in silence for a few minutes. "Do you want to talk about it?"

"It wasn't easy," Mark said after a long sigh. "It was his mom and his sister, Gloria. His sister shed a lot of tears and never said a word. I kept getting the feeling that his mom believed she and her daughter had done nothing wrong with their constant belittling. Mrs. Gentilli told me Joey hung himself in the garage. I feel a little sick having heard that. It sure is sad, Dad," he said. "It makes me incredibly thankful for the love and kindness I've been shown all my life."

"None of us would have it any other way, Mark," said his dad as they neared home.

That evening at a somewhat subdued supper, neither Marty nor Linda asked about the meeting with Mrs. Gentilli. They realized it was private school business and wasn't to be discussed. "Looking a bit ahead," said Marty, "Linda and I were talking about Thanksgiving, and were wondering how you men would feel about having everyone here."

"I think it would be great!" Chuck said. "By that time the triplets will be about six months old and it will be fun to see how Michael and Laurie have been dealing with it all. I'm sure it's been one heck of a challenge."

"You can say that again," Linda said. "I have my hands full with one baby. I can't imagine three at the same time!"

"You do so well with William Francis, Linda. I'm sure you'd have no problem," said Marty warmly. "So, we'll plan on Thanksgiving at our house if your parents and Laurie & Michael are willing to make the drive up from Minneapolis. Thanksgiving is on a Thursday, of course, and it sure would be nice if they could all stay the weekend."

"No school on Friday," Chuck said. "Works out great for Mark and me."

"Before we invite Dad and Mom, I'll write Laurie tonight and see what she thinks," said Linda. "It's been a while since we've written, and I've been wondering how things have been going. It seems since we've been separated, we've been so wrapped up in our busy lives. I guess that's just the way it has to be for now with all our little munchkins. I'll be very happy if we can all be together for Thanksgiving."

It didn't take long after dinner for Linda to get started with her letter writing, after William Francis got his dinner, that is. He had just eaten three hours ago, but Mark and Linda had quickly come to understand that life at a month and a half is all about eating and sleeping. William Francis clamped onto Linda's nipple and sucked like his life depended on it. It didn't take long before his eyes began to close and his mouth dropped from her breast. "Well done, little man, it looks like bedtime for you," Linda whispered as she kissed his forehead. Minutes later, he was sound asleep, and Linda was at her desk writing to her sister:

Chuck Dowdle

September 21, 1975

Dear Laurie,

Hi, sis! I think about you all the time, am so happy to have finally found the time to sit down and write. At dinner tonight, we were all talking about how we'd love to get together with everyone here at Chuck and Marty's for Thanksgiving, including Mom and Dad, you and Michael and, of course, the triplets! Now that I'm sitting here writing and thinking about it, the more I'm feeling like it would be a huge chore for you and Michael to travel with the babies and pack all the baby food and diapers and carriers and everything you'd need for whatever amount of time you were able to spend here. It was impulsive on our part to suggest Thanksgiving in Perham. It would obviously be much easier for you if we all came there. How was that for a sly way of inviting everyone to your place? Mark has Friday off from school, so we'd have a long weekend for visiting. Talk it over with Michael and let us know what you think.

This morning after everyone left for work, I was sitting on the sofa feeding William Francis and the sun was beaming through the window. It was warm and cozy, and I started daydreaming about how our lives were before we got married and had children. I know you well remember our first dance at St. Benedict's with Michael and Mark, and then the lovely Christmas dance at St. John's a couple months later. Things were so simple back then, right?

I was also thinking about the abortion debate Mark and I participated in at St. Ben's. I sure had a hard time keeping my composure when I found out he was my opponent. You'll recall I had the task of proving abortion should be legal. I think about our precious babies, and it's hard to understand how anyone can make the decision to end their pregnancy.

We're going to be busy in the spring! Guess what? We're building a house right next to Marty and Chuck's! Remember the lot with the pine trees? Well, those trees aren't going to stay, not all of them at least! As soon as the ground has thawed, the contractor will begin excavating, and between now and then we'll be working on the plans. Mark and I are so excited. Dr. Bigler, who has a local practice, just moved into a house he had built on the other side of us, so we'll be living between Chuck and Marty and a doctor! Handy, right? Dr. Bigler happens to be on the Perham School Board, which brings me to more news to share.

Mr. Pfenninger and I talked again recently, and he said the World History and Business Law position I had been offered for this year would be held for next year if I want it. So, with William Francis and the new house and the potential to earn more income, Mark and I have a lot to think about.

I miss you, Laurie, and hope we'll be able to be with you on Thanksgiving.

—Love, Linda

September 28, 1975

Dear Linda,

I'm sorry it's taken me a whole week to get back to you. Life has been a little hectic around here to say the least! I finally had the time to talk to Michael and Mom and Dad about Thanksgiving, and of course we want everyone to be together. We agreed it would be much easier if all of you could come to our place. Mom and Dad are hoping Chuck and Marty will stay in their guest room, as they really enjoyed spending time with them. We're so lucky to have the parents and in-laws we do, Linda!

Ah, yes, reminiscing over our college days. Dating and dancing and debates. Seems like a lifetime ago. How things have changed! We all had such big plans for graduate school at the University of Minnesota. I was fortunate to be able to complete the nursing program, but with three kids, I know my nursing knowledge is just going to be used at home, at least for a while. By the way, it's great you'll be teaching at Perham High School next year! Not the law career you planned on, but I think it will be very satisfying. You'll be a great teacher!

Congratulations on the new house! That's so exciting. We have house news, too! We're buying our house from Mom and Dad! They gave us a really good deal, and we were able to swing the down payment and monthly payment thanks to Michael getting a promotion. He's working part time in the pharmaceutical company's lab, and the rest of the time he's out on the road meeting with clients. The company decided to take advantage of his biology and chemistry background, and as a result, his salary was almost doubled. Needless to say, all of this is coming at a very good time!

Sometimes I find myself dreaming of how much easier it would be with just one baby. I love motherhood, but it seems I'm always exhausted! Joseph Christopher already has a tooth showing, and wants to chew on anything and everything. All three are learning to pick up small objects and pieces of food. It's so interesting to watch them develop and observe how they're so alike, yet so different. The boys are willing to have their bottles held for them during feedings, but not Gretchen Marie. Miss Independent! I can't believe they're already six months old. They'll be walking before we know it!

That's the news from here. Mark and I are very excited about having everyone here for Thanksgiving. I miss you and can't wait to see you and adorable William Francis! Our love to all of you.

—Love, Laurie

OCTOBER 27TH WAS VETERAN'S DAY, A MONDAY, AND NO SCHOOL, thus a three-day weekend for Chuck and Mark. "OK, Super Dads, good luck!" laughed Linda as she kissed Mark and Marty and she headed out the door for a fun day of shopping in Detroit Lakes.

Everything was smooth sailing at school for Mark. His Braille classes were rolling along, so much so that the students had started practicing with articles from the Braille set of *World Book Encyclopedia* and were enjoying the challenge. This made Mark very happy, of course, and it pleased the administration as well. In the beginning, they hadn't had any idea whether the new Braille course was going to work out, especially with an instructor who was blind, but Mark had proven to be an exemplary teacher, and the class was a hit with students and parents alike.

October 31st soon rolled around, and all the kids were excited about their plans for Halloween evening. Marty and Chuck and Linda and Mark settled in at home with popcorn and hot cocoa and readied themselves for a night of doorbell ringers. "Fun to think back on my Halloweens as a kid," said Chuck. "We sure got away with a lot. Let me tell you about my favorite Halloween night."

"Uh oh," laughed Mark, "here we go. Something tells me I've heard this one before." Marty knew what was coming as well, but she just smiled and let it ride, knowing there was no stopping her enthusiastic storyteller-husband.

"I'm all ears," said Linda as she smiled at her father-in-law.

"Well, it was Halloween night, Linda," he said as he began his tale. "As usual, I was tagging along with my older brother, Bill. Being with the older boys, especially on a night like Halloween, was a guarantee of action and excitement. They didn't go to parties in those days and didn't go door-to-door saying, 'Trick or treats, money or eats!' And the older boys didn't go around soaping windows. They always planned bigger trouble designed to drive the Crookston police crazy." Chuck paused and smiled as he reminisced.

"That's the way it was in 1938 when I was ten and my brother was thirteen," he continued. "As soon as we'd finished eating dinner, we were out the door and headed downtown. It was already dark, and by the time we reached Main Street, a large group of boys had gathered, their plans already in place. The ringleaders began walking north on Main Street towards the Hill Addition, and I overheard one of them saying how fun this was going to be, outhouses begging to be pushed over!"

"This sounded exciting! It would be a new experience for me, no doubt about that, and a chance to hang out with the older crowd, so I ran along after them. As they rounded a corner, a familiar voice shattered the night air. "Boys! Hold on! I want to talk to you!" It was Art Roy, the Crookston cop with whom none of the boys wanted to cross paths, especially right now.

"Run like hell for the railroad tracks!" yelled the ringleaders. "It's Art!" Instantly, all of us began racing up the steep hill leading to the tracks.

Linda looked wide-eyed at Chuck. "Weren't you scared?" she asked.

"Petrified!" said Chuck. "I was sure Art was going to drag me down before I made it to the top! My lungs were aching and I could hear him gaining on us. In a move of desperation, I lunged at an older boy's hip pocket, and just like that, he pulled me up the hill to the railroad tracks. We all began running toward Pine Street, which happened to be the street where my grandpa and grandma lived. I was panting big time and knew I couldn't keep up with the bigger kids, so I was trying to do some quick thinking. I had to evade Officer Roy and survive! The older boys made a sharp turn and headed right between my grandparents' house and a neighbor's house. As they raced across the back yards to the alley, I could hear Art's shouting growing ever closer. He sure did sound angry. It sent chills up and down my spine! I figured I was doomed. As soon as I reached my grandparents' house, though, I dove to the ground and rolled under their neighbor's car. I held my breath and didn't move a muscle as Art tore by, close enough for me to hear him panting as he passed within a few feet. When I peeked out from under the car, I could see his flashlight waving in the distance. I was saved! I crawled out slowly and raced for home!"

"Wow! said Linda. "That's quite a story! What did you tell your parents?"

"I just told them what happened. My mom said I shouldn't be hanging around with the older boys, that there was bound to be trouble. Boy was she right! When my brother came home, it didn't take long to discover he'd fallen into the outhouse hole when they were pushing it over! His buddy, Louie Salem, came to his rescue and pulled him out!"

"Oh no! You've got to be kidding!" Linda gasped, as Mark and Marty shook their heads and smiled, having heard this one a few times before.

"True story," said Chuck laughing, "and not only that, but Mom made Bill strip outside, cold as it was, scrub himself down with soap and hose off before he could come in the house."

"Nothing like that ever happened in Coon Rapids, I can tell you that," said Linda as she laughed. "You Crookston guys were pretty wild!"

To add to the excitement of Chuck's tale and their Halloween evening at home, the doorbell rang and they could hear a large group of older kids milling about in front of the house. Chuck got up to answer it, and when he opened the door he was greeted by a rambunctious bunch of Mark's students. "Trick or treat! Money or eats!" they yelled out.

"I think I might know those kids," said Mark as he smiled and made his way to the door.

"Hi, Mr. Dowdle!" they hollered out enthusiastically when they saw him.

"Well, this is an unexpected Halloween treat!" said Mark, as he indeed recognized his students' voices. "C'mon in for a visit! We'll see what we can come up with in the way of eats!"

The invitation they'd just overheard took Marty and Linda by surprise as the group made their way into the house and filed into the living room. "That's quite a crowd! And they look hungry!" whispered Linda to Marty. "What are we going to feed them?"

"We'll come up with something," Marty whispered back with a smile. "You kids make yourselves comfortable and visit with your teacher," she said after greetings had been exchanged and she and Linda and Chuck headed to the kitchen.

"OK, gals, what do you think?" asked Chuck.

"How about peanut butter sandwiches and hot cocoa?" said Marty. "It would be easy and I have plenty of everything."

"Perfect!" said Chuck and Linda in unison.

"Those kids sure seem to enjoy Mark," said Linda, beaming with pride as she heard the animated conversation and laughter coming from the living room.

"And vice versa," said Chuck.

"It's just really nice all the way around," said Marty as the kitchen trio went to work.

"What have you all been up to tonight?" asked Mark as he sat in the living room, happily surrounded by the visiting students.

"We've just been ringing doorbells and wishing everyone a Happy Halloween, Mr. Dowdle," said a female voice.

"I know who you are," said Mark smiling.

"Who?" she said.

"Judy Mondt!" he answered. "I'd recognize that lively voice anywhere!"

Another student spoke out, and it soon became an entertaining game of recognize-the-voices for Mark until he had identified everyone in the room: Eugene Klinnert, Charles Meyer, Lorraine Lueders, Robert Przybylski, Allan Arvig, Colleen Belka, Bill Huebsch, Joyce Frank, Ken Anderson, and Linda and Laurie Hertel.

"Make way! Here come the treats!" said Chuck as Marty, Linda and he paraded into the living room carrying two platters piled high with halved peanut butter sandwiches and a dozen steaming mugs of cocoa.

"We didn't expect such fanfare!" said Judy Mondt as the chatter continued and everyone enjoyed their spontaneous meal. "We just wanted to stop by and tell you how much we enjoy your classes, Mr. Dowdle, and how much we like having you as our teacher."

There was unanimous agreement from the students as Mark looked Judy's way and then turned his head from side to side to take in all the kids seated on the floor. He paused, dropped his eyes downward for several seconds, looked up and said, "You have no idea how happy you've made me by coming by here tonight. Your kind words mean so much, and I want you to know I love having you as my students."

"Thanks, Mr. Dowdle! We love you, too!" said the enthusiastic visitors.

"Well, as much as we've enjoyed this, we'd better be on our way," said Ken Anderson after the last sandwich disappeared. "Thanks so much for inviting us in and thanks for the sandwiches and cocoa!" The rest of the students voiced their appreciation as they stood up, gathered their hats and jackets and said their goodbyes.

"See you on Monday, Mr. Dowdle!" they called back as they filed out the door and headed out into the brisk autumn air.

"Those sure are some nice kids, Mark," said Linda as Marty and she gathered up the empty mugs.

"No complaints here," said Mark smiling. "You're really going to enjoy working with them next year, Linda, I know that."

Right on cue, after everything was cleaned up and the foursome was settling in once again, a whimpering came from down the hall. "We were having so much fun, I almost forgot I have a baby to feed," laughed Linda. "Luckily, he didn't!" While she was nursing William Francis, Chuck turned the porch light off and the living room lights down low so any kids who were still out would bypass the house.

"I like the end of the month," said Mark as they chatted.

"Why's that?" said Marty.

"Oh, I don't know," he said. "I guess it's because I know a new month is just ahead. A fresh start, feels good, like new socks," he said smiling.

"And it doesn't hurt that payday is the last day of the month!" laughed Linda.

"I sure remember those early years when Marty and I barely survived from paycheck to paycheck," said Chuck. "We've been working long enough now that we don't have to worry about being able to cover the bills and make it to the end of the month, and we don't get as excited about payday as you young kids do. Don't get me wrong, it always brings a smile to our faces when there's money in the mailbox!"

"Speaking of mailbox, I forgot to mention I got a letter from Laurie today," Linda said. "She told me it would make things a whole lot easier for them if all of us could come to their house for Thanksgiving. She said they'd love to have us and hoped we could stay a few days."

"I think it would be wonderful," said Marty.

"She said Mom and Dad would love to have you and Chuck stay with them again, for however many days you'd like," said Linda.

"Sounds great to me," said Chuck as Marty smiled, already looking forward to spending time in their home, with Grace, especially.

"I'm so looking forward to seeing my parents and Laurie and Michael and the triplets!" gushed Linda. "Just everyone! It's been too long!"

Mark had been sitting quietly, taking in everything that had been said. He began thinking about how he was going to have to wrap up all his schoolwork during the last week of November. "Boy!" he said. "Time sure flies when you're teaching!"

William Francis let out a big yawn. "I think the little guy just told us it's time for everyone to head to bed!" said Linda.

———◆·◆———

WHEN NOVEMBER 26TH ARRIVED, MARK COULDN'T BELIEVE another month of classes had passed. And now he had four whole days with no school, Thanksgiving tomorrow and three bonus days to visit with his brother, Laurie and the triplets, and Linda's mom and dad. "What's not to like about that!" he thought.

Everyone woke up bright and early on Thanksgiving morning. After a light breakfast, they piled into the car, Chuck at the wheel, and were soon on their way to Coon Rapids. Marty sat in front, Linda and Mark in the back with William Francis nestled between them in his bassinet. As was their custom whenever they drove any distance, they prayed the Rosary together. They hadn't gotten beyond the third decade when a light snowfall began dusting the highway. "As predicted," Chuck said. "I knew the forecast was for snow in the Minneapolis-St. Paul area this morning, but seems it's reaching us about the same time."

There was already a foot of snow on the ground when they pulled up in front of Laurie and Michael's house. Linda was the first one out of the car, cuddling William Francis in her arms as she carefully made her way up the freshly-shoveled walkway. Laurie had been waiting excitedly for them to arrive, and when she saw her sister, she flung open the door and greeted her warmly, squeezing her bundled nephew between them. "Linda!" she exclaimed, "I'm so happy you're here! William Francis looks so tiny!"

"He may be small, but he's a lively little guy as you'll soon see!" said Linda.

Marty followed Linda into the house, and Chuck and Mark picked up the rear carrying the luggage. "Take off your coats and come to the kitchen, everyone," said Laurie after a round of greetings and hugs and oohing and aahing over the baby. "With any luck the triplets will nap a bit longer and we might have time for a peaceful lunch!"

"Where's Michael?" Mark asked.

"He went to the supermarket for a few things and will be home any minute," she said.

No sooner had Laurie spoken than the front door opened and a snow-dusted Michael came in, a bag in each arm. "Hi, everyone!" he said cheerfully as he set the groceries down on the kitchen counter and took off his coat. "I'm sure glad you made it with all this snow!"

After a second round of family hugs and more adoration for William Francis, everyone settled in at the kitchen table. "Sure smells good in here!" Mark said.

"We put the turkey in the oven a couple hours ago," Laurie said, "so it will be close to ready when my parents show up later this afternoon."

"I can't wait!" said Mark.

"I know, Brother. Just like old times," Michael said enthusiastically as he put his arm around Mark's shoulders. "Wonderful family and great food! Let's pray and get to eating so we're ready to gorge ourselves again when dinner rolls around!"

After enjoying tuna-salad sandwiches and fruit salad, they all moved to the living room and cozied up in front of a blazing fire. They were warm and comfy and fed and happy, everything calm and peaceful. Knowing there were triplets in the house, it felt too good to be true! And, of course, it was.

First came a call from the wild, like something right out of the jungle. "Uh, that would be boisterous John Christian," Laurie said with a smile. "He's typically the first to wake up in the afternoon and the last to fall asleep at night." John Christian's howl was immediately followed by a second loud cry. "That would be Joseph Christopher, not one to be left out when it's time for a meal," she said laughing. "Just wait a minute, and a third sound will soon follow." Sure enough, after a few moments of silence, a subtle whimpering filled the air, gentle like quiet music or a soft breeze. "And that would be precious little Gretchen Marie," she said.

With the cacophony of howling and crying and mournful whimpers, the three-ring circus of sound was in full swing. "Sounds like feeding time at the zoo!" laughed Chuck.

"That it is!" said Laurie as she stood up. "Everyone c'mon with me and check out the little critters!"

Linda felt a bit stunned in realizing how completely different her sister's life was with three babies versus her life with just one. William Francis hadn't let out a peep since they arrived, and she knew he wouldn't until later in the afternoon. He was on a schedule, and he always seemed happy and content. The triplets were on a schedule, too, but even so, Linda couldn't imagine how exhausting it must be to have three babies!

Everyone got up and headed down the hall to see the trio, who turned off their sound machines momentarily when they saw the row of faces peering down at them, but it wasn't long before they again let their demands be known. They were hungry and wanted to be fed! But, first things first, and that would be three sets of dirty diapers to be dealt with! "Never a dull moment, I'll tell you that!" said Michael as he struggled to remove a kicking John Christian's full diaper and began wiping his little behind.

"Doesn't smell nearly as good in here as it does in the kitchen, I'll tell you that," said Mark as everyone laughed.

By the time the diapers were changed, three little bellies were satisfied, and everyone had had their time cuddling the triplets, William Francis woke up, right on schedule. He ate his meal, soaked up a bounty of affection from Michael and Laurie, then went back down for another nap. "Perfect timing!" said Michael when the doorbell rang, announcing the arrival of his in-laws.

"We won't be eating until 5:00 or so," said Michael after a round of greetings and hugs. "Let's head to the living room and get caught up on what everyone's been doing since the last time we were together."

"Start us off," said Laurie as she smiled at her husband seated next to her on the couch.

"Well," said Michael, beaming at his wife, "you can see I'm married to a rock star of a mother. I head out in the morning and she's here all day taking care of three babies! I'd probably last an hour, if that! Everything's going great at work," he continued. "We're doing some interesting experimentation with drugs, pretty technical stuff, as in boring for most people, so I'll spare you the details. Suffice it to say it's challenging and exciting for me, and the increase in pay is pretty darn satisfying as well!"

"Welcome to a man's world. My work is challenging and exciting as well, but no big paychecks are rolling my way," said Laurie as everyone laughed. "I can tell you one thing, though. My nurse's training has come in handy more than once!"

Mark sat listening, taking it all in. As with Linda and Laurie, he and his brother were sure living in different worlds. "Go ahead," said Linda as she put her hand on his thigh. "Your turn."

"Well," said Mark as he paused for a moment, "I have to say I truly love teaching. It's exciting and challenging and fun and satisfying all at the same time, every kid different, every class different, every day different. The young kids are so honest, and my students seem to yearn to learn and grow. It's rewarding in so many ways. I was nervous about how I'd do, especially being blind, but it feels like it's working out. My two Braille classes are already reading and are just beginning to write in braille, and my three English classes would read all day if they could!"

"Sounds like it's a real joy for you," said Laurie.

"It has been," said Mark somberly, "except for a recent tragedy."

"What happened?" Grace asked in a concerned voice.

"Well, one of my 9th grade students, a boy, committed suicide," said Mark slowly as Grace gasped. "He had a cleft palate and a lisp and was being teased about it at home, including by his own mother."

"That's terrible!" Grace said.

"I know," said Mark with a sigh. "It was rough. I had no idea until it was too late. It affected me deeply, and Linda of course, and obviously all of his classmates as well. Outside of that, things have been going well."

"It sure was sad," said Linda with a sigh. "On a brighter note, it looks like next year Mark and I will both be in the classroom. The principal offered me a job teaching World History and Business Law. Mark and I talked it over and I plan on accepting the position. We haven't worked out the details of childcare for William Francis, but we have some time to figure it out. I'm sure it will all come together."

"Good for you, Linda!" said Chuck as everyone chimed in with their congratulations.

"How are you and Chuck doing with all the action at home, Marty?" Grace asked as the conversation moved on.

"I'd say the changes have all been for the better," she said.

"I'll second that!" said Chuck.

"We help Linda and Mark however we can, Chuck with Mark's teaching and me at home with Linda and William Francis," said Marty. "We're just enjoying each other's company and the fun of having a little one around again. It's going to be pretty quiet when they move into their new place, but wonderful that they'll be right next door!"

"How's the house planning going, Mark," Walter asked.

"You'll have to ask the boss about that," he laughed. "Linda's in charge."

"Not really, Daddy," she said, "but I have had a lot of time to meet with the builder, much more so than Mark. Most all of the plans are finished. They'll start building the basement as soon as they can break ground in the spring. We're sure excited!"

"It's going to be fun watching it go up," Chuck said. "I've always been sort of a sidewalk superintendent."

The family conversation continued well into the afternoon and the house felt near to bursting with the tantalizing aroma of Thanksgiving preparations. "Gather round, everyone, it's time to eat!" said Michael as Laurie carried a bowl piled high with stuffing from the kitchen and set it on the table.

"I smell a feast!" said a grinning Mark. "Just like old times!"

"I hear you, Brother!" Michael said. "Those old times remind us of one thing, great food and a whole lot of it!"

After everyone had found a seat, Laurie asked her dad if he would say grace, and Walter happily consented. "Father in heaven," he began, "thank you for sharing your earthly bounty with us. We are grateful for the peace and love and joy you have showered upon us. Amen."

"Amen!" said everyone in unison.

"Wow! Pretty short Thanksgiving prayer, Dad," said Linda.

"Especially coming from you!" said Laurie kiddingly.

"Well," he said laughing, "I looked at the faces of those two hungry husbands of yours and decided I'd best not make it any longer than need be."

After everyone had enjoyed yet another memorable Thanksgiving feast, they settled comfortably in the living room by the fireplace. No sooner had they done so when the baby zoo came alive once again. The triplets had one last feeding before bedtime, and by the time that ritual was completed, all of the adults were ready to call it a night as well. After a round of good-bye handshakes and hugs, Marty and Chuck headed out with Grace and Walter. It wasn't long before everyone in both houses, little ones and grown-ups alike, were sound asleep.

The rest of the week was spent visiting, playing with the babies and eating leftovers. When Sunday morning arrived, everyone was up early for breakfast and then church, after which the Perham group got packed up and ready for the drive home. Their holiday away had been a welcome respite from the daily grind, but it was time to get on the road and return to their familiar routines.

The new school week began on Monday, December 1st, and although Chuck and Mark had enjoyed being away and visiting with family, they were ready to get back in the saddle for three weeks of teaching before Christmas vacation. Marty and Linda didn't so much feel that way. Linda cherished every minute of visiting with her parents and sister and wasn't too eager to pull herself away, and Marty had gone shopping with Grace in downtown Minneapolis and would have been happy to do a little more of that! But now they were home, and everyone's work-day life was once again in full swing, even Prince's.

Mark wasn't too sure how Prince would take to the snow when they walked to school that morning, but he seemed to like it, even stopped for a couple of curious tastes. "Come, Prince," Mark commanded. "We've got work to do."

When he met with his first period Braille class, Mark found everything just as he had left it, including the empty desk that had been occupied by Joey Gentilli.

The winter weather seemed to invigorate the kids, and Mark had planned to tap into that energy by embarking on an intense writing program with his afternoon English classes, starting with dramatic, narrative and expository activities and ending with poetry. However, his dad mentioned that it wasn't a good idea to assign a lot of writing before Christmas vacation. If he did, it would all have to be read by the two of them, and corrected and graded, and that was no way to spend a couple of weeks off.

"We're going to be doing a lot of writing before the end of the semester," Mark told his 7th graders, "but so as to not spend my entire vacation buried in papers, all of our activities will be oral between now and Christmas break." The students' relief and happiness over the good news was audible, that is, until Mark reeled off a lengthy list of activities in their near future. "We'll be doing monologues, dialogues, plays, letters, logs, diaries, autobiographical sketches, memoirs, biographical sketches, chronicles, short stories, essays and various forms of poetry," he said, smiling as his words were met with a chorus of moans and groans.

"It will work like this," Mark continued. "We'll begin with a new topic each day. It can be a person, place, thing, idea, quality or activity. Any of you can propose whatever you'd like and we'll go with it. That's when the fun begins!" The 7th graders looked around at one another. They knew their teacher's idea of fun didn't always match their own. "Everyone ready to begin?" he asked. No one said a word, so he stood up and said, "Prince!" And then he said, "I love my dog! I don't know how I ever got along without him! We had to go through a lot of intense training, but it has paid off in more ways than one. Prince and I sure have become good friends. We've developed a mighty relationship with one another. We've bonded!" Mark stopped speaking and said, "What I've just done is called a monologue. It's just thinking aloud to oneself. Now the next activity is to turn the monologue into a dialogue. I need one of you to come up and begin talking with me about Prince. Any volunteers?"

At first no one said anything, and then Mark heard someone rise from a desk. "I'll try it, Mr. Dowdle," said the student.

Mark recognized Eileen Wallace's voice and said, "Okay, Eileen. Thank you for volunteering. This activity's very straightforward. All you and I have to do is begin talking to one another about Prince and we'll be doing a dialogue. Are you ready?"

"Ready," Eileen said.

"OK, well, I bet you wondered what kind of English teacher I was going to be when you walked into this classroom for the first time and saw I was blind and had a dog," he said.

"It was unexpected and a little unusual, Mr. Dowdle, but I love dogs, and I immediately looked forward to whatever the experience would be."

"What's it been like for you so far?" asked Mark.

"It's been wonderful!" Eileen responded. "When we read *A Long Way to Go*, I was hooked from the start. The book was about kids like me, and they had a big problem to solve."

Mark paused and said, "And just like that, class, there's a spontaneous dialogue. Well done, Eileen. Thank you for volunteering. For that you've earned an 'A' for your effort. I'd like you to stay up here for the next exercise as well." Mark turned towards the class and said, "The next activity is to turn the dialogue between Eileen and me into a short play. We do that by adding some action. One or more of you may participate in the play we create, but let's limit it to five."

"I'll do it," said Leroy Rosenthal as he rose from his desk. "Here's some action." He approached Prince and grasped his leather handle and lifted it so Prince had to get on his feet. A surprised Prince growled!

<u>Eileen</u>: (sharply) "I don't think you should do that, Leroy!"
<u>Leroy</u>: (with a smirk) "Why not? You earned an 'A.' I want to earn one, too."
<u>Mark</u>: (quizzically) "Leroy, what are you doing?"
<u>Leroy</u>: (releasing Prince's harness) "I was going to take Prince for a walk around the room."
<u>Mark</u>: "Prince growled and got upset, which is his way of letting you know that's not a good idea."
<u>Eileen</u>: "He knows Mr. Dowdle is his responsibility. Prince is here to do a job and doesn't want to be taken away from that."

"OK. Well done, both of you," said Mark. "So class, you were able to see how we went from a monologue to a dialogue to a short play, just like that. And we had Leroy here creating an unexpected conflict for our play," he added. "I interrupted the action since I'm not sure what would have happened if he'd kept pulling on Prince's harness."

"Do I get a grade?" asked Leroy.

"Yes, you do," Mark said. "I'm giving you both an 'A' for your participation. We'll continue this tomorrow," he said as the bell rang. As the 7th graders walked from the room, several were talking about what Leroy had done. It didn't seem to bother Mark. He just waited patiently for his 8th graders to arrive so he could try out the same program with them, and then with his 9th graders at the end of the day. The hours flew by and both classes participated eagerly, especially when Mark used the same beloved topic, Prince!

Before Christmas vacation, he got as far as the short story with the program. All of his students had taken advantage of opportunities to get up in front of the class, and even the more-reserved were becoming comfortable with doing so. Mark liked the sound of their enthusiasm as they participated orally, and he hoped when they returned after the holidays and began writing, they'd be just as eager. On Friday, December 19th, as they were leaving for vacation, he joked with them and said, "Get plenty of rest during your two weeks off, because we'll be starting in on writing when you return."

CHRISTMAS WAS GOING TO BE VERY DIFFERENT FOR LINDA AND Mark this year. Having just spent Thanksgiving with Laurie and Michael, they decided they'd spend Christmas at home, make it more restful and relaxing for everyone. Chuck and Marty had picked out a big Christmas tree, and Chuck was busy setting it up in the living room by the time Mark and Prince got home from school.

"Wow! It sure smells good in here," said Mark as he entered the house and sniffed the pine-scented air.

"The tree will be fancied up in no time," Chuck said. "Your lovely wife and mother are getting the decorations out as we speak and have volunteered to do the trimming, so we can just sit back and watch them have all the fun!"

The men didn't have to wait long. Marty and Linda soon came into the room lugging two bulging suitcases. "Whew! This one is heavy!" Linda said.

"Packed full with ornaments and decorations we've collected over a lot of years," Marty said reflectively, "and more of the same in mine.

Some are things Chuck and I salvaged from our parents, so they have a lot of sentimental value."

"It's so great that you've hung onto them over all this time," said Linda. "I can't wait to see everything."

"Ah, Christmas memories," Mark said smiling. "My favorite will always be when Michael and I surprised everyone and proposed to our gals, complete with engagement rings!"

"That was wonderful all right," Marty said, "a Christmas memory we all treasure! And look at you now. You're married, you have the sweetest of little sons, a job you love, and you're about to move into a new house. So many memories ahead just waiting to be made!"

Everyone voiced their agreement and the decorating began. Prince lay contentedly on the living room carpet by Mark's side, relaxed and seeming to enjoy the sight of the colorful bulbs being strung around the tree. When the trimming was complete and the lights were plugged in, Prince jumped up and stared.

"That sure got Prince's attention, Mark," said Chuck. "He stood up in a hurry when he saw the tree light up!"

"Is the angel on top?" asked Mark.

"Sure is," said Chuck. "Dressed in white with a sparkling gold tiara, you know the one. Same one your mom and I've used since before you and Michael were born!"

Linda held William Francis up so he could fully experience his first Christmas tree. It was interesting to watch his eyes flutter about, from top to bottom and side to side as he took in all of the ornaments and colorful lights. He couldn't yet move his head around as much as he wanted, but he sure was trying. "Only four months old and already he's working at controlling his little body," Linda said.

"That's the way they learn," Marty said. "Before you know it, he'll be moving his whole body around and crawling. You'll be one busy girl trying to keep track of him! I certainly remember what it was like with the boys."

"I can hardly wait," Linda said. "I have to say, it's been easy for Mark and me so far, thanks to all the help from you and Chuck. We sure are thankful."

"That we are!" Mark chimed in.

"It's been a real pleasure for us, no question about that," said Marty cheerfully. "Especially wonderful for me to have another woman in the house, Linda."

"Especially wonderful for me to have a woman, period," laughed Mark.

The two-week Christmas vacation seemed to go by much faster for Marty and Chuck than it had during past years, likely because of the new little family that had been added to their holiday routine. The days of sitting by themselves over the holidays, waiting for their sons to come home from college, those quiet times were a thing of the past. This was the new action-packed next chapter, and the proud grandparents couldn't be happier!

———◆———◆———

ON THE FIRST DAY BACK AT SCHOOL, MONDAY, JANUARY 5TH, 1976, Mark was in for a big surprise. It was about five minutes before the bell rang when he heard a boy's mature voice.

"Good morning, Mr. Dowdle! My name's David Overton. I'm a new student here and I'm in your class!"

Mark looked in the direction of the voice and said, "Well, good morning, David. Thanks for introducing yourself. No one told me I was getting a new student, so this is a surprise. We're happy to have you." Other students were filing into the room, and Mark asked Ken Anderson to show David to his seat, that which had belonged to Joey Gentilli.

"Sure, Mr. Dowdle!" Ken said enthusiastically. He turned towards David and was stunned to see that the new student had no eyes! "Uh… hi," he stammered. "I'm Ken. Your desk is right over here."

What Mark couldn't see happening in this little drama was the efficiency with which David sat down, opened a case he was carrying, took out his personal braille machine and placed it on his desk. He was ready to go to work! Mark's 9th graders took full notice of this, especially when they realized the new student was blind just like their teacher, and he didn't have eyeballs!

David was a personable, outgoing kid, and it didn't take more than a few minutes for him to fit right in with the rest of Mark's first period Braille class, as comfortable as if he'd been there from the beginning of the school year. By clicking his tongue and snapping it down from the roof of his mouth, David was able to use the echo effect to guide himself fluidly through the crowded hallways as he made his way from class to class. It was amazing and impressive to see!

Mark also had David for 9th grade English at the end of the day, so this added a bit of excitement for those students who weren't in Mark's first period Braille class. "For anyone who has yet to meet our new student, I'd like to introduce David Overton," said Mark.

David waved a hand in the air as he acknowledged the welcoming greetings of his classmates. "I'm blind as I'm sure you all noticed, but I make up for it with excellent hearing, so watch what you say about me," he said with a big smile as Mark and the students laughed.

"Okay, let's get started," said Mark. "We're going to begin by reviewing the oral activities we practiced before Christmas vacation. After that we'll do some work with essays and poetry and then begin writing." By the expression on David's face, you could tell he was eager to participate.

That evening, Mark told Chuck about David and also about getting his English students ready to write. He wondered what his dad thought about his plan to have the kids select a single idea or theme and develop it into a play, short story, essay and poem. "I've never tried that," said Chuck, "but I like the sound of it. Interesting and challenging to control the form and the content while developing the theme in four different writing forms."

The next day, Mark heard what his students thought about the plan. "Mr. Dowdle," Jean Wendt said when he explained the assignment to his 7th graders, "won't that get sort of boring?"

"Not unless you make it that way, Jean," said Mark smiling.

"Do you mean we're going to have to try and say the same thing in all of that writing?" asked Jerry Theodorson.

"Exactly right, Jerry," Mark answered. "Let's get started. After you've picked out a topic and have thought about what you want to say about it, synthesize it to one sentence on a piece of paper and hand it in so I know where you're headed, and then you can begin writing."

The 8th graders weren't too happy with the redundant-themed assignment, but that was sort of par for the course with 8th graders. Mark had noted early on that they were usually the biggest complainers and most argumentative. The 9th graders typically just went with the flow, were mellow and got right down to work.

By the end of January, all of the writing was completed and corrected, and both Mark and Chuck were impressed with the results, especially with what the 7th graders had produced. One 7th grade girl, Stephanie, developed the following theme in her four compositions: *It takes talent, skill, determination and courage to be successful in life, but compassion and self-understanding are needed as well.* After Mark and his dad finished reading her compositions, both agreed she was one mature 7th grader and a very capable writer. What grade did she get on her writing? Why, an 'A,' of course! "I sure am impressed!" Chuck said after he and Mark had finished reading all of the compositions. "I may give my seniors the same assignment, see if they can do as well as your students. Especially Stephanie. That girl can write!"

Before the school year ended, word got around about the excitement that was being generated in Mark's English classes. One afternoon he was visited by Mr. Pfenninger and members of the School Board. Prince, who had been lying by Mark's desk while the students were quietly working on an assignment, rose to his feet as if to welcome the guests when they entered the room. "The School Board is visiting some classes today, Mr. Dowdle," the principal said, "and they've been hearing so many good things about what's been happening in yours that I thought I'd let them see for themselves. We'll just stand in the back of the room if that's OK."

This, of course, got the attention of Mark's 9th graders and was a complete surprise for Mark, but most notable was how calmly he responded to the challenge. "Of course," he said warmly. "Welcome to our class. We recently completed an extensive writing program, so we'll give you an example of what that consisted of." Mark's students were anticipating what he was going to do, as they'd been through the sequence of dramatic, narrative, expository and poetic activities over and over. They knew them by heart and were not shy about demonstrating their knowledge. Mark faced his class and said, "Dogs," a monologue." Just like that, one of his 9th graders rose from her desk and began a monologue about her Golden Retriever, and then another student was on his feet and a conversation began taking place about her dog, and then three more students joined them and a play began happening.

"Okay," Mark said, "someone write a letter to a friend and tell them about the play you saw at school today." That's when it happened! David Overton, the blind student, jumped up from his desk, clicked his way to the front of the room and began dictating a detailed oral letter.

The School Board stood entranced at the back of the room, not just by David, but by all they'd witnessed, clearly impressed with how easily and confidently the students had performed. "I have to hand it to you and your students, Mr. Dowdle," one of the Board members remarked as he was leaving with the others, "these kids certainly know what they're doing. Very impressive. Both you and they are to be congratulated. Thank you for letting us come into your classroom."

"You're very welcome. Come back any time," said Mark as he closed the door behind the last departing member. "Guess we showed them!" he said with a big smile as he looked out at his class. The students could feel how happy they'd made their teacher, and they were beaming with pride over what they'd accomplished for an appreciative and important audience.

Near the end of the school year, things were far from uneventful. David Overton had easily adjusted to the action-packed pace of school and had become very active, both in and out of the classroom. One day during the noon hour, some of his close friends talked him into trying out a bicycle on the blacktop. Nothing about that was a good idea, but after a few assisted practice runs, they succeeded in having him weaving around like he'd been sighted and able to ride a bicycle all his life. David was clearly one amazing kid, willing to try pretty much anything!

It was a Friday afternoon, the last day of school, when a major mishap occurred. The kids were understandably excited and wanted to get out of that place as fast as they could after sixth period. The movement in the hall was fast and furious towards the exit door, and David was moving right along with the crowd. He clicked, clicked, clicked as he weaved his way through the throng of rambunctious students. He was practically running when he got to the heavy glass door leading to the outside, and when he reached out to open it, his hand slipped on the horizontal bar and his lower arm crashed through the plate glass. "David!" yelled several nearby students as blood began spurting from his wrist, "You're bleeding!" A teacher quickly approached him and said very calmly so as to not add to the intensity of the situation,

"David, let's go see the nurse. Looks like you've got a pretty good cut there." As they headed towards the office, the teacher pulled a handkerchief from his pocket and wrapped it round David's wrist, applying gentle pressure to slow the flow of blood.

"Did I cut a nerve?" Can you tell? Do you think I did?" David asked excitedly. "I sure hope not! I have to be able to use my Braille machine!"

"We'll have the nurse take a look at it," said the teacher as he escorted David into her office.

Considering it could have been a much more severe injury, David was lucky, and his last-day-of-school tale had a happy ending. After being sent off to the hospital by the school nurse, the wound was closed up with a dozen stitches, and after a few days of taking it easy, David was good to go for the rest of the summer.

THE PERHAM DOWDLES SPENT MOST OF THEIR SUMMER AT HOME, watching Mark and Linda's house being built. It was entertaining for all of them except Prince, who tried to cover his ears with his paws to avoid the noise. And it was dusty, but by the middle of June, the framing began, and by the end of July the new house was totally enclosed. Mark and Linda could hardly contain their excitement, especially when they were told that it would be move-in ready before school started back up in September!

On Sunday, August 8th, Mark and Linda celebrated William Francis's first year of life by going to Mass with Marty and Chuck. The next day was Mark's birthday, so they decided to celebrate his a day early along with his son's. It was a delightfully-sunny Sunday morning, and William Francis didn't let out a whimper all during Mass. Father Donnay greeted them as they were leaving and said, "That sure is a good little fellow you've got there, Mark. You and Linda must be naturals!"

"Linda, yes!" laughed Mark. "Me, I don't know, but it sure helps that we've been living with some experienced parents for the past year!"

"I'll say!" said Linda. "I don't know how we would have survived without them!"

As Marty and Chuck walked towards the car, they talked about what life would be like after Linda and Mark moved out with the baby.

"I know they'll be close by," said Marty wistfully, "but I'm going to miss them and the daily commotion nonetheless."

"It will be different, but I think having them next door is the perfect separation of space," laughed Chuck.

The housing change wasn't the only adjustment on the horizon. Linda would soon be starting her new career at Perham High School. Lucky Linda! She'd be teaching World History and Business Law to seniors while the babysitter would be running around trying to keep track of William Francis, who was already walking and exploring.

On Saturday afternoon of the following week, the contractor showed up on Chuck and Marty's doorstop holding a ring of shiny silver keys. He handed them to Linda, who happened to have answered the door. "As promised, all set to move in!" he told her gleefully. "I hope you and Mark and that adorable baby of yours love your new home!"

"Thank you, Mr. Johnson! I know we will!" gushed Linda. "We already do and we haven't even moved in yet! Thank you, again, for everything and thank you for bringing the keys by!"

"You're very welcome, Linda. It was a pleasure working with all of you. Give my regards to Mark and Chuck and Marty," he said as he smiled and walked away.

Linda couldn't contain her excitement as she ran into the house to tell her husband. "Mark!" Guess what I have!" she said as she hugged him.

"Must be something good!" laughed Mark as Linda continued her embrace.

"Listen!" said Linda as she jangled the keys in front of him. "Keys! I have keys! Mr. Johnson just gave us the keys to our new house, honey! I'm so happy!"

"Well," Mark said, "with hugs like this I'm thinking we should move into a new house every year!" By this time Marty and Chuck had joined the merriment and they all had a good laugh.

———◆·◆———

WHEN SCHOOL STARTED THE DAY AFTER LABOR DAY ON TUESDAY, September 7th, 1976, Linda, Mark and Prince all left their new house together to begin the new school year. Mark already felt like a veteran, but Linda was very nervous.

"Be kind to them, Linda," Mark said smiling as they entered the school and walked away from each other towards their classrooms. When Mark got to his, Prince sniffed around the freshly-painted room until he was satisfied that all was well, then laid down next to Mark's desk.

The beginning of the school year was exciting. Mark settled in with his new Braille and English classes and Linda with World History and Business Law. Teaching came easy for her, as she was clearly a natural in the classroom. She loved being an instructor and thoroughly enjoyed being around the kids. Mark got off to a good start with his English classes as well. This being his second year, he had his students mastering his writing program in no time at all and the results were impressive.

Near the end of the year, Mark began doing a lot more with poetry than he had the year before, and the efforts of his students made him very proud. One assignment required them to create an autobiographical poem with the following directions: *Write one verse of poetry for each year of your life. Before you begin writing, discuss your early childhood with your family so you'll have a good idea of what you were like as a youngster.* One of Mark's 7th grade students, Tom Juarez, had a lot of fun with the assignment:

> *At one I spoke my very first words.*
> *I lay in my playpen and watched the toy birds.*
> *I walked and ran when I was two.*
> *I got some teeth and started to chew.*
> *At three I learned to ride a trike.*
> *I also met a friend named Mike.*
> *I learned to swim at the age of four.*
> *And I decided to ride my trike to the store.*
> *I went to school when I was five.*
> *And I waited for Santa Claus to arrive.*
> *I lost some teeth when I was six.*
> *We played cowboys just for kicks.*
> *I went to Disneyland when I was seven.*
> *It was…really…it felt like heaven!*

I played in Little League Baseball when I was eight.
I was growing and so I put on some weight.
We traveled to Texas when I was nine.
We saw the Grand Canyon and it was fine.
Once more we went to Disneyland when I was ten.
It felt good to see it again.
When I was eleven, I was in sixth grade.
I didn't want to go to 7th…I was afraid.
Well, now I'm twelve, alive and free.
And every single night I thank God that I'm me!

All Mark could think of when Chuck read that poem to him was how thankful he was that he was who he was, just as God had made him, blind and all. His childhood had been filled with love and caring by his family and all those who surrounded him, and now his life was enriched daily by his enthusiastic and caring students.

As the second year came down to the last week, Mark had his students write a letter to one or both of their parents for their final exam. "Write anything you wish," Mark said, "just be aware that this composition will be a big part of your final grade, so give it your best effort." The students did just that. Mark and his dad were especially impressed with student Laurie Zeller's creative letter:

Dear Plant Sitter (Mom),

While I'm gone on vacation, living it up, you will have the pleasure of watching over my plants. I think you'll enjoy getting to know them. They kind of grow on you after a while! I water them every Saturday, and I'd appreciate it if you could keep the same routine. You can use the jar that is on the cedar chest. You will have to fill the jar three or four times to water all the plants. There is also a bottle of plant food on the cedar chest. Put a full dropper of food in each full jar of water. After you have watered them, they like to take a shower. Just squirt them a few times with the sprayer. Any time you have to spare, you can always go and spray them. They love it! Repeat this same routine every Saturday. Thank you very much for doing all of this for me. Now for a few comments about each plant so you can get to know them better:

You once knew Mike, but he started dying on you. I took him from the garbage can and revived him. He might feel badly toward you for abandoning him the way you did, but don't let his attitude get you down. At the present time Mike isn't doing too well, and he might die on you. Don't feel too badly if he does, because his time has come. He is "over the hill" and has lived a long and happy life. Treat him with extra care, however, because he will be very moody. When and if he does pass on, the necessary arrangements to take care of him have already been made. Be sensitive towards him.

Leroy is the healthy spider plant. Right now he is about to bring his first child into the world. Assuming you have never witnessed the birth of a baby spider plant, I will tell you what needs to be done. First of all, I'm sure you can see the skinny shoot with the beginnings of a baby in progress coming from Leroy's center. If a flower happens to appear near the new baby, don't panic! This is how Leroy shows his excitement over the new addition to the family. Leroy was just a baby himself when I started caring for him. He's come a long way since then. This is a very emotional time in his life and he will often need your encouragement. Please give it to him along with his weekly watering. Note: I'm sure Leroy can handle the birth on his own, so there is no need to call a doctor. He would prefer a natural childbirth.

The Fish Family plant is known as a "Moses-in-the-Cradle" in the plant world. Fish is the family name. The children are the smaller sprouts on the right side of the pot, and Mom and Dad are on the left. They're just an average family; the kids fight, Mom worries, and Dad loves to watch or listen to baseball games. This family, like most, loves each other. They have faced the fact that they are literally stuck together. Treat them as you would any family.

Tillie is the Asparagus Fern. You also once knew her. She was turning yellow because you didn't give her enough light. She is now located in a well-lit spot and will soon turn back to her natural shade of green. Tillie and Mike have been through a lot together and are very close friends. She will be very upset if he dies. Keep her next to Mike at all times (unless he dies). If he does, you must break the news to her very carefully. She is a very sensitive plant and might consider suicide if he leaves her. Love her and be her friend.

Allie is the luscious "Boston Fern." She is the beauty of the bunch, but will never admit it. She is very modest and quiet. When she does participate in worthwhile conversations, her advice and opinions are highly respected. She has many true philosophies, but she doesn't go around preaching them. You've got to get them out of her while she's off guard. I'll bet everyone could benefit from her beliefs if she would only open up and express her thoughts. Try your best to get her involved in discussions. You'll be glad you did!

Curley's true identity is unknown. He was adopted while very young. It is difficult to find out about the adoptee's past. The agency keeps the papers secret because it's a confidential matter. Anyway, Curley has been living everywhere and has never been secure. His former parents (who adopted him) didn't give him the care and attention he needed. Curley's outlook on life was very negative because of his harsh upbringing. Since I've loved him, he has almost changed his attitude completely (for the better). He still feels hate toward people who have hurt him. It will take Curley a while to realize you want to help him, but don't give up. If you open up to him, he'll do the same to you.

Laurel and Hardy are avocado plants. Hardy is rather unusual. He grew full instead of tall and skinny like Laurel. They are just like the true comedians. If you are feeling down and depressed, they will do everything they can to cheer you up. They keep the other plants entertained with their humor and wit. It would be a gloomy place around here if it weren't for them. Although they always seem to be happy, it doesn't mean they really are. They need as much love as any of the others.

Piggy is the fat Piggy-Back plant. She is really a hog, but Hoggy would sound dumb for a name. Piggy drinks and drinks and never seems to fill up. She is still just a baby, but she is huge for her age. Piggy lives alongside Sonny and Cher, the fish. Every once in a while, she may be caught dipping into the fishbowl for a thirst quencher. However, this is unusual for her breed of plant. They generally don't like to get their leaves wet. Piggy, I guess, is just as unpredictable as most females. She loves to gossip. She can tell you just about anything you need to know about any of the other plants. Whenever you talk to her, get ready to listen!

Nicky is my favorite of all of the plants. I know I shouldn't play favorites, but it's hard for me not to. Nicky is a cousin of the well-known "Weeping Fig." He stands over five feet tall and is filled with enough love for the entire plant population. He has a personality that many of us envy. His spirit keeps everyone's hopes up, and life is never dull when you're around him. He is an all-around great guy and is well-liked by many. I'm sure you will find it a pleasure to work and care for him.

This takes care of the majority of my precious plants. The others (seeds and little sprouts) also need love and lots of water. That's it! Aren't they unique? Just care for them to the best of your ability and you'll find that they'll grow bigger and better. If you find yourself bored and depressed, just go into my room and visit "My Plant World." The plants will love your company, and best of all, they will never reveal any secrets that you might want to tell them. Try it sometime. It will make you feel better and it will make them feel loved. Thank you very much for your help.

"That kid had a lot more on her mind than just plants," Chuck said to Mark after finishing reading the last sentence to him.

"She sure did," said Mark. "That's what I'm finding so exciting about teaching English, the experiences my students are willing to share with me when they write!"

There wasn't that kind of sharing in Linda's World History and Business Law classes. They were fact filled and straightforward, but she enjoyed her teaching, too, and she and Mark had a lot to talk about every day after school.

⸺⸺◆⸺⸺

DURING THE NEXT FEW YEARS OF THEIR TEACHING CAREERS, LINDA and Mark settled into a comfortable and enjoyable routine. They were constantly impressed by the quality of their students' work, Mark especially so in the fall of 1981 when David Jager, a delightful 7th grader, joined his classroom. He had recently arrived from Brussels, Belgium, where he had been living in an apartment with his parents and sister.

David was a small boy who wore his pitch-black hair in a Dutch Boy cut, an easy target for students who wanted to bully him. And they did, even the girls! Here's what David recounted when Mark had his students write diaries:

There was a mad rush that particular morning. I was late. Tenna was early, my things weren't organized and breakfast was cold. We shoved off in the cold morning air to the bus stop. *The bus was late, as usual, and was an old funky model a garbage lot would refuse. It inched us to the school and let us off. I waited for the halls to open, and when they finally did, it was Paul's turn to use his locker first. I waited around and used mine after it was kicked shut by Cheryl McCarter four times. I grabbed my things and fumbled into the Drama room. People were sweet and sarcastic, like usual, and one student put on his freaky acts. No matter how noisy some students are, they can't seem to stand the sound of my playing the piano, even though they bang on it themselves.*

I ambled on to P.E. to assume my role of punching bag. Brett Wittner would do anything to make me fight him. I was kicked around until Mrs. King-Claye came and took roll and we went out to the field to play speed-a-way. I had a fun time even though we lost. I came into English after a fight about the band during break, and for once I was a little bit in control.

World Geography was next, followed by lunch. Then I rushed off to Reading and listened to Mrs. Branvold while I was anticipating my math grades. I came to Math and sat quietly at my desk and waited. I was appalled when I saw that I had a 'D' and a 'C.' I gathered up my stuff at the bell and went to the bus stop. I couldn't risk getting jammed by Cheryl after school anymore.

Home was a relief. I spent my time practicing and reading by myself and enjoyed a large dinner. School and all my other troubles were forgotten in another world. Oh, I almost forgot to tell. It was a pretty good day for me at school.

After Chuck read David's diary to Mark, both he and Mark felt saddened by the bullying David had been dealing with. The next day Mark quietly pulled David aside after handing back the students' their diary entries at the end of class. "It made me very unhappy to learn what's been going on with you and Cheryl and your locker, David," he said. "It's not OK and I intend to put a stop to it." He did, immediately, and that day he became David's friend.

That friendship blossomed shortly after David handed in his next composition, a story about a real experience he'd had with his family in Brussels. Mark viewed the story as a teacher/student masterpiece, as it put into practice everything Mark had been working so hard to convey to his students about writing, and he was very pleased. The story was about a bird, and David titled it, *To Be Wild:*

To Be Wild

We lived in a small apartment in Brussels, Belgium, a small home where my family had stayed for several months, a place to rest and keep away from the squeezed, overcrowded life of the metropolis. The apartment we lived in was owned by a rich middle-aged landlady, Madame Lebrun, who lived in the second story with her husband and only daughter, Cynthia. Our apartment was furnished with a large glass table in the dining room where I would do my homework at night. We ate in the kitchen, the warmest room of the apartment, where we could gather to talk about our different adventures of the day.

But outside our kitchen door was the area I loved so much, the area where my story takes place. It was a large garden surrounded by a high stone wall, the house and refuse of several animals, a hiding place from the polluted environment of the city. It was a beautiful area, always fresh and verdant from the rainy weather, carpeted with ground moss and wild blossoms from which sprang two large poplar trees stretching out and sheltering the many birds that came to nest in their tangled branches.

It was late in the afternoon when the bird fell. It came tumbling down wildly from its nest perched up high in the tree, and landed on the carpet of moss and grass beneath it. My younger sister, Sheila, was the first to notice. She was a young girl, age five, with the fresh, energetic curiosity of all young children. "David!" she cried. "A bird fell from the tree!"

I was sitting at the dining room table completing my homework, papers and folders scattered in all directions. I turned around in my chair.

"A what?"

"A bird!" There was a look of excitement on her face as she pointed out the window and I ran towards it and looked outside. The bird lay on the ground, hopping wildly about and fluttering its wings.

"Let's go get it!" she cried.

She grabbed my hand eagerly as we set out for the kitchen door. We entered the garden and ran to the foot of the tree. It was a small baby bird, hopping about on one foot, the other torn and bleeding. Its wing was also badly damaged and fell limply to its side while the bird beat the other furiously, desperately trying to fly back to its nest.

"What should we do?" Sheila asked, looking up at me with large, inquisitive eyes.

"Pick it up, I guess," I said. She released my hand and stepped back, fixing her gaze on the injured bird as I reached out my hand to touch it as it rested up for another struggle. I closed my fingers securely around it and picked it up. It gave out a cry of pain as it struggled to be released from my grasp. It was warm, and its heart was beating rapidly as I cautiously carried it to the kitchen. Sheila came up close to watch, fixing her large eyes on it.

It was a small baby dove, covered with a fresh, white coat of feathers carefully preened by its mother. I walked slowly through the door and carried it inside. It was warm in the kitchen, the stove burning on the other side of the room. I set the bird gently on the table and walked to the sink to get some water. I filled a small glass from the cupboard and set it on the table. I lifted the bird and lowered its tiny, pointed, orange beak into the water. Sheila was watching all the time, on tiptoe, as the bird stood there, posed, beak in the glass, and I waited for it to drink. It seemed to be frozen in my hands, immobile. I felt the beating of its heart and the warmth radiating from its small body into my hands as the room held its breath. It was silent, tense, Sheila peering anxiously at the head posed above the water.

"It isn't drinking," she said. A feeling of frustration came over me as I stood and waited.

"Don't worry," I said. "It will."

"But it isn't!" she said.

I lifted the bird and set it on the table. I looked it over with anxious eyes, trying to discover what was keeping it from drinking, but found nothing. I lifted it again and lowered its beak a second time into the glass, still not understanding why the wild bird refused to drink. I gave up a few minutes later, confused and frustrated by a bird for which I had the highest hopes, but which would not take anything from me. Why wouldn't it accept my offerings?

I left the table and walked away. A few minutes later I returned with a small shoebox stuffed with cotton and rags, ready for another try with the water. No matter how hard I prayed, waited or used force, it wouldn't drink a thing. It would only stay posed there stupidly while I forced its beak into the water. I was confused and bewildered. I had no knowledge of wild animals and birds. In my young life, I had known only domesticated pets, those associated with the human world. An animal, for me, was a plaything, a relation, a being that I could take care of, something that I could trust and with which I could live. But this bird was only a source of frustration for me, a being that refused all my love and attention.

Mother walked into the room and set a bag of groceries noisily on the kitchen counter. She did not see my patient as she walked in, but turned around to notice it. I hadn't the faintest idea of being discovered, and here I was, standing in front of the table, the bird tucked away in the box. I placed it behind my back as Sheila quickly ducked under the table, ready for another scolding session to take place. Mother stood in front of me, hands on her hips.

"What are you hiding?"

"Nothing, Mother," I said as I squeezed uncomfortably against the table and gripped the box in my hands. She didn't look satisfied. "Mother, please! I don't have anything, honest! I…"

In one swift, deft movement, she shot out her hand and grabbed the box. A look of compassion came over her face as she held it and looked inside. The bird was carefully tucked in rags, covered with several handkerchiefs and a pillow under its head. She stood facing me and looked me straight in the eye. Then came the fateful words.

"You can't take care of it inside."

"But, Mother!" I cried. "It'll freeze out there!"

"You don't understand…"

"Yes, I do! You want the bird to freeze!"

"Calm down," she said. She sat me down and explained. "The bird is wild, David. It won't survive in here."

"Mother, it'll freeze outside!"

"Birds are used to it. They live outside. It will die in here."

I refused to listen. I turned away and closed my ears. She stood up, sighed and quietly brought the box outside the kitchen. I ran after her. She stopped and grabbed me firmly by the shoulders.

"You have to keep it outside."

"Mother, no!" I tore myself from her grasp and ran for the box. I secured my hands around it and brought it to my room, locking the door behind me. I was frustrated, angry and confused. I looked at the bird, now lying silently in the box. Its eyes had lost their glaze, the lids had closed over them, and its *wings were badly swollen at the joints. I hesitated. I looked out the window upon the garden and the large tree that spread out before me. A nest lay in one of the branches, swaying gently in the wind. I looked around my room, the lamp, closet and bed, the walls that enclosed the place. It was compact, tight compared to the spacious free area that lay beyond the window. It was jostling, alive, not prefabricated with dead materials. The bird was a creature born to live in a free environment, born to be wild. I brought it downstairs and placed it outside. I was uncertain, afraid, unsure of my mother's words, but something told me that she was right.*

That night I brought the box inside to feed the bird. Father was there to help me, waiting with a bowl of bread crumbs soaked in milk. The bird was pale now, wan looking, its feathers disheveled and gray. We tried to feed it with a matchstick, slowly pushing food down its throat. It would only take a little at a time, swallowing slowly. We gave it as much food as we could, and I brought it back outside.

There were no stars, the sky was clouded overhead, and I could hear the faint, distant rumbling of thunder. I hesitated and then placed the box gently on the ground.

Dinner was silent. I was thinking of the bird all the time, lying in its box. Sheila was silently praying by herself, having forgotten about it. I sat on the couch and stared into the blazing fire, flickering and dancing. Confusion, anger and hope were all choked up in me as I sat thinking. I was scared.

I went to bed late that night after trying to feed the bird a second time, and I lay awake for an hour listening to the faint rumbling of thunder playing with the trees. Lying silently, I drifted to sleep, dreaming of the bird, its coat of feathers a dazzling white, its eyes a glossy black, flying back to its nest in the brilliant green branches. I awoke in the middle of the night, rain beating on the window. Thunder was shaking the windows, together with the bright yellow flashes of lightning. I felt sweaty and uncomfortable in my bed, uneasy and frightened. The thought of the bird sent a lightning bolt down my spine.

I scrambled out of my bed and tiptoed down the stairs into the kitchen. It was dark and cold, the fire in the living room only a pile of dying embers. A thunderclap exploded and shook the window, followed by a bright flash of lightning. I was trembling. I approached the kitchen door slowly and grasped the doorknob. The door flung open, and a large gust of wind swept me into the beating rain. I groped around in the dark, searching and calling out. A black shape emerged a few feet ahead of me. I grabbed it. It was the box, but empty. I looked around, hoping to find some trace of the bird. A shadow stood a few feet before me. I looked at it, unbelieving. A flash of lightning illuminated the yard. I saw the bird lying before me in the pale-yellow light, dead! A chill of terror went up my spine while I stood in the downpour, unbelieving, frightened.

I dashed through the door and ran up the stairs into my parents' room. My father turned on the lamp to find me standing sopping wet before him. Confusion and terror were all mixed up inside me and came out in long, hysterical sobs.

"What's going on?" he asked.

"It died!" I cried. "It's dead!"

We held the funeral in the morning under the tree, with a small procession of children. The sky had cleared and the sun was shining through, the garden still as alive as ever. I found the bird lying on the ground in a puddle of water, its head turned to the side and its feet sticking up in the air. I picked it up and placed it in a shoebox and called the children around the neighborhood for a funeral procession. It was a solemn one, I standing by the grave as Father read from an old Bible. I left after a half hour and walked back into the kitchen. I looked out the window upon the old stone wall. Two birds, a couple, sat perched upon it, calling out for their lost, dead child. I wanted to yell, "It's dead! It's gone! Over with!" But I knew they wouldn't understand.

Wild will never mean the same to me again, and the word 'wild' will always remind me of the painful and emotional experience that led me to its meaning.

IT SEEMED TEACHING HAD BECOME SUCH A VITAL PART OF MARK'S life, especially the writing aspect, that he had little time for anything else, even for his son, William Francis, who was now in the 1st grade.

It was near the end of the school year when Mrs. Pauline Bernauer, William Francis's teacher, had the children write a story about the most important people in their lives. William Francis could hardly wait to get started, and when he was finished, he could hardly wait to share what he'd written with his dad and mom. On the last day of class, school papers in hand, he ran home and rushed into the house. He called for his parents, but all he got in reply was a husky bark from Prince in the back yard, so he raced outside.

"You're looking pretty hot and sweaty!" Linda said as she sat relaxing in the shade with Mark, lemonade in hand.

"You must have run all the way home," said Mark with a smile.

"I did!" said William Francis breathlessly as he handed Linda the sheaf of papers.

"What's all this?" she asked.

"It's my writing from this year," he said "The most important one is right on top. I wrote it this week. Can you read it to Dad now?"

"Sure," Linda said as she took the top paper from the pile and placed the rest on the patio table next to her. "What's this story about?"

"Just read it, Mom," he said, "and you and Dad will find out."

"I'm all ears!" said Mark.

"*My dad is blind,*" Linda began reading. "*He's a teacher at my school. A lot of the time when my dad is home he is busy reading papers. My grandpa helps him since he can't see. Sometime me and my dad go out for long walks with our dog, Prince. Those are the times I like the best, the times when we're together. My mom is a teacher, too. She's a really good cook! She's really nice and I like talking with her. My mom has more time to spend with me since she doesn't have all those papers to read. When I come home from school she always asks how my day has been. My mom and dad are the most important people in my life. I love them very much, and I love Prince, too.*" Linda glanced over at Mark when she finished. She could see his eyes had teared up. "What a nice paper, William Francis," she said as she gave him a hug.

"It sure is," Mark said as he reached out to embrace his son. "You're a born writer!"

"Are you sad, Dad?" William Francis asked as he witnessed a tear streaming down his dad's face.

"That writing came straight from your heart," Mark said affectionately. "It was just so good that it got to me."

"You must be thirsty, William Francis," said an emotional Linda, smiling at her son. "How about a glass of lemonade?"

"Sure!" said William Francis.

Linda turned her head from her son so he wouldn't see her tears as she stood up and headed for the house. "It's the end of the school year, time for us to celebrate!" she called back over her shoulder.

While she was gone, William Francis looked up at Mark and said, "Maybe we can celebrate by going to visit Uncle Michael and Auntie Laurie and Gretchen and John and Joseph! Please, Dad!"

"Maybe we can," Mark said. "I'll talk it over with your mom."

After supper that night, with William Francis off to bed, Linda and Mark sat down and had a long talk about what their son had written. Mark felt like an arrow had pierced his heart. "That little guy's words really got to me," Mark said somberly. "I'm definitely going to ease up on the hours of school work I do at home and spend more time with him."

"That would be wonderful," Linda said. "He certainly treasures your time with him."

"I'm going to make a real effort," Mark said, "and there's no time like the present to start making it happen. Also, while you were getting his lemonade this afternoon, he leaned into me and basically pleaded for us to visit his cousins this summer. What do you think?"

"I'd love to, of course!" laughed Linda. "It's been too long since we were together, and we've got some catching up to do. I'll write Laurie and see if there's a weekend that would work out for them."

Early the next morning after breakfast, Mark asked William Francis if he'd like to go fishing. His son was thrilled, and it didn't take long for him to gulp down his cereal, get dressed and be waiting at the door. "Ready, Dad!" he yelled out.

"Easy there, William Francis!" laughed Linda. "I'm still packing a lunch for you two."

"And we have to gather all our fishing gear," said Mark as the two walked hand in hand into the garage.

Little Pine Lake was just a ten-minute drive from the house, and it wasn't long before Mark and his son had their lines out and floats bobbing on the serene lake water.

Linda enjoyed fishing, too, but she wanted today to be a special time of bonding for Mark and William Francis. Besides, a few hours to herself to relax in the peaceful back yard sounded heavenly, and a good time to get a letter off to her sister.

June 5, 1982

Dear Laurie,

I hope things are going well for you and Michael and the little ones. I can't imagine how busy you must be! It's been a while since we visited, and we'd love to come and see all of you. The last day of school was yesterday, so we're done for the summer! Yesterday afternoon the three of us were sitting on the back patio and I suggested we do something to celebrate. William Francis didn't hesitate for a second, said he wants to visit all of you! So, there you have it, Sis. Out of the mouths of babes come important requests. It just so happens that the one made by our young son matches my request as well! I miss you so much! Just let me know if there's a weekend coming up that would work out.

—Love, Linda

It didn't take long for Laurie to answer her sister's letter. Before the next week was over, Linda got the answer she was hoping for.

June 11, 1982

Dear Linda,

I was so glad to hear from you! I've been missing you, too, more than you know, even though it seems I'm busy every second with the triplets. We'd love to see all of you, of course! What would you think about getting together next weekend, June 19th - 20th? We could make it an extended one if that works for you! You could come Friday, any time, and stay Saturday, Sunday and Monday, or as long as you wanted! We could celebrate Father's Day on Sunday and have Mom and Dad come over for dinner. Sound good?

Unless I hear otherwise from you, we'll just expect you on that Friday. I'll call Mom and Dad and tell them the plan. I know they'll want Marty and Chuck to stay with them, as always.

Thanks for making us a part of your summer celebration! See you soon!

—Love, Laurie

The first thing Linda did after receiving her sister's letter was tell William Francis that he'd soon be visiting his cousins. Needless to say, that evoked quite an enthusiastic reaction. He began jumping up and down and yelled out, "Dad! Dad!" as he ran off to look for his father.

"Whoa! Must be big news!" laughed Mark as William Francis located him in the back yard and Prince stood up to assess all the commotion.

"Mom said we're going to see Gretchen and Joseph and John next week, Dad!" said William Francis. "She just told me!"

Marty and Chuck were happy about getting away for a few days as well. They were looking forward to seeing their son and daughter-in-law and grandkids, and interested in hearing how Michael was doing with his work at the pharmaceutical company. And, of course, time spent in Grace and Walter's home was always enjoyable. The triplets were seven years old now, having just celebrated their birthday on June 7th, and it would be fun to see how they'd grown and changed. William Francis was soon to follow, would be turning seven on August 8th.

Chuck pulled up in front of Laurie and Michael's Coon Rapids home around noon on Friday. As everyone piled out of the car, the first ones who came running out to greet them were Joe and John. Gretchen waited shyly by the door and walked to meet them with her parents.

"Hi, everyone! Hi, William Francis!" the boys yelled. William Francis quickly noticed how tall and husky Joe and John were as they stood in front of him. He suddenly felt very small as he took a step back and gave a quiet hello.

Once they were all in the house, though, it didn't take long for the cousins to get reacquainted and feel at home with each other. "Do you want to go outside in the front yard and play?" his cousins asked. Play is always a magic word with kids, and in no time at all they were outside involved in a speedy game of tag. "I'll be it!" Gretchen shouted, as the three boys scattered. She at first chased her brothers, who didn't have a chance of outrunning their light and trim and quick sister. With those two soon tagged, she turned her attention to William Francis, who ran towards the sidewalk to get away from her as rapidly as possible.

William Francis was light and fast as well, and Gretchen quickly realized she had a challenge on her hands. As they raced down the sidewalk, Gretchen's brothers called out, "Run, William Francis, run! Don't let her catch you!" Gretchen was gaining on him, and just as she was about to tag him, her shoe caught a crack in the sidewalk. She cried out as she stumbled forward and flew flat onto her stomach, hitting her head and chin on the concrete.

"She's bleeding! I'll get Mom and Dad!" yelled Joe, as John and William Francis ran to Gretchen's side.

"Mom! Dad! Come outside! Hurry!" Joe screamed as he ran into the house. "Gretchen fell and hurt herself!"

Laurie was the first one out the door and gasped when she saw Gretchen lying on the sidewalk. "Honey!" she cried out as she ran to her. Blood was dripping from Gretchen's chin onto the concrete as she lay motionless. "Call an ambulance, Michael!" she ordered as he ran to her side. Michael didn't hesitate, turned and raced back to the house. When Laurie bent over Gretchen and examined her more closely, she saw blood was also seeping from the back of her head.

Linda and Mark rushed from the house hand in hand, Marty and Chuck right behind. "Oh, Mark, this looks bad," Linda whispered to him when she saw the blood and Gretchen's small unmoving body. "She's just lying on the sidewalk."

William Francis ran to his mom and saw tears in her eyes as he looked up at her face. "Mom," he said as he began to cry softly, "Gretchen was chasing me and we were running real fast and she fell. I'm worried that she's dead!"

"She's not dead, William Francis," said Linda as she hugged him with gentle reassurance. "She probably hit her head pretty hard on the sidewalk and knocked herself out. It will take her a bit of time to wake up."

Joe and John stood quietly by, watching intensely for any movement. "The ambulance is on the way, should be here in a few minutes!" yelled Michael as he bolted from the house and ran to Laurie.

Laurie looked up at her husband and said worriedly, "I hope they get here soon, Michael. She's breathing very shallowly and I've stopped the bleeding, but she hasn't moved." It seemed there was nothing anyone could do but wait. It was eerie and terrifying, the little body so full of life one moment and lying motionless on the ground the next.

Everyone was relieved to hear the wailing siren of the approaching ambulance, and within ten minutes the EMT's had assessed Gretchen's condition, loaded her onto the gurney and were enroute to the hospital.

The three kids quickly piled into two vehicles with their parents and Chuck and Marty and headed to the hospital.

"I sure hope Gretchen wakes up soon," said Joe quietly.

"Me, too," said John. "Is she going to be OK, Dad?"

"They're taking very good care of her," he said quietly. "We'll know a lot more when we get to the hospital and can talk to the doctors after they've examined her. How did this happen, anyway?" he asked.

"We were playing tag," John said. "Gretchen was chasing William Francis down the sidewalk and she tripped on a crack and fell."

"The sidewalk's going to get fixed, that's for sure!" said Laurie as they pulled into the hospital parking lot and made their way to the Emergency Room.

"The doctors are examining her now," said the nurse who came out to speak to them. "Mom and Dad, you can come with me to be with your daughter. We'll give the rest of you an update as soon as we have one."

Gretchen had been transferred to a curtained-off bed in one of the ER treatment areas. She lay motionless, the doctors and nurses hovering over and around her. After observing her closely for a few minutes, one of the doctors, a neurosurgeon, was about to speak when Gretchen opened her eyes and blinked several times under the bright lights. "Where am I?" she whispered weakly.

Tears streamed down Laurie's face as she approached the side of the bed. "You took quite a fall on the sidewalk when you were playing tag in the front yard," she said. "You're in the hospital getting all fixed up."

"I'm so tired, Mom. I don't remember…," whispered Gretchen as her words trailed off. Before she could utter another, her eyes sagged sleepily and she was out once again, breathing deeply. The doctor motioned for Michael and Laurie to follow her out of the examining room and into the waiting room.

"She just woke up!" said Michael to the rest of the family. "She's asleep again now, but was able to speak to us." There were audible sighs of relief around the room.

"I'm Dr. Pederson," the neurosurgeon said as she introduced herself to the group. "It's expected that she'll be tired and sleepy after taking such a hard fall and hitting her head. It's a very good sign that she awakened so soon after her trauma. I want to keep her in the hospital overnight, keep a close eye on her vital signs and make certain she's OK. It looks like she'll need a few stitches as well."

Laurie was the first to speak. She told the doctor she was a nurse and certainly supported keeping Gretchen in the hospital overnight for observation. With that, the doctor was off and said she'd talk to them again in the morning after she made her rounds.

"That seemed like a pretty quick evaluation by Dr. Pederson," Michael said after they'd left the hospital and were driving home. "I'm surprised she didn't spend more time with Gretchen."

"I'm sure she knows what she's doing, Michael," Laurie said. "She's a specialist and Gretchen's just one of many patients."

Everyone was feeling somber as they headed home, Joe and John, and especially William Francis, who had joined his cousins in Michael and Laurie's car for the drive back to the house. They couldn't stop thinking about Gretchen. Joe and John loved their sister and felt it was their responsibility to protect her, and William Francis was having feelings of guilt because she was trying to catch him when she fell.

"Let's all gather around and say a Rosary for Gretchen," suggested Mark once they'd arrived home and were settling in. "We can pray for a quick recovery."

"That's an excellent idea," Laurie said.

"Why don't you lead, Mark," said Chuck.

"Sure," he said. No sooner had he begun with the sign of the cross and the first few words when the doorbell rang and Grace and Walter arrived.

"It's so good to be here!" Grace said to Michael as he ushered Walter and her into the living room.

"And where's my favorite granddaughter hiding out?" Walter asked with a smile.

"Well, sit down and Laurie will catch you up on our day," Michael said after hugs and greetings had been exchanged all around.

Grace and Walter listened intently as Laurie proceeded to recount every detail of their traumatic afternoon. "Oh, my, what a terrible thing for all of you to go through," said Grace, "especially sweet little Gretchen!"

"Thankfully, she seems to be doing okay," Laurie said. "She's very tired, was sleeping soundly when we left the hospital. We're hoping she'll be able to come home tomorrow."

"We were just starting to pray the Rosary for her when you arrived," said Linda. "Would you like to join us?"

"Of course," Walter said with an anxious tone in his voice. "I'm sorry we interrupted, but we came a little early so we'd have time to visit with everyone before supper."

"We're glad you came when you did, Walter," Michael said. "We all know there's power in prayer, so the more of us praying for Gretchen, the better." Michael looked in Mark's direction and asked, "Ready, Brother?"

"Ready," said Mark smiling. He waited until everyone was silent, and then he began. *"I believe in God, the Father almighty, Creator of heaven and earth, and in Jesus Christ, his only Son, our Lord, who was conceived by the Holy Spirit, born of the Virgin Mary, suffered under Pontius Pilate, was crucified, died and was buried; he descended into hell; on the third day he rose again from the dead; he ascended into heaven, and is seated at the right hand of God the Father almighty; from there he will come to judge the living and the dead. I believe in the Holy Spirit, the holy Catholic Church, the communion of saints, the forgiveness of sins, the resurrection of the body, and life everlasting. Amen."*

"Amen," said everyone in unison.

It was already six o'clock and nobody had mentioned anything about food. It had been a frenzied afternoon with Marty, Chuck, Linda, Mark, William Francis and Prince showing up, Gretchen having an accident, and Grace and Walter arriving early. However, all the action didn't seem to bother Joe or John. They were feeling rested after dozing off on the drive home from the hospital. "Mom, are we going to have dinner soon?" Joe asked.

"Oh, my!" Laurie said. "So much for being a good hostess! Everyone must be starving! So much has been happening, I haven't taken a second to think about eating. Everything's pretty much ready, I just need to warm up a couple of things in the oven."

"We'll help you, Laurie," Grace said cheerfully as she followed her daughter into the kitchen with Marty and Linda close behind. It didn't take the four ladies long to get things rolling. "Okay," Laurie said as she opened the refrigerator and began handing things out. "Mom, why don't you work on setting the table since you know where most everything is. Marty, you can help with that if you don't mind, and Linda and I will get the food ready."

"Certainly," said Grace. "C'mon, Marty, we can handle this," she laughed as they headed for the dining room. "Plus, it'll give us a chance to catch up."

It gave Linda and Laurie a chance to do the same, and they took advantage of it. They talked about school and how the kids had done in the 1st grade. Linda began telling her sister about the paper William Francis had written about the important people in his life. "It was really insightful," she said, "and Mark and I were pretty taken aback by what he said."

"What did he say that surprised you?" asked Laurie.

"Well, he basically said his dad was blind and was a teacher and was always busy with Grandpa reading class papers and that neither of them had much time to spend with him. We thought it was pretty sad when we read it, but it's true," Linda sighed.

"Wow! I bet you and Mark had a long talk after that revelation!" said Laurie.

"We sure did," said Linda. "William Francis wrote that he liked how I talk with him and take the time to ask how his day has gone. Can you believe that, Laurie? He said I was a teacher and a good cook as well, but the one thing he most valued from me and Mark was our time."

"Boy, what did you two decide to do?" asked Laurie.

"What else!" she said. "Make darn sure from now on that we make ample time for him and learn to listen!"

"That's good advice for every parent," said Laurie.

"Now tell me about your three!" said Linda enthusiastically.

"I could talk for hours on that," laughed Laurie, "but let's save it for later. I think we'd best get this meal on the table! Grace and Marty had the place settings in order and joined Laurie and Linda in delivering the food. Laurie led with the ham she'd warmed in the oven and Linda followed with a crock of Boston baked beans. Next, Grace carried in a large bowl of potato salad and Marty followed with a basket of buns and fresh butter. They didn't have to call any boys to the table, big or small. As soon as the array of aromas filled the air, Mark was on his feet. "That ham sure smells good!" he said as he and Prince led the hungry brigade to the dining room.

"Wow! This is quite a feast!" Walter said enthusiastically as they all found their seats.

"I had planned on having dessert, too," Laurie said apologetically, "but with everything that happened today, I just didn't have the time."

"No need to feel bad about that," said Grace as she cast a loving glance at her daughter. You've all had quite a day, and this is wonderful! And besides, dessert has already been taken care of." Walter smiled, as he knew what Grace meant. He had watched her prepare a pineapple upside-down cake early in the morning. The cake was to be a surprise and was still in the car.

Joe and John looked at their grandma curiously. "What did you bring, Grandma?" Joe asked enthusiastically.

The boys were used to being teased by their grandma, who just smiled at her grandsons. "Oh, you'll see soon enough," she said. "Right now it's time to pray and enjoy this beautiful food!" The boys weren't about to continue quizzing their grandma, and all heads bowed down as Michael began to pray. *"Lord, please bless this family, and especially Gretchen, who is here tonight with us in spirit. Please help her to heal. Lord. We're very fortunate to have your mighty gifts before us on this table, and we thank you for them. Amen."*

The prayer ended and the passing of the food commenced! There was soon a chorus of yums and smacking lips as everyone dove into their plateful of food. "This ham is wonderful, Laurie," said Walter as he looked lovingly at his daughter. "I sure like the way you prepare it."

Laurie smiled and said, "Thanks, Dad, but the honors go to Mom. I just do it the same way she does, just like everything else I make!" Everyone laughed and kept right on eating.

The trouble with fixing supper for a large family is that it feels like it takes hours to prepare and only minutes before it vanishes. "Where's the dessert you brought, Grandma?" asked Joe after he and his brother had cleared their plates.

"Hmmm…I don't know. I can't quite remember," kidded Grace. "Let me think…"

"Grandma!" said John. "You're teasing us! I bet it's in your car, right?"

"Well, now, I'll have to go out and take a look," she said.

"Can we go with you?" asked Joe.

"Sure," she said, "but first let's clear these dishes." Joe and John sprang into action. They knew whatever Grandma Grace had made for dessert, it was going to be good! As soon as the table was cleared, Grace headed for the front door. The boys were right on her heels, determined not to let her out of their sight. "It's pretty heavy," she said as they neared the car, "so I'll have to be the one to carry it inside." When she opened the trunk, Joe and John nudged in alongside her, and when they looked down they saw a magnificent pineapple upside-down cake!

"Wow!" they said in unison.

"Made it special just for you," said their grandma as she put an arm around each of them.

"Yum! Thank you, Grandma!" said John. "It sure looks good!"

"I can hardly wait!" Joe said. "It's one of my favorite desserts, Grandma! Thank you!"

As Grace picked up the cake from the trunk and walked towards the house with her grandsons leading the way, she couldn't help but think about how happy and appreciative her grandkids were for the little things in life like a surprise dessert, not that this dessert was so little!

"We need to save a piece for Gretchen, Joe," said John to his brother, thoughtful as they always were with their sister.

By the time the family was back at the dining room table and busy polishing off Grace's delicious cake, dusk had settled in and everyone was feeling the fatigue of a long day. "I think we'd best be heading home if we're going to get up early and get to the hospital," said Walter.

"I agree, Walter," Chuck said. "Marty and I will get our things and be right with you."

It had indeed been a wearing and emotional day, and it didn't take long for everyone to nod off that night, everyone except Laurie, that is. "Oh, Michael," she said with a big sigh as he was about to doze off, "I hope Gretchen's doing OK!"

"She's in the best of hands," he said drowsily. "Try to get some sleep. We'll be at the hospital early in the morning." Seconds later, he was breathing heavily and fast asleep. How do men do it? Laurie couldn't help but smile as she looked lovingly at her husband. Here she was, wide awake and unable to stop thinking about Gretchen, and there he was, sleeping soundly by her side. But, then, hers was pretty typical behavior for a mother, especially one who was a nurse, well aware of the potential dangers of a fall such as her daughter had taken.

Even though she'd slept fitfully, Laurie was the first one up in the morning, and by the time the others had gathered, she had breakfast on the table as was ready to eat and run. Everyone sensed and shared her eagerness to get going, and by 7:00 a.m. they were all out the door and on their way to the hospital.

When they entered Gretchen's room, they were in for a big surprise. She was sitting up in bed, eating breakfast. However, her face and head looked very funny. The doctors had sutured her chin, which was swollen and bandaged, as well as the wound at the back of her skull, with layers of gauze wound around her head like a turban. Her brothers laughed when they saw her. "You look like you're wearing a hat!" Joe blurted. Gretchen giggled and took another bite of toast, so everyone knew she was going to be all right.

"Oh, honey," Laurie said as she kissed her daughter on the forehead, "it's so good to see you sitting up and eating. How do you feel?"

"My head hurts a little in the back," she said as she looked up at her mom, "and my chin hurts a little, too. But it's not so bad. Plus, I have a lot of new nurse and doctor friends," she gushed. "I want to be a doctor someday, or maybe a nurse just like you!"

Laurie smiled, as did everyone when they heard Gretchen's words. "I'll say this about our little granddaughter," said Chuck, "she has spunk!"

Dr. Pederson entered the room quietly and observed the abundance of family love before greeting everyone warmly. "This little one has been an ideal patient," she said as she moved to Gretchen's bedside. "She's very brave and never complained while we were fixing her up, not even when we shaved her hair in the back! She'll be able to go home this morning after I complete the discharge papers, if that's OK with her. I don't know…you may want to stay for a few more days of fun with us, right Gretchen?" she said as she winked at her young patient.

Gretchen smiled shyly at Dr. Pederson, and everyone could see the two had bonded.

On the way home, the kids were pretty subdued, so it was easy to hear William Francis whisper, "I'm sorry for making you fall, Gretchen."

She looked at him with a wan smile and said softly, "It wasn't your fault, William Francis. It was that dumb sidewalk." The adults smiled when they heard her say that, because they knew she was on her way to a full recovery. However, when they got home, Gretchen seemed very happy to just curl up on the sofa and rest quietly. Prince sensed she had been hurt, and settled in by her side as she petted him tenderly.

This wasn't exactly the visit everyone had planned, but they were all feeling very grateful and determined to make the best of all that had transpired. "Tomorrow's Father's Day," Grace said enthusiastically, "and I want everyone to come to our house for supper!"

"Are you going to make a pineapple upside-down cake, Grandma?" Joe asked.

"Oh, no," she laughed. "I have something even more special in mind. You'll just have to wait to find out what it is." What she wasn't telling anyone is that she planned to make Gretchen's favorite dessert, angel food cake with pink frosting!

Sunday was a true day of rest. Everyone slept in, even Laurie, and by the time they'd eaten breakfast and gotten home from eleven o'clock Mass at Church of the Epiphany in Coon Rapids, there was still plenty of time for the adults to visit before heading to Grace and Walter's for supper.

The boys were soon outside, running and playing tag again, just like nothing had ever happened. However, Joe and John couldn't hold a candle to William Francis's speed. He may have been a slender little guy, but like Gretchen, he was fast! It didn't take the boys long to wear themselves out, and they were soon back in the house and ready to rest. Gretchen was feeling tired as well and headed to her room for a nap, so the adults had some quiet time to talk about what had been happening in their lives and their plans for the future. "Well," said Michael, "the kids just turned seven this summer, so we're going to be hanging around home for a few more years, at least until they're eighteen and headed off to college."

"I can't believe it," Laurie said. "We had such grandiose ideas when we left St. Ben's and St. John's, got married and started grad school. That just goes to show, the best laid plans don't always pan out."

"That's for sure!" said Linda laughing. "It seems we're all happy with our decisions, so kudos to us!"

"I know I am," said Mark as he leaned over and kissed his wife. "I never thought of myself as a teacher, but the job has been totally satisfying and rewarding. I don't know what life might have been like as an attorney. I'm guessing somewhat boring compared to what I'm doing now, so I'm just going to enjoy every day of being with my students for as long as I can."

"Me, too," Linda said. "We won't be getting rich anytime soon, but it really is enjoyable work. How about you and Michael?" she asked as she smiled at her sister.

"We're in way over our heads in keeping up with our lives!" Laurie laughed. "All you have to do is look around our house to see we're living in a zoo! Given how active the boys and Gretchen are, it's going to be a long time before I have a chance to practice my nursing."

"Outside of the home at least," laughed Michael. "We ought to buy stock in bandaids given our three little wild ones."

"That's for sure," said Laurie. "I definitely have my hands full with the kids, but I love being a mom and Michael is able to make a good living for us, so it's all working out."

"I can see how happy you are," said Linda. "How's your work going, Michael?" she asked.

"Well, my company's been having me spend more time in the lab," Michael said. "There are a lot of exciting studies being financed and new medicines being developed. In a way, I'm not disappointed that I wasn't able to become a doctor. I've always been intrigued by research that leads to new discoveries, and that's exactly what my company is allowing me to focus on."

Laurie, Linda, Michael and Mark chatted on, taking full advantage of the uninterrupted time while all the kids were resting. The four grandparents, meanwhile, were enjoying each other's company at Grace and Walter's, talking about the kids and grandkids and retirement!

"I plan to put in a few more years and then call it quits," Chuck said. "I love teaching English, but with all the papers to read, I think I spend as many hours working on class-related things at home as I do at school. I'll stick it out for another six years and then start enjoying retirement."

"That'd be 1988, Chuck," Grace said. "Is there a particular reason you picked that year?"

"Not really," he said, "other than that I will have turned 60 and am getting tired of correcting all the writing assignments. Don't get me wrong, I love communicating with my students by reading what's in their heads and hearts and giving my feedback, but I'm not going to miss hauling home a stack of papers every week."

"How do you feel about Chuck retiring, Marty?" Walter asked.

"I'm fine with it," she said. "I'll be especially fine with it when I can come home from work and dinner's waiting!"

"Did you hear that, Chuck?" said Walter, grinning broadly as Chuck smiled.

"It's hard to believe I've been working just about as long as Chuck," said Marty. "No papers to correct, but being a physical therapist takes its toll. I'm sure I'll be ready to retire along with Chuck when the time comes."

"How about you, Walter?" asked Chuck.

"To tell you the truth, I haven't given it much thought," he said, "even though I know it's time to start doing so. We aren't getting any younger, and it would be nice to do some traveling and other things Grace and I have talked about."

"I think you've been consumed by your building work the same way Chuck has been by his dedication to his students and Marty to her patients," said Grace. "It's been a lot of years of your lives, and you'll no doubt miss it very much."

"I know you're right, Grace," Marty said.

"Unfortunately, I think we've all been living too much for our work," Chuck said.

"I don't know about that," Walter said. "I love my work. I don't see anything wrong with that. You have to have money to buy a home and eat and take care of your children, and the only way to make money is to work."

"True enough," said Chuck, "but there are things in life that are just as important as work, especially when you're raising a family. Linda and Mark were reminded of that when William Francis brought home a story he'd written about the most important people in his life. He said his dad was blind and didn't have much time to spend with him because he was always correcting papers. He said his mom worked, too, and that she was a great cook, but what he liked most was when she took the time to sit with him and talk. That was what he most treasured, being able to share time with his mom and dad."

"I'll bet that was an eye opener for Linda and Mark," Grace said.

"More than you can imagine," Marty said. "Linda was glad to hear William Francis liked her cooking, but she most valued his expressing how much he liked talking with her. Now Mark and Linda are making a concerted effort to spend more time with William Francis."

"That's very interesting," Grace said. "It seems Michael has been heavily involved in his work, too, and Laurie, of course, has been one busy woman from the day the triplets were born. I've never heard her say anything about them wanting to spend more time with her. I know the boys are typically outside and Gretchen's most often found with a book in her hands when she's not out playing with one of her little friends. Oh, speaking of Gretchen, there's an angel food cake in the kitchen waiting for some pink frosting. I thought I'd surprise her since it's her favorite dessert."

"That's so thoughtful of you. I'll come and help," Marty said cheerfully.

"Thanks, Marty!" said Grace as they headed out of the room. "How about you start in on the frosting while I work on supper?"

"I'm happy to do that," said Marty.

Time flies when families, young or old, are having fun, especially families that love one another. Grace and Marty could be heard chatting and laughing as they worked together in the kitchen, Walter and Chuck contentedly engaged in conversation in the living room. The minutes rolled by, and when the front doorbell rang, they all knew their peaceful afternoon was over!

"Happy Father's Day, Dad!" Laurie and Linda chorused when Walter opened the door and greeted the gang.

"Thank you, girls! Thank you very much!" he said happily. "And Happy Father's Day to you boys as well!" he said as he embraced Mark and Michael. "Come in, everyone, come in! You're just in time for dinner!"

It didn't take long before they were all seated at the large dining room table. "Everything sure looks scrumptious, Grace!" said Michael enthusiastically.

"Well, I couldn't have done it without Marty's help," Grace said as the two exchanged smiles. "I hope everyone likes it! Roast beef has always been one of Walter's favorite Sunday meals, as we all know, and I thought I'd better please him with it today since it's Father's Day!"

"And I sure do appreciate it!" said Walter enthusiastically as he looked lovingly at his wife. "Let's pray so we can get down to eating!

Father in heaven, thank you for this beautiful meal we're about to enjoy and for the two beautiful women who prepared it for us. Amen."

"Wow! That was pretty short for you, Dad!" Laurie said, laughing. "You must be hungry!"

"I am! I am!" he said as he forked up several slices of tender beef from the serving platter. "But let's eat now, talk later, like our little patient." Gretchen squirmed in her chair and looked down. Unlike her brothers, she was shy and never one to seek the limelight.

"Dr. Pederson said Gretchen was a perfect patient," Laurie said, "and Gretchen told me when she grows up she wants to be a doctor just like Dr. Pederson, isn't that right, honey?"

When Laurie said that, everyone looked at Gretchen, and Gretchen, blushing, looked around the table until her eyes met her mother's. "I love Dr. Pederson," she said softly.

No one said anything as they let those words sink in, and then Laurie said, "I love her, too, honey. Dr. Pederson is a very good doctor and she was very kind to you."

"You were an excellent patient and you will no doubt be an excellent doctor!" said Walter as he beamed at his granddaughter.

After everyone had had their fill of roast beef, green beans, carrots, cranberries, mashed potatoes and hot rolls with butter, the women cleared the table. "Anybody ready for dessert?" called Grace from the kitchen.

"We all are, Grandma!" Joe yelled.

As Grace stood in the kitchen doorway, John asked, "Did you make a pineapple upside-down cake, Grandma?"

Grace smiled at her grandson. "Not this time," she said, "but I don't think you'll be disappointed." This made all the kids curious, and when she backed into the kitchen and came out carrying a large angel food cake with pink frosting, they knew immediately for whom it was honoring.

"Wow!" said the kids in unison.

Gretchen's eyes widened with delight as Grace set the cake in front of her. "Your grandpa can help with the slicing," she said as she handed Walter a knife.

"Well, I think I know someone who's going to enjoy this!" said Walter as he winked at his granddaughter, "unless I eat it all myself!" Gretchen didn't say a word, just smiled as she looked up at her grandpa. "Here you go," said Walter as he placed a generous piece on her plate. "Let's see if you can finish that!"

Gretchen didn't disappoint! She kept right up with the adults and downed every crumb. "Thank you, Grandma. That was so good," she said in a quiet voice as she put down her fork.

After dessert, everyone moved to the living room for some relaxed conversation. They talked about what a wonderful visit it had been in spite of Gretchen's mishap. "Marty and I decided we'll head back to Perham tomorrow after breakfast," Chuck said. "We really want to thank you for the three days we've been able to spend here at your home."

"We sure do," said Marty. "It's been so enjoyable and we truly appreciate it."

It didn't take long the next morning for the Dowdles to regroup at Laurie and Michael's house. Grace, Walter, Marty and Chuck were up and dressed by six, done with breakfast by seven, and at Laurie and Michael's house by eight. Everyone was saying their goodbyes when they noticed Gretchen and William Francis talking quietly near the front door. "I'm sure glad you're feeling better, Gretchen," William Francis said as his eyes welled up with tears.

"Oh, it was nothing," she said, "just a little scratch on my chin and a bump on my head." It was pretty obvious that William Francis was a sensitive little boy and Gretchen was a courageous little girl; it was also obvious that the two cousins liked one another.

Tuesday morning after breakfast, before Marty left for work, Chuck took out some of his favorite student compositions. He'd made copies of them, as he did every year, and he had long thought about someday publishing a "writing" book of his students' best work. The more he'd considered it, the more he liked the idea, and so he dug out the boxes of compositions he'd saved from past years and began organizing them. When Marty saw what he was doing, she knew he was still in school, and she began pondering how she was going to spend her summer.

Mark had his summer project brought home to him in stark fashion during breakfast. He and his son were just finishing their usual bowl of oatmeal when William Francis got up, moved to his dad's side, slid his hand into Mark's and said, "Dad, I want to be a teacher."

Mark was very touched to hear his young son say that, but he didn't know quite how to respond. "Well, where did that come from?" he said.

"Gretchen said she wants to be a doctor," he said, "and I want to be a teacher, just like you."

Mark sat quietly for a moment. He thought about what William Francis had written about him at school, about how he never seemed to have time to talk with him because he was always busy correcting papers. "Well, William Francis," Mark said as he smiled at his son, "I know you would be a wonderful teacher."

"Thanks, Dad," he said. "I want to teach Braille just like you. Can you teach me Braille this summer?"

This kid was serious, but then so was Gretchen about becoming a doctor, and there was no way Mark was going to pass up this golden opportunity to connect with his son. "I'd be happy to do that," he said, "and we can start right now." Mark couldn't see his son's face, radiant with joy and filled with anticipation.

The rest of the week flew by for Chuck and Mark, busy as they both were. It was as if school was still in session, but how would their wives choose to occupy their time? It didn't take long for Marty and Linda to put a plan into action. They went shopping in Detroit Lakes that Saturday, and by the time they got home they had their summer plans all figured out. "This is great!" Linda said gleefully as she and Marty meandered from store to store, enjoying one another's company and checking out the latest summer fashions. "Mark told me to have a good time, and I am!" she gushed.

"Me, too!" Marty said. "I could get used to this! It's so nice to get away from the hospital and cooking every once in a while. Speaking of which, I forgot to mention that you and Mark are invited for supper tonight, said he'd have everything ready when we get home!"

The plotting and planning that took place during lunch between Marty and Linda was going to make Chuck and Mark think twice about having been so encouraging with their wives' shopping expedition. The gals decided they liked shopping with each other so much they were going to do it every Saturday during the summer, checking out all the surrounding towns. After Detroit Lakes they'd be going to Park Rapids, then Wadena, Fergus Falls, Fargo-Moorhead…then start over, repeating the circuit until the end of summer.

Besides shopping each Saturday, they also decided it would be fun to have suppers together all summer, switching off cooking. One would cook Mondays, Wednesdays and Fridays, the other Tuesdays, Thursdays and Sundays, and they'd switch days every other week. Saturdays they'd dine out. "Our husbands can be married to their work," laughed Marty, "but that doesn't mean we have to!"

"Amen to that!" said Linda gleefully. "While Mark and Chuck are working on Braille and book publishing, we can be lighting up our kitchens with creative cuisine! Of course, our hardworking husbands will love that!"

At supper that evening, Chuck and Mark sensed there was something different about their wives, something they couldn't quite put their fingers on, but definitely something different. It was as if they were bursting to tell about their time in Detroit Lakes. "Okay," Chuck said as they began eating, "You two must have had quite a good shopping day. I've never seen you so giddy. Tell us about it."

"We had more than a good day," laughed Linda. "we had a wonderful day!"

"We're all ears," said Mark, smiling.

"Well," said Linda, coyly, "Marty and I started brainstorming during lunch, and we've figured out the entire summer for all of us!" This had the men intrigued, so Linda explained the weekly-shopping and shared-suppers plan, Marty enthusiastically interjecting here and there.

The men got a big kick out of their wives' exuberance. "But you left out Saturdays," Mark laughed.

"Saturdays you two get to take us out to supper or have it ready when we return from a hard day of shopping!" said Linda gleefully. "Your choice!"

Chuck couldn't quite believe his ears, but he was all for it. "It will be fun for you gals," he said. "I'll even clean the house and help Mark do the same while you gals are gallivanting around. Maybe we can all go fishing on Fridays and see if we can catch our Saturday supper."

"Oh, can we, Grandpa?" William Francis asked excitedly.

"Depends on your mom and grandma," Chuck said teasingly. "Seems they have things pretty well planned for the summer."

Marty and Linda smiled and nodded in agreement with one another, and just like that, it was a sealed deal.

Chuck started his book project by first reading the compositions he'd saved from his just-finished school year. The more he read, the more enthusiastic he became. He began with two short letters written by an 8th grader and a 7th grader. The assignment was to write a letter to an elected official. The two Chuck selected had both written letters to the President of the United States. The first read as follows:

May 12, 1981

Ronald Reagan
President of the United States
The White House
Washington, D.C.

Dear President Reagan,

There is a big problem that is bothering me. I'm sure it bothers everyone else, also. It is inflation. Inflation is extremely and ridiculously high. Gas prices are pathetic! By the time I get my license to drive, I won't be able to afford gas, let alone a car! I know you hear complaints about that from everyone, but I think it's time you did something about it. Please do your best!

Sincerely,
Kelly Boyce, 8th Grade
Perham, Minnesota

The second letter Chuck selected read as follows:

April 19, 1981

Ronald Reagan
President of the United States
The White House
Washington, D.C.

Dear President Reagan,

I'm writing this letter to you to show my concern about our economic policies and the budget cuts you are making in many of the social programs made to support many of the people of this nation. I certainly support some of your cuts, but taking the money and putting it into military expenditures is a different matter. What you are doing, in fact, is taking money collected to support the nation and spending it on what inevitably will be used to destroy it. I do understand that the strengthening of the military is important to our national security, but I do not believe that we should go to such an extent as to start an arms race. We already have enough nuclear warheads to destroy every Russian city 300 times. Isn't that enough?

Sincerely yours,
David Jager, 7th Grade
Perham, Minnesota

After the letters, Chuck moved on to the logs. He couldn't help but to again include student David Jager in his book-project plan. David could really write, and he had a sense of humor. The assignment was to keep a record of what happened during a 24- hour period. David decided to make an entry every half hour, and it turned out to be fascinating stuff, very insightful concerning what was happening in his life on an almost-daily basis:

10:30 a.m.—It is amazing how many different things can happen in a half hour. In that period of time, Mr. Dowdle gave us four assignments. He keeps us working hard, but I enjoy most of it. I enjoy his policies, especially. He gave an assignment to people who were throwing plums in the library during his absence, telling them to write a 1000-word description of a plum. One student looked like he had swallowed a lemon whole. The punishment seemed to be getting to the "Plum Throwers," for, after all, it takes a lot of creativity to draw out 1,000 words from a round, smooth, red ball, and some students aren't very well equipped for that kind of writing. So far, I have been keeping records of everything I have been doing in the past half hour, and I'm spending my time writing a letter to Christina Arbunic.

11:00 a.m.—For the past hour I've been writing the letter. I'm not sure if I've been telling too much to a stranger, but it's about time that everybody in my class should get to know each other better. I told her about the big events coming up this month.

Chuck Dowdle

11:30 a.m.—Ms. Peppit is continuing to talk about Scandinavia. The information is very interesting. It seems like I was born to put pencil to paper and write, write, write. That's exactly what I've been doing, paying a small amount of attention to my lecture and dutifully scribbling notes on the side. It's pleasurable, but I'm looking forward to when she shows us the film.

12:00 noon—The film proved to be very interesting. To my surprise, it fit exactly what I thought about the country, a free, clean, medically- and industrially-efficient society where everybody stays nice and warm and well protected in the government's lap. But the film saw quickly through that form of government; boredom prevails. Drinking and alcoholism are very frequent. Juvenile delinquents and crime and violence are rather frequent. The picture looks tempting, but I'm glad I'm right here in the U.S.A.

I'm in the middle of an empty lunch conversation that has to be kept going by small pushes of vulgarity and some disgusting jokes. They're fine when you hear them, but after you think about them seriously, you find your stomach out of line. It seems that all these people (including me sometimes) are all sex, sports and music oriented. It seems that all conversations and jokes point toward those three things. "Wanna go listen to some music? Did you hear the one about the fifteen-cent screw? Did you see that hit John made last night playing the Cardinals? Man! That thing went sailing!" Those are the things I usually hear. Nevertheless, it's just plain comforting to stay around in a group and listen to each other, even though it may be as indecent as anything!

12:30 p.m.—I've been spending my time reading an article on U.F.O.'s in Read Magazine. It's pretty fun and amusing.

1:00 p.m.—Ms. Branvold is showing us how to do mapping. The method is pretty boring, but it seems fun to draw out and complete.

1:30 p.m.—It's about time to leave for math, and I'm anticipating my test grades. I expect to get at least a 'C' or 'B' on one of them. For the rest of the time, I'm talking to my friends.

2:00 p.m.—I've been in math for about half an hour. I'm absolutely shocked! I got an 'F' on my area and circumference test and a 'C-' on my make-up test for area and perimeter. For the rest of the time, I'm listening to the lecture.

2:30 p.m.—The lecture is finished and we have to complete a sheet on finding the area of rectangular solids. When I think of it, I really am *interested in geometry and mathematics, but all that has been marred with my past experience with math.*

3:00 p.m.—I've been waiting for the bus to come and watching all the activity going on between students. They seem to be happy just sitting around and talking to each other.

3:30 p.m.—I'm eating my snack at a table right now. I spent most of my time looking out the window on the bus while the others screamed and yelled in the back. I knew I didn't want to join them, but if I didn't laugh or look at some of the things they did, I'd find myself square and repressive.

4:00 p.m.—I'm having a fascinating time reading "Flowers for Algernon," the story of a retarded man experiencing extreme intellectual growth and suddenly finding himself on the other side of the intellectual fence. It also explores the conflict between his old self and his new super-intellectual self.

4:30 p.m.—I've been working on my math, and then taped a funny interview with my sister. She played a super-eccentric pianist while I was a conventional interviewer. It was hilarious and we couldn't stop laughing when she went into her hysterical fits.

5:00 p.m.—I've started my piano practice after spending half an hour working on this assignment. It's really interesting to work on when you think about it.

5:30 p.m.—I was very concentrated during my practice today, so I decided to make an account of the last hour instead of half an hour. What a miracle it is to let one's self get absorbed in a concentrated hour of work! Everything surrounding you seems to fade, leaving only you and the music. Time flies during such moments. What I find most surprising is the way an hour passes in what you thought was fifteen minutes. I also think it's amazing that the number of objects around you is suddenly forgotten. When I come to the end of a practice, I suddenly become aware again of my surroundings. "There's the window and there's the couch!" I find myself saying when I look around and become familiar once again with the daily world.

6:30 p.m.—We had a fascinating conversation about art and photography. My sister's argument was that even though photography showed you exactly what was there, painting was more accurate because it gave you the feel and sensual imagery of the place. We found that in both painting and writing, you could smell, see and even feel the place the artist or author was portraying.

7:00 p.m.—*I've been helping Sheila do the dishes and clean. Since Mother has been gone, Pa expects a lot more of us in terms of work. We are often arguing about something, but most of the time we get along.*

7:30 p.m.—*I've started reading* The Two Towers *by Tolkien after breathlessly finishing* The Fellowship of the Ring. *There is something magical about Tolkien's writing that won't let you put the book down. The air seems to change when you read his descriptions. When he describes the dark forests of Mirkwood, everything turns gray, and when he describes the bright lands of Lothlorien, the entire world grows golden, sweet and singing. You always feel like one of the group when you read a Tolkien adventure.*

8:00 p.m.—*I'm still absorbed in my reading. At this point, Frodo and companions, including Gandalf the Wizard, are traveling through the halls of Moria.*

9:00 p.m.—*The reading was too engrossing to interrupt. Frodo has left the halls of Maris after a battle with an army of Orcs. While crossing a narrow stone bridge to escape from them, a balrog comes from the water and seizes Gandalf, dragging him to his fate.*

6:30 a.m.—*Good morning! I had a good sleep, even though I felt like a log when I got up. I'm late for breakfast as usual, and I have to start my morning mad rush to get ready before Tenna comes to pick us up.*

7:00 a.m.—*Tenna came, and we're waiting at the bus stop. I usually have enough time to make finishing touches on my homework while I wait for the bus.*

7:30 a.m.—*The bus has come, and I'm on my way to school. I usually keep quiet on the way.*

8:00 a.m.—*I'm in class right now after finishing some school business. Now it's time for the Pledge of Allegiance and the morning bulletin.*

8:30 a.m.—*Paul Huberty and I have just completed a small telephone exercise assignment. It's amusing to perform on stage in front of the class, and I find it more enjoyable every time I do it.*

9:00 a.m.—*Right now I have come to gym. We watched the other exercises 'til the end of the period in Drama. A lot of them were hilarious.*

10:00 a.m.—*I decided not to bring my notebook outside, being involved in a fast-moving game of speed-a-way. It's great fun to run around the field. It gives one a sense of control. I'm still having problems with other students, especially during roll call. A lot of the students can't miss a chance of giving me a good punch before the P.E. teacher arrives to take roll. A lot of it has gone too far, so far that the teacher gave me her personal permission to rearrange the face of my chief tormentor. I can't wait 'til Monday when I can improve his looks.*

10:30 a.m.—Here I am again, back where I started. I spent the break discussing a new band we're forming. I think with enough musical people in our group, the whole project could turn out to be an exciting and enjoyable experience. For the last half hour, I've been working on other assignments, and now I've completed this one. That's all for "A Day in the Life of David Jager."

—David Jager, 7th Grade, 1981

The next two papers Chuck read were autobiographical sketches. Students thought of an event which influenced their lives, and if they finished early, they could make up a "fictional" person and write about that person's life for extra credit:

Birth Order

I think the most important event in my life was being born the last child. I think that if I had been born the first child in my family, I would have had many more responsibilities dumped in my lap. I think a lot more things would have been expected of me. Also, I would have had two younger bratty brothers. If I had been a middle child, I would not have had as many responsibilities as my older brother. I would look up to him and try to be "big" and do what he did. I would look down upon my younger brother, sometimes, and be bossy other times. I would help him and show him how to do things.

I am sometimes glad that I am the youngest, and sometimes not. Things are expected of me, but not as much as my two older brothers. The times when I wish I was the oldest are when both my brothers are bossing me around. I wish I could boss them *around and yell at* them *without them hitting* me *back!*

Sometimes I wish I was the middle child so I could be friendly with and talk to an older brother, and yet still have a younger brother who looked up to me. But I happen to be stuck with being the third and last child, and there's nothing I can do about it.

—Suzanne Dieter, 7th Grade, 1981

The New Corpus Eaton 412

The year is 3008, and finally man has found a way to immortality! It was simple: no drugs, no miracle pills nor chemical aids of any kind. It works out like a car. When the engine runs down, a person buys a new one and is fine. Now humans can live as long as they want by buying new bodies.

My name is Eaton 412 and I am a prime corpus, fresh from the factory. I am complete with precision-working brain and nervous system, all of my organs have received the Good Housekeeping Seal of Approval. My skin is guaranteed to last and retain color for a lifetime or your money back. My facial details are also sculpted in the latest fashionable looks for men. Blood surrogates are made 100% germ resistant with cell nutrients included for good health. Sex hormone levels are high and reproductive-system organs are working at the peak of efficiency. Spermatozoa (if desired) are fashioned to give your children your desired genetic traits, including emotional characteristics. The digestive system is complete and the stomach is double lined to prevent ulcers. The intestines are compactly designed to absorb ten times more food nutrients per square inch than normal human capacity. The skeletal system is designed to resist pressures up to 100 pounds per square inch and is made of an ultra-pure, silicate organic mixture for an extremely-light and fracture-resistant skeletal structure.

Muscles are made to perform super-athletic feats and resist stress, preventing arthritic conditions. My brain is designed and compacted to retain huge amounts of information, and knowledge of complete fields can be programmed into me with computers. The purchaser's entire knowledge—emotional, factual and autonomic—will be emptied from him and can be programmed into the likes of me by computer.

I can be obtained with a down payment of only $13,000 with 20% interest added to the balance, paid in monthly installments. Find me at fine body shops.

—David Jager, 7th Grade, 1981

Chuck kept reading through memoirs, biographical sketches and short stories, and by Friday he'd read through all the student works he'd saved from 1961 to 1981. The next step was to organize the papers according to the category of writing and year written. Then came the difficult part, deciding which ones to include in his book.

"That's your project, honey," Marty said when he asked her about it. "I'm busy enough working at the hospital and planning menus! By the way, I'll be cooking next Monday, Wednesday and Friday. Try to arrange your week so we can all go out to Big Pine Lake on Friday and hopefully catch a couple of walleyes for supper. And remember, Linda and I are going shopping tomorrow, so we'll expect you and Mark to have supper on the table and our houses spic and span when we get home," she added with a teasing smile.

Chuck just moaned, then laughed and said, "You girls are really serious, aren't you?"

"You bet," she said, "and you haven't heard the half of it yet! Linda and I also decided it would be a good idea for her and me and William Francis to go to daily Mass this summer. We'll never get a chance to do that once school starts."

"Sounds good to me," Chuck said.

"Linda said Mark's all for it as well. He thinks it would be a great way for William Francis to start the day, and it would give them both time to relax before their daily braille studies. I guess our little grandson is quite serious about learning."

Linda arrived shortly after breakfast to pick up Marty for their shopping adventure. They were going to Park Rapids, which was only a short distance from Perham, but by the excited looks on their faces when they headed out the door, you'd think they were going to Minneapolis!

They immediately began chatting about their newfound freedom and fun day ahead. "What did Chuck think about our summer plans, Marty?" Linda asked as they were driving to Park Rapids.

"He was all for it," she said, "and he liked the idea of us going to daily Mass. I know he'll appreciate having the uninterrupted time to work on his book project."

"It sounds like it's all going to work out," said Linda. "I'm sure happy about it!"

"Me, too!" said Marty enthusiastically. "By the way, how's William Francis coming along with the braille lessons? It's such a wonderful thing that Mark's doing with him."

"He's doing great," Linda said. "That little guy is really eager to learn. He and Mark have been going over to the high school track in the mornings just to break up their day, and of one thing I can assure you."

"What's that?" Marty asked.

"William Francis has bonded with his dad like never before. It's pretty special to watch them work together and then walk out the door hand-in-hand when they go to the track, Prince right with them. He isn't getting any younger, but there's no way he wants to be left behind."

Mark realized how much he'd been missing out on with his son shortly after he began spending more time with him that summer. "Gee, Dad," William Francis said one day as they trotted around the track together, "I sure do like being with you and Prince."

"And I sure like being with you!" Mark said as William Francis began picking up the pace. "We'd best slow down so Prince can keep up."

"How old is he now, Dad?" William Francis asked.

"Well," he said, "I got Prince in 1973 when he was two, and now it's 1981, so that makes him ten years old."

"Prince is older than me!" said William Francis.

"He sure is," said Mark, "and the way they figure it in human years, he's somewhere around 60 years old."

"Wow!" exclaimed William Francis. "Prince is even older than you, Dad!"

"That's right," Mark said. "He's even older than Grandpa!"

When they got home, Prince headed straight for his water bowl. He was one thirsty dog after running around the track.

It seemed like this was going to be an ideal summer for the Dowdles. The ladies loved their newfound freedom and Saturday shopping, Mark and William Francis continued to enjoy their braille lessons and time jogging together, and Chuck was heavily and happily involved with his book of student writings. However, on Saturdays the men's routine was dramatically altered. When the gals arrived home exhausted and ravenous after their day of fun, they had no idea what to expect. When they sat down to a delicious meal such as beef roast and fresh vegetables with chocolate cake and ice cream for dessert, in houses that were spic and span, they were in awe! If facial expressions could have spoken, theirs would have been shouting for joy! The ladies went shopping in

Wadena, Fergus Falls and Fargo-Moorhead the next three Saturdays, then repeated the Saturday shopping circuit through the end of summer with the same five cities.

--------············•·•·•··············--------

CHUCK WAS READY TO START SCHOOL. HE'D COMPLETED HIS BOOK, an accomplishment of which to be proud! He had fifty copies printed to use in his English classes for the 1982-83 school year and shared the book with Mark for his classes as well.

Clever Mark wasted no time in creating a braille copy. "Can I try reading that, Dad?" asked William Francis when his father showed him the finished book.

"Sure," said Mark. "Let's see if you can." He nearly burst with pride when his son did just that, methodically figuring out each word as he moved down the page. That boy was bright and motivated! He was determined to become a teacher like his dad, and it showed.

Linda was so pleased with how Marty and she had spent the summer, she wrote her sister before school began and told her all about it.

September 1, 1982

Dear Laurie,

The last weekend of vacation is rapidly approaching! We head back to school on September 7th, the day after Labor Day, and I just had to write and tell you what we've been up to this summer, also to find out how Gretchen's been doing since her accident.

You're not going to believe this. After we got home from visiting you, the following Saturday Marty and I drove to Detroit Lakes and went shopping and out to lunch. That's when it all happened! We decided to plan out our whole summer with a different shopping and lunch expedition every Saturday! It will go something like this: 1) We all get up early and go to Mass each morning after breakfast; 2) After Mass, the men work on their projects while Marty and I plan our meals for the week; 3) Marty and Chuck have us to their house for supper three days a week and we have them to ours three days a week; 4) On Saturdays, Marty and I go shopping while the men are on house clean-up duty. Not only that, they also prepare supper, have it waiting for us when we return! 5) On Fridays, we all go to Big Pine Lake and try to catch some walleyes for whomever happens to be cooking that night. Needless to say, Mark and Chuck were pretty surprised when we told them about the summer plans, but they bought into it, good natured as they are, and Marty and I have been having the time of our lives!

Mark's teaching William Francis how to read and write in braille, and he's taken to it like a duck to water. Before the two of them get started on a lesson each morning after Mass, they go to the high school and jog around the track with Prince while it's still cool outside. By the time they get home, Prince is tired out and content to spend the rest of the day taking it easy.

Chuck worked all summer on a wonderful book he created for English teachers. It has thirty or so creative-writing assignments, each illustrated with student writings he's saved over the last twenty years! He had a local print shop run off fifty copies for Mark and him to use in their English classes. He's pretty proud of it, as well he should be! Mark and he are ready to get back to school and get started, but I'm sure not. Marty and I have been having too much fun!

Well, sister, that's what's been happening with us. When you have time, I'll be eager to find out how the summer's been going with you and Michael and to get an update on Gretchen and the boys. We sure do miss you all!

—Love, Linda

School started and time once again began passing rapidly. Linda hadn't yet heard back from Laurie, and was relieved when she finally did.

October 24, 1982

Dear Linda,

You may be thinking I'm quite the slacker for not answering your letter sooner, but things have gotten pretty hectic around here now that school's started and I'm working part time at the hospital. I know that's going to surprise you, but Michael and I talked it over and decided it would be good for me to get out of the house and begin practicing my nursing skills again now that the kids are in school. So far, it's been a blessing! Michael pitches in as soon as he gets home from work, so that's made it doable.

We're getting ready for Back-To-School-Night this Friday and Halloween next Sunday. I'm sure the classrooms will be decorated with Halloween stuff and all the kids' work. I hope they have some of their writing. That's what Gretchen likes to do, write! Not so much Joseph and John. They're outside boys through and through. They have a whole lot of energy, and it's a challenge for them to sit still. Not so Gretchen, though she sure loves running, just like William Francis. If you saw her now, you'd never guess she'd had that bad fall. By the way, she has her heart set on becoming a doctor and reminds us of it often. It sure will be interesting to see what all the kids end up doing!

Michael has been busy with his work. He recently got another advancement with extra pay because he's doing more research in the lab. It seems the pre-med studies he did at St. John's gave him an excellent foundation for what he's doing now.

I was flabbergasted when you told me about your summer, how you and Marty had planned it all out, including your shopping Saturdays. Your husbands are gems! And good for you and Marty! If I tried that here with Mom, something tells me it wouldn't go over so well with Walter and Michael. Of course, we're talking taking care of three little ones instead of just one, but still, it's a tempting proposition!

We sure do miss all of you. I can't wait to see you again.

—Love, Laurie

LIFE WAS QUITE DIFFERENT FOR THE TWO YOUNG FAMILIES, ONE raising three children and the other just one, one with a nurse and medical researcher parenting and the other with two teachers. Another notable difference was William Francis growing up with a father who was blind and the close companionship of a dog. That was just the way life was and has always been with families. They all travel different roads, some more complicated, some less so.

William Francis kept loving school and advancing his braille skills, but it seemed he was yearning for even more of a challenge. That wasn't the case for Marty and Linda. They were just enjoying life as it was and already looking forward to summer so they could get back to their shopping routine. Neither realized it would come to such a rapid halt when Chuck retired.

"One more year," Chuck said when he wound up the 1986-87 school year, "and that's going to be it." It wasn't that he was tired of teaching, he still loved it, and loved his students. It was all the hours he spent in the evenings and on weekends doing school-related work. He just wanted to be free! His writing book had been very successful with both his and Mark's classes. The students enjoyed reading what other students had written before they themselves tackled the same assignments, and Chuck enjoyed reading what his students had written, but there was still the time-consuming chore of reading and responding to a couple hundred compositions every weekend.

"Why don't you try something different with one of your classes before you retire, Chuck?" one of the school counselors suggested on a cold February day.

"What do you have in mind, Jerry?" Chuck asked his longtime school friend.

"Well, I was thinking about you taking one of your writing classes over to the *Friends House*. Have the students pair off with a resident and do an interview."

"Hmmm, that would definitely be interesting," he said, and on Monday morning, April 13th, 1987, Chuck headed off with twenty-seven 8th and 9th grade students on a field trip to *Friends House*. It turned out to be quite an experience, which Chuck later discovered was being covered by the local newspaper thanks to his counselor friend, Jerry Hardy.

When the kids arrived at *Friends House*, they paired off with a resident to conduct their interview. The next day in class they sat down to write biographical sketches of the *Friends House* residents they had interviewed. A good example appears as follows:

"Anna Frey"
By Sheba Fulton

Anna Frey has done much for herself and her community during the last eighty years of her life. She has lived to tell of World War I and World War II, the Great Depression and many other major events in world history that affected her life.

Anna was born in Vienna, Austria, in 1907. Her family was very well-to-do and she lived a happy and comfortable childhood. Unlike the average child today, Anna was nursed and taken care of by her nanny and governess for many years in her early life. She was always very close with her family and relatives, which was common with families such as hers. One person who was very influential in Anna's childhood was her aunt, with whom she often traveled.

Anna attended a private girls' school in the suburbs of Vienna during most of her high school years. Afterwards, she attended a business school and then a millinery school to learn a trade so as to make money if she had to, although ladies such as Anna were never usually expected to work, but instead were supposed to get married and have children.

Education was always important to Anna, and it later came in handy when she had to support her husband and herself as newcomers who came to America with little money. In school, one of Anna's best friends was her cousin, so she did not spend as much time socializing and spending time with other girls. Anna always liked school, and she was especially good at math, but in some ways it was hard for her because she had somewhat of a minor case of dyslexia.

Dating in Anna's teenage years was a serious matter that was never usually pursued until a girl reached sixteen or seventeen. Anna really worries about teenagers today because there are so many temptations such as sex, drugs, alcohol, etc. In her day, teenagers were happier and not so pressured, although parents were strict about what their children did and where they went.

Anna Fry's life was greatly affected throughout World War I and the Great Depression. She was always aware of some outside world event going on, partly because her family suffered financially at times. Many people went hungry then, but her family tried their best to help those who were not as fortunate as they were.

In 1938, when Hitler became a threat to Austria, many thought the whole affair would blow over, but Anna and Hans, her husband of four years, knew trouble was coming and fled to England and then to America, where they would spend the rest of their lives. To this day, Anna can still remember hearing the sound of the Nazis marching on the streets of Vienna. Her brother had also fled, to Australia, and her sister to India, but her parents were not so fortunate. They were taken to a concentration camp where they barely survived on potato peelings for two years. They never really recovered from their lack of nutrition for such a long period of time. Anna's parents never wanted to talk about their experience in the camp when they finally reached America.

When Anna was 31 and Hans, a Doctor of Law, was 42, they reached America with less than ten dollars between them and no work. It was during the Depression, and the unemployment rate was high. But Anna kept her spirits up and began making hats to support her husband and herself until he found a job. Anna knew that the one thing no one could ever take from her was her education. She and Hans lived in Chicago and remained there for the next forty-five years.

Anna became interested in Social Work because of her love for people, and she began to get involved in the community. Her job as a Social Worker included involvement in a Housing Committee, Neighborhood Watch and other community groups.

When Anna became 77 years old and her husband turned 88, they agreed that moving to a warmer sheltered environment where they could be helped out would be better for both of them. So, in that year, 1984, they moved to the Friend's House retirement home. So far, they've been at the Friend's House for three years and they love it! They have a lot of neighbors and friends with whom to talk and go places, and Anna is still involved in community work and enjoys it very much.

Anna is a very courageous woman. She came to America with nothing but hope and faith that she would find a better and happier life for Hans and herself. And she did! Anna has spent 45 years of her life helping others make better lives for themselves, just because she likes people and cares. Indeed, Anna Frey is a very special woman!

Chuck was very surprised the next day when a picture of Anna Frey with the two students who interviewed her, Sheba Fulton and Andrea Lambert, appeared in the local newspaper with a short article. The article caught the attention of the principal as well, and he asked Chuck to write up the assignment for the school paper so all the teachers, parents and students could share the experience.

"Friends Meet Friends"
By Chuck Dowdle

On Monday, April 3rd, twenty-seven 8th and 9th grade students and I took a walking field trip to Friends House to conduct interviews with nineteen of the adult residents. Jerry Hardy, one of our school counselors, suggested the possibility to me back in February, but March was flu-bug month for many of us, and we weren't able to act on the idea until just recently. It was an exciting experience for the kids and notable for the residents as well.

Friends House is a Quaker-sponsored adult community for singles and married couples. We made contact with them for a number of reasons:

1. *We wanted to develop a good-neighbor relationship between them and our school.*
2. *We wanted to give the kids a rich cross age, cross-cultural experience with older adults who have had a variety of educational, job, travel and life experiences.*
3. *We wanted to give the kids practice with interviewing people, taking notes and writing first-hand biographical sketches.*
4. *Lastly, we wanted the kids to learn that older people are not only interesting themselves, but are interested in them and love and care for them very much.*

When we arrived at Friends House, I introduced the students to the residents and thanked them for inviting us. They moved off in groups of two, three and four to begin the hour and a half interview. I talked to Donna Lockhardt, a registered nurse and Friends House liaison, and she familiarized me with the complex.

When it was about time to leave, the residents and students began walking back to Commons B, our meeting place. The kids and residents were still talking up a storm! It was pretty neat to behold. Eyes were sparkling and faces were all smiles. It was evident that no age barriers existed. Friendships had developed easily and I know we all gained from meeting one another. While walking back to school, the kids were sharing stories about the new connections they'd made, and I gave them time to do that in the classroom the next day as well. After the kids complete their biographical sketches, we're going to put them in a book for our new friends at Friends House to keep, and to remember.

The *Friends House* excursion turned out to be a great assignment and a welcome diversion from the routine Chuck had been following, but not enough to make him change his mind about retiring!

When June rolled around and school was once again out for the summer, Marty and Linda happily resumed their routine of shopping and supper exchanges. Chuck and Mark, on the other hand, were at a bit of a loss to figure out what to do with themselves. William Francis had been reading and writing braille for five years under his dad's tutelage, and would have been accomplished enough to take over for his dad in the classroom had Mark let him. His interest in teaching hadn't waned, but he had a few years to wait on that.

"So, you think you still want to be a teacher?" Chuck asked his grandson on a hot Fourth of July afternoon while they were splashing around in the above-ground swimming pool.

"I sure do, Grandpa!" William Francis said enthusiastically. "I haven't changed my mind."

"That's good," Chuck said. "I think it's wonderful. And you'll be a fine one, too."

Although it was their weekend shopping day, the gals decided it might just be a good idea to stay home on the busy 4th of July holiday. Giving their husbands a well-deserved Saturday break, they cleaned their own houses and made a heaping bowl of potato salad to go with a platter of crispy fried chicken. And not one home-baked pie, but two, apple and cherry!

It was seven o'clock, still warm and humid outdoors, when they all came inside and sat down to eat. About an hour later, just as the sun was beginning to go down, fireworks began making whistling sounds and the scent of smoke began wafting through the open windows. Mark was the first to hear a thrashing noise outside. "What's that?" he asked as he cast a concerned gaze towards the back of the house. "It sounds like someone's in the pool!"

Chuck jumped up, threw open the screen door and ran to the backyard. What he saw was a first. Prince had fallen into the pool and was paddling around like crazy in an attempt to make his way out. It was understandable why he couldn't. The sides were high, and Prince was old. How old? Sixteen, over 80 in human years! "What do you think you're doing there, Prince?" Chuck said as he grabbed his collar and helped him up and over the side and onto the deck.

"Is Prince okay, Grandpa?" William Francis yelled as he came running outside and saw the big wet dog splayed out on the pool deck, panting.

"He's fine," Chuck said, "just got himself into a bit of a fix. It's a good thing Mark heard the splashing or Prince may not have been so lucky. He's a tired old dog, can't save himself quite like he used to."

"I know why Prince did that, Grandpa," said William Francis.

"Why's that, William Francis?" he asked.

"Because dogs go crazy when they hear all the bangs and whistles from the fireworks," he said. "It makes their ears hurt, so they go wherever they can to get away from the noise."

"Where'd you learn that?" Chuck asked.

"From my friend, Tony," William Francis said. "He said once his dog got so scared with the fireworks that he jumped in the clothes dryer!"

"I think we'd better bring Prince inside," Chuck said. "We'll have to be more careful next year. He isn't getting any younger!"

Little did Chuck realize when he uttered those words that Prince would meet his demise long before the next 4th of July. It happened during the second week of school on Friday, September 11th, 1987, a day that would be forever burned into Mark's memory. He'd stopped taking Prince to school, as his beloved dog had grown appreciative of the rest and comforts of home. Mark missed having Prince by his side, but was able to get around with a cane.

Mark and William Francis were the first ones home from school the day it happened. William Francis left his dad's side and ran through the house to the back yard where they always left Prince during nice weather. "Prince!" William Francis yelled as he opened the back door, but no wobbling dog came to greet him. William Francis checked the side of the house where Prince had his water dish. It was empty. "I can't find Prince!" William Francis yelled as his dad stepped out the back door.

"He's around here somewhere," Mark said assuredly. "Why don't you run over to Grandpa and Grandma's and see if he's there."

William Francis sure could move. He tore through the back yard to his grandparents' house and began calling for Prince, but to no avail. No one answered his knock at the front door, so he ran to the side of the house through the open gate towards the swimming pool, calling for Prince again, but with no response. He leapt up the wooden steps to the pool, and that's when he saw the large lump under the cover. William Frances felt an instant surge of fear electrocute his body. What if Prince had lost his balance and fallen in while trying to get a drink! He slowly bent down to investigate, peeled back a bit of the cover and let out an audible cry. There was Prince's golden head, sopping wet, his teeth clenched together like he was trying to prevent water from entering his mouth. William Francis felt warm all over and hot tears poured down his cheeks as he pulled the plastic further back and saw Prince's bloated belly. "No, Prince, no!" he cried as he dropped the cover and raced back down the steps towards home.

"Did you find him?" Mark called from the living room when he heard his son run in through the back door.

"Dad! Dad!" William Francis yelled. He was gasping and crying as he reached his dad.

"William Francis, what's wrong?" asked Mark anxiously.

"Prince is dead, Dad!" he cried.

"No!" said Mark, looking stunned. "That can't be!"

"He is, Dad! He is!" cried William Francis. "I just found him!"

Mark's face filled with shocked pain. "Where is he, Son?" he said as he stood up.

"He drowned! He's in Grandma and Grandpa's pool!" yelled William Francis.

"Are you sure he's not breathing?" asked Mark anxiously as William Francis guided him quickly out the back door.

"Yes, Dad! I saw him! He's bloated and his eyes are closed and he's not moving!" sobbed William Francis.

They walked briskly next door, and William Francis held his dad's hand as they climbed the wooden steps to the pool deck. He guided him to the edge where Prince lay partially covered in the water, lifeless and floating on the surface. "He's right here, Dad!" cried William Francis.

Mark knelt down and reached into the water. What he touched confirmed what William Francis had told him. He ran his hand along

Prince's wet back and bloated body, then slowly moved his fingers up towards his head. Mark explored Prince's face, wincing as he located Prince's closed eyes. His fingers rested there, and, unable to speak, he dropped his head to his chest, tears streaming down his cheeks. William Francis looked up at Mark and remained silent, fully realizing his dad had lost his lifelong, irreplaceable companion.

"We'll tell Grandma and Grandpa as soon as they get home," said Mark quietly as he slowly raised his head and stood up.

"I'll tell them, Dad," William Francis said bravely, and when Marty and Chuck got home from work, he did just that. Chuck went out to the pool to confirm the devastating news for himself and then he and Marty and William Francis walked next door together.

"I'm so sorry it happened this way, Mark," said Chuck as his son met them in the doorway.

"He was a beautiful part of all of our lives," said Marty, tears streaming down her face, "most especially yours."

"We all knew his time would come sooner rather than later," said Mark, wiping his nose. "I just wasn't ready for it today. It's a hard way to say goodbye. I'm glad he didn't suffer."

"I'm sorry, Dad," said William Francis as he embraced his father.

AFTER SUCH AN INAUSPICIOUS START TO THE SCHOOL YEAR, THE rest of it was pretty tame in comparison. One of Chuck's former students, now a senior a Moorhead State Teachers College, requested and was given his permission to do her practice teaching in one of his 9th grade English classes during the second semester, and this helped to make Chuck's last year of teaching a piece of cake! Marty, knowing this was going to be her last year on the job, left the house singing every morning. She was looking forward to relaxing and reading and traveling to places other than her and Linda's Saturday shopping treks to Detroit Lakes, Park Rapids, Wadena, Fergus Falls and Fargo-Moorhead. Mark and Linda loved teaching at Perham High School, and William Francis, a soon-to-be 9th grader, was looking forward to joining the track team and running the 440, the same distance his cousin Gretchen would be running for her high school.

When the end of the 1987-88 school year arrived, it made Chuck a bit melancholy knowing he wouldn't be coming back to teach, but joyful just the same! He received many touching send-offs from his students, including these words written in his yearbook:

Dear Mr. Dowdle,

Another year has come and gone. Incredible, isn't it? It was a wonderful year, full of exciting books to read, essays to write (yes, I did enjoy them), and topics to be debated. One of the only times I've looked forward to an argument was in your class! In our debates, you always found a way to prove me wrong, yet, for some reason, that just made me feel more firmly that I was right! Your arguments taught me that with most issues, one must take a stand in order to have his/her opinion heard. You have always taken a stand on the issues over which we debated, and this in itself made the issues seem much more important.

All around, you made English a class I looked forward to every day. Thank you! Have a wonderful summer and a relaxing retirement. I consider myself really lucky to have been your student and friend.

—Leah Mundell

May 28th, 1988, was a memorable day, a day of total liberation from work for Marty and Chuck. No more school and no more hospital. Would they miss it? You bet! But it was pretty nice knowing they had the freedom to do whatever they wanted, whenever they wanted.

All the relatives arrived on Saturday for a retirement celebration. Walter and Grace drove up from Coon Rapids early in the morning. Laurie, Michael and the triplets arrived a bit later, and Chuck's brother, Bill, and his family drove up from Columbia Heights, arriving in Perham around noon, just in time for lunch. It was a great time in life for the retirees, and it was a festive afternoon of high spirits, bountiful food and lively conversation.

"We're onto something big at my company, Mark," Michael said discreetly to his brother as they took a break in the action and sat together in the corner of the living room. "If we're successful, it may have a dramatic impact on your life."

"What is it?" Mark asked curiously.

"Minneapolis General Pharmaceutical has created a laboratory to study diseases of the human eye," said Michael.

"That's wonderful, Brother!" Mark said.

"Not only that," he whispered, "but the company has appointed me lead scientist of what will be known as the Minneapolis General Pharmaceutical Eye Research Institute."

"Wow!" Mark said, "I'm impressed. Sounds like a big deal."

"It is, Brother," Michael said. "A bit intimidating to think about the huge responsibility that's been placed on my shoulders, but then I think about how wonderful it would be if we were able to discover a way that helped people to see again, especially if you're one of them!"

"Whoa. I'll say. I'd owe you big time," laughed Mark. "I can't imagine regaining my vision. What have you done so far?"

"That's just it, I'm not an expert on the human eye. I'm no doctor, remember?" Michael said laughing. "But I'm learning, starting with the basics. You're not going to believe this, but the first thing I did when I was appointed was to read the *World Book* 'Eye' article.

"Good place to start," laughed Mark.

"Yeah, Dad would be proud," chuckled Michael.

"What did you learn?" asked Mark.

"A lot," Michael said. "Do you want to hear it?"

"Sure," said Mark. "You know me, always ready to learn something new."

"Okay, then, here goes," Michael said. "As it turns out, the eye doesn't actually see objects. It actually sees the light they reflect or give off."

"Hmm," Mark said as a thoughtful look crossed his face. "I don't know why, but when you said that, I thought about Christianity and how our work is to assimilate and reflect Christ's light so we have a positive effect on others. Sorry, I got sidetracked there. Go ahead."

"OK...the eye can see in bright light and in dim light, but it can't see without light," said Michael.

"Makes sense to me, and I'm no doctor," said Mark smiling.

"So, light rays enter the eye through transparent tissues," Michael continued, "and then the eye changes the rays into electrical signals. The signals are sent to the brain, which interprets them as visual images."

Mark let out a big yawn. "Interesting stuff, really," he said laughing.

"Almost done," said Michael, "then you can ask questions." Mark smiled as Michael continued droning the information he'd gleaned from the encyclopedia. "There you have it!" he said enthusiastically when he'd finished.

"Sounds like you memorized the article word for word," Mark said.

"Pretty much," laughed Michael.

"The funny thing is, I memorized that article a long time back from the braille set of the *World Book Encyclopedia*," said Mark.

"Why didn't you tell me?" groaned Michael.

"Because you didn't ask," Mark said smiling. "No harm done, Brother," he added. "It was a good review. I'm happy for you, and excited as well. Keep me posted on what happens."

"I definitely will," said Michael.

"Hey, you two," Chuck called as he came in to replenish the chip bowl. "C'mon outside and join the party!"

The rest of the afternoon was filled with piles of food, lively conversation and interesting life updates. Grace happily informed everyone that she and Walter had decided it was time for them to retire as well.

"Good for you!" said Chuck.

"That's such a nice surprise," said Marty. "I thought you were going to wait a while."

"We were, we were," said Walter, "but the more we thought about it, the more we liked the idea of not working."

"I hear you on that!" laughed Chuck.

"Looks like the torch is being passed," Linda said smiling.

"What does that mean, Mom?" asked John Christian.

"It means we all have to work hard and make something of our lives so we can help our parents when they're older, just like they helped us when we were young," Laurie said.

"I'm going to be a teacher," said William Francis proudly.

"I'm going to be a doctor, so I'll be able to take care of Grandma and Grandpa if they get sick," said Gretchen confidently.

Her brothers just looked at each other, didn't know what to say. John and Joe didn't have a clue about their future careers. Their aunt saved them by breaking the silence.

"Those would be some very lucky students and very thankful patients," said Linda. "Who knows? You might be working at the same hospital as your mom someday, Gretchen!"

"And William Francis might be teaching at Perham High School with you and Mark!" laughed Laurie. "John and Joe don't yet know where they might be headed, but whatever it is, I know they'll be good at it," said their mom affectionately.

"There's plenty of time ahead for them to decide," said Linda warmly.

"Well, I think you'll all be coming to watch John and me play hockey in the pros," said Joe as he and his brother exchanged high fives.

Everyone got a kick out of their bravado. "Hey, it could happen," said Michael smiling. "Anything's possible with those two!"

"This is boring," whispered Gretchen to her cousin once the adults got into talking about work and their retirement futures. "Let's go to the high school and run around the track."

"Sounds good to me," William Francis said. "I'm going to try out for the track team even though I'll just be a freshman."

"Me, too," Gretchen said. "I sure hope we both make it!"

"What are you going to run?" he asked.

"The 440," she said.

"Me, too!" said William Francis.

It was beginning to get real warm, hot actually, by the time they got to the school, so they started slow with an easy walk around the track. When they'd completed the loop, Gretchen's brother, Joseph, said, "Why don't you and William Francis race a 440 against each other? See how fast you can go."

"Good idea. Do it, Gretchen," said her brother, John. "It's been a long time since we've seen you two run after each other." John, of course, was alluding to the time they'd been playing a fun game of tag and Gretchen ended up in the hospital.

"We'll time you!" said Joe eagerly as he looked at his watch.

"Okay," Gretchen said hesitantly, "if William Francis wants to."

"Sure," he said. "It'll be fun."

They exchanged quick smiles as they readied themselves in the starters' stance at the line. "OK, on the count of three," said Joe.

"One, two, three, go!" yelled John, and they were off!

Running side by side on the all-weather track was a lot different than racing down a cracked-concrete sidewalk, and they both knew it. When they reached the halfway mark, Joe called out, "One minute!" At that point, neither runner was going to let the other pass, regardless of how tired or breathless they were feeling. As they rounded the final turn and hit the straightaway for the final one hundred yards, John and Joe began shouting encouragement as though the runners were about to set a new world record. Gretchen and William Francis pushed all the harder and were neck and neck when they threw themselves across the finish line. It was impossible to tell who'd won, not without a photo-finish camera at least!

"Wow!" said John. "That was a dead heat! You two were fast!"

Both Gretchen and William Francis were sprawled out on the track, panting heavily and laughing at the same time. "What...was...our...time?" Gretchen finally managed to utter between gasps.

"I'm not sure, I got so excited," said John, "but I think just under two minutes."

"Not as fast as I'd hoped," Gretchen groaned.

William Francis sat up on the track and said confidently, "It's not bad, Gretchen. We'll get faster. It'll just take time and training. Hard to believe a guy like Butch Reynolds could make it around that same distance in a little over forty seconds!"

When the kids got home, Laurie was first to greet them. "Where have you been?" she asked. Then she looked at Gretchen and said, "You're all sweaty! What have you been up to?"

"Gretchen and William Francis raced around the track while Joe and I timed them, Mom," John said. "You should have seen how fast they were! It ended up being a tie."

"Good for you two," she said. "We're just sitting down to eat, so you kids get washed up and come to the table. We've been waiting for you."

"OK, Mom," said Gretchen as the foursome raced down the hall.

"They'll be right here," said Laurie as she walked into the dining room. "Joe said Gretchen and William Francis raced each other around the track while John and he clocked them. By the looks of their sweaty faces, you'd think they were training for the Olympics."

Joe and John were the first to get to their seats. Those two huskies never missed a meal, especially when either of their grandmas was in on the cooking. "Well, boys, who won the race?" Walter asked.

"I think it was a tie, Grandpa," Joe said. "We couldn't even tell. They flew around the track!"

"We were timing them," John said, "but we got so excited cheering that we forgot to click the stopwatch when they crossed the finish line."

"We're pretty sure they made it under two minutes," said Joe.

"Wow! That's good! Now let's say a prayer and enjoy this food!" Chuck said as Gretchen and William Francis found their seats.

The supper-table talk was mainly about Grace and Walter's and Marty and Chuck's retirement, far from entertaining as far as the kids were concerned. "What are you two going to do with all that free time?" Michael asked. Walter looked at Chuck and Chuck looked back at him. Both men shrugged in unison and laughed.

"They don't have to worry about that, Michael," said Grace. "Haven't you already learned that we women can concoct an array of never-ending projects?"

"Oh, yeah," Michael said, groaning, "I know all about the honey-do list!"

The weekend passed rapidly. Everyone went to Mass at St. Henry's on Sunday and then came home for a backyard barbecue and swim fest. Monday was Memorial Day, and the families went out to Big Pine Lake for a picnic and fishing. Just like that, Tuesday rolled around, time for the Minneapolis gang to pack up and head home. "Thanks a lot for a great weekend, Charlie," said his brother, Bill, as he and Pearl were loading their trunk. "We really enjoyed the company and I loved the fishing."

LITTLE DID CHUCK REALIZE HIS BROTHER WOULDN'T BE WITH HIM much longer. Bill died of cancer a year later on June 23rd, 1989. Chuck asked the priest if he could give a eulogy at the funeral Mass, and the priest said it would be fine. He suggested Chuck write it out. "People get very emotional at funerals," he said, "and they often forget what they wanted to say."

Chuck took his advice, typed it up on an old manual typewriter in the basement of Bill and Pearl's house the day before the funeral, and was glad he did. The large Columbia Heights church was filled to capacity, and he did get choked up when he began speaking the following words about his brother:

"My name is Chuck Dowdle. I'd like to say a few words about the brother I admired and loved, and who will always be with me. I can already hear Bill saying, "Charlie, Charlie, let's not go overboard now.

First, let me give you a little family background. We're from Crookston. Bill was the eldest of five children. I was second and our sister, Betty, was third. Our sister, Cathy, who died at an early age of Parkinson's disease, was fourth, and our brother, Jerry, was the last. Our dad died of a heart attack and our mother is still living. Bill was a lot like Dad. He loved life, he enjoyed a good time and he loved people! When he was in the hospital, he said, "I sure wish I could go quickly like Dad did."

I got to know my brother real well when we were growing up. We shared a bedroom for about fifteen years. We shared brotherly secrets and experiences. We shared a paper route and delivered during sun, rain and freezing blizzards in the early hours of the morning. When Bill was a senior at Cathedral High School and I was a freshman going to my first school dance, I didn't know how to dance, so Bill taught me the fox trot, albeit reluctantly. It seemed that Bill was always looking out for me in a sensitive and nurturing way.

He taught me how to fish the river and he introduced me to sports, which he loved, especially baseball and ice hockey. He was catcher for the hometown American Legion baseball team and captained his high school hockey team. We used to go outside in the winter with Mom's pillows stuffed in our pants and take turns shooting pucks at one another. Bill even played football when he was a senior. He played end. Can you imagine a 5'7", 120-pound end?

For a short time after graduation, Bill worked for the Great Northern Railroad as a fireman on a passenger train from Grand Forks to Seattle. He hated it, and that's when he decided to come to Minneapolis and look for a job. I remember seeing him off at the Greyhound Bus station. I had saved up some silver dollars to give him as a going-away present. When he left, it was like a part of me left, too. Bill got a job at the Honeywell Regulator Company, and he worked there for 42 years. He retired at 62 and died two years later at 64.

I'd like to tell you how Bill died, because I think he lived like he died, filled with courage, faith and love.

Pearl, his wife, said, "On Monday of last week, the doctor was going to come into Bill's hospital room and tell the family the results of some tests, and Bill wanted the whole family to be there. I think Bill knew what the results were going to be, because after everyone was in the room, he said, "Close the door, honey. We don't know what the doctor's going to tell us, how much time I have left, but I want to spend it with my wonderful family, and I want to tell them all how much I love them, including the sons-in-law and the grandchildren. And I want to tell them to love everybody and to love their spouses as much as I love you." Pearl said everybody began crying and telling Bill how much they loved him when he said that, and Bill said, "That's all right. It's good to cry. Now lighten up!"

My wife, "Marty," (nee Marilyn Kirkwood), and I entered Bill's room for the first time last Thursday morning just as a cancer specialist was beginning to explain to Bill and the entire family that his chances of surviving were extremely slim. Bill took the news fearlessly and calmly. My wife and I visited with Bill and Pearl all day, and my brother and I got to talk about all the good times we had had together, and I got to tell him how much I loved him.

Pearl, who'd been sleeping by Bill's side since he entered the hospital, called us early Friday morning and said Bill's blood pressure and pulse had dropped. The whole family got there before Bill gave up his life at around eleven a.m. It seemed like he was just struggling to wait until they all arrived. As he repeatedly made the sign of the cross, his dying words were, "Can't take it anymore! Bye bye! I love you!" And then Bill stared at the ceiling as if seeing a vision, and died.

I'd like to close by speaking directly to my brother. You folks can listen in…

Don't worry about Pearl and kids, Bill. They're following right in your footsteps. You'd be proud of them. After you died on Friday, the whole family went to Hillside Cemetery and purchased two lots, one for you and one for Pearl, and right next to Pearl's mom and dad whom you loved so much. I remember how you fell in love with the whole Carlson family when you met Pearl. You put faith in Pearl and the kids to carry out your well-laid plans, Bill, and they're doing your bidding to a 'T'. Bill, you taught me what it means to be a man *when you lay dying and asked God's forgiveness for any hurt you may have caused anyone. Not to worry, Brother. You were too gentle, kind, sensitive and thoughtful to hurt people. Father Jim Studer, the priest who gave you the blessing of the sick and dying, said never in his life had he seen a greater demonstration of faith in a dying man. You're home free, Brother!*

Lastly, Bill, let's talk a little about love. Do you remember when you wanted to go on a double date with me because you'd met this real neat gal from Columbia Heights? You wanted me to check her out. I didn't know who to go with, and you said, 'How about that Kirkwood girl you went to high school with? She lives in Minneapolis.' Those two gals became our wives. We sure knew how to pick them, Brother!

Bill, it has to be true that home is where the heart is, because the love your family is showing for one another right now is extremely touching. I think you taught us all a good lesson about how to go about understanding and caring for people. Your whole family seems to have developed your touch, Bill. They love one another!

I think you knew all along you were going, Bill. You just waited so all of us could be here with you. Your spirit lives, Brother. Thank you for showing us the way. We love you!"

On the drive back to Perham, Chuck and Marty reminisced about how their own parents had passed away, about how fragile life was, and about how they intended to spend whatever time they had left. Marty said the past year since retirement had been relaxing, and that the traveling they'd been doing was fun, but now she wanted to begin doing something more regular, something helpful to other people.

"What do you have in mind?" Chuck asked.

"I'd like to volunteer someplace where they really need me," she said.

Chuck glanced over at his wife and smiled. "I know just where that place is," he said.

"Where?" she asked.

"The hospital, of course!" Chuck said. "Where else? You know they can always use extra help, and no doubt they'd love to have you back!"

"Well, maybe so," she said. "I'll go over there tomorrow and see what they say."

What they said when she walked through the hospital doors was how much they missed her, and when she told them she was thinking about volunteering a couple days a week, they embraced the possibility of her return with open-armed enthusiasm.

Chuck spent a lot of his retirement time continuing to sell *World Book Encyclopedia*. When he wasn't doing that, he could be found running around the high school track and bicycling to get his exercise. Both Marty and he were avid readers, and it was enjoyable for them to have time in the evenings to kick back and absorb good books.

Retirement was a harder adjustment for the Johnsons. Walter was having a difficult time getting used to life without work, the absence of building and the business he so loved. He found himself feeling restless and a bit overwhelmed with all his free time, which made their home environment more challenging for Grace, but she, on the other hand, was enjoying her retirement immensely. She was happy to be able to spend more time with Laurie and the triplets.

They were different kids now, fourteen and in the 10th grade. They were putting serious thought into their career plans, and Gretchen hadn't wavered. She was going to be a doctor, no question about it! And she was a real whiz at science! Her brothers were more interested in following in their grandpa's footsteps, not in building necessarily, but something in business. Like his cousin, Gretchen, William Francis was steadfast about his future plans. He was going to be a teacher, just like his dad.

LIFE MOVED RIGHT ALONG FOR ALL THE DOWDLES UNTIL THE YEAR 2000. That's when major changes began taking place. The most challenging one occurred shortly after Chuck and Marty's 49th wedding anniversary on June 9th. Over the past year, Marty had mentioned having on-and-off stomach aches and had noticed a big, hard lump in her belly. Sadly, she was diagnosed with Stage IV ovarian cancer on July 19th and died just four weeks later. Needless to say, it was a devastating time for Chuck and for all the family. He sat down the day after losing Marty and wrote these words:

"Marilyn Kirkwood"

On Sunday, August 20th, 2000, at 11:40 a.m., the love of my life, my wife, Marilyn "Marty" Kirkwood Dowdle, my buddy and best friend, died of ovarian cancer. As she took her last, soft breaths, I held her hand and told her how much I loved her. She died peacefully, with no pain, no nausea, and a smile on her face.

Earlier that same morning, she'd been going through hell. She was receiving Demerol via a computerized pump, and I was pumping an extra shot into her body every ten minutes. It wasn't enough to handle the breakthrough pain. When my daughter-in-law, Linda, came in, she immediately called Home Hospice, and Patty Shribbs, an angel as far as I'm concerned, came to the house. She asked if I wanted Marty to have suppositories to relieve the pain. I said, "Yes!" as I certainly didn't want her to be suffering. Patty gave her two Nembutal suppositories and the pain subsided. It was a bittersweet moment for me, relieved as I was to have my wife free of pain and nausea, at the same time feeling the mighty sadness of impending loss.

That evening I put on one of our favorite songs, "All the Way," sung by Frank Sinatra, and I started dancing around the living room as if I was holding Marty in my arms. I soon began hyperventilating and crying uncontrollably, and it feels like I haven't stopped since. For those of you who've been there, you know what I mean. Why, I'm crying like a baby as I sit and write this, but I don't care. I want all my tears to flow out naturally for the person I loved more than anyone else in my life, more than anyone else in the world.

My two sons run a close second in the love department. I don't know what I would have done without them, both of them. The day after their mom was told she had cancer, Michael arrived early the next morning from Coon Rapids to be with her, and Mark and he sat on either side of their mom, Mark with his head pressed gently against hers and Michael holding her hand while they talked.

Michael drove us to Minneapolis to consult with a surgical oncologist, who informed Marty that she basically had three options: 1) Do nothing; 2) Inject the liver, which was already three times its normal size; 3) Have surgery. Marty prayed about it all that night and opted for surgery. We were all feeling a level of relief, cautiously optimistic that the surgery would be successful and that she'd be on her way to recovery. Sadly, that's not the way it happened.

After a week in the hospital in Minneapolis, where my sons and I took turns spending days and nights in her room, we were finally able to bring her home to Perham. She had a Fentanyl patch for pain and Compazine for nausea, but, as it turned out, neither was adequate. Fortunately, Michael's wife, Laurie, took time off from work and arrived in time to help out.

Needless to say, it was the most difficult week of our lives. Marty was experiencing a great deal of incisional leakage and breakthrough pain, and it was gut wrenching for all of us to witness her tearful pleas for it to just be over. "All I want to do is die! Just help me die!" were her cries, but there was little we could do beyond staying at her side and praying for the pain medication to take effect. Believe me, if Marty had had the necessary pills within reach to end her life, she would have wanted to take them, and I would have assisted. She and I shared a belief in the right to die without unnecessary pain when one is terminally ill, which she obviously was. The doctor had given her a prognosis of less than six months.

Marty lived just three weeks after surgery, four weeks from the time of her diagnosis. Difficult as those four weeks were, they weren't completely devoid of smiles. One of the two drugs she was taking caused her to hallucinate. She said she heard Tex Beneke playing and saw Spanish dancers. We both chuckled over that. She also had a good laugh when I came home with my head shaved right before she went into surgery. I figured if she was going to undergo chemotherapy and end up losing all her hair, I wanted to be right there with her. She wasn't exactly thrilled with the look. I think her comment was, "Oh, no!" My bald head did provide us all with some much-needed comic relief over the days to come.

Marty could have opted for chemotherapy after her surgery, but having been told by the surgeon postoperatively that the cancer was incurable, she chose not to do so. She was already weak from the surgery, and could actually tolerate pain more than nausea, so she was firm in her decision to forego chemotherapy. After being at home for a week post-surgery, Marty was re-admitted to the hospital for care of her incision and pain stabilization. While she was there, Mark and Linda and Laurie took turns relieving me so I could check on things at home and try to get a few hours of sleep.

I sing the praises of my wife! She was a fortress of courage. I sing the praises of all women! They're the saints of this world as far as I'm concerned. I know my wife was. She put everyone before herself, always. She was the inveterate volunteer, and was always gently suggesting that it would be good for me to give it a try. Now, I think I will.

So, there you have it. Surgery in Minneapolis one week, all hell breaking loose the second week, back in the hospital the third week and discharged to home on Hospice Care the next.

Let me tell you a little about that fourth and final week with Marty. So many beautiful moments were had in the midst of the pain and sadness. Her sons were able to have many intimate talks with their mom, I'd say talks that were life changing for them. Marty was so thankful she had the opportunity to say goodbye to each of us in this way, and so were we. We will treasure those moments until the day we die. "Don't sweat the small stuff, boys," I heard her tell Mark and Michael. And then she said mournfully, "You both look so sad! I could just hug the two of you every time I see you!" Which she'd always done.

We all treasured the way we sent Marty off, a love-filled celebration of her life! She was cremated as per her request, and after a funeral Mass at St. Henry's in Perham, her ashes were buried in the Perham Catholic Cemetery. While we were all gathered, I read a poem titled, "I'm Free," which captured the way Marty felt about death:

I'm Free

I could not stay another day
To laugh, to love, to work or play
Tasks left undone must stay that way
I found that place at the close of day.
If my parting has left a void
Then fill it with remembered joy
A friendship shared, a laugh, a kiss
Ah yes, these things, I too, will miss
Be not burdened with times of sorrow
I wish you the sunshine of tomorrow
My life's been full, I savored much
Good friends, good times, a loved one's touch

Perhaps my time seemed all too brief
Don't lengthen it now with undue grief
Lift up your heart and share it with me
God wanted me now, he set me free
Don't grieve for me, for now I'm free
I'm following the path God laid out for me
I took His hand when I heard Him call
I turned my back and left it all.

—Author Unknown

"Of all the time I knew Marty, I never heard her say a negative thing about another person," said Linda as the family was leaving the cemetery.

"Same for me," said Laurie, "not one word."

They were so right. That was Chuck's wife through and through, always thoughtful, gentle, sensitive and kind to others.

"I remember the worst she could say about William Francis when he was fussing up a storm and she was walking with him and cuddling him, trying to give him comfort," said Linda smiling. Her words were, "He's a little tiger. He's a real puzzle."

They drove home, had lunch and talked about all the good times they'd had together. Marty would have wanted it to be an environment of celebration and love, and they honored her wishes as best they could in spite of their broken hearts. When Marty and Chuck were talking about God during her last week at home, she had said, "Chuck, my God is a nonjudgmental, compassionate, merciful God." The way she felt about God was the way she lived her life. Chuck loved that woman!

Marty's passing was not the last of a death spiral that was about to take place in the family. Walter and Grace hadn't attended the funeral, as they'd been experiencing health problems of their own. Walter had suffered a heart attack and was confined to the house while Grace looked after him. Sadly, they were soon both gone. Walter died of a second heart attack on November 19th and Grace died the following month on December 18th.

The holidays were a difficult and mournful time for all the Dowdles, especially so for Laurie and Linda. Chuck was the only one left of the old guard, and he did his best to comfort his daughters-in-law and grandkids. At the same time, he didn't know quite what to do with himself. The house was hollow and lonely without Marty. It felt empty, as did his heart.

After several more weeks of feeling intensely lost, Chuck decided to get away, to get himself into a less-sad environment for a while. He decided he'd take a flight to the west coast, rent a car and head south down the coast, rekindling relationships with friends and relatives along the way. And he did just that! His first stop was in Cambria, California, for a visit with Carmelle Johnson Matthes, an old high school friend whose husband of 50 years had recently passed away.

Carmelle had been a close friend of Marty's, and Chuck had been in the same grade with the two of them at Cathedral High School in Crookston, Minnesota. He never really got close to either until after being discharged from the Navy on Thanksgiving Day in 1947. He asked Carmelle out to a New Year's Eve dance at the Crookston Armory. They danced the night away, and then walked home hand-in-hand through the snow, cuddling into the warmth of a large, cozy sofa upon arriving. It was a memorable date for Chuck, and now here he was, meeting up with her again, and as it turns out, just as smitten by her charm as he had been decades ago. To say he was riding high on a cloud when he continued south the next day barely touches the towering tip of the joy he was feeling, especially after so many weeks of utter despair.

The next stop on his California journey took him to Tustin, California, where he visited with an old teaching friend and his spouse. The first thing Bill Wegner's wife, Marge, said to Chuck when they sat down and began talking was, "There's something different about you. I can't quite put my finger on it, but there's definitely something different." Boy, was she right! Chuck was in love!

His last California stop before heading home was in San Diego to see his cousin, Bill Carter. Bill's wife had passed away, and he was alone, too. When Chuck told him he'd stopped to visit the former Carmelle Johnson in Cambria, Bill said, "It's pretty obvious you have strong feelings for her, Charlie," and he was right.

After Chuck left his cousin's house and began driving back to San Francisco, he thought about stopping to see Carmelle again before flying home to Minnesota, but he thought the better of it and begrudgingly passed on by. Instead he wrote to her when he got back to Perham, and she wrote back to him, and after many more such exchanges, they developed a loving distance relationship. Carmelle eventually flew to Minnesota to visit him, and that clinched it! They were married on April 21st, 2001. Chuck sold his house and moved to Cambria, California, and he never looked back. That's what love will do!

The seeming hastiness of their father's actions threw Michael and Mark for a loop, their wives as well, but change was a fact of life. Everyone knew that, they just needed time to adjust to the new reality and to being so far away from Chuck...Dad...Grandpa. For Michael and Mark, it was doubly challenging, as it felt like they were not only suffering the loss of their mother, but in some ways their father as well.

The grandkids had an easier time of it. They all flew to California with their parents for Grandpa Chuck's wedding, and much to his joy, they liked Carmelle from the moment she walked down the aisle, all smiles and looking radiantly in love. When Gretchen learned Carmelle had been a nurse, the two of them began chatting with one another like colleagues. Gretchen was on her way to becoming Dr. Gretchen Marie Dowdle, currently in training at the University of Minnesota in her area of specialty, Ophthalmology.

Gretchen's brothers, ice-hockey players extraordinaire, graduated from St. Thomas University in St. Paul, Minnesota, with B.A.'s in Business Administration. The two of them were now happily working together in sports marketing.

William Francis followed in his father's footsteps and was teaching English and Braille at Perham High School. The successful Braille program had become so popular that William Francis had begun giving workshops in other Otter Tail County towns and throughout Minnesota, and was tutoring younger students as well. Much like his father, one of those students had been blind since birth, and had been learning braille since he was four years old.

Michael and Mark continued to find their work exceedingly satisfying and rewarding. Whenever their families got together, a lively discussion ensued. Exploration had begun at Minneapolis General Pharmaceutical Eye Research Institute into the sight-restoring potential of gene therapy and retinal implants, and impressive progress had been made since Michael had been appointed Lead Scientist in 1988. This interested Gretchen and her father immensely. They felt fortunate to be on the informed and cutting edge of whatever advancements might be made to benefit the blind population, thinking especially of Mark, of course. Mark was curious as well, as one would expect, but not in the same way. Happily living his life as a blind person was all he'd ever known, and he rarely entertained thoughts of it being any other way.

CHUCK WANTED MARK AND MICHAEL TO APPRECIATE FIRSTHAND how their dad's life had changed over the years, and he and Carmelle decided to fly the entire family out to California for their 15th wedding anniversary on April 21st, 2016. Sons, daughters-in law, grandkids and great-grandkids! Everyone was invited, and, wonderfully enough, all were able to make it, even Gretchen, who now had a busy ophthalmology practice.

The gregarious gang arrived at the San Luis Obispo airport the day before the celebration. Chuck and Carmelle picked them up with two vehicles, a large rented van and their own family sedan. The first stop was the Cambria Pines Lodge, where Chuck had arranged for them to stay, very convenient in that it was located right across the street from their house, and a hearty breakfast included!

After a good night's sleep and a short, but restful morning for the travelers, Carmelle and Chuck picked up the group at 8:15 a.m. and drove to Santa Rosa Catholic Church in Cambria in time for the 8:30 Rosary. Only about a dozen people typically showed up to pray the Rosary, which was followed by 9:00 Mass, but on this morning the front rows of the church were filled with Chuck's family, all seventeen of them! Michael and Laurie sat with their two sons, who were married and had children of their own, three daughters for Joseph Christopher and his wife, Maureen, and two daughters for John Christian and his wife, Elizabeth Ann. It was interesting that the robust ice-hockey-playing boys ended up having all daughters, but they loved it that way, and they loved their girls. Gretchen Marie sat in the pew behind her brothers with her husband, Charles Latovsky, and their two year-old son, Charlie Junior. Gretchen hadn't married until she was 38, but "Charles was definitely worth waiting for," she always said with a beaming smile. An ophthalmologist as well, the two of them didn't waste any time starting a family. And William Francis, who'd yet to marry, sat with his parents, Mark and Linda. When Chuck began the Rosary by making the sign of the cross and saying, *"In the name of the Father, and of the Son, and of the Holy Spirit,"*…everyone had their rosaries in hand and began reciting the Apostle's Creed together. It was beautiful to hear all the voices praying to God with such love and sincerity.

After the Rosary and Mass, Father Mark Stetz, the pastor, asked everyone to remain seated and announced that Carmelle and Chuck were going to renew their wedding vows. This surprised everyone, and they whispered excitedly in anticipation, especially Joe and John's five teenage daughters. Father Mark motioned for Carmelle and Chuck to approach the altar, and when they stood in front of him, he smiled and began to speak, *"Since it is your intention to enter into marriage and declare your consent before God and His Church,"*…Joe and John's five daughters began giggling. They'd been to weddings before, but never to one where a grandpa and grandma were renewing their vows. Getchen smiled knowingly and cuddled little Charlie to her breast. Chuck's sons, Michael and Mark, were a different story altogether. When they heard Father Mark ask Carmelle and Chuck to join hands, the boys were riveted by what was about to happen. When their father began saying his vows, tears formed in his and Carmelle's eyes and theirs as well. The twins couldn't help but to think about what it must have been like on June 9th, 1951, when their father spoke those same words to their mother.

"Please join your right hands and repeat after me," Father Mark continued. *"I, Charles Dowdle, take you, Carmelle Dowdle, to be my wife. I promise to be true to you, in good times and in bad, in sickness and in health. I will love you and honor you all the days of my life."* When Chuck had finished, Father Mark turned to Carmelle. "Your turn," he said with a smile.

"I, Carmelle Dowdle," she began in a strong voice, *"take you, Charles Dowdle, to be my husband. I promise to be true to you in good times and in bad, in sickness and in health. I will love you and honor you all the days of my life."*

At this point you could have heard a pin drop in the church. Father Mark turned towards Chuck and said, *"Chuck, here before God, do you take Carmelle to be your wife?"*

Chuck answered loud and clear. *"I do,"* he said.

"And you, Carmelle," Father Mark continued. *"Here before God, do you take Chuck to be your husband?"*

"I do," she answered brightly.

Father Mark faced the twosome. *"You have declared your consent before the Church. May the Lord in His goodness strengthen your consent and fill you both with His blessings. What God has joined, men must not divide. Amen. Chuck, you may now kiss your beautiful bride,"* he said warmly. Chuck reached for Carmelle, embraced her lovingly and kissed her with the fervor of a newlywed. The family-and-friend-filled church broke out with joyful applause as the newly-vow-renewed couple turned toward them with the widest of smiles.

"That was something, Dad!" said Mark as Linda and he walked alongside Chuck and Carmelle on the way out of church. "It was so moving to hear you and Carmelle re-commit to each other like that. Hearing those vows made me think about what it was like when you and Mom got married."

"It was sort of the same," said Chuck, "but different, of course. We were so young, but there was a Mass, just like today, and your mother was beautiful, just like my lovely bride is today."

"Well, I just want to say I'm very happy for both of you," said Mark. "You're a lucky man, Dad."

"As is Carmelle a lucky woman," piped in Linda as she winked at her father-in-law.

"Being here to hear the two of you exchange your vows was worth every bit of the travel, Dad," said Mark. "Thank you both for your generosity in making it happen. Linda and I and William Frances appreciate it very much."

"As do we!" said Michael as he and Laurie caught up with the family in the parking lot. "I'm so glad we were all able to be here. Thank you, Dad! And Carmelle, too!"

"It was beautiful little ceremony, it really was," said Laurie. "Thank you both."

"Well, thank you all for being here," said Carmelle.

"Yes, thank you," said Chuck. "We'll see if we can continue making it worth your while for the rest of your time here. Now everyone listen up," he said when they were about to get into the two vehicles. "Our next stop is the Moonstone Beach boardwalk for a meander along the ocean. Load up, everyone!"

Most of the family had never experienced the ocean. Lots of lakes in Minnesota, of course, but no ocean! The exceptions were Gretchen and Charles, who'd traveled extensively around the country, and Michael, who'd attended conferences on both coasts. As they neared the ocean and could hear its roar, the teenagers got real excited. When the car and van pulled into full view of the ocean, the girls squealed in delight and gazed in awe as the bright morning sun lit up the water like diamonds.

With the vehicles parked, it didn't take long for everyone to pile out and make their way to the boardwalk. "This is really neat, Dad," said Mark as father and son walked along slowly, Chuck guiding Mark along. "The air smells so fresh and I love the warm breeze against my face," he said happily.

Gretchen, Charles and two year-old Charlie picked up the rear when they started out, but once Charlie's feet touched the boardwalk, he was off and running. "Wait for me, Charlie!" Gretchen called as she raced after him. In seconds he was at the head of the line, running as fast as he could to get away from his mother. Needless to say, he didn't have a chance against the former track star. Gretchen was just as lithe and speedy as she'd always been.

They gave themselves a couple of hours to meander along the boardwalk and down on the beach, and by noon everyone was ready to head back to their lodging, eat some lunch, get a little rest, then dress for the 5:00 p.m. anniversary dinner. They all thanked Carmelle and Chuck profusely for the Rosary, Mass, vow renewal and walk on the beach, and it was clearly apparent that everyone had enjoyed their memorable morning together.

The anniversary dinner was held in the Fireplace Room of the Cambria Pines Lodge, so called because a large stone fireplace graced an entire corner. Four round tables, each with five chairs, were positioned so that everyone could appreciate the warmth of the fireplace. The tables were covered with white linen tablecloths, and in the center of each was a crystal vase holding a red rose. The Fireplace Room looked out upon a spread of green grass and pathway to a rose-covered trellis, often used for Lodge weddings.

Chuck and Carmelle were already in the Fireplace Room when the family members began arriving. "Take a seat wherever you want," Chuck said cheerily. "This is going to be a bit different than your usual sit-down wedding dinner." As soon as the teenage girls heard this, they all opted to sit together. Gretchen, Charles and little Charlie sat at a table where one of the waiters had placed a high chair, and Chuck and Carmelle joined them. Laurie, Michael, Linda and Mark sat at a table with William Frances, and Joe and John sat with their wives, Marie and Elizabeth Ann.

Michael got the celebratory ball rolling by clinking his water glass with his dinner knife, motioning for his dad to give his "bride" a kiss. Chuck rose to the occasion immediately. He gazed lovingly into Carmelle's hazel eyes, lowered his head and pressed his lips gently against hers. The teenage girls giggled, not able to imagine what it would be like to be married for fifteen years, or married at all for that matter! Everyone broke into spontaneous applause, and even little Charlie got into the act by rambunctiously banging his spoon against the highchair tray.

"This is turning out to be a very lively day," said Chuck as he turned in Michael's direction and smiled at him, "and I'm enjoying it immensely," he added as everyone laughed. Laurie managed to divert little Charlie's attention as she pulled an enticing snack baggie from her purse and replaced his noisemaker with a cracker. "It's time to eat," said Chuck, "so let's begin by thanking God for this beautiful day." Chuck bowed his head and prayed: *"Lord, thank you for being so good to us! Merciful God, guide us as we travel on our separate journeys and be with us always and forever. We ask you in Jesus's name. Amen."*

When he finished, you could have heard a pin drop, all heads bowed. There was silence until little Charlie once again took charge, happily resuming his percussion act. He was hungry and it was time to eat! Everyone burst out laughing and the fun began.

The waiters entered the dining room with menus folded under their arms, placing one in front of each person. Chuck rose from his chair and said, "I forgot to mention, Carmelle and I want you to order whatever you'd like from the menu. Anything! That works for everyone, right?" he said smiling. He got a roomful of smiles in response, and that was his answer.

After a delightful dinner, everyone oohed and aahed as two waiters carried a giant layered cheesecake into the room, splendidly aglow with fifteen white candles. It became quiet as Mark pushed back his chair and rose to speak. "I can feel," he began in whispered, measured words, "that this special day for Carmelle and Dad has been a special day for all of us." As he spoke, it was easy to sense the intimate bond that had developed over the years between Mark and his dad. Tears welled up in William Francis's eyes as his dad continued speaking, and one could easily tell a uniquely-intimate bond had developed between him and his dad as well.

The dinner fanfare lasted two hours, including devouring the entire cheesecake! Everyone was tuckered out after the long and wonderful day together, especially little Charlie, whose head was bobbing and weaving in random motion over his tray. Chuck and Carmelle said their goodnights and told everyone they'd be by in the morning to pick them up for the Rosary and daily Mass. The teenagers groaned when they heard the early morning hour, but they were the first ones waiting outside when Chuck and Carmelle arrived.

After church, Chuck gave everyone the itinerary rundown for the day. "First, we'll check out what is known as the Fiscalini Ranch Preserve and get in a good walk," he said cheerfully. "Then we'll take a short drive north to see the elephant seals at the Piedras Blancas Elephant Seal Rookery. After that, we'll drop you off back at the Lodge so you can rest up before heading across the street to Dowdles' Diner for the salmon dinner Carmelle and I will be preparing." Faces lit up when they heard 'salmon dinner.' They all loved fish!

Carmelle and Chuck had anticipated feeding a hungry gang, and had brought home four large salmon filets and three large pumpkin pies from Costco. Of course, ice cream was essential with pumpkin pie, thus they'd bought two gallons of their favorite Tillamook vanilla at the local Cookie Crock grocery store. But first came the Fiscalini Ranch Preserve and elephant seals.

As the two vehicles left Santa Rosa Catholic Church and wound their way north along Main Street through what was called West Village, all the women in Chuck's rental van were trying to catch a glimpse of the quaint little shops. "Will we have some time to check these out tomorrow, Grandpa?" asked Gretchen.

"I don't see how I can possibly refuse," said Chuck, laughing. "I'm totally outnumbered!" The van took a left on Windsor Boulevard, crossed Highway 1, drove past Shamel County Park and soon arrived at the Fiscalini Ranch Preserve. Everyone oohed and aahed as they drove past the luxurious oceanfront Seacliff Estates.

"Wow! I wonder who lives in those!" said an awestruck Kathleen.

"People with a lot of money, that's for sure!" said her sister, Patricia.

The day turned out to be beautiful, warm and sunny with a cool breeze, perfect for a short meander along the ocean. "Look at those birds!" Genevieve shouted. "What are they doing?"

"Those are pelicans," Chuck said. "They're fishing for their dinner." It was an amazing sight to see as one pelican after another dove into the water at full speed. As everyone ambled along the walkway and neared the end, Kathleen noticed a huge rock in the ocean near the shoreline. "What's all the white stuff on that rock?" she asked.

"Did you see all of those black birds sitting on it?" Chuck asked.

"Yes," she said.

"Well," Chuck said smiling, "the white stuff is guano."

"Guano?" she asked.

"The dictionary would define it as the excrement of seabirds and bats, but it's more commonly known as poop," he said smiling.

"Ewww. No wonder it stinks!" she said, plugging her nose.

"I know," Chuck said laughing. "The good news is it gets washed away regularly, every time the tide comes in."

On their drive north to see the elephant seals, the girls' curiosity was really peaked. "We're going to see seals that look like elephants?" they asked.

"I read about them in *World Book* a long time ago when I was learning about ocean life," Mark said. "I remember it saying they can grow over 20 feet long and weigh up to 8,000 pounds!"

"And get this," said Chuck. "When they're mating, the bulls fight over the females with such gusto that they get all bloodied up in their attempt to surround themselves with a harem." This really got the teenage-girls' attention. They could hardly wait to see a big male in action!

They didn't have to wait long, because the elephant seals were just a short drive north along the coast on Highway 1. Once there, everyone piled out of the two vehicles and headed along the fenced-in walkway, following the cacophony of sound from the hundreds of seals that populated the sandy beach. The girls were hoping for some entertaining action, and there was plenty to be had! In addition to several males fighting over the females, they were able to view baby seals from a close-up vantage point. "I read that the newborn elephant seals can weigh as much as sixty pounds!" said Mark. "Those are some big babies!"

There was a lot of animated chatter on the drive back to Cambria Pines Lodge. Everyone seemed to have enjoyed both Fiscalini Ranch and the elephant seals. It had been a great day! Now they were looking forward to a bit of rest and a delicious home-cooked meal.

Around four o'clock, one family member after another left the lodge and headed across the street to Carmelle and Chuck's house. Mark could smell the aroma of salmon and fried potatoes before they'd even made it to the front door. "I can hardly wait!" he said as he held Linda's hand and headed up the front-porch stairs. "I feel like I could eat a whole fish!"

"Easy, now. You need to save some for the rest of us," she said kiddingly.

After everyone arrived, Carmelle pulled two sizzling salmon slabs from the oven and placed them on the countertop trivet along with steaming potatoes, fresh broccoli, homemade cranberry sauce and a basket of hot rolls. "Okay, everybody, dinner is ready!" she said triumphantly. "This is a very informal buffet. Just line up, take a plate and silverware, and help yourselves! Feel free to sit inside or out on the deck, your choice."

"All of us teenagers can go outside," said Kathleen, "then there'll be more room inside for all the adults."

"Thanks for offering that, Kathleen," Carmelle said. "That's very kind of you."

"Before we start loading up our plates, let's pray," Chuck said. *"Bless us O Lord and these Thy gifts, which we are about to receive from Thy bounty and goodness, through Christ our Lord. Amen. Oh, and Lord,"* Chuck added, *"please bless the cook!"*

Carmelle smiled and said, "Okay, everyone, dish up!"

"This is really good, Carmelle!" Michael said as he made headway into a large chunk of salmon. "I think it's the best salmon I've ever had!"

"And the broccoli's great, too!" Mark added. "Tastes like it's fresh from the garden."

"I like the rolls!" said Patricia.

"The cranberries are extraordinary!" said Chuck. "Just had to get my two cents in."

"This man would eat cranberries with everything if he had the chance," Carmelle said, laughing. "I don't know where that came from, but he sure does love them!"

"He's always been that way," Michael said. "Mom used to say he'd put them on his oatmeal if she'd let him."

Everyone thoroughly enjoyed the salmon dinner, and after the teenagers picked up the dishes and loaded them into the dishwasher, it was time for pumpkin pie, ice cream and coffee. True Minnesotans never served dessert without coffee. It's the unofficial state drink, just like the mosquito is their unofficial state bird.

By seven o'clock, everyone was tuckered out. "You'll be happy with what I have to tell you," Chuck said. "Tomorrow is Saturday, so you can sleep in since we won't be going to Mass until five in the afternoon. And we do have something special planned. After everyone's had breakfast, we're going to tour Hearst Castle, and after that we'll have a picnic at San Simeon State Park, which is right across the highway from the castle. There's a real gentle cove there, so bring your swimsuits if you think you might want a dip in the ocean. Carmelle and I will pick you up at nine o'clock and drop you off downtown so you can do a little sightseeing and shopping, and then at ten we'll pick you up and head out to Hearst Castle."

As the families left, they thanked Carmelle for her hospitality and wonderful salmon dinner. The last two to leave were Michael and Mark. Chuck noticed Mark whispering something to his brother, and then Michael took Mark's arm and led him over to Carmelle, who was putting things away in the kitchen cupboard. She turned to Mark as he placed his hand on her shoulder. "Thank you very much for the delicious dinner, Mom," he said.

Emotion welled up in Carmelle. Tears began forming in her eyes, and she was glad Mark couldn't see them when he gave her a big hug. "I'm so glad you and Linda and William Francis were able to be make the trip," she said as she embraced him. "And you and Laurie and the kids as well, Michael. It's been such a joy for your dad and me to spend time with all of you."

"You and Dad have made it a joy for all of us!" said Michael as he hugged her. "Thank you both for the wonderful dinner and for everything you've done to make our trip special. It's been really great." With that, the boys gave their father a good-night hug and headed out the door. As they crossed the street, the sun was setting and bursting with red, pink, yellow and orange hues behind the masses of evergreens surrounding the Lodge. The perfect ending to a perfect day.

"It's been quite a whirlwind, hasn't it, honey?" Chuck said as they sat in the living room.

"It sure has," she said. "I'll admit I'm a bit tired, but I'm so glad everyone was able to come to California, so happy you're getting to spend time with all the family, especially Michael and Mark. Those are two special boys. They melted my heart!"

On Saturday morning, Chuck pulled up in front of Cambria Pines Lodge at nine on the dot, and seventeen eager passengers were waiting to be ferried downtown. "I'll have to make two trips," he said. "Carmelle is busy fixing our picnic goodies, but it doesn't matter. It only takes a couple of minutes to drive down the hill. So, who wants to go first?"

"Why don't you take all the adults first," Kathleen said. "We girls can wait."

"Sounds good," Chuck said as he opened the side doors. "You're not going to get lost," he announced as they headed off. "There's only one major street running through town and it's called Main Street, can't miss it even if you try. When you finish walking the entire length, you'll end up at the Shell Station and that's where we'll pick you up in an hour. Have fun sightseeing and shopping! I'll drop you off right here," he said as he pulled to the curb at the Main Street intersection and everyone piled out.

"That didn't take long!" said Patricia as he drove up to the lodge for load number two.

Chuck was put to work immediately when he got home. First, he got the ice chests from the garage and filled them with drinks and ice. Then he loaded an array of blankets and swim towels into the van. He helped Carmelle pack all the food into the trunk of her car, and by then it was nearly ten o'clock and time to head back down the hill.

When they got to the Shell Station, everyone was there. "Gee, Dad," Michael said with a boyish grin when Chuck pulled up. "You've changed! You're right on time!"

"We aim to please," he said, smiling at his son. "We aim to please!"

Everyone enjoyed the Hearst Castle tour and San Simeon State Park picnic. The teenagers put on their swimsuits and frolicked in the gentle surf. Gretchen and Charles splashed around in the shallow water with little Charlie. The only problem was he didn't want to get out!

"You all are going to love the picnic lunch Carmelle has fixed for us!" Chuck said as everyone dried off and settled in on the blankets. "She wouldn't let me sample so much as a nibble during the packing, but my mouth was watering at the sight of it. Baked ham, fresh rolls, potato salad, Boston Baked Beans and dill pickles! And tonight for dessert? Blueberry and olallieberry pies from Linn's, our favorite Cambria restaurant. With vanilla ice cream, of course!"

"First the castle, now the feast! I feel like a king!" said Mark as everyone laughed.

"You two certainly have gone to a lot of trouble for all of us," Michael said appreciatively, "and we thank you very much!"

"It's our pleasure, Michael," said Carmelle.

"Absolutely," said Chuck. "That's what family is all about. And who knows? This may be the last time we all have a meal together," he said a bit sadly as he glanced around at everyone. "Let's begin by saying grace: *Bless us O Lord and these Thy gifts, which we are about to receive from Thy bounty and goodness, through Christ our Lord. Amen.*"

It didn't take long for the ham and rolls and potato salad and beans and pickles to disappear. Everyone had worked up quite an appetite, especially the wave-romping teenagers. At a quarter to three, Chuck began picking everything up, and in no time at all, with a multitude of hands helping, they were packed and ready to head home, still plenty of time to rest up a bit and dress for church. "I'm really glad you and Carmelle planned this trip for us, Dad," said Mark. "Thank you!" And planned it was, right to the minute! At three on the dot, they pulled out of San Simeon State Park, and at 4:30 they were all being picked up at the Cambria Pines Lodge and off to five o'clock Mass.

After Mass, it was back to the house for dessert. It was a jolly scene to behold, seventeen people devouring two pies and two gallons of ice cream! "I know your flight leaves at noon tomorrow," said Chuck, "so we'll need to pick you up at 10:00 a.m. It'll take about an hour to get to the airport, and that'll give you another hour or so to check in and get to your terminal."

When Carmelle and he pulled up in front of the Lodge the next morning, the whole gang was waiting, along with a mighty pile of suitcases. It had been an action-packed trip, pleasant, rewarding, love-filled, a trip everyone would cherish and remember, especially Chuck, who'd once again been able to be with his sons.

"We usually say the Rosary when we're on a trip or when we're driving from Cambria to San Luis Obispo," Carmelle said to Gretchen, Charles and William Francis, who were passengers in her car. Would you like to do that?"

"I think that's a wonderful idea," Gretchen said. "We'd be delighted!" It was Sunday, so they said the Glorious Mysteries: The Resurrection, The Ascension, The Descent of the Holy Spirit, The Assumption and The Crowning of the Blessed Virgin Mary. As it turns out, Chuck said the Rosary with the crew in his van, too. When they pulled into the airport parking lot, they were both just finishing.

It was relatively quiet inside the small terminal, at least until the Dowdles and the Latovskys arrived. That's when the hubbub began! When everyone checked in and began saying their goodbyes, Michael and Mark waited by the security gates until all the others had passed through. Their wives, Laurie and Linda, went first, followed by Gretchen, Charles and little Charlie. Next, Joe and John left with their wives, Maureen and Elizabeth Ann and their daughters, Kathleen Annette, Laure Jean, Patricia Marie, Genevieve Suzanne and Mary Maureen. That was quite a sight, five young girls laden with shopping bags!

William Francis hesitated at the security gate, then turned and walked back to Carmelle and Chuck to give them a hug. "Thanks again for your hospitality, Carmelle," he said, "and thanks for treating us, Grandpa. I had a really great time."

After he passed through security, William Francis turned and saw his dad and Uncle Michael in a quiet corner with Grandpa Chuck. The two brothers gave their father a big hug, but before Michael could take Mark's hand and lead him away, Mark put both hands on his father's face, his fingers holding it in a warm embrace. "We love you, Dad," he said.

Carmelle and Chuck waited for the plane to taxi down the runway and lift off before they headed back to their cars. When Carmelle turned to Chuck and saw tears in his eyes, she knew what he was thinking, that he likely wouldn't see his sons, his beloved "Twin Lights," ever again.

EPILOGUE

"Twin Lights" was written by Chuck Dowdle in his imaginings of a vastly-different life course had his twin sons survived and been his only children. Michael and Mark Dowdle were born prematurely on August 9th, 1953. Both died the next day, Michael at 12:05 p.m., Mark an hour later at 1:05 p.m. The boys weighed one-and-a-half pounds each at birth. Dr. P.B. Schoeneberger delivered the twins, and Chuck's wife, Marty (Marilyn Kirkwood), had a near-death, out-of-body experience during the delivery.

The twins were baptized by Sister M. Giovanni Becker, OSF, and confirmed by Father Nicholas Donnay, the pastor at St. Henry's Catholic Church in Perham, Minnesota. With Marty still hospitalized, Chuck and his young daughter, Kathleen Annette, attended a brief funeral service conducted by Father Donnay at St. Henry's. The twins were placed together in a small white box and buried at St. Henry's Catholic Cemetery in Perham. The Dowdles went on to have four more daughters: Laure Jean, Patricia "Allie" Marie, Genevieve Suzanne and Mary Maureen.

After Marty, his wife of forty-nine years, died of ovarian cancer on August 20th, 2000, Chuck took a road trip down the California coast, connecting with relatives and friends along the way. One of these was Carmelle Matthes in Cambria, California, who'd recently lost her husband after fifty years of marriage. Marty, Carmelle and Chuck had all graduated from Cathedral High School in Crookston, Minnesota, Class of 1946. Chuck and Carmelle were married on April 21st, 2001, and have been enjoying life together in Cambria ever since. In addition to his five daughters, Chuck has nine grandchildren and six great-grandchildren.

Chuck Dowdle began writing "Twin Lights" in 2011 when he was 83 years old and completed the book in 2021 at age 93.

Made in the USA
Columbia, SC
12 December 2021

50983301R00245